Praise for the Alexa Glock For

Molten Mud Murder
The First Alexa Glock Forensics Mystery

"Johnson provides a fascinating view of New Zealand and insights into the Māori culture… Armchair travelers will have fun."
—*Publishers Weekly*

"The novel is a page-turner par excellence with vivid characters and an enthralling plot, all wrapped up in a most charming evocation of New Zealand's landscapes, people, and local politics. I highly recommend this debut novel!"
—Douglas Preston, #1 bestselling coauthor of the Pendergast series

"Johnson gives us a compelling picture of modern New Zealand overlaid by Māori culture with its strict taboos and amazing artifacts. Alexa hopes to stay in New Zealand, and if this leads to a full series, my fingers are crossed that she gets her wish."
—Margaret Maron, *New York Times* bestselling author

The Bones Remember
The Second Alexa Glock Forensics Mystery

"At the exciting climax, Alexa uses her wits, not a gun or martial arts skills, to take out the bad guy. Hopefully, this refreshingly normal heroine will be back soon."
—*Publishers Weekly*

"Ready for some armchair travel with a hint of *Jaws*? Sara Johnson provides the ride in her second New Zealand–set Alexa Glock Forensics Mystery, *The Bones Remember*. Once you discover, with this dauntless forensic investigator, the wilds of Stewart Island, you'll want more pages. And the shark attacks and treachery along the way will keep the pages turning."

—*Kingdom Books Mystery Blog*

Also by Sara E. Johnson

The Alexa Glock Forensics Mysteries
Molten Mud Murder
The Bones Remember

THE BONE
TRACK

THE BONE TRACK

AN ALEXA GLOCK FORENSICS MYSTERY

SARA E. JOHNSON

Poisoned Pen
PRESS

Published by Poisoned Pen Press, an imprint of Sourcebooks
P.O. Box 4410, Naperville, Illinois 60567-4410
(630) 961-3900
sourcebooks.com

Library of Congress Cataloging-in-Publication Data

Names: Johnson, Sara E, author.
Title: The bone track : an Alexa Glock forensics mystery / Sara E. Johnson.
Description: Naperville, Illinois : Poisoned Pen Press, [2022] | Series:
  Alexa glock forensics mystery ; book 3
Identifiers: LCCN 2021023601 (print) | LCCN 2021023602
(ebook) | (trade paperback) | (epub)
Subjects: GSAFD: Mystery fiction.
Classification: LCC PS3610.O37637 B659 2022 (print) | LCC PS3610.O37637
  (ebook) | DDC 813/.6--dc23
LC record available at https://lccn.loc.gov/2021023601
LC ebook record available at https://lccn.loc.gov/2021023602

Printed and bound in the United States of America.
SB 10 9 8 7 6 5 4 3 2 1

For my sister, Jennifer

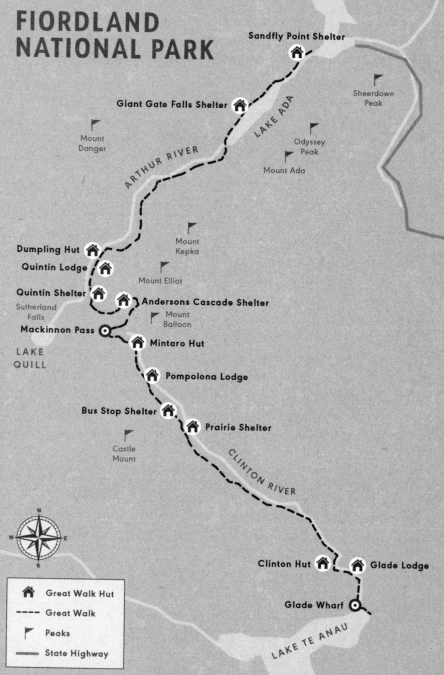

FIORDLAND NATIONAL PARK

MILFORD SOUND/
PIOPIOTAHI

Sandfly Point Shelter

Sheerdown
Peak

Giant Gate Falls Shelter

LAKE ADA

Mount
Danger

Odyssey
Peak

ARTHUR RIVER

Mount Ada

Mount
Kepka

Dumpling Hut

Quintin Lodge

Mount Elliot

Quintin Shelter

Andersons Cascade Shelter

Sutherland
Falls

Mount
Balloon

Mackinnon Pass

Mintaro Hut

LAKE
QUILL

Pompolona Lodge

Bus Stop Shelter

Prairie Shelter

Castle
Mount

CLINTON RIVER

N
W   E
S

Clinton Hut

Glade Lodge

Glade Wharf

LAKE TE ANAU

Legend

🏠 Great Walk Hut

--- Great Walk

⚑ Peaks

—— State Highway

Prologue

She gripped the cold metal handrails—they vibrated as if alive—but her feet wouldn't budge. The swing bridge taunted her. *Cross me if you dare.* She believed people should be able to control fear: simply put mind over body. But her body was betraying her. The medical term for fear of bridges was gephyrophobia, and this one-person-wide catwalk over the river gorge gave her the classic symptoms: racing heart, sweaty palms, trouble breathing.

The river was so far down and the wooden slats so flimsy-looking. A thunderous waterfall churned the water, blocking all sound, and the rain made everything blurry. She turned and squinted to see if the others were coming. She didn't want her fear on display.

The trail was empty. She'd better hurry.

"One, two, *THREE*," she yelled and rushed forward.

Halfway across, one of her hiking poles snagged the safety netting where the handrail sagged lowest, barely waist-high. She wobbled, jerked the pole free, and rushed across the remaining undulating planks. On the far platform, her victory shout was drowned by the waterfall.

She descended three steps to firm earth and stood still, regaining her composure. Composure was important for a medical professional. Composure and control. Slowly, ecstasy replaced fear; she was proof a person could overcome adversity. She'd done it her whole hungry life.

And look at that. The rain had stopped.

She walked across a clearing and stared into the deep woods where the trail picked up. She sensed watching eyes.

Nonsense.

She leaned her poles against a tree, slid her backpack off, and stuffed her raincoat into it. The waterfall, picture-perfect in a shaft of sunlight, cascaded in white membranes over three ledges. She retrieved her phone and walked to the cliff's edge for a clear view. Who could she send a picture to? She thought of the young man she'd met at the Queenstown pub. His deep-brown eyes and baby-soft hair. His beard against her cheek, his hot breath in her ear. She'd lowered her guard. Let the pressure and drive and strife dissolve in his attention.

Had she given him her mobile number? No. She'd said the battery was dead. He wrote his number on a scrap and slipped it into her pocket. His fingers rustled about, probed, and played.

She would cut back on alcohol as soon as she got home.

Her boot dislodged a pebble. It rolled off the precipice, bounced, and disappeared in froth.

She'd take a selfie and send it to him when she had service. She turned her back to the cliff, leveled her chin downward, held the phone at a flattering angle, and tilted her head. Click. She'd add filters later. Satisfied, she faced the river again, soaking up sunshine. No one was crossing yet; she would still be the first to reach the lodge. She liked being first. Deserved it. She sensed movement behind her. A dark-winged force. Sensation stabbed into her back, pushing her into the air, her legs and arms flailing, the phone flying from her fingers.

THURSDAY

Chapter One

Nine bodies. That's how many were excavated three days ago on the coastal road near Wellington, New Zealand.

Alexa Glock stepped around someone's outstretched legs in the airport waiting area and continued pacing. Nine times 206, the number of bones in a mature skeleton—more, if the remains included children. She hoped children weren't involved.

She imagined the driver's face as his bulldozer lifted the bones. "What the hell?" he probably said. He would have cut the engine, jumped from the cab, hoping and praying the bones weren't human.

The skull, its large eye sockets leaking dirt, brought the road construction to a halt.

"Stared right at me," he told the project's archaeologist.

A loudspeaker announced the arrival of an Air China flight. Alexa was waiting for her younger brother, Charlie. His plane was an hour late. He had left North Carolina twenty-four hours earlier. He didn't know that tomorrow morning, on the way to the hiking trip they were taking, they'd make a pit stop so Alexa could meet with the archaeologist who was keeping the location of the bones secret.

"We don't want stalkers and gawkers," she had said.

The bones would probably be historic remains of the

country's indigenous people, the Māori. They were being stored until she could get there. The local *iwi*, or tribe, would take guardianship if they were historic.

But what if they weren't old bones? Alexa's specialty—teeth—would tell the tale.

The loudspeaker made her slosh her coffee. Air New Zealand Flight 47 from Los Angeles had arrived. Her phoned pinged.

I'm here. What's for dinner?

Alexa panicked. Buying the food for backpacking was enough, wasn't it? She hadn't prepared anything beyond that. And why was Charlie talking dinner? It was ten o'clock in the morning.

Weet-bix, she texted back. She had tried some of her Kiwi roommate's cereal, doused it with milk. It had turned to mush.

She was apprehensive about seeing Charlie, who was four years younger than her thirty-seven, and married with two little boys. They weren't close. She was apprehensive about the hiking, too. Except for running, she wasn't outdoorsy. She preferred analyzing bite-marks or blood spatter to communing with family or nature.

She downed the last of the coffee and stood by the swinging doors. A gaggle of teenage girls tussled over who would hold a homemade poster that said "*Kia Ora,*" the official Kiwi greeting, like *aloha* in Hawaii.

Dazed passengers emerged. Charlie, in wrinkled khakis and a plaid flannel shirt, backpack over his shoulder and dragging a wheelie suitcase, was last. He stiffened when Alexa bear-hugged him.

She let go and stepped back. "You made it! How was the flight?"

"Long. I'm starved."

"We can stop at McDonald's on the way to my apartment." She took the wheelie suitcase from him and started walking.

"McDonald's? I didn't fly halfway across the world to eat at McDonald's."

"They have different things on the menu. Georgie Pies."

"I don't want pie."

God almighty, he was still a pouty kid. Alexa dodged a mother who had her toddler on a leash—was that legal?—and headed for the exit. "They're meat pies."

"Is Milford Track open?"

That was the hike they were taking—the Milford Track. "What do you mean?" Alexa waited for Charlie to evade the leashed tot and catch up. Crow's-feet around his eyes startled her.

"They had a perfect storm—thirteen inches of rain in one day, more the next—and it closed down the track. Hundreds of people had to be evacuated by helicopter. Don't you listen to the news?"

Auckland, where she lived, was on the North Island of New Zealand, and Milford Track was way down on the South Island. "When was the storm?"

"Two weeks ago. I've been following it. I can't believe you haven't heard."

"I've been busy. I have to get to work today."

"Work?" Charlie stopped walking. "I've only got two weeks. You're working?"

"Just a bit." Alexa kept walking. "I have reports to finish. I figured you'd want a shower and a nap," she called over her shoulder.

The reports turned out to be routine, except for the final one. That's where Alexa lost track of time. A woman claimed a man attacked and robbed her in a parking garage. In the struggle the attacker bit her arm. A close-up photo showed the bite-mark—a shallow puncture of the skin—above the woman's left wrist. Alexa compared it with a photo of the alleged victim, who had a noticeable gap between her top incisors. "It looks self-inflicted,"

Alexa told her boss Dan Goddard at Forensic Service Center. "We'll need her dental X-rays to confirm."

They stared at the side-by-side photos. "Why would someone do that?" Dan asked.

"Could be a response to pain or to keep from screaming," Alexa said. "Or she could have made up the attack."

She didn't get home until seven. She unlocked the door and found Charlie reading a Milford Track guidebook on the sofa.

"So much for 'I won't be long.'"

He had called twice, and each time she had begged for another hour.

"For your information," he said. "The Milford Track reopened two days ago. We're lucky."

"That's good." She stepped around his bulging backpack. "What all do you have in there?"

Charlie ignored her. Alexa set her laptop and tote on a kitchen chair and scuffed out of her Keds. "Did you get a nap?" She could tell he had taken a shower but hadn't shaved. His sandy-brown-colored hair was short on the sides with a quiff on top. The trendy cut was probably his wife's idea.

"I went out for an early dinner with your cop roommate before she left for work."

"You went out to eat with Natalie?" Alexa hadn't ever done that. She rarely saw Natalie, who worked the six p.m. to six a.m. shift four days a week and spent her off time at her boyfriend's. This made her a perfect roomie—or flatmate as Kiwis said—for someone who didn't want one. Housing prices in Auckland were double compared to Raleigh, and she was making half the money she had at her old job at the North Carolina State Bureau of Investigation.

"We ate at a restaurant called Lord of the Fries."

Alexa laughed. "Did Frodo serve you?"

"Did you know Natalie and Trevor split up?"

Alexa was stunned. She didn't even know her roommate's

boyfriend's name. "I suppose you know Natalie's hopes and dreams, too?"

Hazel eyes were the single physical characteristic the brother and sister shared. Charlie's sharpened. "Some of them. She's nice."

Alexa bit her tongue and put leftovers in the microwave. While the electromagnetic waves zapped the Thai curry, she popped them each a Speight's beer.

"Smells good," Charlie said. "I'll have some, too."

She laughed again. Charlie had a good appetite like she did. She dished up the curry and told him about the bones. "They're storing them near the site. It's probably a burial ground. We have an early flight to Wellington. An archaeologist is picking us up. I'll examine the bones, and then we'll fly to Queenstown."

"So you're working tomorrow, too?"

Charlie loved his job as a geotechnical engineer. He was a rock and soil geek. One of his main duties was analyzing sites to see if they were right for construction projects. "They're building a road," she placated. "Maybe you could dig around or talk with the site manager."

He crumpled his beer can. "Maybe."

FRIDAY

Chapter Two

Dr. Ana Luckenbaugh, who was around Alexa's age, drove with one hand on the wheel and used the other to fiddle with her thick, dark hair. Her scuffed work boot was heavy on the gas pedal. She had whisked Alexa and Charlie away from Wellington Airport, promising to have them back for their two p.m. flight to Queenstown. En route to examine the bones, she explained her involvement. "I'm an archaeologist for Beckett & Associates in Auckland. We specialize in cultural heritage remains."

"I live in Auckland, too," Alexa replied brilliantly. She had made sure to get the front seat, relegating Charlie to the back of the RAV4, squeezed next to a monstrous child-restraint seat. Riding in the back made her carsick.

"The roadwork has halted, and now the construction company is seeking permission to continue."

"From whom?"

"New Zealand Pouhere Taonga, a historic heritage agency. If this is a Māori burial ground, the road will have to be rerouted. We think teeth are the key. That's why you're here."

There were plenty of cultures that held negative beliefs about disturbing remains. Alexa shifted in the seat.

Cook Strait, which separated the North Island and South Island, lapped a rocky shore out the window. The wind off the strait tried to wrestle the wheel from Dr. Luckenbaugh. She chuckled. "Wellington is the world's windiest city, eh?"

"Really? Did you know that, Charlie?" Alexa turned around. Charlie was slumped against the car seat, asleep.

They talked about their jobs. Alexa loved conversing with fellow professionals. From the evidence in the back seat, this one had a child. "You don't mind the traveling?" Dr. Luckenbaugh asked.

"No. I like it."

"Traveling gives me a break from my she-devil daughter. She's four. But I miss her."

Alexa noted the archaeologist wasn't wearing a wedding band but knew that didn't mean much. Charlie wasn't wearing one either. She supposed she should ask something about the kid, but she didn't know what. "Have you ever done work with the police?"

"Occasionally." Dr. Luckenbaugh didn't elaborate. "The *kōiwi* are being cared for by a representative of *ngā hapū iwi*." She turned onto a steep road.

"What does *kōiwi* mean?"

"Human remains." Dr. Luckenbaugh eased to a halt at a stop sign. She lowered her window, and Alexa could smell the sea. "After the area was blessed by the *iwi*, I conducted a grid search, labeled the caskets according to sector. The bulldozer damaged one casket, but we were able to reconstruct it."

Alexa was glad she wasn't facing all commingled bones. "When did Māori begin using caskets?"

"It varied, depending on *iwi*. But by the early twentieth century, most Māori used caskets or coffins."

"Have you recovered artifacts?" Clothing, pottery, weapons would be clues to the age of the bones.

Dr. Luckenbaugh pressed her lips together.

They were in a neighborhood of single-storied homes, funny New Zealand cabbage trees—their buoyant green afros rocking in the breeze—and blooming hydrangeas. Dr. Luckenbaugh pulled into a driveway behind an SUV. The house was an L-shaped ranch with green trim. A detached garage at the end of the driveway had been converted into a workshop. Alexa felt bad. It was hardly the construction site she had promised Charlie.

Dr. Luckenbaugh turned off the ignition. "A *kaumātua*—an elder—is with the bones. His name is Harry Blackburn. I'll do the speaking."

The archaeologist's eyes, Alexa noticed, were hazel like her own. She and Dr. Luckenbaugh could be sisters.

Charlie woke with a start. "Where are we?"

Alexa grabbed her crime kit and opened the car door. "You better wait here."

"In the car? Really? This is epic, Lexi."

There was nothing she could do to appease him. She joined Dr. Luckenbaugh, who rapped three times at the workshop door.

The door opened. The elder had graying hair swept back from a broad forehead and dark eyes.

"How are you, Mr. Blackburn?" Dr. Luckenbaugh asked.

"Fair." His stout body blocked the workshop. "Who is this?"

Alexa began to introduce herself, but Dr. Luckenbaugh held up her hand. "This is Ms. Glock from Auckland. She is a forensic odontologist. She'll examine the bones."

"Their fate must be decided." The elder folded his arms across his chest and spoke in Māori to Dr. Luckenbaugh *"Ko te kino tenei..."*

The archaeologist's face creased as she listened. When the elder finished speaking, she turned to Alexa. "Mr. Blackburn believes you'll be in grave danger if you examine the bones."

"Danger?"

Mr. Blackburn gave a single nod. His voice was gravelly. "The viewing of bones can unleash misfortune to the living. Or worse."

Alexa kept her face neutral. "I'm good."

The elder stepped aside.

SATURDAY

Chapter Three

Alexa pushed her shoulders against the bus seat the next morning, the vibration from the rough and curvy road like a fifty-
cent motel massage. The bus was transporting them to Te Anau
Downs, where they would catch a boat to the start of the hike.

Rounding a curve, the bus slowed, then halted. Three orange
cones blocked half the narrow road where the pavement had
collapsed into a fast-flowing roadside stream.

"Damage from the storm," Charlie said.

After waiting for an oncoming car to pass, the bus crawled
toward the cones. Alexa held her breath that the remaining
road—possibly undermined by the gushing water—would
hold. The Māori elder had warned of grave danger.

The road held. She exhaled and thought of yesterday's bones.

Teeth *had* told the tale. And the caskets. Several had Māori
carvings in the wood: spirals—Tiki, fish. It was as if she could
feel the etchings, worn and subtle, on her fingertips now.

Under Mr. Blackburn's and Dr. Luckenbaugh's watchful eyes,
she had examined the skulls and teeth. She replayed the scene in
her mind. The opening of each coffin. The sweet waft of earth
and must and mystery. The empty eye and nose sockets. The
macabre grins. The teeth preserved.

She snorted.

Charlie, who'd snagged the window seat, frowned. "What?"

"I was just thinking. Death is excellent dental care."

"You are so weird."

"Want to know why?" He hadn't shaved again, and his hairstyle wasn't so quiffy.

"No."

He was still a little touchy that she'd been working so much. She really didn't blame him.

"Teeth decay while we're alive, right? Like now, from the syrup you slathered on your pancakes at breakfast." She had ordered "brilliant bacon and egg butty," a sandwich of bacon, drippy fried egg, and onion jam. She would have to expand her palate more often. "And the bacteria in our mouths. The sugars and bacteria that cause decay don't survive death. That's why teeth are so resilient."

Charlie seemed to consider this. "There are minerals found in tooth enamel. So teeth are like rocks."

Not really, Alexa thought.

Charlie shook his phone. "I can't get a signal."

"I told you there's no cell reception. I only brought mine to be a backup for my camera." She said it like "no biggie," but being cut off from the outside world made her nervous. The whole hiking thing was making her nervous. "Hey, Charlie…" She waited until he slipped his phone into his pocket. "Yesterday, when I was looking at those bones…"

"And I was stuck in the car like a kid…"

"The Māori elder told me looking at them could bring me misfortune or danger."

Charlie's eyebrows went up. "That's BS. You don't believe that, do you?"

She scratched her ankle. "No."

The first casket had held a surprise. She opened her mouth to tell Charlie about it, but then shut it. The bones had a right to privacy. Nestled in the crook of the adult skeleton's arm was an infant so young that the fontanelle was visible in the skull. Mother and child. The sight had touched Alexa's heart, made her think of her own mother cradling her, loving her, protecting her—and then up and dying of cancer when Alexa was six and Charlie two.

She avoided eye contact with Mr. Blackburn and Dr. Luckenbaugh as she gently manipulated the adult's jaw so that she could examine the teeth.

"No sign she had dental treatment," Alexa said. An examination of the pelvis would confirm the skeleton was female, but Alexa was pretty sure.

Dr. Luckenbaugh took notes on her pad. "That's a clue. New Zealand's School Dental Service began in the 1920s. It was years later before it reached Māori children."

Mr. Blackburn sighed. Alexa could smell his peppermint breath as she counted the mother's teeth. "The wisdom teeth are erupted," she said. "So the remains belong to someone late teens or older." The teeth of children are a fairly reliable means to estimating chronological age, but after the eruption of the wisdom teeth, it was harder.

She poked a lateral incisor. "I see minimal signs of decay. No Coca-Cola cavities."

Dr. Luckenbaugh frowned. "No what?"

"Sugary drinks cause cavities. These teeth indicate a healthy diet."

"The precontact Māori lived on fern root, fish, shellfish, birds, and some crops," Dr. Luckenbaugh said.

Alexa retrieved her magnification glass from her crime kit and studied the teeth again. "There are also flat wear planes."

"Eh?"

The elder startled her. She explained. "There is flattening of the molars."

"From chewing fern root, probably," Dr. Luckenbaugh said.

Alexa tongued her own molars. "Fern root?"

"The rhizome of the bracken fern. It wasn't very nutritious, but it was available year-round. Even boiled, roasted, or pounded, it was hard to chew."

Sometimes Alexa's cooking was like that. She moved to the next intact casket. That skull was missing several teeth—maybe lost prior to burial—but the remaining ones were in good shape, and the molars also showed flattening. An hour later she had examined all nine skulls, plus the infant's. Given the condition of the teeth and the use of caskets, her best estimate was that the burials took place between 1900 and 1930.

Dr. Luckenbaugh nodded. "The artifacts confirm that. I removed them so they wouldn't influence your judgment."

"Radiocarbon tests can give you a more definite answer."

"No need," the elder said, folding his arms across his chest again.

"The road will need to be rerouted," Dr. Luckenbaugh concluded. "Thank you for this information."

Alexa thought reinterring the bones quickly was a lost opportunity.

As if reading her thoughts, Mr. Blackburn added, "There is nothing to be gained from further violation." He then spoke in Māori to Dr. Luckenbaugh. Alexa recognized *urupa*, the word for burial ground. He bowed his head.

She looked for a final time at the casket that held the mother and child, closed now to prying eyes, and knew he was right.

———

Getting to the Milford Track was complicated. Dr. Luckenbaugh had rushed them back to the airport to catch their eighty-minute flight to Queenstown. At the Queenstown airport, they rented, at Charlie's insistence, a sporty red Mazda. He drove the two hours from the airport to Te Anau, leaving his grudges behind, and managing the left side of the road well.

They spent the night in side-by-side rooms at the Explorer Motel in the village. She supposed they could have shared a room, but, well, she hardly knew her brother. A Christmas here, a wedding there. Her two visits to meet her nephews. Benny was the first baby she had ever held. She didn't like the way the month-old infant had howled in her arms, waving his tiny fists. Mel had scooped him up like Alexa was pinching him. Alone in the motel room, she completed her reports on the skeletons and emailed them to her boss and Dr. Luckenbaugh, with whom she had exchanged business cards.

She and Charlie would have plenty of time to bond during the hike. They would share huts for three nights with other hikers; no tent camping was allowed. Each hut held forty hikers, and they were usually full. She shuddered.

This morning, after their caloric breakfasts, they drove to the Milford Track Visitor Center. "Good morning," Alexa said to a dark-haired ranger. "We're checking in."

"Welcome. From the states, eh?" He was young, maybe Māori.

Charlie nodded.

"Weather is fine today. Rain is forecast for tomorrow."

Slogging through rain did not excite Alexa. She had only been backpacking one other time: a high school Appalachian Trail new-boot nightmare. Her heels had blistered, ruining the experience. Not this time. She looked down fondly. Her sturdy boots were broken in.

"What name is the reservation under?" he continued.

Alexa panicked. Her friend Mary had made the reservations. "Um. Horomia."

"Who's that?" Charlie asked.

Alexa kept quiet.

The ranger filed through a stack, humming tunelessly. "Eh, here we go." Then he stared at Charlie. "You don't look like a Mary."

Charlie looked at Alexa. "What gives?"

"Oh, well, I was supposed to hike with Mary, but she…" Mary Horomia was the one friend she had made during her fellowship at University of Auckland. Mary had been excited to show her around, and they had decided on hiking Milford Track when the semester was over. She had died in a car wreck, just two months ago, and Charlie was her understudy. Only he didn't know that.

"…she had a car accident. My brother, Charlie, is filling in."

"Highly irregular." The ranger clicked on his computer. "It says here that Ms. Horomia is a New Zealand citizen, and Ms. Glock has a work visa."

"That's right," Alexa said.

The ranger squinted at Charlie. "But you are not a citizen of New Zealand, mate, is that right? And you don't have a work visa?"

"Right," Charlie said.

A heavy woman, maybe fifty, with thin blond hair and a double chin, spun a rack of postcards on the other end of the counter.

"There's a price difference," the ranger explained. "Hut reservations for Kiwis and visa holders are seventy dollars a night. For international visitors, it's a hundred forty a night. That will be an additional two hundred ten dollars, please."

Alexa blanched, but dug out her credit card. She hoped Charlie wouldn't ask about Mary. Her friend's death was a raw spot; she was still grieving.

A postcard fluttered to her feet. Alexa picked it up while she waited for her credit card, and studied it: VISIT TE ANAU GLOWWORM CAVE. "Maybe we'll go here after the hike," she said to Charlie, showing him the picture.

"Give the woman her card," Charlie said.

She handed the postcard to the woman who opened her mouth as if to smile, revealing a small gap between her top teeth, but then shut it.

"Here are your tickets," the ranger said. "The huts are almost full—there are thirty-five people in your cohort. The hut master will collect tickets each night."

"Hut master?" Charlie asked. "That sounds kinky."

The ranger laughed. "If kinky is mopping loos and trail work, you're dead on. This is only the second day the track has been open since the storm. There are downed trees blocking the path in several places."

"But is it safe?" Alexa asked.

Charlie rolled his eyes.

"Yeah nah. You hike at your own risk, of course. We get thousands of people each season." He handed them their tickets and a map. "Write in all the hut books, though. Leaving a trail helps us find you if something does go wrong."

Alexa didn't like the sound of that.

The ranger pointed out the window to a bus. "Just two buses a day. Milford trampers only. This one is about to leave. It will take you to the boat. After the boat ride, you'll start the hike."

Plane, car, bus, boat. *All that is missing is a train*, Alexa thought.

The bus driver pulled the doors shut after Charlie and Alexa boarded. They found side-by-side seats halfway down the aisle, stowed their backpacks on the overhead rack, and braced themselves as the bus pulled forward.

"Stop," a man behind them called.

The postcard woman was running across the parking lot, her open raincoat flapping like bat wings. The driver halted and opened the door. "Your lucky day."

The woman was huffing from her parking lot jog. She slid her pack off and sat across from Alexa and Charlie.

With a lurch, the bus of Milford trampers pulled out of the lot. Kiwis used the word *tramp* instead of *hike*. And *track* instead of *trail*. Alexa swallowed, checked her cheap watch, and leaned back for a catnap.

Charlie nudged her shoulder ten minutes later. "Look at

the waterfall." He hadn't mentioned the hut tickets. Probably because she'd paid.

The water crashing over a cliff caused her heart to race. It looked so powerful, so indifferent. Her mind was leaving the skulls behind.

A college-aged woman bounded down the bus aisle and leaned over Alexa. "You don't mind, do you?" She thrust her camera toward the window.

Alexa shuffled her hiking boots to make room. "Have you seen Dad lately?" Alexa asked.

"Dad and Mom spent Christmas with us."

The burn scars that flowed like an ugly stream across Alexa's back, hidden from anyone who didn't know her intimately, tightened. She shuffled her boots again, forcing the college woman to back up and leave their space. "Rita is not your mom."

"She's the only mom I've ever known. You're the one who has a problem with her."

Her back scars were a barometer. The greater her stress, or anger, the more they constricted. She took a deep breath. Dad's marriage to Rita was a long time ago and a hemisphere away.

The light in the bus faded, eclipsed by dark trees on either side of the road.

"Who turned off the light?" Charlie asked.

"They're black beech," floated a voice from behind. "Endemic to New Zealand."

The owner of the voice, a lightly bearded man, smiled pleasantly when Alexa turned to see who had been eavesdropping. His accent meant he was endemic, too. She was pleased another Kiwi besides Postcard Woman was on the hike. Mary had said mostly foreigners scarfed up the reservations. "Black beech sounds like a fungal disease," she told him.

"You're right," the man said. "They're prone to sooty mold."

The wheels of the bus crunched across gravel. Out the window Alexa saw a gray lake, gray mountains on the far side, and chunky gray ducks churning the still surface. A long single-file boardwalk stretching into Lake Te Anau looked too much like a pirate's plank for Alexa's comfort.

Chapter Four

Alexa grabbed her backpack, looped it over one shoulder, and followed the passengers down the bus aisle. "I don't know about this," she told Charlie.

"Are you shook?" he asked. "You're in good shape. You got this."

She basked in his kind words.

As if the lake's mood had changed, its water was now ruffed by wind. Not a single boat was in sight.

She weaved her other arm through the backpack strap and hoisted it so that the weight was distributed and stepped off the bus. Her biggest packing dilemma had centered on her crime kit. It weighed over twenty pounds. No can do when backpacking. To compromise, she created a mini-kit in one of those draw-string gym bags that teenagers use and filled it with a variety of evidence bags, sealing tape, tweezers, scissors, caution tape, dental probe, fingerprint powder, brush, lifting tape, white backing cards, ruler, gloves, pad, pen, the magnifying glass Dad had given her on the cusp of graduate school, and her Maglite. She added a tiny vial of distilled water, swabs, and transport tubes, because—well—you never know when you'll need to take a DNA sample. She patted one of the side pockets of the pack, checking for the compact and water-resistant Olympus Tough camera with an extra battery. Her regular camera, a digital SLR with various lenses, was too bulky. This was vacation, not work.

The cool, fresh lake breeze drew them to the shore. Alexa stood on the shingly beach and sniffed deeply. Charlie picked up a rock, pulled his arm back, cocked his wrist, let it fly. One. Two. Three skips. Alexa clapped. When she had called to invite Charlie on the hike, he had readily agreed. "It's been a rough patch. I need a break."

With a start, she realized that she hadn't asked about his rough patch. She was a crap sister.

Still no boat. Alexa turned and surveyed her fellow hikers. People spoke in various accents and languages: Kiwi, Australian, Middle Eastern, German, Chinese, and loud American English coming from the young woman who had taken a photo out of their bus window. She was chasing two other young women with bug spray.

Alexa immediately felt itchy. She took off her backpack and rummaged for the repellent, used it liberally, and handed it to Charlie. "You don't want sandfly bites. I read that they're the biggest danger on the trail." As he sprayed, she counted: twenty-six people, sixteen of whom were women—roughly half were older than herself. Two women in their seventies were taking selfies in front of the beautiful background. Everyone looked fit except Postcard Woman. Shuffling along the shoreline, she looked like a misfit on a Sierra Club outing. A boy, maybe twelve, ran after another boy shouting, "Chuck it to me." The eavesdropper, Sooty Mold Man, stood by himself and looked to be sizing up the crowd, too. He caught her eye and smiled. Alexa looked away, flustered.

A second bus—gleaming and modern—pulled into the lot. Luxe Tours blazed on its flank. With a pneumatic whoosh, its doors opened, and a man with a clipboard hopped off, beckoning to his followers, all beelike in matching bright yellow rain jackets, except for one teenager. He had probably refused to wear something people three times his age were wearing. Alexa counted thirty-four yellow jackets, adjusting packs, sucking nectar from their matching water bottles, and buzzing with excitement. She was surprised by the numbers because the huts only accommodated forty people, and the ranger had said only thirty-five were booked. Where would the extra people sleep?

"Let's gather by the tree," Clipboard Man chirped, walking backward. His long brown hair was kept out of his face with a hippie headband. Surprised—*who was this guy?*—Alexa followed. A woman turned. "Are you with Luxe Tours?" She wore substantial makeup—eyeliner, thick mascara, lipstick, and foundation that clashed with her outdoors attire. Her odor—bug spray or perfume—made Alexa step backward.

"With what?"

"Luxe Tours."

"Um, no." Alexa noticed she wore a name tag: *Kia Ora. My name is Diana Clark.* Someone had Sharpied *Dr.* in front of Diana.

"Didn't think so." Dr. Clark swung around, making for Clipboard Man in purposeful strides.

Alexa was pretty sure the doctor had dissed her. She rejoined Charlie, who was talking with Sooty Mold Man. She interrupted. "Who are those people?"

"The luxury trampers," Sooty Mold said. "There are two ways to do Milford Track. Independently, freedom hikers we're called, sleeping in the huts, no guide. Or you can go guided. Luxury trampers pay thousands of dollars to have a guide, sleep in fancy lodges, and eat fancy meals. It's too posh for me."

"Man," Charlie said, "that's not too posh for me."

Alexa agreed. "Do the lodges have restaurants?" Maybe the hike wouldn't be so bad if she could stop for a bacon butty and a flat white.

"For the luxe hikers only," the man said.

Alexa tried to process. "So we start at the same place, but

spend the nights in different huts?" All these people bunched together on the trail sounded nightmarish. The man studied Alexa as if Charlie weren't there. Her face flushed.

"Huts and lodges are staggered about a mile apart. I'm Steadman Willis, by the way. Call me Stead."

"I thought this was supposed to be a wilderness experience. Sounds like the trail will be crowded," Alexa said.

He laughed, showing off straight teeth. "Fiordland has 1.2 million hectares. There's plenty of track for everyone. What's your name?"

"Alexa. This is my brother, Charlie."

His eyes stayed on Alexa. "Are you American or Canadian?"

"American." His focus was—well, she couldn't decide— flattering or creepy. Her mind flashed to Bruce Horne. He was the detective inspector she'd worked a couple cases with. She licked her lips at the delicious memory of kissing him. Only they shouldn't have. It was during a case, and he'd been her boss.

But still.

The chugging of a long, low boat diverted her attention. It appeared from the right of the fiordlike lake, its bronze-green paint shimmering in weak sunlight, and serenely turned— barely creating a wake—to align with the pier. Along its flank were twelve square windows encased in brass. TAWERA was painted below the windows.

"It looks like a steamship," Charlie said. "I wonder how old it is?"

"She's been ferrying people to Glade Wharf for decades," Stead said. His eyes widened at a moving mass of Luxe Tours hikers descending single-file on the narrow pier. "That's cheeky. They think they're entitled. We were here first."

"The best views are front right," Mr. Clipboard shouted to his swarm. A younger woman, also with a clipboard, stood by his side, smiling broadly.

Alexa got in line behind some Yellow Jackets walking the

gangplank. *This is it,* she thought. *No turning back now.* A gray duck glided close to watch the parade with its topaz eyes. Lake water nipped and sloshed against the pilings.

A portly skipper extended a hand to help her aboard. She grabbed it, flashing back to her last travel case when she'd jumped aboard a boat.

But this was vacation, not work.

There were empty bench seats on the deck and an open door to the cabin. A colorful array of backpacks leaned against the railings. Alexa kept hers on and entered the cabin. To the right of the aisle, the double seats were claimed by Luxe Tours hikers. The doctor woman had scarfed the front seat that had more legroom, and now she removed her yellow jacket. She appeared to be lecturing the woman sitting next to her. Alexa was surprised the boat wasn't listing from unevenly distributed weight. She leaned her backpack against the inner wall where she could keep an eye on it, and plopped in the first seat on the left, scooting over for Charlie. He paused and looked around. "Better views outside, I bet."

She followed his eyes. The three American women—maybe college students—were opting for the deck as well. Alexa felt a twinge of sadness as she watched Charlie leave. Their time together was so brief.

Stead shoved his backpack under the seats and said, "Mind if I join you?"

"No. Sure."

She tensed, thinking she'd have to make conversation, but Stead popped back up and asked if she'd like a tea or coffee. She spotted the beverage counter at the rear of the cabin. "Coffee, white," she said. "No sugar."

They exchanged pleasantries as the *Tawera* eased northward. Stead worked in Greymouth.

"Where's that?"

"It's the largest town on the South Island's west coast. What do you do?"

Alexa guessed Stead was in his early forties. "I work with Forensic Service Center in Auckland. I'm a traveling forensic investigator."

"Not on duty now, I hope?" His eyes were creek-stone brown, not blue like Bruce's, and his brows were blond. His ball cap hid his hair. When she didn't comment, he continued. "I'm an engineer. I work with piezoelectric composites. I might be transferring to Auckland soon."

"Pi-zo what? I hope you're not on duty, either." Stead laughed, and Alexa liked the sound of it. "My brother is an engineer, too. Geotechnics." She could see Charlie standing against the rail, a grave look on his face.

In the cabin, Mr. Clipboard clapped his hands for attention. A whistle dangled around his neck. Alexa squinted, but couldn't make out the writing on his name tag. "Say goodbye to civilization, folks."

She snorted. They had been in the middle of nowhere since they'd left Te Anau, which wasn't exactly somewhere.

"The ride is an hour," Mr. Clipboard continued. "I'll regale you with facts as we make our way. Most of Lake Te Anau is in Fiordland National Park and Te Wāhipounamu World Heritage Site. Te Wāhipounamu means 'place of greenstone.'"

Alexa perked up. She had learned about greenstone on her first New Zealand case.

"After all the rain and flooding we've had, the rivers should be full of what the Māori call the stone of the gods. You might find some on your tramp. You can't sell it unless you're Māori, but you can have it polished and made into jewelry."

Now Alexa was excited.

"Rat shit," Stead said. "The rivers aren't full of it."

"It wouldn't be valuable, if they were," Alexa agreed.

The guide's spiel continued. "Lake Te Anau is the largest lake on the South Island and the second largest in New Zealand. Who knows what lake is largest?"

"Lake Taupō," Stead shouted.

"Correct!" Mr. Clipboard dashed to fist-bump Stead. "Lake Te Anau was carved out by huge glaciers," he continued.

Alexa liked how he pronounced glacier: glah-see-er, like it had three syllables.

"Deep and cold," Clipboard Man was saying, "Lake Te Anau..."

Alexa tuned out. She finished her coffee and watched a river feeding into the lake. The ferry struggled with conflicting currents and responded by turning course, slightly into the fray. Blue and pink lupines lined the shore, and the mountains beyond them were capped with snow—even in February, which was summer in the Southern Hemisphere. She reviewed the hike: thirty-three miles spread over four days. The hardest part, according to Charlie's guidebook, which she had borrowed last night, would be Day Three, when they climbed Mackinnon Pass. It was nothing compared to Mount Mitchell in North Carolina, which was twice as high. Not that she had hiked it; she'd climbed Mount Mitchell in a car.

But still.

"Cave of swirling water!" Stead shouted. He had turned sideways with his legs stretching into the aisle.

Alexa tuned back in.

Mr. Clipboard—well, Alexa could see that his name was Clint Knight—said, "This bloke is right again. The Māori name for this lake is Cave of Swirling Water. There is a myth that says a Māori chief happened upon a sacred spring not far from where we are now." The guide pointed out the window to the dark shoreline. "He asked his wife to keep it a secret. But when he departed on a journey, the wife showed the secret place to her lover, who looked into the spring to admire his reflection."

A gull squawked, and another one fussed back. Alexa watched through the open cabin door as Charlie leaned over the rail, taking photos.

"The man's reflection unleashed a raging torrent from the spring, flooding the village and forming Lake Te Anau. Whatever you do on the Milford Track…"

The lake had narrowed, and Alexa spotted a pier.

"…don't look at your reflection in the water."

Chapter Five

A plastic wash bucket sat at the end of the pier. The skipper stood by it and told everyone to slosh their boots through it. "We don't want to contaminate paradise," he said.

"What do you mean?" Alexa asked.

"It helps prevent the spread of nonindigenous flora and fauna. Milford Track goes through ancient forest. There are hundreds of plants that only grow right here in Fiordland. The spread of non-native species could devastate them."

Thinking of *Jurassic Park*, Alexa double-dipped, hoping to kill wayward hitchhikers.

At the lake's edge she adjusted her backpack straps and cinched the waist belt, immediately relieving pressure from her shoulders. The reflection of mountains in the lake—midnight-blue giants—wavered, then stilled. She expanded her hiking poles—trying to remember what the woman at Macpac—New Zealand's equivalent to REI—had said about the proper length. She had never used poles before, but Charlie, in a pre-hike phone call, had insisted.

"They're for old people," Alexa had protested.

"That's why you need them," Charlie said. "You're what? Forty?"

"Thirty-seven," she retorted, taking the bait.

The clerk told Alexa they'd help her maintain balance and alleviate stress on knees and muscles, so she'd caved. They weren't cheap, either.

Stead had followed her to the lakeside. He whipped off his ball cap and swatted a fly. What little hair he had was golden brown. "You aren't going to hike with those on, are you?" he asked, pointing to her poles.

"Hike with what on?"

"The rubber boots."

Alexa studied her leather hiking boots. The dude from Greymouth was not making sense.

"Those are for walking on hard surfaces," he said, pointing to the tips of her poles.

The tips did look like they were wearing funny black boots.

"Pull them off," Stead advised. "What you need on the Milford Track is a good pointy tip." He showed her his pole. The sharp tip glistened. Then he flipped it and stuck it in the soft ground, making little divots.

Alexa pulled off the rubber boots and felt like throwing the stupid things in the lake, but that would be introducing non-native plastic. She thrust them in a pack pocket and dug out her sun hat.

"Do you have bug juice on?" Stead asked.

Mr. Boy Scout was beginning to irritate her. "Bug juice? In America, kids drink bug juice at summer camp."

Three fit hikers marched toward the trail like they were late for a business meeting. Alexa didn't understand the rush, but to each his own. She pulled her hat on.

Charlie bounded over, his eyes alight. "Let's take a photo." He pointed to a green and gold Department of Conservation Milford Track sign.

"Hand me your phone. I'll take it," Stead said.

"Thanks, man." He turned to Alexa. "You're not going to wear that, are you?"

She didn't know what he was talking about.

"That hat. It looks like Dad's old fishing hat."

Alexa jerked the hat off and stood on one side of the sign, frowning, Charlie on the other, smiling. The sign said Glade Lodge was twenty minutes, and Clinton Hut an hour and a half.

"The wussy Luxe hikers only have a short walk." Charlie said.

Alexa looked at her watch: one o'clock. Her stomach immediately rumbled.

Stead laughed. "Our trek isn't that much more."

"Hand me your phone," Charlie said to Stead. "I'll take one of you."

"No worries," Stead said.

"You've hiked the Milford before?"

Stead nodded.

Alexa wondered if Stead was going to walk with them, but he said, "Catch you later," and set off.

The waterfall woman and her friends rushed over. "Would you take our picture?" she asked Charlie. "We're nurses from Austin."

Charlie took the purple phone and mentioned he was from Asheville. The nurses squealed. One was wearing bright-pink Crocs. How could you hike in Crocs?

The Luxe guide, Clint, waved a camera. "Gather for a group photo."

Alexa took that as a cue to get moving. "Come on, Charlie. Let's go."

He was talking breweries with the nurses. "I'll catch up with you."

So much for bonding. Alexa put her hat back on, squared her shoulders, and faced the path. The first step into the wide unknown felt momentous. She noticed the birdsong—*swee, swee*—and searched her memory for step quotes: "One small step for man, one giant leap for mankind." "A journey of a thousand miles begins with a single step." "One step closer to the edge." Too ominous. "Step one in crime scene investigation is to establish security." She liked that one best, and took her first step on the Milford Track. Her reverence was broken by catching up with the senior hikers, who were conversing in German. Alexa hoped to be in such good shape at seventy or seventy-five.

"Hello," Alexa said.

"G'day," one woman said.

"*Guten Tag*," said the other.

Alexa skirted a mud puddle and passed them. The big storm left high-water marks—silt and weeds—in zigzags along the path. Around a bend came a sweet smell of something blooming. Or was it something decaying? Decomposing bodies emit a sickly sweet odor. Alexa sniffed suspiciously. It bothered her that she couldn't locate the source of the fragrance, but she hiked on. Her cop friend in Raleigh had said every time he was in public, even dressed in civvies and messing around with his kids, he felt suspicious of people walking toward them at a park, of every car that drove by when he walked the dog, of every door that opened when he was in a restaurant. Not an easy burden. Was the same happening to her, keeping her always on alert?

A bird—dark on top, yellow belly—darted across the path. She could hear the rush of water behind a carpet of emerald ferns and a maze of trees festooned with what looked like Spanish moss. She shivered, well aware that moss was parasite-ridden.

Where was Charlie? She looked behind her. The trail was deserted.

Alexa tried to concentrate on the here and now. Be in the moment. She focused on bright-green moss, roots, rocks—some flecked with mica, some coated with lichen. A sharp, sweet bird trill. The click of her new poles. The small holes they made with each placement. Her breathing. Bruce. He was newly divorced and recently moved to Auckland. Alexa fantasized he'd moved to Auckland because that was where she lived. The thought both thrilled and panicked her. Auckland Central

Police Department, where he was their newest detective inspector, was across the street from Forensic Service Center. They had met for lunch last week, and Bruce looked stressed. "Do you have a place to live?" she asked.

"A loft apartment in the Brickworks area. Two bedrooms." He snared her eyes like two bedrooms was a secret message.

Her heart hammered. Their attraction was undeniable, but if she yielded, gave herself over, melted, she'd end up leaving him. It was her modus operandi. In Raleigh, she'd done it to her live-in boyfriend, Jeb. And he wasn't the first.

Bill—back in college—and Harry, too.

She didn't need a therapist to tell her this was preemptive self-preservation.

Straddling a downed tree focused her on the path again. She followed the trail to a clearing, grateful she didn't have to watch out for copperheads like back home. There were no snakes in New Zealand. Bears, either. On one side of the path, a meadow stretched to a sparkling river. A side trail had been worn by hikers wanting to reach its banks. Glade Lodge, the destination for the Luxers, was on the other side of the path, one hundred yards away. Alexa had expected something fancier than the long green building. The middle section was gabled, with tall windows. Single-storied wings flanked it.

"G'day. It was 3,053 steps to get here," came a voice from behind her.

Alexa was blocking the path and moved over. A woman around her age smiled triumphantly, her face shiny with sweat as if she had jogged. Alexa didn't have patience for people obsessively counting steps. "Are you wearing an ankle monitor?"

The woman looked confused, then smiled again. "Yep. I reckon you're joking." Her accent sounded Australian. Alexa was beginning to recognize the difference between the Australian "yep" and the Kiwi "yiss." The woman waved her wrist to show off her tracking watch. "I'm diabetic. Logging my steps helps me know how much I can eat. Do you mind taking a snap of me for Facey?"

Alexa accepted the woman's phone and took a photo for her to post to Facebook. "Have fun," she said to the step-counter, and set off across the meadow to the river where she could keep an eye out for Charlie. She was hungry and wished he'd show up. The water was an intense aquamarine. Glacial melt, she surmised. Something about refraction. She dropped her poles and leaned her pack against one of the few trees shading the bank. She scrunched past boulders and across smooth stones to the edge. She didn't have to worry about seeing her reflection because the water ran swiftly. She scrutinized the shallows for greenstone. What did raw greenstone look like? Might not even be green. Dad and Rita had given Charlie a rock tumbler for his tenth birthday. The directions promised to turn ordinary stones into sparking gems. She'd been too impatient to wait the two weeks to see if Charlie's ugly driveway rock had metamorphosed into a swan.

She heard the nurses, like howler monkeys, before they came into view. Charlie was in their midst. She waved her hat to get his attention, but of course this attracted the whole troop, who invaded her space in leaps like their backpacks were weightless. None of them had old-lady poles or a fishing hat.

"How's it going?" Charlie asked. He poked the tips of his poles into the earth so that they stood on their own. He introduced Alexa to the nurses. "This is Hannah, Carlie, and Jennifer."

"Alexa, what's the temperature?" Hannah asked, and then laughed.

"Hannah," Jennifer admonished. She had a thick braid and glasses. Alexa thought she looked the most sensible of the three until she saw Jennifer was the one hiking in pink Crocs.

"Couldn't resist," Hannah said. "You must get it all the time. People asking for the weather or to play a song."

Alexa was used to Glock jokes, not Alexa jokes. She addressed

Charlie. "I'm starved. Let's eat." She hiked over to the tree and rummaged for the bagels she'd packed for their first lunch. For a surprise she had added two pink coconut sponge cakes, something the Kiwis called lamingtons. Charlie was contributing apples. Mel probably had him eating healthy.

"Look." Hannah pointed upriver, and Alexa's eyes—followed her finger. She saw a long swing bridge, sagging slightly in the middle, spanned the river fifty yards upstream. Two figures jounced across. Alexa thought they might be the German women.

The nurses rushed off.

"They've got a lot of energy," Charlie said. He picked up a rock and examined it. "This is limestone. There might be fossils in it."

Alexa nodded at the ugly rock to be polite. She handed Charlie a bagel. They stood there munching and watching the nurses jump up and down on the bridge. It made Alexa queasy.

Charlie took a large bite of bagel. He had cream cheese on his chin, but she didn't tell him. "Let's sit by the trees."

She rooted for the bright-green ground cloth the Macpac clerk had recommended. "Rains all the time on the Milford Track. Sit on this so your bum doesn't get wet." Of course it was in the bottom of the damn pack, and all her careful packing was now in disarray.

Charlie laughed. "Alexa, do you know Siri?"

"Shut up." She spread the cloth below a sun-warmed boulder, ten feet from the river, and sat to eat lunch with her brother. She couldn't begin to figure out when the last time she had eaten lunch, alone, with him. Good things were happening in New Zealand.

After five minutes they watched four new hikers cross the swing bridge. How many hikers could the bridge support? She held her breath until they all reached safety.

Charlie talked about his latest project. "It's a dam-remediation, near Cashiers, blah, blah. The seepage analysis found…"

She liked his enthusiasm about work, but her attention was

on a pair of gray ducks as they paddled against the current, then turned and rode it to where they started. Then they did it again. "Do ducks play?" she asked.

"What? Haven't you been listening?"

"Yes. Dam-remediation." She ate the last bite of her bagel and doled out the pink coconut cakes.

Charlie's eyes got big. "That looks like a Hostess Snoball. No way Mel would let the boys eat one of these."

The pink concoction was pretty bad; Alexa ate it anyway. For the calories. She unzipped her side pouch and got her camera. Through the telephoto lens she saw the ducks had rosy bills. One had a strand of algae hanging out of his.

Voices made her start. Two women were making their way to the river. One was the Dr. Diana Clark woman. Alexa remembered her cutting comment about Alexa not being a Luxe hiker. The other, shorter and stouter, jabbed the flat ground with her hiking poles as if gigging flounder. Alexa scooted back against the boulder and motioned for Charlie to do the same. She put her finger to her lips, indicating for him to shush.

"Quit trying to lord your posh life over me," came an angry voice.

"Oh, for Christ's sake, Rosie, be grateful I invited you."

Charlie looked at Alexa, his eyes big again.

"You only invited me because that Paul man from your office canceled."

"So what? You should still be grateful. Get you out of your little rut. Teach school. Fix dinner for Roy. Watch tellie. The problem with you is that you're always in my shadow, eh? The younger-sister plant that can't reach the sun."

Charlie caught Alexa's eye and made a face. She had to bite her tongue not to laugh out loud.

"That's important to you, isn't it? Your fans being grateful. Like this trip. They wouldn't be so grateful if they knew..."

"Knew what?" The doctor's voice turned venomous.

Alexa's urge to giggle evaporated.

"How free you are with your pad. How chummy you are with your drug rep. That you enjoy kickbacks."

A cloud covered the sun. Alexa felt trapped.

"Think of me as you enjoy your three-course dinner and wine tonight—something you wouldn't be experiencing without me."

Alexa heard the crunching of boots on the shingly ground. Then river burble. The remaining sister kicked a boot toe into shingles.

Chapter Six

When the second sister was gone, Alexa let out a whoosh of breath. "What was that all about?"

"They've got some Cain and Abel stuff going on. Glad they aren't in the hut with us."

She made Charlie go first on the swing bridge, and waited until he was across. She held both hiking poles in her right hand and clung to the railing with her other. Queasiness came as soon as she took a step. That icky roller-coaster feeling.

She was halfway across when someone stepped on behind her, causing the bridge to undulate. The panic she had been keeping at bay ambushed her; her heart raced and sweat dampened her armpits. She sprinted to the end. Charlie hadn't even waited. She could see his back disappearing into the forest. She swung around to glare. The woman who had dropped the postcard at the ranger station marched woodenly to the end, not even holding on, no hiking poles in sight. Alexa forced herself to replace the glare with a weak smile. "That was scary, wasn't it?"

"What?" The woman's face was expressionless. She no longer wore the long raincoat.

"That bridge. The way it wobbled."

She shrugged, her ferny green eyes on the path ahead.

They walked together awkwardly as the track veered from the river. "I'm Alexa," she said to break the silence.

"Gina."

Alexa smelled cigarette smoke on Gina's clothes and thought it odd for a hiker to smoke. "Where are you from?"

"Burswood."

Alexa hadn't heard of Burswood. The heavyset woman's face looked drawn, and Alexa hoped she was okay health-wise. "I live in Auckland. So you're hiking alone?" *Idiot.* Gina was hiking with her. "I mean, like overall?"

Gina gave a croaky laugh. "Giving it a go."

"That's brave. I'm doing it with my brother." She pointed. "He's up ahead."

Gina stayed silent.

Conversing with the reticent woman was draining Alexa's reserve of conviviality. Better save some for hutting. After a climb during which Gina huffed and puffed farther behind her, the trees gave way to a corridor of mountains, and Alexa ran to catch up with Charlie.

They remained silent as the path meandered in a narrow valley between snowcapped mountains, the vistas worthy of song. Alexa hummed "The Sound of Music" as she dug out her camera. "Stand there," she told Charlie, and clicked. The mountain on the left had a clear-cut swath starting halfway up and ending in a jumble of trees, boulders, and scree blocking the path. The sharp scent of freshly split wood spiced the air, and several root balls were taller than she was. A jerry-rigged wooden ladder had been placed between downed trees and big branches to help people navigate over the wrack.

"This was a recent landslide," Charlie said. "Probably happened during that storm."

She stowed the camera and went first over the ladder, hoping she wouldn't sneeze—didn't noise trigger avalanches? When a helicopter suddenly appeared, buzzing down the corridor, a heavy load of something dangling from its belly, she found herself scurrying from rung to rung, certain the vibrations would cause another avalanche.

She kept up her rapid pace and didn't wait for Charlie to catch up until there was a small lake between the path and closest mountain. A black bird perched on a drowned tree and scolded her with caws.

"What's your hurry?" Charlie asked, panting.

She was glad when the path rejoined the river. A sign said Clinton Hut was twenty minutes away. "I'll hike ahead and get us bunks," Charlie said.

"Okay." It was only four o'clock. Panic wedged in her mind as she watched Charlie head off: what would she do until bedtime? She'd rather be at the lab, where she could find out what happened about the woman who bit her own arm, or even better, start an article for the *Forensic Examiner* on the overlap of archaeology and odontology.

Overlap. Get it? She laughed at her own dental joke, but the flattened teeth of the Māori had intrigued her. The coffins were probably sealed now.

Clinton Hut was three forest-green single-storied buildings connected by decking. The fit businessmen—that's how Alexa thought of them—were playing cards at a picnic table. They nodded as she climbed the three steps to the deck. "Made it, did you?" one asked.

A squawk made her start. Two olive-green parrots played tug-of-war with a severed backpack strap near the cardplayers. One parrot dropped its end and eyed her, cocking its head. Alexa removed her hat and stared back.

Stead was sprawled on the bench of another table, sipping a beer, a collapsible fishing pole beside him. He gave Alexa a *what-took-you-so-long* smile.

She had seen parrots on her last case, but these looked larger. "Are they kakas?" she called to Stead.

"They're kea. The only alpine parrots in the world. Watch your stuff."

The kea followed Alexa like a security guard as she walked to Stead's picnic table. It squawked and spread its wings, flashing orange, and took flight. Alexa had an instant vision of the parrot caught in her ponytail. She waved her arms. The bird dive-bombed Stead instead and flew off with his Dodgers baseball cap in its beak.

Stead lunged at the bird. "Tosser. Give me that."

The kea landed on the corrugated hut roof and went to town, shredding the cap with reptilian talons and razor beak. Alexa tried not to laugh as she secured her own hat in a side pocket of her pack. The cardplayers jumped up to take photos. A couple other hikers emerged from the hut to watch the Dodgers massacre. Within two minutes the ball cap was in strips.

"Guess he wasn't a fan," Alexa said, dropping her pack with a thunk.

Stead rubbed his bald spot and didn't laugh. She hoped he might offer her a beer, but he stayed quiet. She hefted her pack and walked into the closest hut, searching for Charlie.

"Take your boots off!"

She looked at a frowning woman behind her. The line of hikers' boots against the outer wall should have cued her. "Sorry." She backed up and tugged off her boots.

The woman was part of the family of four, all in socks. They pushed past her into the hut, fanning in different directions.

Poles hung on hooks above the boots, so she looped hers on one and hoped nobody would steal them. She entered the hut in socks.

"Here, Daddy," the boy said.

"No," the woman said. "Those bunks are too close to the door."

Alexa thought her accent was Australian.

"There are two sleeping huts. I'll check the other," the dad said. "Take those for now." He pointed to four bunks.

Over half the twenty bunks had been claimed. Her heart surged at the sight of Charlie stretched on a bottom bunk near a window. His backpack lay on the top bunk.

"Hey, Lexi. Primo spot." He pointed up.

"Thanks."

Charlie removed his backpack so Alexa could spread her sleeping bag on the bunk. She noticed the low ceiling and that she'd barely be able to sit upright. "The hut master is giving a guided hike at five o'clock. After that, we can eat," he said.

"More hiking?" She saw he was excited, so she said okay. Plus—what else was she going to do? She searched through her pack for her Tevas and slipped them on over her socks. *Hello, Fashion Police.* She grabbed her toiletry bag and asked Charlie for directions to the bathroom.

There were four stalls with flushing toilets, and six metal sinks with ledges and crappy mirrors. No showers or hot water, but this was the wilderness, right? Alexa scrubbed her hands and face at the sink, reset her ponytail, and sprayed on more bug repellent.

When it was guided hike time, she and Charlie followed Ranger Beckett Harker past Clinton Hut. His droopy white hair and beanpole height made him easy to follow. "Been hut master for twenty years." He stopped on a wooden platform and welcomed around fifteen hikers, including Stead, the nurses, and the German women. He stomped his boot on the platform. "This is a helicopter landing pad. You'll hear a greater number of helicopters in the area, due to the storm. They're moving material to repair the track." He pointed to four MINI Cooper-sized white mesh bags full of rocks. "To fill in washout. Each bag holds a ton of rock. Won't shovel itself, though."

Alexa remembered her earlier helicopter encounter. "Can the noise from the rotors trigger avalanches?"

Ranger Harker gave her an appraising look. "It's not

avalanche season, lass. That's May through November. It's land-slide season now."

"Should we be worried about landslides?" she persisted.

"Eh, slips are more frequent after heavy rain."

Great. "So—yes?"

"*Yiss.* Landslides have been occurring round here for millions of years."

"Are there warnings?" one of the nurses asked, her eyes big and round.

The ranger rubbed his chin. "Trees cracking, boulders knocking together."

"If that happens—what should we do?" the nurse asked.

"Run."

Alexa, swatting tiny flies, did not like that advice. Stead, now wearing a fleece beanie, caught her eye. She blushed, and then got mad at herself for her schoolgirl reaction.

"We'll head toward the river," Ranger Harker said, leading the way as Charlie peppered him with questions about granite and marble and glacier moraines. They talked rocks until the ranger stopped and pointed to tracks. "We've had a recent visit."

The group crowded around him.

"A kiwi," Ranger Harker said. "See three toes and how the prints are in a straight line?"

Alexa pressed close to Charlie. "Did you know there are no indigenous land mammals in New Zealand? That's why there are so many flightless birds like the kiwi. They don't have to fly away from prey."

"Shush. I want to hear what the ranger is saying," he grumbled.

They ambled to the riverbank, the mood light as shadows darkened. Ranger Harker used a stick to dislodge a rock in the shallows. "The Māori have hunted greenstone in the Clinton River for centuries. Of the three types, the rarest and most valuable, bowenite, is found in Milford."

Stead used his hiking pole to turn over a few rocks, too.

"Have you ever found any?" Charlie asked the ranger.

"Yes, and I turned it in. The Ngāi Tahu tribe have all mining rights."

Stead grunted.

"The Luxe guide said we could keep it," Alexa said, "so long as we didn't sell it."

Ranger Harker frowned. "No *pounamu* can be removed from the park without permission from Ngāi Tahu."

"The Crown doesn't have any business saying who owns greenstone," Stead said.

"The law is the law," Ranger Harker said. "People stealing greenstone is a problem. Thieves even use helicopters to cart away boulders of it."

"Greenstone shouldn't belong to any one person or group over another," Stead insisted.

Alexa hopped from one rock to another, a few feet into the river, considering the opposing views of Stead and the ranger. *Does everything in the world need to be owned? Who are nature's shareholders?*

"Is this greenstone?" one of the nurses asked, holding a dark speckled pebble.

Ranger Harker studied it in her palm. "I don't think so, but if you had sandpaper..."

"Look," Charlie interrupted, "a trout."

Alexa saw the fish through the clear water.

"The Māori consider *pounamu* a fish deity," Ranger Harker said, turning his back on the river. "This is the end of our guided walk. I will see you all tonight."

Alexa hopped back to shore.

The nurses splashed in the river. "It's freezing," one of them screamed. Charlie began to take off his shoes, but Alexa told him she was starved.

Inside the dining hut, the windows were steamy, and mingled cooking scents made Alexa's stomach rumble. A hiker diced onions at a long stainless-steel counter. Another filled a jug from the sink. The three businessmen were using two of the six gas burners. The tween children ran around their parents' table. The older one tossed a hacky sack up and down. "Gimme it," the younger one screeched. Charlie intercepted it and started playing Monkey in the Middle with them. Alexa found a spot at a table where the German women played cards.

"*Du bist dran,*" one said.

"*Ja, ja,*" the other said, taking a card. "I know it is my turn."

Alexa said hello as she dug food out of her pack.

Charlie threw the hacky sack to the shorter boy and joined her. "What's on the menu?"

"Beef Stroganoff. All you do is boil water. Then pour in the foil bags and let it rehydrate. Presto, eat-o. No cleanup." *Ingenious,* she thought. If it was good, she might try it at home.

Charlie claimed an empty burner, lit it, and put their pot of water on. Alexa watched him talk to the businessmen, admiring his easy way with strangers.

"Mind if I join you?" Stead Willis asked.

Alexa scooched over.

Stead spread a cloth napkin like a tablecloth, and set a dish and spork on it, all very civilized. He wore no wedding band, Alexa noted. Not that that meant anything. "I don't cook the first night," Stead said. "I do takeout."

"Takeout is my middle name," Alexa joked.

"We'd make a great couple." Stead opened a crumpled paper bag and peered in.

Alexa's cheeks heated as she ripped open the freeze-dried dinner bags.

"'Sup, man," said Charlie, carrying the pot of boiling water. Alexa backed up as he poured half the water in one beef Stroganoff bag, and the remainder in the second bag.

"We have to wait six minutes," she said.

Stead laid a barely crumpled pie on his plate, the crust flaky and golden, and spread jam on it with his spork. "Venison pie with plum sauce."

"Crap. That looks good," Charlie said.

After four minutes, Alexa couldn't stand it and attacked her beef Stroganoff. Voices around her rose and fell like swelling waves. Alexa felt a rare sense of belonging as she crunched.

"Did you drag a husband with you from the States?" Stead asked.

"Her? Married?" Charlie snorted. "She loves 'em and leaves 'em."

"Shut up." He made her sound slutty. She closed up her beef Stroganoff to let it cook longer and stabbed Charlie with her eyes. "Do you have my lunch apple?"

"Oops. I ate it."

"Dammit. That was mine." They sounded like schoolkids. She opened her Stroganoff bag again and ate while coveting Stead's venison pie. When she slurped the last noodle, she crumpled the foil bag and looked for a trash can. She had a couple candy wrappers she wanted to get rid of, too. Stead saw her looking. "No rubbish bin. You carry your waste out with you."

"Really? I have to pack my trash?"

"Didn't you know that?" Charlie chimed in. "Pack it in, pack it out."

"The lunch apples your brother ate, for example?" Stead brushed pastry flakes off his hands. "Some tourists throw the cores in the bush, thinking it's okay." He looked at Charlie, his eyes appraising.

Charlie shrugged.

"If you throw the core out, it attracts pists."

"Pists?" Charlie asked.

"Rodents. Stoats and rats."

"Oh. Pests."

"What I said. We're trying to eradicate pists."

Alexa gathered her trash. "How is it you know so much about hiking and wilderness?"

"I spend a lot of time in the bush. I have a bach on the Grey River."

"A batch?" Charlie asked.

"A holiday cottage," Stead explained.

Ranger Harker appeared like a tall ghost and floated from table to table, collecting hut tickets and reminding everyone to sign the logbook.

"You sign for us," she told Charlie. "Our tickets are in my backpack."

As she shut the dining hut door, the world hushed. It had gotten dark, and she turned on her Maglite. A figure startled her. Alexa shone the light at a fully loaded and limping hiker emerging from the woods. She was startled to see Gina—Postcard Woman—shielding her eyes. Where had she been since they crossed that swing bridge together hours ago? Maybe she had had a Rip Van Winkle nap. "Hi," Alexa said, lowering the beam. "Are you hurt?"

Gina mumbled something and clomped into the closest bunkhouse.

So much for trying to be friendly.

Ranger Parker stood in a circle of soft light, his face ghoul-like, when Alexa returned. She sat next to Charlie, who handed her a mug of Sleepytime tea.

"It will rain tomorrow, heavy at times," the ranger was saying. "Some of the smaller creeks might flood the track. You need to use judgment crossing them."

She wouldn't need her sun hat. Charlie didn't need to know that it *was* Dad's old fishing hat. Alexa had borrowed it when she left for college and never returned it.

The ranger held some photos. "This is Hirere Falls Branch." He showed a dry creek bed. "This photo is only hours later." He glided around the room, holding the next photo so that everyone could ooh and ah at the raging torrent. "Anything that swift, don't cross."

Duh…

"Last year a twenty-two-year-old from Sydney was swept away, right here. She stuck one foot in the current. It dragged her in so fast her partner couldn't save her. She was found two kilometers downstream."

"*Ve* have hiked in rain before," one of the German women said.

"Yes, but perhaps not in New Zealand," the ranger responded. "If you come to a creek crossing the track, and it's deeper than your ankle, stop. Wait it out or turn around. It's better to be cold and late—than dead."

Alexa's mind flashed to the Māori elder's pronouncement: viewing the bones would unleash danger. Would it come as raging water?

Hikers, including Stead, left the dining hut subdued after Ranger Harker's additional warning of "Don't leave before dawn. Don't want anyone hiking off a cliff like…" Another gloomy tale about a girl leaving before first light and never being seen again.

Jeez, Alexa thought, *that girl's bones are somewhere. Maybe it wasn't an accident.*

Charlie nudged her shoulder. "Well, do you?"

"Do I what?" She watched the German women walk by. What was "good night" in German? *Gesundheit,* she thought.

"Want to go for a walk before turning in? I want to look for kiwi. This is when they're active. And the bathroom rush will thin out if we wait to brush our teeth."

"You heard what the ranger said about hiking in the dark."

"We'll be fine going to the river where we saw those tracks."

"I saw a kiwi on Stewart Island," she bragged, following him into the swiftly cooling night. "You wouldn't believe the blood-curdling calls the females make."

"I bet I could," Charlie said. "Turn your light off. Let's let our eyes adjust."

"To what?" Alexa said, slightly panicked.

The primordial woods, blanketed in darkness, shut her up. Sounds magnified: her breathing, the crunch of gravel, the swish of Charlie's nylon hiking pants, the trill of a bird, the gurgle of water as they approached the river. She strained to hear a kiwi and kept close enough to Charlie that she could grab him. Something damp brushed her cheek as her Teva stepped into a pool of sequin soup. What? Alexa jumped back and stared at the turquoise dots. The surface of the puddle was reflecting stars, she guessed. She craned her neck to see the sky, but the overhang of inky ferns and leaves and branches was impenetrable. She crouched and extended a finger to poke a fairy light. There was no pool of water.

"Charlie, look," she called softly, as if the insects would hear her and turn off their bioluminescent lights.

"What is it?" he said in wonder.

"Glowworms."

He crouched so close she could smell chamomile and spearmint on his breath. "Ben and Noah would love this." But instead of extolling the beauty of the glowworms' glimmer, Charlie sort of shuddered and choked out, "Mel and I have separated."

Alexa fell back on her butt. She scrambled to her feet and looked down at her brother. "What do you mean, separated?"

He didn't raise his head. "I moved into an apartment four weeks ago."

No ring. Rough patch. Alexa shouldn't have been surprised. "But why?"

Instead of answering, his shoulders quivered and he melted into a puddle of rain forest whimpers.

Alexa patted his shoulder. "What about the boys?"

He shook his head. "Mel cheated. I'm not taking her back."

———

Much later, a loud snorer and then a pressing bladder woke Alexa from sleep. That mug of Sleepytime was a bad idea. Alexa had stashed her flashlight in the crack between the mattress and the wall for easy access, but now—in darkness—she couldn't find it. She sat up and whacked her head against the ceiling eave. "Dammit."

She dangled her legs over the side of the bunk, guessed it was two a.m., and eased down, landing on her backpack. She shook a foot loose from a strap, almost toppling, and groped blindly for her Tevas.

Charlie—a gray lump in his sleeping bag—looked dead to the world. Poor Charlie.

She crept toward the door, past supine hikers, and stepped on a land mine of aluminum pots and pans, the clanging and crashing obnoxiously loud.

"For the love of God," a voice bellowed.

She found her way to the door and escaped.

In the bathroom she felt for the switch, forgetting there was no electricity. Peeing in pitch-darkness. Washing in cold water. Scurrying across the deck. The glow of ember. Someone smoking. Was that even allowed? She entered the hut, avoided the cookware, and climbed up to her sleeping bag.

"Bloody hell," its occupant yelled.

Oh, my God. Wrong bunk. She scuttled to the next top bunk, and patted the bag. Empty. She nestled in and cursed the snorer under her breath.

SUNDAY

Chapter Seven

Hot oatmeal with raisins perked her up in the morning. Alexa stood at the dining hut window, scraping the last gummy oats from her bowl. Charlie had already finished and was packing up. The mountains were enshrouded in mist. Beyond the pane of glass, Gina set off, her limp barely perceptible.

Alexa watched as the fog swallowed her. Swirly. Poof. Gone.

The way she vanished worried Alexa. Disappearing in these giant mountains was easy.

While she washed her dish, she looked for Stead. He had either left early or was sleeping in, though Alexa didn't see how sleeping in was possible. People had whispered and zippered her awake before first light. Most of them were already gone. *Were they trying to get the best bunks at the next hut?*

Fifteen minutes later she and Charlie sat at one of the deck picnic tables, tugging on their boots. The sound of an approaching helicopter drowned out the morning birdsong.

Charlie hefted his backpack on. "I'm off. It's ten miles to Mintaro Hut."

"Hold on. I'm almost ready." She double-knotted her left bootlace.

"Nah. I'll see you later. I'm sure we have different paces."

"What if we have to cross a stream?" She made a knot of her

right lace and had to start over. "It would be safer if we hiked together."

Charlie scowled. "It's not raining. If anything looks dangerous, I'll wait for you."

Alexa decided he regretted confiding in her about Mel. Her heart ached as she watched him trudge off. She didn't want a wedding or kids, God forbid. But she wanted Charlie to have them. To be whole. To be the family unit snatched out from under her childhood.

Damn Mel.

She doused herself with repellent as a yellow copter lowered through the mist and landed deftly on the helipad. The helicopter bore the logo Southern Fiordland Aerodrome. A middle-aged man hopped out as Ranger Harker crossed to meet him.

"Damien," he shouted.

"Harker," the pilot answered.

Ranger Harker's voice was animated. "What are you doing here? I heard they pulled your license. Flying too low. Landing in a danger zone."

Alexa stood for a better view.

"Nah, mate. Just a misunderstanding," the pilot yelled. He looked over at Alexa, then back at Harker. "It's all hands on deck because of the storm. Let me use the dunny, grab a cuppa, then I'll be moving these loads to Devil's Elbow." He pointed to the rock bundles surrounding the pad.

"Bugger all. I read that incident report."

The family of four, marching in descending size order, interfered with Alexa's eavesdropping. The caboose tossed the hacky sack in the air as he followed his parents and brother into the woods.

She spent a few moments digging out her raincoat, giving the family plenty of time to get ahead. No one else was around as she left. Her worry about overcrowded hiking trails had been silly.

Pale mossy tresses draped from tree branches as she walked down the canopied track. The ranger had called it goblin moss. It made the woods look haunted.

A light rain started a half mile later. She took inventory to stave off unease: waterproof pack liner—check. Waterproof pack cover—check. Waterproof food sack—check. Raincoat— wearing. Poles. Crap. Her new hiking poles were back at the hut. She planned to use them to test water levels if the paths flooded. She twirled around and headed back.

A sprinkling of people in matching yellow slickers passed her. She realized they were Luxe Tour hikers. Clint, his clipboard encased in plastic, brought up the rear. He'd been photograph- ing the Luxers from behind. He eyed her suspiciously. "Milford Track is one way only," he said. "Northward."

"Thanks for that."

The nurses came next, talking earnestly about night shifts, charting, and paging. The one named Hannah waved at Alexa.

She was glad to pass them without an Alexa comment and have the path to herself again. Not that she wouldn't have minded hiking with Charlie, though. She wanted to ask him why he moved out. *Shouldn't it have been Mel?* She thought of her nephews, Benny and Noah. Her heart ached for the confu- sion they must be experiencing. She'd buy a couple stuffed kiwis for Charlie to take home for them.

The haughty doctor rounded a bend—*what was her name?*— gesticulating to a dark-haired man beside her. Her mauve lips moved rapidly. She barely glanced at Alexa, as if her presence didn't register. "We'll have to expand the theater hours."

"Your schedule is full," the man replied, pulling on his hood. "It would be best to hire another ortho."

"That would eat up profits. We can add Saturday mornings."

Overhearing snippets of conversation was fun. Where was the doctor's sister? Their argument at the riverside had been quite vicious. She heard a noise in the thicket just off the path and jumped. No bears or cougars in New Zealand, she reminded herself. She cinched her waist strap tighter, pulled her hood up, and picked up her pace. Her fingers were cold, but it would be too much hassle to dig for her gloves.

The deck of Clinton Hut was deserted. Her hiking poles weren't dangling from the knobs where she had left them. She worried someone had taken them as she entered the dining hut.

Stead Willis sat at a table, a mug steaming in front of him. He had the room to himself. He half rose upon seeing her, but then sat.

"You're still here?" she asked.

"Tried to catch my breakfast in the river. No luck. Coffee?" He gestured to the mug. The strong aroma was heavenly.

"Sure." She felt uneasy being alone with him but then heard voices.

Stead sprang to the window. "Some Luxe trampers. They'll use the loo and be on their way." He came back to the table and rummaged through his pack for a pot. At the cook counter, he lit the gas, filled the pot, and set it on.

"I forgot my hiking poles and had to turn around to fetch them," Alexa explained. "Now they're missing."

Stead pointed to the ranger's quarters. "Look in there."

The door was cracked. Alexa knocked perfunctorily. "Hello?"

There was no answer, so she pushed it open. Her hiking poles were crisscrossed on the ranger's desk, next to the logbook. She swooped them up and showed Stead.

"Good, that." He was washing a mug in the sink. "Someone left this behind. You don't need to fish yours out."

Alexa retrieved the logbook from the ranger's desk and sat down as Stead concocted her coffee. She remembered how the ranger at the Welcome Center had said to always sign the logbook. She flipped to the last pages, curious where her fellow hikers were from. Austin, Texas. She thought of the nurses. Tianjin, China. Perth, Australia. Tel Aviv, Israel. Bremen,

Germany. There was Charlie's familiar scrawl: *Charles Glock, Asheville, NC.* He had written her name, too, and listed Auckland as her home. Alexa thought about this. Auckland felt like an experiment yielding unexpected results. A good job. Bruce. But it didn't feel like home.

"Here you go." Stead set the mug in front of her, and took his seat. Junk was spread over the table. The collapsible fishing pole. A waterproof map. Trowel. A baggie of sandpaper. A knife.

Stead must have seen her eyes linger on the knife. "For gutting fish," he said.

"Thanks for the coffee." She met his gaze, held it, took a sip. She could get used to a man making her coffee. More comfortable talking about work than personal stuff, Alexa asked what a pi-zo engineer did.

"Anders is a growing company. Couple offices here and there. I work mostly with aviation noise control."

"That's interesting." Like counting sheep is interesting. New Zealanders were sensitive about sheep jokes, she'd discovered. But counting teeth. *That* was interesting.

Stead asked about her job, and Alexa told him about her most recent case. "I got chased by a sea lion," she added.

Stead's laughter was drowned by thwapping. It sounded like a copter was landing on the roof. No noise reduction here. He hurried to the window.

Alexa took another sip of coffee, set it down, and waved goodbye, glad to be setting off again. The yellow Southern Fiordland helicopter hovered above the landing pad area, a long line and hook hanging from its belly, the tall grass stirred into a frenzy. One load of rock was gone. Alexa guessed the delinquent pilot—if Ranger Harker had been correct—was back for a second load. She watched as a bundle was hefted into the air as if it were a bag of bones.

Bones. What made her think of bones?

The helicopter pilot wore shades and a shiny helmet. She

wondered if he recognized her from earlier when their eyes had met over the tongue-lashing Ranger Harker gave him. Probably not. Might not even be the same man.

It was peaceful, reclaiming the path, the rain gentle, the leaves shiny, the branches of one tree heavy with deep red berries. She thought of Bruce, smiled softly, and wondered when she would see him again. A fantail bird kept just ahead, teasing, tweeting with nervous energy, and opening its tail feathers like a deck of cards.

A dead fantail in a house was a Māori omen of death. She shrugged off worry; she was outside, and the bird was alive. She imagined its beating heart, so fast, and imagined her own, slow and steady. She stepped over a gnarled root, then another, and wondered if underground they were connected to the same tree. She knew a whole network of roots spread below the surface, holding hands, sharing nutrients—through fungi—like neighbors sharing a cup of sugar. When the rain picked up, she didn't mind. It was nourishing the roots.

She recognized the spot where she had turned around before: the straight stretch hugging the river, which she noted was running gin-clear, despite the rain. Ranger Harker had said a sign of impending landslide was muddy water. Everything ahead was new territory. She checked over her shoulder for Stead, figuring he'd catch up with her.

She was alone.

Hiking wasn't bad, she decided as time and mile markers passed. A lot of hiking was looking down, navigating roots and rocks and life.

At mile marker seven, the path turned into a stream. She tried hiking on the higher ground to the side of the path to keep her boots dry, but the slant and slide made her succumb to sloshing through. Within her hooded world, sound was amplified. The rain pelting her pack. The slosh and suck of her boots through mud. Her breath. She jogged up a small rise, leaving the flooding track behind. At the top, she could see a wide flat valley, the Clinton River on one side, mountains on the other, and the trail like a gray highway through the middle. It looked like a bowling alley, Alexa thought. Maybe a mile ahead, she could see the forest begin again.

Openness was refreshing after the cloistered woods.

The gray hulks guarding the left side of the trail were almost vertical. Thin waterfalls gushed down their sides in silver streaks. She trudged down the hill and onto the flat corridor. A No Stopping, Avalanche Area sign fueled her stride.

A sharp crack made her freeze.

Don't stop.

A blur on the mountainside caught her eye. A tilt of trees. Thunderous roar. Vibration beneath her boots.

She turned tail and ran.

Chapter Eight

Alexa leaped over rocks and staggered up the slick hill, away from the corridor of mountains, back toward Clinton Hut, struggling against a stream of mud. She slipped, face-planted. One pole went flying. She couldn't breathe or scream in the muck as her body slid down the hillside, her backpack weighing her down. She struggled into an upward-facing-dog position, her hands sinking until she found purchase and flipped over, sat up, pawed sludge from her eyes and nose, and spat mud. From here she had a front row view of Mother Nature's force: a slew of boulders, branches, and mud obliterated the trail she'd just vacated, terminating at the river's bank. Both sides of the swath were visible—the debris at the bottom spread half a football field wide. The sound of another crack made her crab backward. God almighty. A car-sized boulder careened from the mountainside, gained momentum, bounced like a giant's beach ball, detonated the pileup, then rolled to a stop in a ditch.

Alexa's heart drummed heavy metal and her breath came ragged. The boulder would be embedded for a thousand years.

She was nothing but a speck in time.

She blinked a raindrop out of her eye and spit more mud onto the ground, bit down, felt grit. She spit again. The hiking pole she hadn't dropped was tangled on her wrist. She yanked it off, glad she hadn't gouged herself, and groped under her slimy pack cover for her water bottle. She fumbled it open and gulped while sitting in a stream of mud and rain. She was spared. She wiggled her wrists and ankles, flexed her knee joints, checking for injury. Her right knee was sore, probably hit a root, but the mud had softened her fall.

A sound made her start. She realized she was whimpering. Like Charlie had been last night. A few more feet down the path and she'd have been flattened by Mother Nature. The danger the Māori elder had warned her about had been unleashed.

I believe in science, not curses.

She wiped her nose and jumped up. What if someone was buried alive? What if Charlie was hurt? She turned. Surely Stead, or someone, would hurry along and know what to do. The path was deserted. Did anyone besides her even know there had been a rockslide? How far had the sound carried through the rain?

Think.

She searched for her missing pole. Couldn't find it. Backpack on or off? She'd be faster with it off, so she unbuckled the waist belt. But no. The first aid kit was in it. She clipped the belt as her mind jerked into gear. The first step in crime scene investigation—even a Mother Nature crime scene—was to make sure it was safe to enter.

Was it?

She edged forward, aware it had only been minutes since the landslide. She spotted her missing pole, grabbed it, and started down the rain-slicked hill, toward the open valley, feeling like a contestant on *Survivor*. She stepped past the listing AVALANCHE DANGER sign, listening for cracking or crashing, ready to run. She scanned the mountainside. The sliding mass had sloughed a trail, narrow at the top, and wider at the bottom where mud, rocks, and trees had catapulted to the river.

A gust of wind lifted her sodden ponytail as she stepped around the giant boulder. She pulled her hood up as a bird flew overhead, tweeting complaints. It landed on an uprooted tree. King of the jumble. First eyewitness on the scene: a robin. It occurred to her that most landslides happened without witnesses. As far as she knew, this one had. She'd heard and felt the barrage, but her back had been to the tumult as she ran for safety. Again she wondered if anyone else knew about the slide. Was this front-page news? Or commonplace? She didn't think anyone had been directly in front of her, but you never know.

She schlepped to the debris field, scanning for a backpack or hiking pole. Movement. "Anyone need help? Hello?"

"Hello, 'ello," echoed back.

She leaned forward and cupped her hands on either side of her mouth. "Charlieee. Charlie?"

Only wind and echo answered.

Time for a plan. She was closer to Mintaro Hut than Clinton Hut. It was maybe four miles away. She wanted to go forward, to where Charlie was. She peered at the swath, ready to retreat at the slightest shift or movement. Climbing through the rubble was stupid. Dangerous. Skirting the debris and rejoining the trail—she could see it lonely, unscathed—on the other side, was her best bet, even if it meant she'd have to wade in the river.

She studied the sky. No indication the rain would cease. The river was rising. She bushwhacked along the chest-high debris field, stomping on ferns and sinking in shifting scree, to reach the bank. It was hard to believe this was the same river where a trout flickered through its crystal depths last night. Rubble, bisected by the trunk of a tree, stretched five feet out in the turgid water.

Go, go, go, she told herself.

She stepped in shin-deep, shocked by ice-melt temperatures, and staggered against the mean current. She jabbed her poles down for stability, pulled, then couldn't extricate them. *Damn.* One was wedged between two solid things, the other was stuck in mud. She pulled again, got one loose. Tugged the second, almost falling when it released, the current pressing her backward. She dangled the poles from her wrist and staggered farther out, stubbed a boot against a hidden rock, stumbling like a drunk. If she fell, her backpack would be an anchor. She unbuckled the waist belt so she could slip out of it, and then lunged for the trunk of the downed tree. It would be safer to climb over the trunk, rather than go farther into deeper water. She heaved herself up the slimy cold bark, and over. Dropped down. Staggered in dammed water up to her thighs, then her waist. She yelped, thought of drowning, of Charlie. Of the curls he'd had when he was little. She pulled herself around a jagged branch. Jerked a snagged pole free. *Oh, my God, a bird's nest—* three tiny green eggs—nestled in a crook. Unbroken. Perfect. She freed the nest, carrying it above the whirling eddies, and heaved her leaden legs toward shore. Five more steps. Four. Three. Her numb feet hit solid ground.

Deliverance.

Her breath came staccato. Her pants and boots were water-logged. Entering the river had been risky. The icy force of it. But she had made it.

She settled the nest on the ground and struggled out of her backpack. Food. She needed carbs. Too many drawstrings and buckles for her stiff fingers. She panicked that the food would be wet, ruined, but the pack cover and pack liner and waterproof food bag had worked. She marveled at the high-tech magic, mentally thanking the woman at the outdoors store for insisting, and scarfed cheese and crackers and dried salami, right in the rain like a crazy woman. She shivered, imagining the enzymes in her stomach breaking down the food, sorting sugars and fats, and converting calories into energy and heat.

Time. Her watch wasn't waterproof.

She shook her wrist, pulled up her sleeve, and stared. The minute hand caressed the four, crept toward the five as if this were an ordinary day. She noted the time: 1:30. No wonder she'd been hungry.

Alexa stored the food bag and retrieved the nest, worried for the eggs. Spotting a solitary stunted beech spared by the rock-slide ten feet away, she squelched through mud and rocks to reach it. She lifted a leafy branch and stood on tiptoe. "Here, guys." She wedged the nest into a gnarled crook sheltered from the rain and admired the delicate promise of new life. She backed out, praying Mama would find them. Not that praying for her own mama had ever worked.

She turned and almost stepped on a hand that was jutting from a pile of rocks.

Chapter Nine

She stifled a scream. The hand was skeletal. Bare bones. This wasn't a landslide victim.

Or a current one.

Confusion whirled in her head. What was going on? Was this another burial ground? Had the landslide exposed the bones? But that was strange. The debris from the landslide ended a couple yards away. This spot near the river was undisturbed. Maybe vibrations from the tumult had exposed it.

She shrugged out of her backpack again and knelt, wondering how many of the twenty-seven bones of the human hand would be present. Bone-scatter—usually by animals—might be minimal if they'd been buried. She removed a pebble, exposing the two bones of the thumb. Opposable thumbs, Alexa reflected, allowed early humans to make tools, build shelter, forage food, caress their babies. Alexa flexed her cold fingers and then made a fist. The human hand evolved not just to enhance dexterity, but also as a weapon. When the fist clenched and the thumb folded, the hand became a club with which to strike an opponent's skull. Male-to-male combat to win the female. Violence in pursuit of procreation.

Stay on task, she chided herself.

She removed a rock from the wrist. The sight of the ulna and slightly larger radius stopped her. This wasn't a severed hand. These were arm bones. That meant there was probably an entire skeleton.

She jumped up and backed away. She hadn't noticed before, but the hand and lower arm extended from a mound of rocks. River rocks the size of fists. Jesus. This wasn't random disarray. This was a grave.

Alexa wanted to call Bruce. He could notify the local cops. But she was in the middle of nowhere, where cell phones didn't work. For all she knew, another landslide could be brewing, like an earthquake aftershock. She thought of Stead and other hikers who would be coming this way. They would see the landslide. Would they forge the river forward like she had? Or turn back, tell the ranger? She figured the latter, especially since the rising river was inundating her route. The tree she had lumbered over was barely visible now. What if the river continued to rise? She was maybe forty feet from the bank. She could smell the river's breath. It was like an animal, roiling by, waiting for opportunity. Urgency and the danger of another landslide helped her make a plan. *Take photos. See if there is a skull and peek at the teeth. Hightail it to the closest hut.* Mintaro was maybe two hours away. The Luxe lodge was closer.

She walked over and ducked into the shelter of the beech tree and leaned the backpack against the trunk. She flexed her hands, trying to warm them, and pulled out the crime kit sack and camera. She reviewed the basics in crime scene photography: Adjust for lighting. Shoot distant first, then medium range, then close up. Include a scale. Had she packed a ruler? She opened the sack and peered in. *Yep.*

Ready, she slipped on latex gloves, pulled her hood up, and left the foliage, her wet pants clinging to her calves and thighs. She backed up from the grave, the churning river behind her, the chaos of the landslide past the grave filling the viewfinder, and clicked. Her hands were shaky; she had to work to steady them. Then she photographed from the other side, toward the river, and took panoramas of the hostile grandeur.

She approached the grave. Mid-range shots established spatial relationships. How close the bones were to the beech tree. How far to the landslide rubble. Mid-range photos sometimes included evidence. A knife left in the body. Bullet casings. A cigarette butt. Body fluids. If this was a crime scene, Alexa had no idea what the evidence might be. A rock? A Māori war club? Could this be a Māori who had come to Milford for greenstone?

Was she unleashing more danger by looking at the bones?

I believe in science, not curses.

She placed the ruler next to the hand and shot several pictures. Based on the position of the hand, she believed the deceased was lying on his or her back. She retrieved her probe to count the visible bones. She wished Dr. Luckenbaugh, the Wellington archaeologist, was by her side, in case these were old bones.

Out of nowhere, a large bird of prey—a hawk, she thought—swooped so close to her head she felt the breeze. A damn pterodactyl from Gondwanaland, trying to carry her away. She did not like this place.

She stood on shaky legs and peered over the grave, guesstimating where the head would be. She knelt above the spot and removed stones, one by one, wondering about the hands that had placed them. Were they shaking? Grieving? Bloodstained? Raindrops splotched a protruding rock. When she tried to pry it up, she realized it was the smooth curvature of the frontal bone—a forehead. Alexa hopped up to retrieve her dusting brush and the spoon from her cooking supplies. She checked the river.

The tree trunk she had clambered over was gone, submerged.

She brushed mud, spooned out hardened dirt, repeated the process until an eye socket—somewhat square—gaped, then the second. She started to dig soil out of the orbits but caught herself. Eye sockets contain delicate bones that the spoon would damage. Her gloved hands no longer shook, and she was barely aware of the steady rain. She exposed a sunken nasal cavity and wiped a raindrop off her own nose.

A beetle crawled across the left cheekbone. She flicked it off, exposed the right cheek, and then uncovered the jaw. She believed the skull was that of a mature adult—the teeth would confirm—and probably male since the ridge along the brow was pronounced, and the jaw was squared and robust. She thought again of man's ability to make a fist, and marveled at the fact that the male skull evolved to withstand its blow.

Her heart revved as she looked at the teeth.

She thought of the fern-root-flattened molars of the Māori in the caskets. If these molars were also flattened, it would indicate the decedent was pre-1930s. She tongued her own molars, gummed with candied pineapple, and traded the camera for the dental probe, nearly dropping it. Her gloves were wet. She wiped them on her thighs and gently, reverently cracked the death smile and maneuvered the jaw open. She leaned close and inserted the probe.

The third molar held a surprise. Nestled in the well-defined ridges and clefts was a composite filling. The decedent had had a cavity filled. Alexa wasn't expecting this skeleton to have records in some dentist's office. She discovered a second filling, and then a third.

The skeleton was modern, not ancient.

She took three close-up photos while running through a list of the materials used to fill cavities over the centuries: beeswax, gold, porcelain, silver, amalgams of copper, tin, silver, and mercury. Composite fillings mostly replaced silver or amalgam fillings around twenty years ago.

So the decedent could afford dental care, and was most likely buried within the last two decades. She rubbed her hands together, thinking of an X-ray machine. Maybe she could fly out with the skeleton when the authorities were notified. Leave all this hiking business behind, good riddance. But what about Charlie? She couldn't leave him when he had flown 8,500 miles to see her.

Damn rain. She stretched her stiff back and decided to expose more of the skeleton. Look for cause-of-death evidence and remnants of clothing or possessions. She squinted at the river. Stoked by relentless rain, it had crept closer. She marched over and placed a rock five feet from shore. When that rock was submerged, she'd leave. Milford Track stretched long between a valley of ferns, she noted, and was deserted of hikers. She checked the way she had come and didn't see a soul.

She'd take a quick look at the rib cage and get going. She removed more dirt and rocks. Dug with her spoon until it bent, then used her hands and ripped a glove. She found a sharp-edged rock and used it as tool and scoop. Unlike teeth, bone continues to degrade after death. Soil composition, temperature, rain—they all factored.

A glint below the rib cage caught her eye. She rooted around and exposed tarnished metal. Excited, she dug a bit more and took a photo before extracting a three-inch-by-two-inch metal plate with a twirly elaborate design. Her heart fluttered. An artifact. She brushed away a clump of dirt and turned it over to expose a bar and prong. This was a belt buckle, with the barest remnant of leather attached at the prong. She brushed away more dirt, photographed the front and back, and then bagged and tagged and stashed it in the crime kit. There was no more belt leather or sign of other clothing. The constant downpours of the area and the shallow grave had probably dissolved them. She felt lucky the buckle remained.

Alexa returned to the ribs, flattened by disarticulation. She was fairly certain this was an entire skeleton, though she had not exposed the legs. She poked a rib with her probe. Still solid. The mutilation made her drop it. She retrieved the metal probe between the third and fourth rib, noting multiple notches and incision marks, possibly knife wounds marring the bones. She counted six. Seven. Her heart revved. A lower right rib had been severed. She couldn't tell if the notches in the gray-brown ribs had been made by something serrated or smooth. One vertebra was severed. This man would never have walked again had he survived his injuries.

This guy had been brutally stabbed.

Alexa looked around as if a knife-wielding killer might emerge from behind the landslide rubble. *Stupid. The killer is long gone.* Then she freaked when she saw her warning rock was gone, submerged by rising water. There was no way other hikers would be able to follow her route now. She dashed to the tree and packed up everything but the crime scene tape. She encircled the grave with it, weighing down the bright tape with rocks. Florescent yellow would be noticeable from either side of the track and from the air. She found a stick and jabbed it into the muddy earth, tied the last of her tape from it like a flag. The rain weighed it down, but when the sun came out, if it ever did, it would flutter to life. More than she could say for the victim, whom she scrutinized for thirty more seconds. He resembled a person on the beach, half-buried, posing for a picture. She lifted a thumb bone, worried birds or rats might carry it off. Should she take a sample of bone with her? She found her ground cloth, the bright-green one she bought at Macpac. It was big enough to cover just the skull and shoulders. She weighted it down with rocks.

In the end, as further proof of this man's existence and insurance against scavengers, she slid the thumb bone in her pocket.

Chapter Ten

The track toward Mintaro Hut hugged the river. Alexa wished she could leave it behind. She felt like the river was following her, instead of the other way around. She eyed the bulwark of mountains lining either side, spilling their guts in roaring ribbon falls. Remnants of a prior landslip stopped just short of the trail. Alexa figured this was damage from the recent storm. A bag of rocks—like the ones around the helicopter pad—had been set down right on the path. She trampled waist-high ferns and grass verges to get around it.

Fifty yards up was another bag of rocks. BULK BAG was written on the side. She had thought the pilots dumped the rock, instead of setting down the whole bag. Using helicopters made sense. There were no roads. She guessed a ranger spread the contents. First they'd have to deal with the latest landslide.

She imagined the dammed-up Luxers behind her, disappointed they'd have to turn around. Every day new trampers, both independents and Luxers, started the hike. There would be a logjam.

Not my problem. Steadman Willis would be wedged among them. She'd been interested in what he had to say, and had stupidly blushed when he'd caught her eye. Bruce wasn't the only trout flashing in the river.

Now she'd never see Stead again. A tramping crush, crushed.

She looked ahead, tried to see how long she would be in this flat, fraught valley. For a surprise moment, the rain ceased and sunlight flickered across the fern field valley. Milford Track dissolved into mist, the forest obscured. Bush, the Kiwis called it. The landslide and skeleton had cost her two hours. Now was when she should be arriving at the hut. Charlie would start to worry. She picked up her pace, fingering the bone nestled in her pocket.

Another DANGER sign caught her attention. She scurried to read it: AVALANCHE ZONE. DO NOT STOP.

The river widened into a small lake, its surface uneasy, and then it snarled its way out the other end. A distant *whop-whop* brought her to a halt. She searched the sky. The whopping intensified. A yellow copter throttled into sight.

Alexa got excited. If she could get the pilot's attention, he could land. She'd be able to explain about the bones and get him to notify authorities.

She waved her poles back and forth, hoped her bright-blue raincoat would draw the pilot's eye, even though she was a half mile away. The bird hovered over the landslide. Over the bone field. The pilot would see the destruction, the severed path, the yellow tape, and her green tarp covering the bones. Alexa ran in a clumsy circle, sloshing through puddles, flailing her arms. The copter dipped over the tape area, hovering like a fat osprey eyeing a fish. Alexa started running toward it, but after a few yards, the copter lifted and veered off toward Clinton Hut.

Her heart sank. The rain started again. She got mad and beheaded a stalk of grass with her pole. She whacked another. And another. Guillotined husks littered the path. The authorities needed to be notified, and her chance to do that had just flown away. Hiking sucked. She calmed herself by remembering Charlie as a little boy. After Mom died, she and Charlie and Dad had banded together, become a ragtag team. Dad took them on

Saturday-morning hikes. Umpstead Park. Hanging Rock. Neuse River Trail. Charlie, with his mop of uncombed curls, always lagged behind, irritating Alexa.

But he was only four or five. I was awful.

She was glad Charlie had confided in her. She wished she knew how to comfort him. She had failed as a kid. Now it was time to step up. Step forward like she was doing right now. But she didn't know what to say. The path meandered along a mountain flank, farther from the river, making Alexa nervous about another rock slip. Pulsing in the air caused her to turn. She watched the copter maneuver back, enlarging from yellow dot to incoming aircraft, the grass waving in its wake. The rpm of the rotors increased, became deafening. A bulk bag dangled from its belly.

He'd come back with a load of rocks.

Alexa raised her poles, waved them. The copter dipped vertically over the landslide, where she figured it would hover again, but it flew past, toward her. Hope flooded back as she watched, her poles in the air. The copter homed in on her. Yes! But it accelerated instead of slowing, the bulk bag skimming the ground. She could see the pilot's face through the windscreen. Helmet. Sunglasses. Weird again because of the rain. She waved madly. The stalks of grass edging the path flattened in the downdraft, the bag of rocks closing in, coming at her. Alexa ducked.

"Dammit," she screamed at the ground. "You're too low." She looked up, confused.

A ton of rock bore down on her like a runaway freight train.

Alexa dove flat. The copter hovered just ahead. She lifted her head, watched as pendulum physics played out in front of her eyes. The lethal mass of rock was swinging back. She flattened, protected her head with her hands, her mouth pressed against moss. She heard and felt the bulk bag whir by. She wiped her mouth with the back of her hand. Caught her breath. She pushed her chest up with her arms and watched the helicopter and its lethal cargo dart away. She scrambled to her feet, awkwardly because of her pack, and held her hands like WTF.

"Moron," she yelled. She had dropped her poles and now scooped them up.

All she could figure was that the pilot forgot he had the load of rocks, and had tried to land. A huge mistake. She expected an apology. A dip of the bird. A hand signal. Mouth open, she watched the copter circle around, dip, come at her, the bag of rocks still suspended from a chain, careening her way.

This was no apology.

She dove as the bag whizzed by. She could feel the rotor downwash. Feel her heart pound her rib cage. She lifted her head. What goes up must come down, oscillation, she remembered from physics, and waited out Bulk Bag's return path, her skull throbbing in anticipation, the rotor noise deafening. The bag passed in a heavy *whoosh*, lower than her full five feet seven inches, and would pass again, its arc diminished, if she waited. She sprang to her feet and ran. With all her might. A glimpse of green woods ahead, a safe harbor. Alexa tore like Justify, the Triple Crown winner, all the time rationalizing: *He didn't see me. He didn't see me.*

The valley tapered. Trees appeared. Her legs shook as she reached the tunnel of green. Safety. If a bench appeared along the track, she'd sink onto it thankfully. Catch her breath. Call the police.

As if. There was no reception in these three million acres of national park. She stopped, bent over, pack riding up on her shoulders, hands on knees. *What just happened?*

Then she shuddered. The helicopter might land, the pilot might follow her into the woods. Try to kill her again.

Try. To. Kill. Me.

She straightened, cringing as her burn scars protested. She tightened her waist belt to ease the weight on her shoulders and loped ahead like the prey of a large flying carnivore.

It had to be an accident. He hadn't seen her, was trying to find a spot for the rocks.

No. He was trying to knock her head off.

Maybe he was trying to scare her. Have some fun at the expense of the tourist.

An accident. The rain made it hard for the pilot to see. Helicopters had blind spots.

Alexa vacillated for half a mile while checking over her shoulder. *Kill. Fun. Negligence.* The river had twisted off to torment someone else. Mud, puddles, and decaying matter muffled her footsteps. Ferns—high and low—dripped everywhere. Filmy fern. Palm fern. Tree fern. Silver fern. Red stems. Green stems. Furry stems. Furled stems. She stabbed a fiddle fern with her pole, and watched it quiver.

Why the hell hadn't the other hikers, Like Charlie, come to find her?

A crashing sound made her whip around. *Holy crap.* It was one of those New Zealand pigeons on steroids. Four times as large as the pigeons at home. Iridescent and ungainly. Flying low, then high, then off. Kererū. She had seen one on Stewart Island.

If the pilot had been trying to kill her, why? Was it because of the skeleton? Had she released some curse by removing the belt buckle?

Or taking the thumb bone?

The trees, close and tall, had stringy peeling bark and were smothered with hanging vines, goblin moss, lichen, and parasitic orchids. Plants dependent on other plants. Alexa wasn't dependent on anyone. For once, her independence made her feel vulnerable. But not helpless. She had the skills and brain to get out of trouble.

A sign ahead caused her heart to leap. But it was for Prairie Shelter, not a hut or lodge. The deserted shelter consisted of pilings with a tin roof. She stopped to catch her breath, but the openness made her uneasy—so she took a swallow of her water and hit the trail.

For an hour she tramped through steady rain, the trail empty and gloomy. She had no idea how a person could get used to hiking in rain, but she barely noticed it. The pattering on her hood was white noise. She hurried, picturing Charlie's sweet childhood face, and his harder-to-get-used-to adult face—he looked more like Dad now.

The path, banked by a cliff, was flooded. She remembered the ranger's warning about flash floods and jabbed a pole to measure the depth. Eight or ten inches. A rivulet tangling over the cliff was the culprit. It leaped and plunged and blew mist. She stepped over immersed rocks and roots. The path dipped, turned, and led to wooden steps disappearing down a thicket. Alexa gripped the slimy rail, counted twelve slippery steps. At the bottom, a small clearing opened to a swing bridge.

The river beneath it was a crescendo of force.

A waterfall—maybe a hundred feet high—fed the river. Jaw-dropping beautiful, she supposed. A sign said POMPOLONA CREEK. *Ha. Like Niagara is a creek.* She imagined writing Dad and Rita a postcard: *On day two of Milford Track, I found a skeleton and someone tried to smash my head with a bag of rocks. Wish you were here.*

Thinking of Rita always made her back scars taut, always made her think of that day she was thirteen and skidded across the kitchen linoleum in her socks, straight into her stepmother as she poured boiling water from a kettle. The top came off and the water poured down Alexa's back, melting her shirt into her skin. She hated the months afterward—pain, skin grafts, physical therapy. But even more she hated the cold look in Rita's eyes as she watched Alexa writhe on the floor.

Dad, Charlie, and her therapist tried to convince her the scalding was an accident. Her own clumsy fault. And she had, in recent years, started to accept it might be the truth.

But still.

She shuddered and walked closer to the bridge. The unrepentant sky pelted her with rain as she looked down. Volkswagen-sized boulders were slick with moss. Froth and mayhem funneled between them. The violence of nature took her breath.

The bridge was narrow—one-person wide, with a coiled metal handrail. Three wooden steps, covered with nonslip chicken wire, led up to the suspended structure. A sign warned it could support only three hikers at a time. Alexa looked over her shoulder, aware of being alone in the great sweep of forest. No one appeared, but fear settled on her shoulder like a hawk, its talons razor-sharp. She was between a landslide and a wild river.

Damn Charlie. Why had he left her behind?

Chapter Eleven

Alexa couldn't decide whether to hurtle or turtle across the suspension bridge. Each step brought a sway, wobble, warp. Her stomach hollowed. Her balance was challenged. In the middle, as if pulled by a magnet, she looked down at the gushing meltwater, untamed and jubilant. Close. Loud. If she fell, no one would hear her scream.

Go. Go. Go.

She bounced to the other side and jumped down the three steps to the ground. Something caught her eye. Blue metal. She walked along the bank of the cliff, maybe ten feet, and looked over the edge.

A hiking pole was wedged between a rock and a tuft of grass, just out of reach. She got a riding-in-an-elevator feeling in her stomach as she studied it, ignoring the river below. How did the pole get there?

The edge was too steep to lean over to grab it. She used the pointy tip of her own pole, poked it through the strap, and thrust. The mystery pole wouldn't release. She used both hands and jerked upward. It yanked free and dangled from the tip of her pole above the gorge. Suspended. She brought it to the bank. It was blue, with a smooth cork grip and lighter than her own poles. The grip looked ergonomically designed.

She might be someone's hero at the hut when she showed up with it. She retracted it and stashed it in a side pocket of her backpack.

Walking a long gentle hill past the swing bridge restored her body heat and equilibrium. Each huff separated her from creeks and rivers and helicopters. The trauma of the bulk rock bag had replaced the amazement of finding the skeleton. She reached in her pocket. Nudged her cold fingers around in the tiny nooks and corners, first the right side pocket, where she knew she had stashed the bone, and found only a candy wrapper, then in the left, a sealed baggie of clean toilet paper. Nothing else.

Gone. The thumb bone was gone.

Maybe during her lifesaving dives it had fallen out of her pocket. Why hadn't she stored it in an evidence bag in the crime kit? It was her duty as a forensic investigator to preserve evidence. She was an idiot.

Okay, she rationalized, she hadn't lost it willingly, and the evidence could be replaced by one of the other maybe 205 bones left at the scene. Plus she had taken plenty of photographs. She had proof in her viewfinder. But to lose evidence was a big no-no.

The face of the Māori elder filled her mind like a close-up movie scene. The elder's eyes were sad. "I was just borrowing the bone," she yelled. "To prove he exists. I was going to put it back."

She was losing her mind, yelling into a void of freaking trees. She looked around, but no one was coming. Now the body would never be whole. Her first New Zealand case had involved a black-marketed skull of an ancient Māori chief. The separation of head and body had unleashed a storm of evil.

The same had happened here. Someone had tried to kill her while the bone was in her pocket. No way she was going to retrace her steps and look for it. Not with a deranged aviator in the area.

Science.

She almost missed a sign hidden by drooping ferns. RIGHT: POMPOLONA LODGE, 10 MINUTES. LEFT: SIDE TRAIL TO FLOSS FALLS, 15 MINUTES. STRAIGHT: MINTARO HUT, 60 MINUTES. She sighed with relief. Charlie was waiting at Mintaro, but she needed to go to the closest oasis of civilization. Tell someone about the bones and crazy helicopter pilot. She didn't mind keeping Charlie waiting anyway. Served him right the way he hiked off without her this morning. She trotted toward the luxury hut.

On the porch of Pompolona Lodge, she shook off her hood. Was there a boot rule? She looked down at hers, soaked and muddy. But boots were not lined up outside the door like at Clinton Hut. Through large windows she spotted ten or twelve people at a bar or lounging on sofas and chairs, legs outstretched. Laughing. Talking. Drinking. A strange contrast to the solitary track and danger.

She wiped her boots on a mat, opened the heavy door, and stepped into a foyer area.

Heads swiveled her way. Talk and laughter ceased. The animated expression on the woman closest to where Alexa dripped on hardwood floor turned into a frown. As if she were expecting one person, and another showed up. Alexa wanted to yell, "Someone tried to kill me," but smiled apologetically instead, blinked in the bright light, and walked to the bar.

An attentive bartender, twenty years old at the most, came around front. He wore a tight black T-shirt and a black Luxe Tours ball cap. "Welcome. I'll get you checked in, eh? You look knackered. Your name, please?"

"She's not one of us," a man interjected. He sat at a bar stool in his clean trendy hiking outfit, twirling an olive on a toothpick.

Jeez, Alexa thought. "I need to speak with a ranger or person in charge."

"In that case, I'll find the lodge manager," the bartender said. "Can I get you something to drink while I track him down?"

"I'm good." When he left, Alexa unbuckled her waist belt, slid her sodden backpack off and leaned it against her thighs. Then she unzipped her raincoat, feeling eyes on her back. The talk in the lounge resumed, albeit softer. Someone played a jazz melody on the piano—"Stormy Weather," Alexa thought—near a glowing fireplace. She swiped her plastered hair out of her eyes and watched a confident woman, dressed in jeans and red V-neck sweater, pat the piano player on the back and murmur something in his ear. Then she sauntered over to Mr. Unfriendly at the bar. "There you are," the woman said to him.

He looked her up and down. "Feel better?"

Her golden brown hair shimmered. "Helped myself to a little something because of my knee. All good now. Any word on Diana?"

Alexa could tell by their accents that they were Kiwis. The man, dark-haired with a sharp chin, looked vaguely familiar.

"Not yet. She missed tea, but she won't want to miss cocktails."

Alexa knew where she'd seen the man. He had been walking with the haughty doctor this morning when she turned to retrieve her poles.

A door past the bar swung open, startling Alexa. A woman in a black apron bore a tray of muffins or biscuits and set them on a buffet table. Alexa watched her arrange cream, butter, and jams around them. "Pompolonas, as promised," she announced. "Piping hot."

Their scent was tantalizing.

A woman popped up from a couch and crowded the baker. "They look like scones."

"Yes. That's what they are. Just like the ones Quinton Mackinnon served his guests. But with Queenstown salted butter instead of mutton fat."

Another woman, and the Luxe guide, Clint—Alexa recognized him even without his clipboard—made a beeline.

"I'm nervous about climbing Mackinnon Pass tomorrow," the woman said.

"You'll be fine." Clint took a scone and spread it with butter and jam. "I'll be right with you."

"What if there's another landslide?"

"Oh, not happening. No worries."

Alexa's mouth watered as she watched Clint chew. Maybe just one scone while she waited. She saw how dirty her hands were and looked for a restroom. Her backpack would be safe leaning against the bar. She passed through, her boots trailing mud, and saw a sign for the Ladies near a dining room. She observed a young woman, dressed in a black T-shirt like the bartender, filling water glasses at seven round tables. Alexa couldn't help but compare the flower vases and tablecloths with last night's bare-bones dining hut. The far side of the room was a wall of windows framing a huge mountain, its upper third enshrouded in mist.

"Isn't the lodge in that mountain's avalanche path?" Alexa asked.

The waitress looked up, surprised. Her name tag said *Ima*. "We see slides on Mount Elliot all the time. Hear them, too. But we're too far away to be in their paths."

People are freaking nutso to be here, Alexa thought.

She hurried in the Ladies, not wanting to miss the manager, or the warm pompo-scone-os. The liquid soap smelled like lavender. She sniffed deeply, her shoulders easing.

The bartender intercepted her scone plan on her way to the lounge. "That's her," he said to the man with him.

The manager looked harried. He was tall, thin, in his fifties, with longish graying hair. "Vince Bergen. How can I help?"

She introduced herself, and explained that she was an independent hiker. "Is there somewhere we can talk in private, Mr. Bergen?"

"Eh, call me Vince. I'm quite busy. We have a situation."

You're about to have another one.

She followed him to a square paneled office with file cabinets and two messy desks. A large map of Milford Track took up half a wall. She was relieved to see a radio and phone on one of the desks. Vince motioned to a swivel chair, but Alexa launched right into her story.

He interjected after she explained about the rockslide. "We heard. Only seventeen of thirty-six Luxe clients made it here. The rest are stuck at Clinton Hut because they can't get through. Plus a guide."

"An independent hiker, too," Alexa added, thinking of Stead. She explained who she worked for to establish credibility.

"You work at Forensic Service Center? That's the CSI place, eh? Can't get telly at the lodge, but I watch it back home."

"Past the landslide, near the river, I found human remains."

"Someone got killed in the landslide?"

"No. These are old bones." But not *old* old. "I think the landslide jiggled some rock to expose them."

Vince rubbed his stubbly chin. "A dead person?"

"Yes. Skeletal. I need to inform the authorities."

"Who is it?"

She found this an interesting question. "I don't know."

"What authorities?" He remained standing and cracked the knuckles of his left hand.

"Law enforcement." It occurred to her that she would be the one sent to the scene. It was her job to travel to remote crime scenes to carry out investigations. *Oh, the irony.*

"So it's not the missing tramper?"

"I don't know anything about a missing tramper."

"One of our Luxers hasn't shown up. Her party is concerned. Did you see anyone?"

She thought of the mud and rock slamming down the mountain. "I haven't seen another hiker since the landslide. Do you think she got caught in it?"

"No. She was last seen past the slip."

She decided to keep mum about the helicopter pilot until speaking with the police. There was no telling with whom Vince was connected. His lodge must rely on copters for supplies. "Can you get that radio thing working, please? I also need to let my brother at Mintaro Hut know I'm okay. He'll be worried."

"It's a satellite phone. But there's no immediate emergency, eh?"

Why was he delaying? "I need to inform authorities now."

The office door opened and a woman stepped in. She was Vince's age, with chin-length brown hair tucked behind her ears.

"This is Kathy, my wife," Vince said. "Any word on the tramper?"

"Silas told me we had a visitor." Kathy looked quizzically at Alexa, and then at her husband. "No word. We need to call SAR."

"It's hours until dark," Vince replied. "Give her another thirty minutes. Remember the one who came in after dinner? All hyped about seeing a kiwi."

"I remember the hiker last summer, too." Kathy pursed her lips.

What happened to that hiker? Alexa wondered, hoping Kathy would elaborate.

"Our visitor says she found human bones."

Kathy's eyes widened.

Vince grabbed the phone.

Chapter Twelve

"What's your emergency?" the dispatcher said, her voice tinny.

Vince had handed the phone to Alexa. "I have found a human skeleton on the Milford Track." She enunciated carefully. "Near the Clinton River. Male remains. I suspect foul play."

"Is he hurt?"

She regretted mentioning the gender. "It's a skeleton."

"Do you need a helicopter?"

She needed a helicopter like a hole in her head. "I need the police to get here as soon as possible. And a forensics team. Well, forget that. I am the forensics team."

"Say again?"

"Keep the antenna pointing up," Vince said.

There was an antenna sticking out of the phone. Alexa realized it could swivel, and she adjusted it. "Send the police to Pompolona Lodge as soon as possible." She handed the phone to Vince, who then complicated matters by mentioning a possible missing tramper. "No," he said. "Don't send a helicopter. She might show up. I'll notify SAR if she doesn't."

Jeez, Alexa thought. *Let's be ambiguous.*

Vince talked some more and then disconnected. "The Te Anau police will be here at seven a.m."

Alexa had thought they'd come right away but realized that

was wishful thinking. Dusk was creeping over the mountains and rain forest and lake between here and Te Anau. "I won't be here in the morning. I'll be at Mintaro Hut."

"You can spend the night here," Vince said. "We have plenty of empty rooms because so many of our clients can't get here."

"But my brother is expecting me at Mintaro Hut."

"We'll radio the ranger and let her know. She can tell your brother. I also want to see if our missing tramper has shown up at Mintaro. I've already checked once, but maybe she arrived later."

Vince switched from satellite phone to VHF radio. The first question he asked when he made contact with the ranger at Mintaro was if the tramper had shown up. "The Diana Clark woman."

The name of the missing tramper gave Alexa goose bumps. It was the doctor she'd seen this morning.

"Negative, that," the ranger replied. "I would have called. I'll keep looking for her. We've a missing tramper as well. Her brother is concerned. Her name is Alexa Glock?"

"That's me," Alexa blurted.

Vince told the ranger that she was at the lodge and planning to spend the night. "She encountered an unusual situation and has notified the authorities."

"I'll let her brother know she's safe."

Alexa leaned toward the radio. "Tell Charlie I'm sorry." With a jolt she realized she had their hut tickets that the ranger would ask for. She began explaining.

Kathy interrupted. "Invite your brother here. It's only an hour hike. There's light yet."

"Our paying guests might object," Vince said.

"Pshaw," Kathy said.

Alexa leaned toward the radio again. "Tell Charlie Glock to bring his stuff and come here."

The ranger said she'd relay the message.

Worry besieged Alexa as Vince disconnected. What if Charlie refused to come? He'd be all set up at the independent hut, his sleeping bag unrolled, his boots off, feet up, wondering what was taking her so long. She told herself to have faith. Blood was thicker than dry socks.

"I'll have Silas show you to a room," Kathy said. "Dinner will be at six thirty. There will be a talk on Fiordland flora and fauna afterward."

Alexa doubted she'd be able to concentrate on ferns and fantails. She thanked Vince and followed Kathy toward the bar. "How worried are you about the late hiker?"

"Dr. Clark passed her sister on the track, so it doesn't make sense that she isn't here. Her guide and I are about to go out and search."

Alexa knew she hadn't passed anyone. She'd hiked through a whole lot of alone. Unless someone had hidden from her. *That* was a creepy thought. "I can come with you."

Kathy's brow bunched. "Ta, but I'm probably overreacting. You go freshen up, have a glass of wine with the others." The lounge area was even busier. Kathy leaned over the bar to speak to Silas. He came around and scooped up Alexa's backpack. "Kathy said to give you and your guest a double en suite. Follow me."

The thought of sharing a room with Charlie eased Alexa's tension. She'd be safe.

They weaved through clean and animated Luxers—perhaps on their second or third beverage of choice. Only crumbs were left on the scone platter.

"Staying, are you?" a woman asked.

Alexa did a double take. It was the step counter.

They turned down a hallway. Two doors past the Guest Laundry, Silas unlocked a room and handed Alexa the key. "It's the Tauhou room. All our rooms are named for Milford Track birds. Tauhou is Māori for silvereye, a small songbird." He pointed to a rubber mat by the door. "You can leave your boots here. We'll clean and dry them for you."

"Really?" She began undoing the muddy laces, but paused, uncomfortable at the thought of being parted from them. They were her ticket out of here. But that was silly. She pulled them off, her toes thankful, and entered the room.

Pale blue powder-puff duvets topped the twin beds. A plate of chocolates tempted her from the nightstand. The curtain at the lone window fluttered. Outside, foliage sagged in the rain.

Silas set her backpack on a luggage rack and flicked on the overhead light. "The generator goes off at ten p.m., and comes back on at six a.m." He paused and smiled.

Maybe he expected a tip. She considered the twenty-dollar bill she had stuffed in the nether regions of her backpack. That was all the emergency cash she had, and she hadn't expected to need it. There wasn't a single thing money could buy along the Milford Track. She'd leave it where it was. "How often do you get helicopters here?"

He stuck his hands in his pockets. "Once a week, for supplies, and to haul the rubbish and recycling out."

"Where's the helicopter pad?"

His eyes were shaded by the brim of his ball cap. "Round the side. Why?"

She ignored the "why." "What's the scoop on the missing hiker?"

"It's a bit sus, yeah?"

"Sus?"

"Suspect."

"Yeah."

After Silas left, Alexa locked the door and pulled the curtains. She hung her raincoat on a hook and gobbled a chocolate. In the bathroom she found a flush toilet, hot water shower, shampoos and lotions, hair dryer, even lavender-scented soap. She stared at her image in the mirror: cheeks pink, dirt across her forehead, bedraggled ponytail. She got the water running and peeled off her clothes.

The thing about a helicopter is that it couldn't sneak up on you.

The Luxers were advancing from the lounge to the dining room, catching Alexa in their flurry. She searched for Charlie. He wasn't among them. Then she searched for any familiar face—one of the nurses, or the businessmen—but the familiar faces were at Mintaro Hut. She leaned against the wall, disconcerted by the elegance and bright lights when she had nearly been crushed by rock, first in the landslide, then by a bulk bag kamikaze helicopter pilot. *Had that really happened?*

A glass of wine would help. She weaved through the flow, and found Silas squirting the bar with sanitizer.

"Any chance of a glass of wine?"

"Nah yeah."

She was used to this weird Kiwi expression now. "Nah yeah" meant yes. Or at least that's how she interpreted it. "Yeah nah" meant no. There might be nuances she wasn't familiar with. Nuance wasn't her strength. "White. Sauvignon blanc, please."

Silas turned around. Alexa could hear the glug, glug, glug of wine splashing against a glass. "This one is from the sunny Wairau Valley. The Māori called it *Kei Puta te* Wairau, 'the place with the hole in the cloud.'"

Outside, the rain came in sheets. No hole for the sun to shine through here. *Poor Charlie.* It felt delicious to be wearing clean, dry clothes and warm socks. Alexa wiggled her toes. "How many people work at the lodge?"

"Me, Chef, Ima—she waits tables—and a housekeeper. Plus the Bergens. We all multitask, eh?"

Alexa had been doing a lot of multitasking today and could relate. "Any word on the missing tramper?"

Silas handed her the glass. "Nah."

An attractive older couple veered toward Alexa, the woman smiling warmly. "Would you like to join our table?" Her royal blue quarter-zip sweater, sleek black yoga pants, and chunky necklace made Alexa feel dowdy.

"Please do," the man added. He wore a navy turtleneck tucked into clean hiking pants. "I'm Mark, and this is my wife, Debbie. We're from Pennsylvania."

They looked like *AARP The Magazine* models. "Thank you. I'm Alexa. My brother, Charlie, should be along soon. We're from North Carolina."

"Did you hear about the missing hiker?" Debbie asked, taking her arm.

Alexa tried not to spill the wine. "I hope she turns up."

"She's an orthopedic doctor from Auckland. I talked with her about my knee replacement. She's treating her office to this trip. Called it a group jolly. Let's see. There's her anesthesiologist and her pharmaceutical salesperson. Plus her sister."

Stead had said the Luxe hikers paid thousands of dollars for their guided Milford experience. "Dr. Clark must do a lot of knee replacements."

Debbie looked around at the empty spots in the dining room. "We had a lovely conversation with a couple from London last night, didn't we?"

Mark nodded.

"The Drakes their name was." Debbie looked disappointed. "They must be on the other side of the landslide. Such a shame. Their trip ruined by Mother Nature." She stopped at a table and spoke to the couple. "How's Eitan?"

"Fine. He's showering."

"I'm so glad you didn't get separated. Terrible about the landslide, isn't it?"

"They're from Israel," Mark told Alexa. "Eitan is their son."

Alexa gave up trying to keep the new names straight. Her head was full enough.

Debbie waved to the woman in the red sweater Alexa had

seen earlier at the bar. "Cassandra is Dr. Clark's pharmaceutical rep," Mark said.

Cassandra waved back and joined them at a table for six. Debbie introduced Alexa, mentioned that Alexa's brother would be joining them, and then asked, "Has Diana turned up?"

"No," Cassandra replied. "Larry went with some others to look for her."

"Larry is her anesthesiologist, right?"

"Yes. Clint recruited him to help with the search."

Alexa sat back in the plushy chair and sipped wine.

Mark, sitting next to her, whispered, "Debbie makes friends with everyone. Clint is one of our Luxe Tour guides."

Clint was Mr. Clipboard, she reminded herself. Names and faces swirled in her head. She took another sip—the wine tasted like fruity sunshine—and reflected. *Diana Clark: missing doctor. Larry: also a doc, looking for Diana. Clint: a guide who probably felt bad he'd lost a client. And drug rep Cassandra.* Alexa tuned in to what Cassandra was saying.

"Rosie doesn't look worried. If it were my sister, I'd be out looking."

Alexa followed Cassandra's gaze. A girthy woman with choppy brown hair laughed with someone at her table. It must be the sister from the riverbank while she and Charlie hid behind the boulder. They'd been cruel to each other.

"What's that quote?" Mark asked. "Something like 'Siblings are your only enemy you can't live without.'"

Alexa mentally replayed the sisters' spat. *Quit lording it over me. Always in the shadows. If only people knew. Kickbacks. Kiss-up.* No love lost between those two. While she watched Rosie, she contemplated what it meant to be a sibling, if anything. Before this trip, she and Charlie barely had anything to do with each other. And Rosie over there was acting as if siblingship didn't amount to even worry. She was laughing with tablemates instead of out looking for her sister. Would Charlie search for Alexa?

Siblings are enemies we can't live without. That was garbage. Alexa had proved she could live without family interference. But still. She hoped she could change, and open her heart more to Charlie.

And Bruce, too? Her head was swimmy.

A waitress offered a bread basket and a spiel about the menu: Roast pumpkin soup followed by Rangiora duck, tomato and porcini ragu or Lake Wakapitu salmon with kumara crisps, or something something pasta—Alexa always tuned out the vegetarian offers—followed by pavlova for dessert.

"Is the soup heavily salted?" Debbie asked.

"No, just the right amount," the waitress with the Ima name tag said.

"How is the duck prepared?"

"Well."

Debbie looked alarmed.

"I mean, it's choice." The waitress shuffled. "The duck is roasted with red wine, tomatoes, and mushrooms."

"Is it spicy?"

"It's flavored with tarragon, garlic…"

Get on with it, Alexa thought. When it was her turn, she ordered the salmon. "Double crisps, please."

Debbie turned inquisitor after the waitress left. After extracting that Alexa was from Raleigh, currently living in Auckland, and worked in forensics, she expressed surprise that Alexa wasn't married "What? Lovely girl like you?" Debbie studied her. "You still have time."

Her assumption annoyed Alexa. She didn't want to be married. Or have kids.

Cassandra watched the exchange closely. She had strange amber-colored eyes.

"We're happy to have an independent hiker join us," Debbie said.

Alexa mumbled thanks and looked for Charlie. Through the

windows, she could see the rain had slacked, and mist obscured the mountains.

"I'm sure the DOC huts are entirely adequate," Debbie went on. "But Mark and I thought it would be better if my pack was light. My knee replacement was only a year ago. "

The waitress came back with the soup.

"Nice that they cook for us, too," Mark added with a smile.

As he and Debbie bowed their heads to say a blessing, Cassandra leaned toward Alexa, her amber nuggets narrowed. "You aren't a Luxer. Why are you here?"

Alexa narrowed her eyes back. "I'm on official business." She picked up her spoon.

Debbie raised her head. "Bon appétit, everyone."

"Are those your brothers?" Mark asked, pointing.

Alexa dropped her spoon into her pumpkin soup. Droplets spattered the tablecloth. Charlie walked toward their table. Stead Willis trailed behind him.

Chapter Thirteen

Charlie's hazel eyes bore a hole in Alexa's. "I heard about the landslide when I got to the hut, and then you didn't come. I was worried."

Her heart swelled.

"Each time another hiker came in, and it wasn't you, and I thought you were hurt, or, I don't know." He worked his jaw. "I told that ranger woman you were late."

"I'm sorry. I didn't have a way…"

"So you've been hanging out here?" Charlie gestured to the food and her almost-empty wineglass.

"Something came up. I'll explain later." Then she frowned at Stead, who should have been stuck on the other side of the rockslide. She thought she'd never see him again. "How can you be here?"

"I walked with your brother."

The men's jackets dripped on the hardwood as everyone stared at them.

"But you were at Clinton Hut when I last saw you. You were *behind* me. Behind the landslide." His presence didn't make sense.

"I have friends in high places," Stead said ambiguously. "I got airlifted."

Her mouth dropped. Was he buddies with the killer helicopter pilot?

"Ranger Harker called in a copter to assess the landslide damage. I hitched a ride so I could continue my tramp." He looked around the room, even nodded at a woman staring at him from one table over, her soup spoon halfway to her mouth.

Mark cleared his throat. "Please, gentlemen, take off your coats and join us."

Stead stuck out his hand to shake Mark's, and smiled at Debbie and Cassandra. "I'm Steadman Willis. The ranger at Mintaro Hut said there was a missing tramper. Has she been found?"

"No," Cassandra's eyes were glittery. "We're worried about her. Last night at the other lodge—what was the name?"

"Glade Lodge," Mark said.

"I saw someone lurking in the bushes out my window. I think he was spying on us. Maybe, well, I don't know. Maybe he did something to Diana."

"That's scary," Debbie said. "Did you report it?"

"When I looked again, he was gone. So I didn't. But now?"

Alexa wondered if the Peeping Tom story was true. *Who in the world would be peeping through a window in the middle of nowhere?* Maybe Cassandra sought attention. She'd heard of witnesses making things up to feel important.

Stead broke in. "I'm president of the Greymouth Tramping Club and a volunteer with LandSAR. I can lead a search for the woman."

Stead was full of surprises.

"What's LandSAR?" Mark asked, gesturing to the two empty chairs. Charlie sank into one, unzipped his jacket, and helped himself to a piece of bread.

Stead remained standing. "It's a search and rescue organization. We carry out more than five hundred operations each year for lost trampers."

"Oh my," Debbie said. "Do they usually get found?"

"Most do. American, are you?"

Mark and Debbie nodded.

"We had a mother and daughter from the States, the Carolinas, get lost in Tararua Forest Park. They were out for a day hike. It took us four days to find them. The daughter was on the brink. Shared her dying wishes, even." Stead looked out the window. "Your Pompolona Lodge manager is expecting me. There's an hour of light left."

Charlie stood, still chewing. "I'll help look."

Alexa cast a sad glance at her pumpkin soup. "Me too."

Talk ceased as they threaded between tables. "I'll have them keep your dinner warm," Debbie called.

They found Vince Bergen pacing his small office, his hair in tufts.

Stead introduced himself. "I'll take over the search efforts."

Vince's shoulders lowered. He looked at Charlie. "You must be Miss Glock's brother?"

Charlie nodded.

"Fill me in," Stead said. "The ranger at Mintaro didn't know much. Who is missing and for how long?"

"Her name is Diana Clark. She's a medical doctor. She should have shown up here by three or four o'clock." Vince looked at his watch. "It's seven now."

"What have you done to locate her?"

"SAR is on standby. Three people are out searching. My wife, Kathy. She's qualified in mountaineering first aid. Clint Knight, the Luxe guide—he has first aid training, too, of course—and another bloke. They're walking toward the river." He pointed out the route on the wall map.

"Do you have a way to contact them?"

"Both Kathy and Clint have radios."

Stead studied the map. "Get them back here so we can coordinate."

Alexa studied the map, too, pinpointing the area where she'd found the bones. She would show the police in the morning.

"But won't that take time?" Vince asked.

Stead traced the outline of the trail with his finger, and then tapped the Pompolona Lodge dot. "It's better to waste a few minutes than have one search turn into two."

While Vince made contact, a tentative knock made them turn. Rosie stood uncertainly in the doorway and cleared her throat. "Any word on my sister?"

"No word," Vince said.

"When is the last time you saw her?" Stead asked.

Rosie's cheeks were blotchy. "At Prairie Shelter for lunch. Around one o'clock. Who are you?"

Stead introduced himself.

"She finished eating and left," Rosie continued. "She should have beat me here."

Stead tapped the spot on the map. "Has anyone seen her since?"

"Dr. Salvú hiked off with her," Rosie said. "He's searching for her now."

"It's crucial to establish her point last seen. Describe your sister. What's her age?"

Rosie slipped her phone out of her pocket and fiddled. "Diana is forty-six. Here's a picture from yesterday."

Stead took the phone, studied it. "She looks fit, eh? Is this what she's wearing?" He passed the phone to Charlie, who shared it with Alexa. Diana beamed by the MILFORD TRACK sign.

"She wouldn't wear the same outfit two days in a row," Rosie said. "I know she's wearing the yellow Luxe Tours raincoat."

"That will make her easier to spot. What color is her backpack?"

Rosie thought for a moment. "Blue, I think. Yes."

"Does she have a PLB?"

Rosie nodded.

Alexa had learned about Personal Locator Beacons in her last case. "It's an emergency device that can send an SOS to Search and Rescue," she told Charlie.

Stead frowned. "Odd that she hasn't used it. Do you know if it's registered?"

Rosie shrugged. "I have no idea. She always has the latest and greatest gadgets. That's why I haven't been worried. If she were in danger, she would have set it off."

"Does she have any medical conditions?"

"Not that I know of."

Stead hesitated, scratching his chin. "Does she suffer from depression or another mental disorder?"

Rosie studied her silver and white tennis shoes. "Arrogance isn't a mental disorder, but it might be what has gotten Di in trouble," she said quietly.

Stead nodded. "I know people like that. Think they're invincible. Does she have food and water?"

"She has a water bottle and snacks."

Stead's flow of questions impressed Alexa. Her confusion at seeing him evaporated. He appeared to be a take-charge guy. Impressive, even.

Vince broke in. "Kathy says they're ten minutes away. No sign of Diana. We'll meet them on the porch. That's better than everyone traipsing through the lobby, setting off a panic."

"I need you to contact SAR again," Stead said. "See if anything has come through via the PLB. Check if her device is registered. If it is, see if it has GPS tracking. That would tell us where she is. Or rather, where the PLB is."

Vince grabbed a pencil.

Stead addressed Rosie, Charlie, and Alexa. "We're all this woman has right now."

"I'll go change into my boots," Alexa said. "And get my raincoat."

"Grab a torch, too," Stead said.

"Charlie, you can come with me. I'll show you our room." She wanted to tell him about escaping the landslide. And about the bones and the helicopter pilot.

He avoided her gaze. "I'll see it later."

Alexa's heart sank.

Rosie looked down. "I better change shoes, too."

Laughter and talk flitted from the dining room as they scurried by, the sounds incongruous to the task ahead. Alexa glanced at Rosie. "What do you think has happened to your sister?"

"I think she's lost, but doesn't want to admit it." Her tone was matter-of-fact. "Princess Di never admits to being wrong. She's out there somewhere clawing her way back."

The image was unsettling.

The boot mat was empty. Alexa unlocked the door, flicked on the lights, and looked around. No signed, sealed, delivered dry boots. She tried to stay calm about her missing boots. She grabbed her raincoat and flashlight, ate the remaining chocolate, and wondered why the room was so chilly. She snatched back the drapes. The window was wide open. My bad, she thought, remembering it had been open when Silas showed her the room. Someone could climb right in. She closed and latched it.

Maybe her boots were in Guest Laundry. She locked the room, passed the next guest room—Takahe—and poked into the laundry. There were two washers, one spinning clothes in a swirl of suds, and two silent dryers. No boot-drying contraption. Dammit. She missed Clinton Hut where no one touched her boots, though that woman had admonished her for wearing them in the hut. *Who ever heard of boot etiquette? And now boot theft.* She'd find Silas and ask where they were, or hike in her Tevas.

Silas wasn't behind the bar. No one was. Through the windows Alexa could see Stead and Charlie under the porch, and mist from the woods stretching to swallow them. She stepped out of her Tevas, whipped off her socks, stuffed them in her pocket—they were her only dry pair—and pulled the Tevas back on. At least they were better than the Crocs one of the nurses hiked in. She slipped her Maglite into her raincoat pocket and the first aid kit strap over her shoulder. She joined the men on the porch as the search trio climbed the steps.

Stead, wearing a backpack, explained who he was. "I'll be acting coordinator."

Kathy removed her hood and introduced herself as co-manager of Pompolona Lodge. Her face was drawn. "We made it halfway to Pompolona Creek. No sign of her. At least the rain has stopped. I'll go check in with Vince. Be back in five."

"Bugger," said Clint. "This whole thing is alarming. Where is she? I remember you from the boat ride," he told Stead. "Clint Knight with Luxe Tours."

Stead nodded, and turned to the remaining searcher. "Are you the person who last saw Diana Clark?"

"Me?" He shook his hood off, and swiped his dark bangs to the side. His face was flushed. "Dr. Salvú. Call me Larry."

Alexa, remembering how he had swirled an olive on a toothpick at the bar, wondered how many mixed drinks he'd consumed.

"When did you see Dr. Clark last?" Stead asked.

"We ate at that shelter. The rain, don't you see? What time was that, Clint?"

"Half past one."

Around the time I discovered the skeleton.

"We work together," Larry said. "I'm Diana's anesthesiologist. I'll help you get through your surgery. Tell me when you can no longer feel your wallet."

Alexa couldn't believe the guy was cracking jokes.

"Always in a hurry, Diana is," he continued. "Least amount of pain meds, so patients don't need much recovery time. Get them in, get them out. Same with lunch. Diana left the shelter first. I never caught up with her. "

This statement snagged Alexa's attention. Rosie had said Larry and Diana hiked off together. One of them was mistaken.

"Is there anyone else who saw her after that?" Stead asked.

Larry shrugged. "I don't know. Maybe a freedom hiker."

Stead gave a sharp nod. "For now we'll say Dr. Clark's last contact was the shelter at one thirty. That's six hours ago and three kilometers from here. Statistically, the doctor is either lost or hurt."

"But how could she be lost?" Charlie asked. "The path is well marked."

"Maybe she stepped off the path to take a wee," Stead said. "She takes a left instead of a right, and she's lost in thick bush. It happens."

Rosie and Kathy rushed out the door. "Vince has notified SAR," Kathy said. "They haven't received any signal."

"I had a rescue once—a lone tramper was crossing a swollen river and got swept away," Stead said. "His PLB was in his pack, which washed away."

"Did he die?" Alexa asked.

"He got out of the river, but without his PLB, he couldn't signal for help. He died of hypothermia."

Alexa hated sad endings.

Stead removed his hiking poles from his pack and extended them. "Here's the plan. We'll split into three teams."

Alexa stepped close to Charlie.

"I've divided our search range into segments." He looked at Charlie and Alexa. "Segment one is Pompolona Lodge to Pompolona Creek. One of you," he looked at Clint and Kathy, "give them a radio."

Kathy handed Charlie hers.

"That's where the swing bridge is, right?" Charlie asked. "How far away is it?"

"Twenty minutes." Stead looked at Kathy. "You and the two gentlemen"—he indicated Clint and Larry—"will take between here and halfway to Mintaro Hut. Rosie and I will take the High Floss side trail."

Kathy nodded. "Be careful. It's steep and slippery."

Up until this moment, all Alexa could think about was human remains and the whizzing of the bulk bag coming at her head. But on the cusp of night, fear for the missing woman slipped to the head of the line.

"Search ten feet on either side of the trail, when safe," Stead ordered. "One on each side. Stay within voice range of your search partner. Trampers usually take the course of least resistance, so if the terrain looks dicey, avoid it. Every five minutes, call her name, stop, and listen for ten seconds."

"How long do we stay out?" Charlie asked.

"It's coming on dark. One hour. Walk thirty minutes, then turn. If you find her, use the radio. We'll come fast."

Alexa looked at Charlie, who pulled his hood up. "Ready?"

Chapter Fourteen

The side trail to the waterfall was in the same direction as Pompolona Creek, so Rosie and Stead followed them, quashing Alexa's chance to tell Charlie her distressing news. She bumped his shoulder as they walked, feeling weightless without a backpack on, and kept repeating her favorite Robert Frost poem in her head, *"These woods are lovely, dark and deep/ But I have promises to keep/ And miles to go before I sleep/ And miles to go before I sleep."*

Except these woods weren't lovely. The foggy jungle hung heavy, oppressive, waiting to pounce. Hidden birds trilled and screeched. Night lurked around the bend.

"Why aren't you wearing boots?" Charlie asked.

"Someone took them to be dried. It's a service at the lodge."

Charlie shook his head. "How could you lose your boots?"

"I didn't lose them. Don't you listen? And why did you hike off without me this morning?" A clammy spiderweb brushed her cheek. She swiped at it and waited a full minute for an answer.

"I needed to think. Figure things out. With Mel." He kept his eyes on the trail.

She wasn't good with feelings. "Yeah, well, okay."

Stead, all business, was ten feet off the track to her left, gliding ethereally past hulking trees and glistening ferns. Rosie plodded ten feet off the other side of the trail.

"Dianaaa," called Stead.

They froze, listening to collective dripping, a startled bird, the rasp of a critter scampering in the underbrush, then crept forward. After ten minutes Alexa saw the sign pointing to Floss Trail. Stead appeared on the track and said, "See you back at the lodge." He veered off.

Rosie added, "Be careful," and followed him.

They evaporated into the fog.

Before Alexa could launch into her story, Charlie sidled off the path to execute Stead's search protocol. Alexa heard him counting steps. "Wait," she said. "Come back. I have something to tell you."

"Some woman is hurt, and you want to chat?" Charlie called. He crashed through brush like an angry bear.

Fury rose in her like bile. *He* was the one who left *her* behind this morning. This whole damn hiking vacation was a disaster. "Everything is always 'I'll hike ahead. Catch you later. Meet you at the hut,'" she yelled. "Forget that. I have something to tell you now!" She stamped her Teva like a kid, mud splattering her pants, and saw him, Charlie at six, his eyes sad, pleading with her to build a LEGO fort.

Her response: later. She never made time for him when he was a kid.

In the distance Stead called, "Dianaaa. Diana Clark."

Charlie parted two tall ferns, squeezed through, and stepped on the track. "What?"

She hadn't planned on how to tell him. "In case you're interested, someone tried to kill me today. After I found a skeleton."

A small flock of olive-green birds took wing in a cloudy unit.

"What the hell, Lexi?" Charlie looked mad instead of concerned.

"After the landslide…"

Charlie grabbed her arm. "What's that?"

Was he not listening? The earth trembled. She could feel it to her knees, then hips. The trees in her peripheral vision jiggled, leaves and branches waving. A limb crashed through foliage and landed in the middle of the path, three feet away. She put her hands over her head. "Duck," she cried.

Charlie wrapped her in a bear hug and pressed them both to the ground. They crouched like kids hiding in a closet, hoping not to be discovered. But they weren't in a closet. They were exposed, with trees everywhere. When another limb fell, Alexa pulled them off the trail, against a thick tree trunk. They huddled together, tornado drill position, trembling like the fern fronds, waiting for the earth to still.

When it did, the birds stayed mute. Holding their bird breaths. Alexa let hers out in a long whoosh. "That was a tremor."

"Holy shit," Charlie said.

"These are the shaky isles," Alexa said. "Tremors are common."

"Does it mean a big earthquake is coming?"

"I don't know."

Charlie stood and looked around. "I think everything is okay." He squatted and looked her in the eye. "Let's stay a minute. You can tell me what happened earlier. Did someone really try to kill you?"

Alexa nodded. "There was a landslide. You heard about it, right?"

"The ranger at Mintaro Hut told us. Is that what you meant about someone trying to kill you? Mother Nature?"

"No. Hold on. The slide happened right in front of me. I ran the other way. After it was over, I didn't want to be cut off from you, so I waded in the river to get around the mess." She remembered the icy water and force of the current. "On the other side, I found the bones of a human hand. Sticking out from under rocks. Connected to a body." Actually disarticulated but that was TMI.

"Are you kidding? Was it someone caught in the landslide?"

"He was skeletonized. The landslide exposed him."

Charlie's eyes widened. "If it's a skeleton, how do you know it's a guy? Because of what he was wearing?"

She relished his full attention. "There weren't any clothes on the part I saw. They've disintegrated. That's not surprising when you consider all the rain around here. But I did find a belt buckle."

A high pitched *kee-aaa, kee-aaa* was followed by a *chee chee chee*. The birds were reclaiming the forest.

Alexa stared at Charlie's face, inches away, noting his sandy-colored hair had flopped across his brow and the thickening stubble on his square jaw. She thought of how he had tried to protect her during the tremor. "I could tell it was male by the shape of the skull. That's the reason I didn't show up at the hut. I dug around and discovered evidence that the deceased might have been stabbed. The ribs showed…"

"What? The dude was murdered?"

"I think so. The police are coming in the morning."

"Was it someone who died a long time ago? Like those bones in the caskets?"

She thought of the modern dental work. "This guy wasn't as old as them."

"A dead guy. A missing woman. A landslide and an earthquake. What else can happen? Oh, yeah." He shook his head. "Who tried to kill you?"

All together the events sounded implausible. "After I left the bones, a helicopter flew over. Then it came toward me. I tried to flag it down, but it came after me." The next part would sound deranged. "The pilot tried to knock me down with one of those giant bags of rock. He swung it at me."

"What?"

"He tried to kill me with it. I'm pretty sure." The more time that passed, the more she doubted her memory. *Who can trust memory anyway?* Human memory is malleable and reconstructive, she knew. The neurons and connections that an experience wires into the brain can be distorted. That's why she preferred forensic evidence. Like the thumb bone. But then she felt a chill on her neck, as if the rock bag were passing overhead. "It happened twice."

"Lexi, that's…"

"I know. Crazy."

Charlie stared at her, weighing her words and his obligation to her, she imagined. What would be the verdict?

"I saw one of those copters set a bag of rock down near the path this morning. Very dexterous. The pilot was probably focused on his work and didn't see you."

Alexa decided not to argue.

Charlie got to his feet. "Mel won't believe all this." He cracked a smile, and then it vanished, as if he remembered he and Mel had separated. He reached a hand down and pulled her up. "We better keep looking for Dr. Clark while there's still some light."

Since she was wearing open-toed shoes, she stayed on the track, picking her way over fallen branches and around mossy rocks. *Why would the doctor be off the track anyway?* An image of a wounded animal, crawling away to die, popped into her head. She tried to erase the image, but it lingered.

Charlie followed Stead's advice, and Alexa could barely see him off to her left. Fog swirled and thickened as they traipsed. Charlie called Diana's name every five minutes. Alexa froze each time, her ears straining. Only irritated birds answered. She pushed forward, stubbing her toe on a rock, and realized her hiking poles were at the lodge. Charlie didn't have his, either. The trail was flat, so it didn't matter, but she had grown fond of them. In the distance she heard the rush of water, and knew they were nearing the swing bridge and waterfall.

Charlie came out of the woods, and they stood side by side in the flat open space ten feet from the bank, staring at the crashing cataract. Its white froth was the only brightness in the gloaming, and its spray carried to Alexa's cheeks.

Charlie yelled, "Dianaaa," but his voice was drowned out by the thundery roar. "I hope she didn't fall in the river," he shouted to Alexa. "I'll check on the other side of the bridge before we head back."

Alexa stared at the bridge. The thought of Charlie crossing it—narrow treadway, droopy in the center, flimsy safety rail—made her mouth go dry. "We need to turn around or we'll be caught in the dark," she shouted. It was then she remembered finding someone's pole. Right near here. *Jeez. What if it belonged to the missing woman?*

Charlie climbed the three stairs and stepped forward. She decided to wait from the stair platform, to keep a better eye on him. The slick coiled handrail vibrated as she pulled herself up. The volume of rushing water pounded closer and louder. Something whizzed by her cheek. A shadow with velocity. The platform shook. She jumped the three steps in a single sideways bound as the bridge twisted laterally, pitching Charlie over the railing.

Chapter Fifteen

The bridge snapped back as she watched. Empty.

Alexa couldn't believe her eyes. She grabbed the handrail, climbed the first step, and leaned forward. Charlie was gone. The fact was too horrifying to register. "Charlieee!"

Then the bridge jerked like a phantom was crossing. Alexa twisted so she could see underneath it. Charlie was hanging from the sagging center of the bridge. His boots, twelve feet above the rushing river, dangled like rearview mirror charms. Then they kicked to life. He was there, alive.

Don't just stand here.

The stair platform looked stable. She climbed the final two steps, but the bridge, listing to the right, obscured her view of Charlie. She jumped off the platform and rushed to the edge. Her heart dropped like a stone. Charlie was monkeying closer. If he let go, he would be swept away by rapids.

She dropped to her knees, lay flat, and popped her head over the bank. Straight down, in gray dusk, she made out a lip of rock, coated with mist. Large enough to stand on. Closer to Charlie.

"You're almost here," she cried, her voice swallowed. "Keep going."

He swung his hips and moved his right hand along a thick cable. His left hand followed until his hands were inches apart.

Then he swung his hips and shimmied his right hand along the cable again.

Alexa lowered three feet down onto the rock overhang, got to her feet, and pressed her back to the rock wall. The ledge was more spacious than she'd thought. The bridge platform was above her now. If she stretched right, she could touch Charlie's lifeline cable.

"You've got this," she screamed.

Charlie's eyes were panicked-horse big. His mouth opened, but his words were stolen by the roaring torrent. There's no way he would have been able to hang on if he'd been wearing his backpack, Alexa realized. Thrusting his body forward—he was eight feet away—took more effort as the cable sloped upward. The tonnage of water below leaped and roiled.

"Hang on!"

He slid his left hand close to the right, swung his hips again, and moved his right hand along the coiled wire. Five more feet. If he could kick his feet to the rock ledge, she'd grab his waist and pull for all she was worth. For all her trespasses.

She braced and peeked down at another rock lip, just large enough to stand on. If Charlie could get his feet to it, and lean into her, she could grab him by the shoulders and pull him up.

Charlie must have thought likewise, because he thrust his legs like a gymnast. His boots nicked the ledge, dislodging a flurry of stones, and swung back over the water. The momentum caused him to lose his grip, and now he hung one-armed. Alexa covered her mouth. In slow motion, his remaining fingers began relinquishing one digit at a time. In a Herculean effort as his pinkie and ring finger lost traction, he thrust his body through space and landed with a grunt on the lower shelf, chest level to her ledge, one hand wrapped around her ankle, the other clutching rock.

Alexa tumbled backward, landing on her butt. Charlie still gripped her ankle. She leaned forward until she could grab his free wrist with one hand and his collar with the other. "Let go. I have you." He relinquished her ankle, and she snaked her arms through his armpits. They met each other's eyes as Alexa pulled with all her might, straining, leaning back, inching him onto the ledge. When his head and torso were secure, and only his legs hung over, she let go and rolled sideways, her heart sprinting, her arms trembling, her ankle throbbing.

She now understood how a mother could lift a car off her child.

Charlie wormed forward and dragged his legs up. He curled in a ball. The thin strip of skin between the back of his hair and collar made Alexa cry for the fragility of life. She thought of how Benny and Noah had almost lost their daddy. She patted his back, felt his tremors come and go in waves. "You did it. You did it."

Charlie shuddered. She remembered him as a toddler. That duck on wheels he pulled after Mom died. Around and around the den. His way of mourning. His toddler labyrinth.

She wiped her nose and was about to say she loved him when he lifted his head, his eyes wide. "I saw her."

"What? Who?"

"The missing woman." He gulped air. "I think it's her."

His words skipped off her brain like a stone. All she could fathom was the miracle of her brother, panting beside her. "You're safe."

"Lexi!" He raised up, sat back on his haunches, rubbed his upper arms. "We've got to help her. Maybe she's alive."

His words snagged in her cerebrum this time. "What did you see?"

"When I was hanging over the river, I saw a body." His voice was thick. "At the shore, squished between big boulders. I could see legs and a head. It's got to be that woman.." He wiped his eyes and left a smear of blood.

"You're bleeding."

Charlie looked at his right palm. Blood trickled toward his

wrist. He checked his left, and saw it was bleeding, too. Sliced by cable. He wiped them on his pants and got shakily to his feet. "Remember what that Māori man said to you? About grave danger? Guess he was right."

Alexa rose as well, keeping a hand on the rock wall to steady herself. "That's stupid." *But is it? This whole experience is a curse.* Her words evaporated as she looked up at the riverbank, and then at the sky. Between trees she spotted one star, and it gave her hope. She found a foothold, clutched the cliff edge, and boosted herself up. Charlie followed with a grunt. "Good thing this is granite and not limestone."

When they were back to the beginning, at the foot of the listing swing bridge, where she watched her only sibling fly into the air, she asked why.

"A limestone ledge might have crumbled from our weight. You can count on granite."

She remembered something whizzing by her face. "What happened to the bridge?"

"I don't know. Maybe it had to do with the quake. I'm lucky the whole thing didn't collapse."

She took his arm. "I'm sorry, Charlie. For all the times I wouldn't play with you when we were little. For not building LEGO forts."

He met her eyes in the almost-dark. "Where did that come from?"

"I was a crappy sister. I never read to you or played with you." Her throat swelled. She couldn't go on.

"You weren't responsible for me." His voice quavered, too. "You were just a kid. A little kid who lost her mother. Benny wouldn't suddenly take care of Noah if something happened to me or Mel." He went quiet, probably aware that what he said had almost come true.

She stayed quiet, too, amid the symphony of nature, wondering if her guilt would lift.

"Come on." Charlie broke the silence. "We've got to take a look. See if we can help her."

She recoiled. "I'm not going down there. It's too dangerous. You nearly died."

But she knew he was right and followed him as he glided along the cliff above the river, fifteen or twenty feet past the crippled swing bridge. He leaned over, moved down a few more feet, and leaned again. "Look."

She looked, following his finger downward. In the waning light she spotted a log—twenty or twenty-five feet below— wedged between two shoreline boulders. She fumbled in her jacket pocket, past a balled sock, for her Maglite and turned it on. The powerful beam, designed for first responders, turned the log into a human form. She swept the light back and forth, and made out legs, one bent backward. This was definitely a body. She directed the beam past the boulder hiding the torso, and made out a face—pallid and still. She looked for movement while Charlie screamed, "Diana."

The figure was not responsive to light or voice. Charlie screamed again.

"I think it's the woman we heard talking with her sister yesterday," Alexa told him. "When we were behind the rocks."

"Damn," Charlie said. "She must have fallen off the bridge."

"How in the world did you see her?"

"I don't know. The mist cleared and there she was."

Alexa wondered if Diana could have survived. Falls are the second-most common cause of injury-related death after traffic accidents. Height of fall and type of ground were the main mortality factors. Twenty or so feet from here to there, Alexa guessed, with a crash landing on boulders. Her blood went icy. "We need a helicopter to lift her out. Use the radio."

Charlie patted his pockets. "Crap. The radio is gone. I was holding it on the bridge. I dropped it."

Alexa didn't know what to do.

"I'll stay," Charlie said. "You go back to the lodge and get someone."

The track was separating them again. "Are you sure?"

"It's the right thing to do. I don't want her to be alone."

I don't want to be alone either.

Chapter Sixteen

The dark hovered. Alexa pocketed the Maglite, tightened the Velcro on her Tevas, and let her eyes adjust to the grays of the trail and blacks of the trees. She flew down the track like it was noon in Raleigh's Umstead State Park where she'd jogged for years. Cardio combined with yoga kept her burn scars from causing muscle and joint limitation. The payoff was this moment, gliding to the lodge.

But a thought bullied its way in. *Up-current.* With each stride she wondered why—if Diana had fallen off that evil bridge— her body was up-current.

By the time she arrived, night was true. Pompolona Lodge looked like a golden snow globe against an inky curtain. The massive mountains beyond the lodge were invisible hulks, guardians of secrets, their presence felt, not seen. She pounced up the steps and yanked the door open. Luxers, relaxing in chairs and on sofas, gazed at her in alarm. She panted heavily in the lobby like a wild thing. She had déjà vu about wanting to scream for help.

Silas hadn't noticed her. He held a poster of a white-faced owl. "Some believe the laughing owl is extinct, but if you leave your window cracked, its laugh might…"

The dozen or so Luxers stared at her instead of at the owl.

"Did you find her?" Cassandra called.

Alexa pretended not to hear. She wove through the lounge, dodging couches and armchairs. Debbie, the friendly American, sprang from a love seat and intercepted her. "Your dinner is waiting in the kitchen. I told the chef to keep it warm."

A droplet of sweat ran into Alexa's eye. "Okay. Thanks." She pushed past, bumping a footstool. A clatter made her turn. Stead and Rosie had arrived. They must have been trailing her on the track. That gave her the willies. The way someone could be behind you, and you not know. Rosie scanned the gathering.

"She's still not here," Cassandra said.

"We're a bit shook," Stead announced. "A tremor, eh?"

Silas laughed. "Just a wee one. It's all good."

Alexa beckoned to Stead. He followed her, lugging his rescue pack. Rosie stayed behind. The door to Vince's office was wide open. He shot out of his chair when he saw them. "Where's Kathy?"

"She's not back yet?" Stead asked.

Alexa closed the door. "My brother and I…spotted a body in the gorge…near the swing bridge." She leaned her hands on her knees, trying to catch her breath. "I guess it's her. I don't know if she's alive."

"Why didn't you radio the lodge?" Stead snapped.

"Charlie lost the radio. In the river."

"Bloody irresponsible," Stead said.

Just then Kathy opened the door. She pushed into the small room, followed by the guide Clint, and Larry. "No luck."

"Miss Glock has some disturbing news," Vince said, making room for Kathy to stand next to him in the overcrowded office.

Alexa straightened and repeated her story.

"Ah, no," Larry said, his face ashen. "Diana can't be dead."

"We couldn't reach her—she's like twenty feet straight down."

Words from Silas's lecture floated into the office: "Dismal…"

"Shrieks…" "Nocturnal…" Stead shut the door. Alexa circumnavigated a desk and sat in a swivel chair. She planted her feet firmly, stilling it. "The swing bridge bucked my brother off." She gazed at Stead. "That's why he dropped the radio. He nearly died. The bridge is still spanning the creek, but something is wrong. It needs to be closed."

"Bucked him off?" Clint said.

"What else can go wrong?" Vince said.

"Sounds like those backpackers who were crossing the Whanganui Bridge last year," Stead said. "It flipped them in the river."

"All the rain, then the tremor," Clint said. "A cable must have broken loose."

Alexa felt destabilized. "My brother is still there, waiting for us to help." She would need her camera and the caution tape. No—wait. She had used the tape up with the skeleton.

"Does Rosie know?" Kathy asked.

"No. She's in the lounge with the guests," Stead said. "We need to go." He ripped off his knit hat and used it to wipe his forehead. "Larry and Clint, come with me. I have a rescue stretcher. With Charlie, that will make four of us to haul her back." He instructed Vince to call SAR. "Apprise them of the situation."

Kathy twisted her wedding band. "This is tragic. It will make the news."

"I'm coming, too," Alexa said. "I'll meet you on the porch."

"It's not necessary," Stead said. "You can wait here."

Her hackles stood quicker than she did. Her brother was involved, and there might be a death. She was definitely going. "If the doctor is dead, there will need to be an inquest. I'm qualified to investigate."

Stead opened his mouth, saw the look on Alexa's face, and closed it.

Vince cracked a knuckle. "Would you use the side porch? It's at the end of this hall. I don't want to further alarm our guests."

Alexa hurried to her room. Her clean, dry hiking boots, like old friends, awaited her arrival. She unlocked the door and noted Charlie's backpack and hiking poles on the second luggage rack. It made her uneasy that someone had entered. She changed from Tevas to boots, grabbed her camera, debated whether to grab her poles and decided not to—the ground between here and the bridge was flat—and flew to the side entrance porch. The three men were waiting in rocking chairs. Alexa almost laughed. Rocking on the porch was for holidaymakers, not body hunters.

"Let's go," she said.

They set off on what felt like a death march. Alexa's thoughts drifted from one horror to another. The horror of the bulk bag crashing toward her head. The horror of Charlie hanging over the river. His escape made her want to sink to her knees and kiss the earth.

The periphery was soot black. She didn't like it and walked in front of Larry and Clint, and behind Stead. She didn't want to be picked off, like in some horror movie.

When they arrived twenty minutes later, Charlie jumped up from the steps leading to the swing bridge. "You were gone forever," he shouted at Alexa. She hoped he was shouting so his voice could be heard over the waterfall. She gave him a quick hug, which he shook off.

"Show us then, eh?" Stead said.

Charlie walked a few yards up the bank and shone his light on the body below. The others crowded around on the verge.

Alexa directed her Maglite at the body, and Stead did the same.

"Eh, I thought she'd be wearing her yellow rain jacket," Clint yelled over the din. "Every client gets one."

With the added light, Alexa could see a pale moon face, craned toward them.

"It might have washed off when the river was higher, " Stead called. "The water was up to those boulders earlier. She might have been submerged."

"I've been calling her name," Charlie said.

"What?" Stead shouted.

"I've called out her name, but she hasn't moved."

Alexa didn't harbor much hope that Diana—if it was her—was alive.

"No more gawking. Let's follow the bank upstream," Stead said. "The water level is down. We'll be able to get to her."

The steep ledge subsided after a hundred meters. Stead directed them to climb down an embankment and follow the shoreline back to the body.

"What's your plan?" Charlie asked, slipping up to Stead.

Stead held one flashlight in his hand, and had another on a headlamp. "I've got a litter."

"A what?"

"Rescue litter. A collapsible stretcher. We'll get her to the lodge."

The bank below the berm was a mixture of sand, shingle, and rock. White froth pitched and hurtled alongside them. The temperature plummeted. They forged the shoreline by flashlight. *Mere steps from mayhem*, Alexa thought, sidestepping a log. Larry stumbled, but Clint caught him. "You right, mate?" he shouted.

Alexa couldn't hear Larry's reply. She felt hemmed in by river on one side and steep bank on the other. Charlie's broad back was a comfort, though his recoil from her hug smarted. Maybe she'd embarrassed him.

The sight of the body stopped them. The woman looked like flotsam tossed by a tempest. Her torso, clad in a thin gray pullover, was sandwiched between large boulders. Her head rested on another rock, and her legs jutted from the other end, one bent backward. Larry dashed to her and knelt near her head. "Diana. Diana. Can you hear me?" he yelled, nudging her shoulder. No response. He bent close to her mouth. Alexa knew he was feeling for breath. Then he fingered her carotid artery for a pulse.

Time slowed as Alexa awaited the verdict. The swing bridge, intangible in darkness, bridged this world to the next. Had Diana crossed over? Larry shook his head, then opened his arms as if to scoop the broken body up.

"Don't move her," Alexa shouted. "Let me take photographs first." Larry backed up as she turned on the camera and flash. The low battery light flickered. *Shit.* She had a spare battery in her backpack, but not here. She prayed for juice as she moved in, scrunching over pebble and shingle, snapping mid-range and close-up photographs of Diana, then of the area. She was standing in for the pathologist. She needed to capture the scene with the body in situ, but it was hard without proper equipment. She missed the portable spotlight in her full crime kit. She knew the flash wouldn't penetrate the darkness. Again she thought of the pole she had found earlier, embedded.

The camera shut itself down. She was thankful she'd had enough juice to photograph the body.

The men stood shoulder to shoulder. She could feel their eyes watching as she checked if Diana was wearing a watch. A watch might have broken due to the fall, and mark time of death. She felt up the sleeve of Diana's left wrist. It was bare. She checked the right wrist and felt a slinky band—maybe a bracelet—but no watch.

"It's okay to move her now." Diana was wedged tightly. Alexa, holding her beam steady so the men could see, held her breath until they pulled the body free. As Stead strapped her on the rescue stretcher, Larry hung his head.

Alexa shone her beam around. "Where's her backpack?"

"What?" Stead yelled. His headlamp gave him a cyclops appearance.

"Her backpack!"

"Probably fell off, washed away," he answered.

"So she was here, all this time, when we crossed that bridge?" Larry sputtered.

"Might have been," Stead said. "She'd have been hard to see, jammed between those rocks."

That means I passed by, too, Alexa realized. *What if she had been alive?*

The men headed back upriver with their awkward cargo. Alexa lingered, nosing around with the beam of her Maglite, searching for any of Diana's belongings. The boulder where Diana's head had rested was stained dark. Alexa figured Diana's skull had cracked. It made her own head throb.

It took forty minutes to reach the lodge. "Let's put her down," Stead said. "A frickin' hard yakka, that."

"Couldn't see a thing," Charlie said.

The men lowered the stretcher onto the side porch. Larry volunteered to break the news to Rosie. Then he turned to Alexa, his eyes downcast. "I'd rather not examine her. She's my friend and colleague."

Alexa was taken aback. Using one's professional abilities was a better way to honor a friend than bowing out. "I'll handle it. Her. If I get some calories in me, I'm good to go." The litter was in shadows. "Why is the lodge dark?"

"The generator goes off at ten," Clint said.

"They need to override the system. This is an emergency," she snapped.

"Electricity isn't going to help her, Lexi," Charlie said quietly.

He was right, but light would help her examine the body. She and Charlie let Stead and Clint deal with where to put the body, and entered the lodge.

Kathy had been hovering near the porch and ushered them to the kitchen by lantern light. "So it's her? The doctor?"

Alexa nodded.

"And she's...dead?"

"Yes."

Alexa excused herself to run through the dark hallway to her room, switch camera batteries, and wash her hands.

Back in the kitchen, Kathy made a tsk sound and pulled on an oven mitt. She pulled open a warming drawer below the seven-burner stove. "Here you go, luvs," she said like a mother. "Sit. Sit here. I've kept your mains warm."

Alexa swallowed back a lump. Being mothered always made her teary.

Kathy sat the covered plates at a small counter and arranged cutlery and napkins. She turned on a second lantern. "Tomato sauce? Cocoa?" As soon as they had everything they needed, Kathy said she'd check in with Rosie.

"I don't envy her," Charlie said after she left.

They ate by lantern light. The salmon was dry, but the sweet potato fries were moist and delicious. Alexa relished the interlude with her brother. "How are your hands?"

Charlie set his fork down and grimaced as he studied his palms. The flesh was raw and leaky. "Carrying that stretcher was rough."

"I've got antibiotic cream in my backpack. Wash them good and spread it on."

Stead popped into the kitchen. "Diana is in Ruru, and the generator is coming back on any minute. I'll see you folks in the morning."

"Ruru? What's that?" Charlie said.

"All the rooms are named after birds," Alexa explained. She waited until Stead shut the door. "He sure knew what he was doing out there."

Charlie wiped his mouth with his napkin. "He went above and beyond to help. Some vacation he's having."

Vacation. This jaunt in the woods was anything but. "I still don't get how he got to Mintaro Hut."

"He came by helicopter. I saw him get dropped off."

Alexa stopped chewing. "What color was the copter?"

"Yellow."

The overhead light in the kitchen flickered on. They both squinted. Alexa forced herself to swallow. "That's the same color as the one that tried to knock me down."

Charlie pushed his plate away. "I don't know. You might have jumped to conclusions about that. It's been hell of a long day."

She fished the key out of her pocket, handed it to him, and told him to leave the door unlocked.

Ruru beckoned.

Chapter Seventeen

A neuroscientist Alexa admired suggested people die three times. She always remembered this when examining a body. *The first time is when the body ceases to function.* She knocked on Ruru and pushed open the door. Rosie and Kathy stood on either side of a single bed and eyed her solemnly. Alexa nodded, pulled the door shut, and braced herself.

Diana Clark lay on thick navy towels, perhaps Kathy's intervention to protect the linens, and was covered to the neck with a light blue sheet. A bit of collar poked out, indicating Diana was clothed, and the feet under the sheet were large. The doctor, who had ceased to function, was still wearing boots. Her face was bruised and swollen. There was no trace of makeup except raccoon smudges under her closed eyes. If her skull had cracked, it was in the back. The one visible ear had a diamond stud. Her hair, damp and matted, looked like straw against the towel. A river-water and organic scent filled the room, nothing offensive, but Alexa knew the decomposition process was underway.

She set the kit down and walked to the foot of the bed. "I'm sorry about your sister."

Rosie picked a twig out of Diana's hair. "She'd want her hair brushed and styled."

"You'll be able to have that done later. Was your sister married?"

"She's divorced. No children. A cat." Rosie's chin trembled. "Who will look after Panther?"

Kathy came around and hugged her. "There will be time to figure that out later. This is such a shock, eh. Poor lass."

Alexa didn't know if Kathy was referring to Rosie or Diana. "I am a forensic investigator. I can take a look at your sister and maybe see what happened or how she died. And because her death is unnatural, we'll need information for a coroner." She didn't mention that deaths classified as unnatural must undergo an autopsy. Diana's autopsy would provide scientific answers, but Rosie might think it was mutilation or that Diana had suffered enough.

"Larry said she fell off the bridge," Rosie said.

Why would he say that? Alexa wondered. "Would you mind leaving the room? Kathy can fix you a cup of tea."

Kathy squeezed Rosie's shoulder. "Yes, pet, let's get you a cuppa and then send you to bed. There's nothing else you can do for your sister tonight." She looked at Alexa. "We've notified DOC. They'll be sending a crew of rangers in the morning to look at the bridge."

"Good. It needs to be blocked off."

"I'll just give you a key, eh?" Kathy said. "You can lock the door when you leave."

Alexa pocketed the key and sighed with relief when she was alone. *The second death, the neuroscientist said, is when the body is buried. Or cremated. Flesh to ashes, death to dust. Would a lot of people gather to pay their respects to Diana?*

She pulled on disposable gloves. The ritual of donning gloves calmed her and helped her think. In her mind, she pictured an accidental death report form. She took a pen and Pompolona Lodge stationery from the dresser, ready to re-create a report.

Alexa dated it, and wrote: Diana Clark, MD, female, aged

forty-six, White. She wrote the location of the accident as Pompolona Creek, up-current from the swing bridge, Milford Track. She underlined *up-current*. Time of death: 1:30–8:00 PM. Between lunch with her fellow Luxe trampers and Charlie's sighting. First on scene, she wrote her name and Charlie's. For cause of death, she wrote "fall?" An examination would confirm this.

What else was on an accidental death form? Description of incident. There were no witnesses. She decided to concentrate on nature of injury by examining Diana's body. She wasn't a pathologist, but she knew enough about bones to feel if one was shattered.

Before removing the sheet, she studied Diana's face, trying to match its lifeless pallor to the woman on the trail this morning—if this was still the same day—talking to Larry about profits and extending theater hours. As Alexa took a close-up photo of Diana's face, she wondered why the doctor wanted to work longer hours. *Did she need the money?*

Alexa put down the camera and removed the diamond studs from Diana's cold ears. They could snag during her examination. She carefully reattached the posts to the tiny backs, and tried not to be judgmental about bejeweled hiking. The diamonds looked real, but for all Alexa knew, they were zirconia. Nothing wrong with zirconia. Dental implants, crowns, and bridges could be made from zirconia, a white crystalline mineral. She lifted the sheet and reached for Diana's right wrist where she had felt a bracelet when she had checked for a watch, and removed it, too. A slinky gold band. She put the jewelry in an evidence bag and labeled it. She would ask Vince if the lodge had a safe. Diana's fingers were ring-less.

She quickly patted Diana's pockets for a phone. No surprise she didn't find one. Men usually stuffed their phones in their front pants pockets; women stuffed theirs into purses and backpacks.

Diana Clark had been vibrant. Bossy. A woman in charge.

She'd worked hard to become a medical doctor. "Strong women benefited all women" was Alexa's belief. Diana had been in her prime. It was weird that she had gotten too close to the edge of the river. Taking risks was something eighteen-year-old males did, usually under the influence of alcohol, not accomplished doctors.

She started at the front of Diana's skull. She pressed on her forehead, orbital rims, and then temples, manipulating for wiggles and ridges that indicated fractures. Nothing obvious, and the mandible felt stable. She had a quick peek at the teeth: they had been well cared for and professionally whitened. She gently lifted the head and palpated the back of Diana's skull: parietal, occipital, and temporal, upper, middle, bottom, for cracks, lacerations, cave-ins. Her hand came away sticky. The lower left skull was fractured. For the first time she wondered if Diana had taken her own life. Jumped. The main cause of falls from heights was suicide. An investigator with more experience than she had might be able to tell if Diana jumped or fell. Maybe Diana's dominating demeanor was a mask to hide sadness or depression. Alexa wrote "Temporal cranium fracture with probable hemorrhaging" on her report. She blew a wisp of hair out of her eyes and added "Mental status: unknown."

She felt the neck, reflecting how fragile the cervical vertebrae were. Too many teenagers didn't realize this as they jumped from cliffs or dove into pools. Diana's neck did not feel snapped or misaligned. Alexa pulled the sheet back; Diana wore a gray Patagonia pullover. A subtle whiff of perfume from the fabric made Alexa sad. Never again would the interaction of Diana's body scent and whatever perfume it was—Alexa had no idea, and didn't wear perfume—be reproduced. She didn't think a woman would dab perfume behind her ears or between her bosoms if she was going to kill herself. *Plus—who wears perfume while they're hiking anyway? Was Diana trying to attract someone? Larry, perhaps?*

She tugged the sleeve of the right arm. Even though she had been expecting rigor mortis, it was still a jolt to feel the arm's rigidity. Twelve, twelve, twelve, Dr. Winget, her boss at the North Carolina State Crime lab, had emphasized. Twelve hours after death for rigor mortis to maximize, twelve hours of stiffness, twelve hours for the muscles to go flaccid. The body was still in the first of the categories, which meant Diana had died within this time frame. A rectal thermometer would be a better way to determine time since death, but Alexa didn't carry one. She tried not to grimace as she removed the damp pullover.

Diana's upper limbs did not feel broken, and her hands were void of cuts or scrapes. She hadn't tried to break her fall. Determining cause of death was Alexa's objective. She pulled up Diana's lightweight pink T-shirt and checked her stomach. Bloating and discoloration indicated internal hemorrhaging. As she took photos, she used the reddish-purple lividity on Diana's side—gravity had forced the blood to pool here—to confirm she'd been lying on the rocks right-side down, just as she was found. She checked for dual lividity, which would indicate the body had been moved after death. There were no other areas where blood had pooled. The body had not been moved.

She made a note of this on the form and then pressed on the doctor's rib cage, and felt a sickening give of bone. Exploring higher, Alexa noted the left collarbone was asymmetrical to the right, and she could feel it was broken, too.

She added internal bleeding and fractured ribs and clavicle to her accident report. Then she checked Diana's pants pockets. For some reason, this felt like a violation of the doctor's privacy. The left pocket contained a waterlogged tissue and a scrap of paper. Alexa set them aside and felt inside the right pocket. Lipstick. Some brand—Guerlain—that Alexa had never heard of. Mauve Gloves. What kind of color was that? Alexa licked her own lips to moisten them. She had forgotten to pack ChapStick.

The scrap of paper had a name and number on it. The black

ink had bled. Alexa stashed it in an evidence bag, wondering if it was the number of a friend. Perhaps a new friend would wonder why Diana didn't call.

The third death, according to the brain doctor, was in future years when your name is spoken for the last time. According to Rosie, Diana had died with no children. The third death would come sooner for her, than say for Charlie, who had two boys who would in turn grow up and perhaps have children, extending his name on earth.

The third death made Alexa squirm.

She squeezed the doctor's thighbones. The femurs felt intact. When she pulled the sheet back to the doctor's muddy boots, she could see the outline of something pressed against the right shin area, and remembered how the bone had been bent backward. The fabric was stained red. She unzipped the detachable pant leg and pulled it up rather than tugging it over the doctor's boot. The tibia pierced the skin like a jagged spear.

A terrible thought invaded Alexa's mind as she took a close-up photo: *Had the doctor bled to death on the rocks?* The injuries were substantial, but there's a chance she could have survived. She shook the image of a dying woman out of her head and checked the doctor's boots: size-eight Keens, soles showing little wear. She took soil samples from the treads.

She had enough evidence to list cause of death without turning the body over, but Alexa never cut corners. Turning a body solo would be hard. She could use Charlie right now. He was probably asleep. A wave of tenderness flowed through her: Charlie was safe. Better than Charlie to help would have been Larry, the medical doctor. She was miffed he begged off because his emotions were fragile. If nothing else, he could have assisted her by taking the photos.

She added "compound fracture, right shin" to the accident report and then took two pillows from the unused twin bed, set them as a bumper, and used the towels to heave Diana over, first upper half and then lower, cringing at the sight of the protruding bone.

Diana's T-shirt twisted. Alexa straightened it out before pulling it up, and was surprised to see two small tears in the fabric rimmed by a small amount of blood. The tears were too regular in shape to have been made by rock. Alexa pulled the T-shirt up.

What the hell?

Above Diana's sports bra strap, two puncture wounds—like bloody eyes—stared at her.

Chapter Eighteen

Alexa didn't know what to make of the punctures. She studied them: dark red and gleaming, dime-sized, the skin around the holes a puckered crater. The left hole was two inches higher than the right. Something about them was familiar. She backed away from the body and collapsed in the soft corner chair.

Bruce. If only she could call Bruce and get his take on her theory. He was a cop. She wasn't. But her phone wouldn't work in these forsaken mountains. It was tucked into her backpack anyway.

She was pretty sure someone had rammed hiking poles into Diana's back. Hard enough to pierce fabric and skin and thrust her over the cliff.

If she was right, this ugly surprise turned accident into murder.

She closed her eyes and visualized a person running at Diana from behind, choking up on the poles, thrusting into her. She popped up and grabbed Diana's pullover from the spare bed to examine it for holes. There they were. How sharp were pole tips? What were they made of? Could they be honed?

The pullover fell from her hands. What about the pole she had in her backpack? The one she'd found on the cliff edge. Could it be a murder weapon? She wished she had it with her.

The room was deathly quiet. No sound came from the hallway. She looked at the door with alarm. Her heart hammered so hard she pressed her palm to her sternum. Someone could open it at any moment. She wasn't ready to share this news with any Tom, Dick, or Harry who barged in. She locked it.

Her fingers trembled as she photographed Diana's back—full view, mid-range, and then close-ups of the punctures. She set the camera aside and checked Diana's buttocks and thighs for more punctures but didn't find anything except a single sandfly bite.

She studied the wounds with her magnifying glass. A puncture was a wound whose depth was greater than its width. She used a probe to measure: almost 25 millimeters, or an inch deep, and 17 millimeters wide. Definitely a puncture. The edges were serrated, almost starlike. The left one had a dark splinter-like substance. Alexa traded the magnifying glass for tweezers and removed it. She held it up to the light. Probably organic—maybe dirt or wood. She stuck it in an evidence bag and labeled it.

With a grunt, she flipped the body to supine position, causing one pillow to tumble. She straightened Diana's T-shirt, pulled her stiffening arms along her body, and covered her with the sheet. She added "two puncture wounds, upper back" to the accident report, folded it, and placed it in the crime kit.

She yanked off her gloves, logged all the evidence, and then washed her hands in the dark bathroom. She didn't want a mirror to reflect the day's toll on her face. Charlie had almost died. A skeleton with trauma wounds awaited justice on a lonely riverbank. A helicopter pilot played a deadly game of cat and mouse.

Add a murdered hiker.

Someone had blood on their hands. She kept scrubbing hers under icy water.

It hit her like a fastball. Diana's murderer could be sleeping in one of the guest rooms. Or prowling the hall. Had they hoped

Diana would wash downstream? Were they freaked out the body had been discovered?

Knocking made her jump. She turned off the faucet. She could not think of a plan as she dried her hands. She tiptoed to the door to see if there was a peephole. No. She was out of her depth. More rapping.

"It's me. Charlie. Open up."

She yanked at the door, but it wouldn't open. She unlocked it, and this time it jerked open.

"What's wrong with you?" Charlie asked. "You look like you've seen a ghost."

"Quiet," she hissed. She looked both ways down the hallway—empty and dark—and told him to come in.

Charlie had changed into shorts and an ENGINERD T-shirt. He cast an eye toward the body and didn't move. "I'll just wait here. I came to see if you were okay."

"I'm not. We've got a problem."

He entered reluctantly, his brow furrowed. "What now?"

Alexa shut the door and leaned against it. "I found evidence that someone pushed Diana over the cliff."

Charlie mouth dropped open, but no words fell out.

"She's got puncture wounds on her back. I think someone rammed hiking poles into her."

"What the hell? What are you going to do?"

Adrenaline leaked from her veins like air out of a balloon. "I don't know."

"This is like a nightmare. Do you think her sister did it?"

"What?"

"Because of that argument they had by the river?"

"That's jumping to conclusions. I'm not telling anyone what I found out. The police will be here first thing in the morning. They'll take over." Saying this felt like shrugging off a heavy pack. A sudden release of pressure. The weight of all her discoveries wouldn't rest solely on her shoulders.

"Everyone is asleep anyway," Charlie said. "It's midnight."

Alexa collected her belongings.

"You can't just leave her."

"Why not?"

"I don't know. Like when I waited with her…" He finally looked at the sheet-covered body. "While you got the rescue crew. It doesn't seem right to leave her alone."

Alexa considered this. Several cultures believed someone needed to stay with the body from the moment of death to burial. That was a traditional Māori belief, she was sure. But this meant family members or loved ones of the deceased. Not forensic investigators. And Diana wasn't Māori. She took a deep breath. "She'll be okay. Kathy gave me a key to lock the door."

"What if someone tampers with her?"

"Who? Like body snatchers?" She patted her crime kit. "I've documented everything on my camera. The evidence will be safe."

The hallway was deathly quiet. Alexa, spooked, took Charlie's hand.

In their room on the opposite wing, Charlie shut the door of the bathroom as Alexa rummaged through the side pocket of her backpack. She half expected the hiking pole to be gone. She almost extracted it without gloves. That's how tired she was. She slipped on a fresh pair and gently lifted it out. As soon as she held the tip to the lamp, the light flickered off.

MONDAY

Chapter Nineteen

Thwapping interrupted Alexa's jumbled dream. She threw off the duvet and lurched to the window. She whipped the curtains aside and searched the blushing sky. A white helicopter with a pointy nose hovered above the trees and then lowered out of sight. The panes of glass rattled. The flank of mountain towering above the trees made her gasp. With the swing bridge damaged, there was no way out of here but up and over that very giant. The racket eased to a *chup chup chup* and then silenced.

Help had arrived.

A helicopter was another way out. She had been in a helicopter once before, on Stewart Island. She got elevator stomach thinking about it.

Charlie, covers up to his chin, looked too big for the single bed. She wondered how he could sleep through the rotor racket. She washed up and wrestled her sleep-tossed hair into a pony-tail. She switched yoga pants for hiking pants, and pulled on a long-sleeved black T-shirt.

Next, she collected her crime kit and camera and then turned her attention to the hiking pole she'd recovered from the cliffside. After the generator had gone off last night, she had examined the pole with her flashlight, wondering if it had propelled Diana to her death. She had wrapped it in a plastic

Pompolona Lodge laundry bag to keep it safe. Her prints would be on it. She would have taken more care not to contaminate it if she'd known it would be important evidence. She'd examine it in Diana's room. She grabbed one of her own poles, too, for comparison. She fumbled her boot lace in excitement.

Charlie grunted and opened his eyes. The sight of his sleepy face evoked the memory of another sleepover, the two of them, in the backyard. Dad set up a pup tent. She'd been nine and Charlie five. She remembered the sticky katydid-loud night surrounded the tiny tent, and how she'd almost caved, almost retreated to the house, but the sound of Charlie's soft snuffles had finally lured her to sleep. They had eaten leftover marshmallows and chocolate bars for breakfast. It had been brave of him to last the night, she realized now. Maybe he felt protected by her. She snorted at the coincidence. This past six hours she had felt protected by him. "The police are here. I'm headed to meet them."

Charlie sat up and scratched at his nascent beard. "Want me to come?"

"No. Get some breakfast. I'll check in with you later."

"What time is it?"

"Six thirty."

"Breakfast isn't until seven thirty." He flopped over.

In the hallway she passed a Luxe hiker in pajama pants and sweatshirt, carrying a cup of coffee. The woman must have sensed Alexa's envy, because she said, "Coffee is in the lounge."

Alexa made a beeline. The lounge was deserted. She spotted Vince through the window, talking to two police officers on the porch. Both wore checkered New Zealand police caps. The older one, pencil straight, stood with his hands clasped behind his back. The younger man, short and pear-shaped, yawned. She set her things on a nearby chair, filled a mug with coffee, and added milk. *Nectar of the gods*, she thought, sipping. She had read that it took forty-five minutes for full caffeine effects to reach the bloodstream, but she felt more alert two sips in.

As she watched the cops, she wondered how many guests knew they'd been sharing the lodge with a dead woman. She counted: Charlie, the managers Vince and Kathy, Rosie, the guide Clint, the colleague Larry. And Stead. Seven people knew about the dead woman. Plus whomever they'd told in turn. News like this was hard to keep quiet.

But only she and Charlie knew the truth. *Well,* she amended, *someone else knows the truth, too.* She gathered her things and scurried out the door.

On the porch, Vince said, "Here she is now. Good morning, Ms. Glock. Sleep well?"

Was he nuts? She raised her mug. "The coffee is good." She turned to the officers and introduced herself. "I work for Forensic Service Center in Auckland," she added.

The older officer, his blue jacket zipped to the neck against the morning chill, introduced himself as Sergeant Adrian Kramer and his colleague as Constable Joel Bartlett. "We're from the Te Anau Police Department."

"Mr. Bergen radioed you on my behalf. I have two suspicious deaths to report."

Sergeant Kramer said, "Two?"

Vince intervened. "The guest that had the tragic fall. I was just telling you about her. A doctor from Auckland. More tragic than suspicious."

Alexa lowered her voice. "It's better if I showed you why her death is suspect."

Before anyone responded, a man slipped out of the morning haze and hopped onto the porch. Alexa sloshed coffee on her T-shirt.

"G'day," Vince said. "Did you deliver these blokes?"

The porch hopper wore a red jumpsuit with a Queenstown Limited logo. He nodded. "I was told we might have an extra passenger on the way back?"

"That's right," Sergeant Kramer said.

Alexa realized the extra passenger was Dr. Clark. Her heart revved as she stared at the pilot. He wore sunglasses even though it was barely light. That worried her. She remembered her kamikaze pilot had worn sunglasses, even in the rain. She mentally put a helmet on the man, but drew a blank. There was no way to tell if he was the same man, although she ventured she would remember the red jumpsuit. The color red was a warning signal to humans, linked to survival, and therefore more memorable than green or blue. She didn't remember a flash of red, and the copter had been yellow. This pilot was flying a white one. She relaxed.

"Go help yourself to a coffee," Vince told the pilot. "Brekkie will be coming."

Inside, Alexa noticed the pilot's face light up when he saw the coffee station where Stead Willis and a Luxe hiker were filling mugs. A fellow coffee-lover couldn't be all bad. She took a quick sip from her mug and told Vince she had a key to Diana's room, but he insisted on showing them the way. "Ruru, isn't it?"

She nodded. "Does the lodge have a safe?"

"Each room has a safe in the closet." Vince saw how encumbered she was with camera, kit, hiking poles, and mug. "Can I carry something?"

"I'm good."

They passed through the hushed lobby, Constable Bartlett bringing up the rear, and entered the guest wing, passing rooms Kiwi, Weka, and Tui. Alexa wondered if the guest in Tui knew he or she was sleeping next door to a dead woman. "There are some valuables I removed from Dr. Clark's body in my crime kit. Earrings and a bracelet." She looked up at the sergeant. "Unless you want to take possession?"

"Shouldn't we give them to Rosie?" Vince asked. "Dr. Clark's sister?"

"A safe should do for now," the sergeant decided.

Vince unlocked Ruru, which made Alexa uneasy. She was

naive to think she'd had the only key. He flicked the light on and motioned for them to enter.

Alexa set her mug on the dresser and untangled herself from her belongings as she watched the constable venture close to the sheet-covered body.

"Stay back," she ordered.

The constable jumped. He was young; Alexa wondered if this was his first dead body. She dug out the bag of jewelry and handed it to Vince. "I don't think anyone should leave the lodge until the police talk to them."

"What?" Vince looked shocked. "They'll want to be on their way. Directly after breakfast. Weather's fine, and they've a big climb up Mackinnon Pass."

"She's right. Hold the guests," Sergeant Kramer said. "That's all for now. Ta, Mr. Bergen."

Vince mumbled something about inconveniences and left.

The scent of river water was diluted with something else. Excess carbon dioxide was building in Diana's body, causing membranes to release enzymes that were eating her cells from the inside out. She would need to be refrigerated soon, or she'd bloat and stink.

"Just so I am clear," Sergeant Kramer said, removing his hat, "your name is Miss Clock?"

"No. Ms. Glock. Like the gun." She shot Constable Bartlett a warning look, expecting a crack about her name, and it worked. No gun jokes followed. The constable removed his hat, too, and patted his fair hair.

"Ms. Glock then," the sergeant said. "What brings you to NZ?"

"I first came for an odontology fellowship at Auckland University."

"Odon what?"

The sergeant's lower teeth were overcrowded, forcing an incisor to protrude. She wondered if his lip ever snagged. "My specialty is teeth. When the fellowship was over, I took a job as a traveling forensic investigator."

The sergeant pointed to the body. "The deceased is one of your suspicious deaths?"

Alexa nodded. She scanned the room. Nothing appeared disturbed. She lifted her mug and took a last sip.

"And there's another body? Is it related?"

"No." Didn't people listen? She had explained everything to the dispatcher. "I mean yes, there's another body. But I doubt it's related. There are skeletal remains along the Clinton River. I discovered them yesterday afternoon. Maybe the landslide unearthed them. I put caution tape around the scene. A male, I believe. There are stab wounds to several of the ribs."

Constable Bartlett whistled as he jotted down notes.

"Any idea how long the deceased has been there?" Sergeant Kramer asked.

"Old, I bet," Constable Bartlett said.

She smiled, proud of her specialty. "He had composite dental fillings. Twenty years, or less."

The constable twiddled his pen. "There goes my theory. I thought he might be Māori. You know—on the *pounamu* trails. Like hundreds of years ago."

The sergeant shook his head. "Bones by the river. Possibly a murder victim. You're sure?"

That irritated Alexa. Science was never one hundred percent certain. "No. I need a lab to confirm. I need to take X-rays. I believe his clothes have disintegrated, but I did find a metal belt buckle and scraps of leather." It was in the crime kit. She hadn't had time to examine it further.

"He must match a missing persons alert." Sergeant Kramer addressed his junior officer. "Call this in, and get someone to the scene."

The constable flew out of the room.

She was about to tell the sergeant about the murderous

helicopter pilot, but he pointed to Diana's body. "Let's get to the bird in hand, eh?"

Alexa walked to Diana. "My brother is the one who spotted Dr. Clark on the rocks." That sounded like a morbid bar drink. "She was upriver from the Pompolona swing bridge, so she couldn't have fallen off it. You'll want to speak to her colleague Dr. Larry somebody; I can't remember his last name. But you'll want to talk with Larry."

Sergeant Kramer watched her carefully. "Why?"

"He may have been the last person to see her before she disappeared." She let this fact register.

"Puts him square on the suspect list if this is a suspicious death," Sergeant Kramer said. His short gray hair was cut in acute angles. She guessed he was in his mid-fifties. She retrieved a pair of gloves from the crime kit.

The sergeant took her cue and pulled a pair from his pocket.

Alexa pulled the sheet down to Diana's chest and gazed at her face. The skin of her cheeks had loosened, and her colorless lips looked waxy. "When I examined her last night, I made a startling discovery."

"Yes?"

Alexa abandoned the body and fetched her report from the kit. "Here." Back in her room last night, she had crossed out "Accident," and written "Possible Homicide."

When his forehead crinkled, she knew the sergeant had noticed. "There are puncture wounds on her back. I think someone rammed her with hiking poles and pushed her off the cliff."

Sergeant Kramer took out his cell phone. "I'll just photograph this report, eh? Send it to headquarters."

"Okay. But there's no service." When he finished, she said, "You can help me turn her."

All the muscles in Diana's body had tensed. Sergeant Kramer noticed as he helped rotate her. "The march of rigor, eh?"

"My professor used to say that," Alexa murmured. She pulled up Diana's T-shirt.

The sergeant stayed quiet. When he tore his eyes away from the wounds, they went directly to the hiking pole Alexa extracted from her stash of evidence.

"I found this wedged in the cliff side above the body." She remembered lifting the pole by its strap, and how it dangled over the gorge, suspended, evidence almost sacrificed. The star-shaped metal tip protruded an inch out of the shaft. She scrutinized it for human flesh, blood, or fiber. It looked clean. It also looked sharp enough to pierce skin.

"Are you saying it's one of the poles that made these?" The sergeant indicated the wounds on Diana's back.

"It's possible. Are you a hiker?"

"Done my fair share," Sergeant Kramer said. "I use trekking poles."

That didn't surprise her. Most Kiwis loved tramping. "What are the tips made of?"

"For rugged terrain like Milford, carbide is best." He studied the pole. "This is carbide. Black Diamond is a good brand."

"Rosie said her sister liked top-of-the-line stuff." She pointed to the plastic snowflake disc with her free hand. Her pole didn't have one. "What this?"

"That's the basket. Good for muddy ground to keep your pole from sinking too deep."

"Do you think the tips could pierce skin?"

The sergeant reached out a finger, but then retracted it. "With enough force, yes."

"Do all tips look the same?"

"Pretty much. They should be notched, for traction. I imagine the notch pattern varies, though, from brand to brand. I've seen tips that are spiked, probably for ice walking."

Variations would make it easier to match which pole was used to stab Diana's back. "I'll set it aside for now, but later I'll dust it for fingerprints. Mine will be on it, but, hopefully, I can lift some others. I'll take the victim's prints now, for comparison." She switched her attention to the glory of fingertip ridges. "If they match, then the pole probably isn't a murder weapon. But if they don't match..."

Sergeant Kramer finished her sentence. "...they might belong to the murderer."

She smiled. "I should fingerprint each of the lodge guests, too." She stowed the pole back in the laundry bag and placed it on the dresser. "Plus I need to see the guests' hiking poles. For comparison. Or someone might be missing one."

She retrieved her own pole now and studied the tip. It was rounded, with no notches. She had bought the cheapest pair and wondered if this was why.

"We can't force the guests to provide their prints."

She set her pole aside. "You can ask, right? Anyone who refuses would be suspect."

The sergeant nodded.

As soon as Alexa touched Diana's clenched fist, she realized her mistake. Crap. She should have taken the prints the night before, as soon as she suspected foul play. When postmortem rigidity wasn't maximal. She'd freaked out over the puncture wounds and lost her professionalism. Now, with the fingers stiffly curled, it would be difficult.

"What's wrong?" Sergeant Kramer asked.

"I'll have to break rigor." She thumbed through her mental file of rigor mortis data. There were two main ways to break rigor. Brute force or cutting the tendons in the wrist. Cutting the tendons was easier, but would result in blood dripping out of the wound. Too messy. Plus Alexa didn't have a scalpel.

They righted the body.

Alexa took Diana's right hand in hers, took a deep breath, then bent the fingers backward as hard as she could. She did this repeatedly, grimacing. She finally heard a crack.

The sergeant had paled. "When you're finished, we'll fly her out. Closest morgue is in Queenstown."

Alexa had worked up a little sweat. "They'll do an autopsy, right?"

"Yes. It's customary in suspicious deaths."

Alexa thought of Rosie, and the argument she'd had with Diana on the riverbank. "You might want to talk with her sister. I'm not sure she and Dr. Clark got along all that well."

"Are you suggesting she has something to do with Dr. Clark's death?"

She and Charlie argued, too, and she hadn't killed him. "My brother and I overheard them arguing on the first day of the hike is all." Unfortunately, Diana's thumb was still curled.

"What were they arguing about?"

"Rosie accused her sister of lording her fancy lifestyle over her, and Dr. Clark said Rosie was jealous. That was the gist."

"Write down everything you remember about it. We'll have to call in a DI to take over."

Little town police stations in New Zealand didn't have homicide detectives. They were recruited from the big towns like Christchurch, Wellington, or Auckland.

"Dr. Clark is from Auckland," the sergeant continued. "Probably best if we brought in a DI from her hometown."

"Bruce," Alexa blurted.

"Pardon me?"

She flushed. "Ask for Detective Inspector Bruce Horne. He's with the Criminal Investigation Branch at Auckland Central. He recently solved a double homicide on Stewart Island." *With my help.*

"You know this bloke?" the sergeant asked.

She bent the thumb back as hard as she could, twice, a third time, and heard a crack. "He's the best."

Chapter Twenty

Alexa was glad Sergeant Kramer left to make radio calls. She preferred working in solitude. She felt safe with law enforcement on the premises, and maybe Bruce on the way.

Bruce. She allowed herself a second to conjure his blue eyes and the kiss they had shared under a dark sky sanctuary. A steamy scene until Bruce balked. He believed in keeping professional and personal lives separate. She did as well. To a point.

She walked around to the other side of the bed and picked up Diana's left hand to repeat the process, grunting with effort. Breaking rigor was hard. She finally heard the loud cracking of bone and set Diana's left hand down. She longed for her postmortem print kit with its cadaver spoon. The spoon stabilizes and supports the finger, and the curvature picks up ridge detail without having to roll the fingers.

She would never go anywhere again without a full crime kit.

Alexa inked Diana's thumb. Then she ripped off a piece of lifting tape and stretched it over the thumb pad. Then she lifted the tape and carefully placed it on the card, creating a mirror image of Diana's thumbprint. She'd have to digitally reverse the image in a lab. She repeated the process for each digit.

After cleaning up, Alexa studied the results with her magnifying glass. A British anthropologist first published a book on the uniqueness of fingerprints. Sir Francis Something-Or-Other classified the ridges as loops, whorls, or arches. She mentally saluted him.

Diana had a loop. Common, yes, but unique to her. Alexa was excited to lift the latent prints from the hiking pole and compare. They could possibly lead to Diana's killer.

No jumping the gun, Glock.

She covered Diana's body and quickly took her own fingerprints to use for elimination, ridiculously proud of her rare arches. She smiled, thinking back to her fellow lab rats in Raleigh; they'd been stupidly geeky about their fingerprints, too.

Then she studied the pole again. The brand name, Black Diamond, sounded ominous. Under her magnifying glass, the metal tip looked clean, and not altered or honed, but she knew it could harbor Diana's DNA if it had been used to push her off the cliff. She withdrew the distilled water and a sterile swab from her kit and carefully squeezed one drop of water on the swab. Then she rubbed it against the pole tip, rotating the swab once.

One and done.

She stuck the swab in a transport tube, labeled it, and set it aside.

She toyed with the idea of flipping Diana's body again and comparing the pole tip to the wounds, but decided to use the photographs she had taken the night before instead. She'd be able to enlarge them. But first she propped the pole up against a chair, upside down, so she could photograph the tip from above.

She grabbed her camera and scrolled through the hundred or so photos she had taken until she reached the ones of Diana's wounds. When she found a clear, well-lit photo, she tapped the screen. The puncture resembled a small-caliber gunshot wound. She retrieved her magnifying glass for an even closer look: the outline of the wound was stellate.

If she were in a lab, she would superimpose the photograph of the wound on the photograph of the pole tip to see if it aligned.

If it did, she'd have proof a Black Diamond pole resembled the murder weapon.

She tamped down her excitement and readied her scant supplies: black powder, a brush, lifting tape, and backing cards. Work was her happy place.

Where would prints be? The cork handle should be rife, but cork was icky to work with. Any prints lifted would have a distracting pattern running through them. Background interference, it was called. She liked a challenge. She shook her jar of powder, opened it, and butterfly swished the brush across the thin coating clinging to the lid and tapped it on the powder container. Too much powder would obliterate the print. Satisfied, she spun the brush, applying slight pressure on an area of the cork. A partial fingerprint emerged. Excitedly, she set the brush aside and took a close-up photo. Then she secured a piece of lifting tape across the surface of the print, pressed down, and lifted. She transferred the tape to a white card and peered at it under the lamp. It was a mess.

She repeated the process on the metal shaft of the pole with more success, lifting a couple partial prints and two nearly complete impressions.

Holding her breath, she compared them to Diana's prints. She retrieved her dental probe to keep track of ridge features. Back and forth, through her magnifier, she compared cards. Bingo! A print lifted from the shaft matched the deceased's. The pole had probably belonged to Diana.

Then she discovered a non-matching print. Her heart skipped a beat. Excluding her own prints and Diana's, someone else had touched the pole. The murderer? She photographed all the print cards to have backup.

Unlike medical doctors, forensic scientists lacked a Hippocratic oath, but before she pulled the sheet over Diana's face, Alexa promised to apply her scientific skills to find her killer.

She could smell bacon but decided to stop by her room before eating breakfast. Unfortunately, Charlie still had the key—they needed a spare. She knocked, but Charlie must have left. She tried the handle; it was unlocked. She wandered past the unmade beds and into the bathroom to wash her hands again, trying to remove ink traces and the memory of cadaver skin. She squeezed lavender lotion on her palms, massaged it in, and inhaled. Lavender masked the scent of death.

After breakfast she would return to the riverbank. A daytime examination of the scene was prudent. She might find Diana's backpack and second pole. She'd have to get there before the rangers trampled any remaining evidence when they went to assess the bridge. She eyed her camera and crime kit. Leave them here or take them to breakfast? The safe in the closet had a real key and lock. She guessed an electronic safe would be worthless when the generator was off. She opened it and stuffed the retracted and wrapped hiking pole in it; it barely fit. She put the other pieces of evidence in, too: the particle from the wound, the slip of paper, soil sample, the lipstick, the fingerprint cards, and DNA tube. Plus, she had the buckle from the skeleton. She would find Sergeant Kramer and ask him to fly the evidence out with the body.

The most important evidence was the photos. The Olympus Tough camera needed charging again. She slipped the memory card in her pants pocket and plugged the camera in the outlet, gladdened to see the generator providing power. She locked and pulled the door tight.

Please be bacon left, she thought.

The Luxers bunched in the lounge, murmuring quietly in a ring around Rosie. *Ashes, ashes, we all fall down* popped into Alexa's head. From the concerned looks on the Luxers' faces, it appeared she'd let the cat out of the bag about her sister. Alexa tried sneaking past, but Debbie bound over. "Have you heard?"

"Heard what?"

Debbie grasped her elbow. "Rosie said Dr. Clark drowned in Pompolona Creek. She fell off the swing bridge."

Alexa refrained from correcting her. She scanned faces for Charlie and saw him talking with Stead.

"I thought there was something wrong with that bridge," Debbie continued. "The way it shook with every step. It's so terrible, don't you think?"

Alexa extracted her elbow. "Yes, it's terrible."

The Luxe guide Clint entered the room, his clipboard hugged to his chest. Constable Bartlett followed. They stopped next to the easel that displayed the laughing owl poster. The black-eyed owl wasn't laughing.

Clint cleared his throat. "Good morning, Luxers. Thank you for gathering. Those of you standing, please take a seat. We will have a brief update before we adjourn for a delicious breakfast."

The smell of bacon was killing Alexa, but she needed to listen.

Constable Bartlett rocked back and forth on the balls of his feet, his pale blue eyes flitting from person to person.

Debbie gave Alexa's arm a pat and joined her husband on a love seat.

Clint's normal buoyancy had deflated. He raised his eyes and smiled anemically. "We at Luxe Tours take your safety as our number one priority. We have an exemplary record."

Trampers muttered.

"You've lost trampers before," said a man Alexa didn't recognize. He was dressed for hiking, and she couldn't place his accent. Middle Eastern, maybe. "That Japanese hiker. She got lost, just like the doctor."

Clint frowned. "Yes, yes. But we found her. She was uninjured and rejoined the hike the next day."

Was there something fishy about Luxe Tours? Alexa wondered. Maybe the police should look into the company's track record.

Rosie hiccuped. The woman next to her patted her knee.

Alexa counted heads. Seventeen Luxers including Clint, plus Stead—who appeared to be looking right at her—and Charlie. They stood next to Cassandra and Larry. Cassandra held her chin high and stared at Clint. Larry studied his hiking boots.

Kathy appeared with a plate of scones. "To tide you over," she said, setting them near the coffee station.

The aroma was tantalizing, but most of the Luxers remained fixated on Clint. Alexa seized the opportunity to help herself. She was starved. The only other person to indulge was the teen son of the Israeli couple. He gave her a shy smile.

Clint tapped his clipboard. "Unfortunately, there are inherent risks and dangers with tramping that we cannot foresee. As you've no doubt heard, we discovered Dr. Diana Clark's body on the riverbank last night. We aren't sure what happened, but she is deceased. The swing bridge is closed."

The Luxers glanced at Rosie, and quickly away. Then came a volley of comments.

"First the avalanche, and now this," Debbie said.

"How did it happen?" Debbie's husband asked.

"Did she drown?" the Fitbit woman asked.

"We don't know," Clint said.

"Can we continue the hike?" a man with a French accent asked. His head was shaved, and he wore trendy glasses.

The guy was worried about his vacay, Alexa realized, and not about Rosie or the doctor. She looked around at the well-dressed, fit crowd, and wondered how many felt similarly entitled to vacay-uninterruptus.

"We don't know details because there was no witness," Clint said sensibly. "I am turning this meeting over to Constable Joel Bartlett from Te Anau. He and his sergeant are here to help us through this. Thank you."

The scone was delicious. Alexa wiped crumbs off her fingers.

Constable Bartlett stopped rocking. "I know this has been a shock, eh?" He gave a nervous cough. "My sergeant has issued a request that no one leave the lodge until myself or Sergeant Kramer speak with you. You'll be too hard to round up once you cross Mackinnon Pass and reach Milford Sound."

"*La vache*," the French man said. "We have an arduous climb ahead of us."

The constable ignored him. "Please stay in the lounge, or in the dining room. No returning to your rooms until we've talked with you."

"You're dreaming," the Fitbit woman said. "I need to get my insulin supplies."

The constable looked alarmed. "What's your name?"

"Emily Wolf."

"You can come first, Ms. Wolf, so that we can clear you for leaving. Mr. Bergen is finding a room for interviews. I know you all want to help us investigate what happened."

The Luxers watched Constable Bartlett leave. Then they headed toward the dining room, shaking their heads and speaking in somber tones. Alexa thought Constable Bartlett handled the briefing well. Vince raced around the corner, his face grim. He searched the crowd, his eyes alighting on Alexa, and scurried over. "Come to the office, Ms. Glock. Call for you."

She frowned, her bacon dreams dashed.

In the office Sergeant Kramer spoke into the satellite phone. "Here she is now." He handed it to her, and whispered, "It's that detective inspector bloke from Auckland. Keep the antenna pointed up."

"Hello?"

"Alexa? Can you hear me?" His voiced echoed.

"I can hear you, Bruce."

"Are you all right?"

Her face colored. She turned her back on Vince and Sergeant Kramer. "Yes. But there's a lot going on."

"Fill me in."

"Hold on." She turned and asked Vince if he'd leave the office.

"Leave my own office?"

"Ta," said Sergeant Kramer. "You can show me the room we can use for the interviews."

The sergeant was quick on the uptake. Alexa nodded her thanks. When the door shut, she sank into a desk chair. "Bruce? Are you there?"

"What's going on?"

It was hard to know where to start. She pressed the desk stapler with her free hand.

Bruce was impatient. "Kramer said you had two suspicious deaths. What have you gotten into this time?"

She wanted to staple him for that remark, but took a deep breath instead. "My brother and I discovered a woman's body on a riverbank below a cliff. I believe she died of blunt force trauma from falling off the cliff. She has puncture wounds in her back. I think someone pushed her off by ramming into her with hiking poles."

"Repeat."

Alexa rotated the antenna upward and repeated her account. "She was pushed off a cliff?"

"That's what the evidence suggests. I also found a Black Diamond hiking pole above where the body was. We are detaining all hikers until we question them."

"That's good."

"She's a medical doctor from Auckland. Her sister and two colleagues are here with her." She gave Bruce their names.

"Don't let the colleagues or sister leave. I'll start by interviewing them."

She depressed the stapler. "I told you we're holding everyone until we clear them."

"Don't release the sister or the colleagues," he repeated. "I'll get Constable Cooper to dive into Clark's affairs at this end. Her phone and computer records. Her standing in the medical community."

The mention of Constable Cooper jerked Alexa back to her first case in New Zealand. Alexa had suspected the young Māori of committing the murder, but had been wrong. "Coop," as her colleagues called her, hadn't forgotten. "But Constable Cooper is in Rotorua."

"I recruited her to Auckland." Bruce had been her mentor in some career-shadowing outreach program and a couple years later hired her.

Alexa switched gears. "There's more. Yesterday, I discovered a skeleton along the river. It became exposed during the landslide we had."

"The what?"

"A landslide. Mudslide. You know. Slip. An avalanche without snow. This isn't avalanche season." Her geology eruption silenced Bruce. "I saw it happen." That bus-sized boulder careening down the mountainside. *Jeez.* "I did a preliminary examination of the remains and discovered multiple stab wounds to the rib cage."

"Bloody hell. How old is the skeleton?"

"He has composite resin fillings."

Bruce huffed.

"Twenty years or less. We might be able to identify him through dental X-rays."

"Any personal effects?"

"A metal buckle. There could be more. I didn't fully examine the remains." She imagined her voice zooming skyward, hitting a satellite hovering over the Tasman Sea, and bouncing back to Bruce in Auckland. "One more thing." She checked the antenna and scooted to the edge of her seat. Now or never.

"Spit it out."

"A helicopter pilot tried to kill me."

Chapter Twenty-One

Telling someone besides Charlie eased her anxiety. Bruce stayed quiet as she described the ton of rock swinging toward her head. "At first I thought it must be a mistake. Like he didn't see me. Or forgot he was carrying the bulk bag. Then he turned the copter around and came at me again. I had to run for the woods."

"This was soon after you found the body?"

"Found the skeleton."

"Then there might be a connection. Didn't you put ribbon around the scene?"

She bristled. "Of course I taped the scene. Used every bit of ribbon I brought with me on my *vacation*."

"I'm just confirming."

Alexa adjusted the antenna and recounted all the details she remembered: yellow helicopter, white bulk bag, helmet, sunglasses. It wasn't much, but how many yellow copters had been buzzing around Milford Track yesterday? A handful, or less.

"I'll contact Civil Aviation Authority to see the daily concessions."

She wasn't clear what Bruce meant, but it sounded as if he was taking her seriously. "Talk to the ranger at Clinton Hut." She almost called him Gloomy Gus. "Ranger Harker. A yellow copter landed there early in the morning. Harker had words with the pilot." The ranger had called the pilot by name, but Alexa couldn't remember it. "About flying in the danger zone."

Silence.

"Bruce?"

"*Top Gun*. Danger zone. I wanted to be a pilot when I saw that movie."

"Me too."

"Could the helicopter pilot have used the rock bag to knock Dr. Clark off the cliff?" Bruce asked.

She knew he was trying to connect the two incidents. "I don't think so. There were too many trees."

"Don't leave the lodge until I arrive early afternoon. Keep an eye on the sister and colleagues and anyone else who knew the doc. If this is murder, they're the main suspects."

He was right. Most victims were killed by people they knew.

She found Vince, and he showed her how to dial out on the satellite phone. She called her boss, Dan Goddard, at Forensic Service Center in Auckland and spent ten minutes updating him.

"Strange," Dan said. "If you had been here, I would have sent you there."

She agreed it was strange.

Breakfast was buffet-style, but Silas was cooking eggs to order. He cracked them with one hand, and shimmied the pan over the gas flame. "I saw you on the porch talking to the cops," he said.

Alexa nodded.

He lowered his voice. "This is bad news for Luxe Tours."

She watched the egg whites sizzle. "What's the scoop on the Japanese tourist who went missing last year? Were you around?"

"Nah yeah." He added salt and pepper to the eggs. His ball cap was on backward, and she could see a tint of ginger in his brownish hair. "Like Dr. Clark, she was seen at lunch and she didn't show up that afternoon at Quinton Lodge. That's the next lodge for Luxe hikers, right? After Mackinnon Pass. She was, like, in her seventies. They found her in the middle of the night." He slid her eggs onto a plate.

"Was Clint her guide?"

"I don't remember. Guides come and go with each bunch."

Bruce would need to check out Mr. Clipboard, for sure. And Kathy and Vince.

Two slices of bacon wasn't enough for the day ahead. Alexa nestled a third by sunny-side-up eggs, their yolks beautiful orange bursts, and scanned the dining room. Luxers ate in huddles, talking in animated tones, their faces lively. It was human nature to be titillated by the misfortune of others, Alexa realized.

Rosie was missing. Cassandra and Larry sat together. Larry was buttering toast. Cassandra had pushed back from an almost-full plate. Could they have plotted to get rid of Diana? But didn't their livelihood depend on the doctor? Or Larry's did anyway. She added a slice of melon to her plate and joined Charlie and Stead at a table.

"What are you smiling about?" Charlie asked.

She hadn't known she was smiling.

Stead looked miffed. "Can you get your mates to let me leave?" he asked.

"The policemen aren't my mates."

Stead's backpack rested against an empty chair. "I was happy to lead the search and get the poor woman's body back here, but I have a schedule to keep."

Alexa added more salt to her eggs and took a bite. "You've been a big help."

"What did the cops say?" Charlie asked.

She covered her mouth with her napkin. "They're calling in a detective I know."

"Why do they want to interview me?" Stead asked.

Alexa hoped Charlie had kept quiet about Diana's wounds. "It's not just you. It's everyone. They're just following procedures."

Stead leaned back on two chair legs. He had been alone at Clinton Hut when she had returned for her poles. The sound of a helicopter had made him dash to the window. "Did you know that helicopter pilot at the hut yesterday?" she asked casually.

Stead looked startled. "Which one?"

"The one who showed up while I was there. When you made me coffee. You had a bunch of stuff spread on the table."

Stead righted the chair.

She chewed half a slice of bacon, then swallowed. "Did you know that pilot?"

"There was all sorts of copters yesterday. I know a DOC pilot. But that wasn't him."

"What's your DOC friend's name?"

Stead hesitated. "Bill Little. He's the one that gave me a lift to Mintaro Hut. After the landslide blocked the path, DOC ordered several helicopters into the area to assess the damage. There's a lot of money riding on the Great Walks. Since I was stuck on the Clinton Hut side, I waved one down."

Alexa remembered forking over her credit card to pay extra for Charlie's tickets. She also wondered if Stead was changing the subject.

"The season has already been disrupted by the big storm a couple weeks ago. Now this," Stead said. "They'll have to fork over more refunds."

"Your friend flew you over the landslide?"

"What a mess. I imagine he's there today, rerouting the track. I'd hike backward and help if it wasn't for the swing bridge."

She thought he had a schedule to keep. "Did you see caution tape near the debris field?"

His brown eyes flickered. "Yeah. What was that all about?"

Across the room, Constable Bartlett approached Emily, the Fitbit woman. Maybe he was about to start the interviews. "There's your chance to talk with one of the officers about leaving," Alexa said, ignoring his question.

"I'll have a word then," he said, leaving his backpack behind. Alexa glanced at Charlie as she chewed, gathering courage and calories. Now was the time to have the talk. She had been worried about breaking the news that continuing Milford Track was on hold for her. "Um, Charlie?"

He raised his eyebrows.

"I'm not going to be able to hike today. You can go on without me." She expected him to protest, but his face stayed calm. "When my duties are finished I'll catch up with you in Te Anau. We can go to the glowworm cave," she added lamely.

Charlie shook his head as if she were daft. "I'm not leaving you. At least not for ten more days. I'll be your bodyguard."

"I don't need a bodyguard," she said reflexively.

He scratched at his new beard growth. "Kathy stopped by and said the next wave of Luxers has been canceled because of the landslide and bridge. We can stay another night if we need to."

She smiled. Things were looking up with the men in her life. Charlie wasn't jumping ship, and Bruce was on his way. Bruce's command that she stay in the lodge until he arrived was an obstacle. She decided to leap over it. "You can come with me to the swing bridge." Returning to a scene of the crime in daylight was protocol, and evidence would be trampled as soon as the rangers arrived to inspect the bridge. "We better go. I want to see if we can find any of Dr. Clark's things. She should have a backpack." She lowered her voice. "And maybe there's some clues left by whomever rammed into her."

Charlie looked excited. "Like what?"

"Anything suspicious." She stood, knocking into Stead's backpack. She grabbed a strap to right it, but it toppled over. "Damn. What does he have in here?" She could see him across the room talking with Constable Bartlett.

Charlie set it right with a grunt. "My arms are killing me."

She thought he was talking about the backpack but then

flashed to his death-defying cable swing. "Your brachium saved your life."

"My what?"

"The three muscles in your upper arms. Your biceps brachii, your brachialis, and your triceps brachii."

"Whatever. They hurt."

"You can be my assistant."

"Ha! Like you made me wait on you when you were recuperating from your accident. You took total advantage. Bring me a Coke. Bring me Cheetos."

Her back scars pulsated. Charlie had been there that March afternoon twenty-four years ago. She could see his little-boy-self holding the refrigerator door open, his face twisted in confusion as she screamed. She remembered her stepmother's cold eyes, too. All the other details were a blistering blur. "It wasn't an accident."

Charlie's mouth gaped. "You aren't still convinced Mom scalded you on purpose? I saw you skid across the floor into her."

"Don't call her Mom."

"I'll call her what I want. Maybe it's time to take down your shrine to our birth mother."

She wanted to hurl a comeback, but threw her napkin on her plate instead. He was right. Maybe Rita's eyes had been shocked, not cold. Mom, her real mom, wouldn't want her to be bitter. Wouldn't want her to shut people out. Her chest ached as if her heart was cracking open, letting in a ray of light.

———

They doused themselves with bug spray in their room. Alexa opened the safe with the little key and removed the evidence; she was hoping Sergeant Kramer could get it to a lab ASAP.

"Hey," she said to Charlie, "before we go, look at the buckle

I found on the skeleton." Alexa pulled on gloves. "Can I have a piece of your notebook paper?"

Charlie had a spiral notebook. Alexa had seen him writing in it. He tore out a fresh sheet—college rule, she noted. She gingerly removed the buckle from the evidence envelope and set it on the paper.

"Why don't you wash it off?" Charlie asked.

"That could damage evidence." She wished she had a cleaning brush. She considered her toothbrush, but ended up using a facecloth provided by the lodge to gently dislodge dirt. "Look. A pattern."

"Swirls," Charlie said, leaning closer. "Like snakes. Or eels."

"Eels are a big deal to the Māori." Alexa got her magnifying glass and studied the buckle. Each corner had spirals, reminding her of fern fronds. The middle looked like intertwined creatures. She searched for a manufacturer mark or engraving, but couldn't find any. She took a photo of it with her cell phone. "Any idea what type of metal it is?"

"There's hardly any rust. Maybe it's zinc," Charlie said. "Do you think you'll be able to trace who the guy is through the buckle?"

"I think his teeth are a better bet," Alexa said.

Charlie laughed. "You and teeth. A love story."

She left the key in the safe lock and collected her jacket, poles, crime kit, and charged camera. "Let's go."

Sergeant Kramer was in Vince's office. Alexa was trying to be a team player. She notified him of her plans to visit the scene. This was a trait her boss at Forensic Service Center suggested she work on. Well, he was only the latest boss who advised this. Alexa concluded that men didn't like take-charge women, but admitted that her boss, Dr. Winget, a woman, made the same comment during a performance review.

"The scene needs to be secured," Sergeant Kramer agreed.

"Hold off on interviewing Dr. Clark's staff and sister until

Bruce gets here, well, I mean, DI Horne. He said to not let them…"

"…leave until he gets here," Sergeant Kramer finished. "I talked with him after you did. If the weather holds, he should be here by one."

"Is the weather going to get bad?" Charlie asked.

"A front is moving in this afternoon. More rain. We're getting ready to transport the body now. I've informed the morgue in Queenstown to expect a delivery."

Instead of unwrapping the buckle again, Alexa showed the sergeant her photo of it. "What do you think? Does the design mean anything?" He tapped the screen to enlarge it. "*Koru* or spirals symbolize new life and growth." He pointed to the middle. "These might be eels, a Māori treasure and source of food."

"No thanks," Charlie said.

"So the man wearing the buckle might be a Māori," Alexa said.

"Could be," the sergeant said. "Māori still make pilgrimages here to hunt for greenstone."

He promised to get the evidence to the nearest forensic lab.

"Is there a lab in Queenstown?"

"No. We use Forensic Service Center in Christchurch. FSC is who you work for, right?"

"The one in Auckland. The evidence will receive priority, given that this is murder." She double-checked that the time, date, and her name were clearly marked. They were all stored in paper bags except for the pole and the note that had been in Diana's pocket. "Look at this." She held up the clear evidence bag that held the slip of paper.

Sergeant Kramer held the bag by one corner. "It's torn off a pad, maybe." He pulled glasses out of his shirt pocket and slipped them on. "Written in black ink. D, E, something something, space, J, A, C. Jacob? Jack? That's a three area code, which could be anywhere on the South Island. I can't make out any other numbers except double nine." He took a couple photos and gave it back to Alexa. "Odd, eh? Don't most people exchange names and numbers using their mobiles?"

"Hardly," Charlie said. "Now it's more like 'Follow me on Instagram.'"

Alexa didn't do Instagram. A qualified forensic document examiner might be able to eke out more from the scrap. She had an urge to be in a lab, safe with science. She added her business card to the collection, which included her accident/homicide report, and handed it to Sergeant Kramer. She had to trust the chain of custody would work properly and that the evidence would be preserved in a legal manner. "What about the skeleton?"

"We can't get to the scene until this afternoon. We're short on people. Today is our annual Te Anau Downs Classic."

"A horse race?" Charlie asked.

"A sailing regatta."

Alexa frowned. With the swing bridge out of commission, there was no way to hike back to the skeleton. She felt a sense of urgency that the bones not be neglected. "Boats are more important than bones?"

"Lighten up, Lexi. The bones can wait another couple hours."

"What if it were Mel?" she countered. "You wouldn't want to wait."

The morning forest sparkled as they started down the track. A musical whistle followed by a screech made Alexa search the trees for a tui, a New Zealand bird that makes cuckoo-clock noises. They walked side by side, their argument tucked away for later. Charlie shook a branch laden with pink fuchsia-like flowers, causing a mini shower to rain on Alexa.

"Stop!"

"You're an old lady."

Alexa almost poked him with one of her poles, but caught herself. That would be in bad taste, given Diana's wounds. The temperature hovered around fifty degrees. She picked up her pace to warm up and checked over her shoulder.

Charlie looked, too. "Who are you looking for?"

"No one. Just checking."

"For the helicopter pilot?"

Alexa shook her head, but wondered if she could be in danger. The copter pilot had tried to kill her with the bag of rocks. Perhaps the pilot had freaked out over the discovery of the skeleton because he was the person who had stabbed the victim.

Maybe he hadn't wanted her to reach the lodge and notify the authorities.

Too late. Telling others of her discovery made her safer. Plus she had photos.

Two murders. It was hard to fathom. Diana's murderer could be someone sitting in the lodge right now. Worried. On the defensive. Dangerous.

Or having a second cup of coffee, feet up, satisfied. That was the more chilling thought.

Alexa reviewed protocol as she skirted a rotting log sprouting ears of lichen. Now that she'd established a crime had taken place, she needed to consider areas where evidence could be. She had begged some twine from Vince, because her caution tape was used up. The most likely area was where the perpetrator interacted with the victim. She envisioned the cliff bank above where the body was found. Evidence could also be found in pre-crime and post-crime areas.

"…asked me to bring home a kiwi."

"What?"

Charlie frowned. "Haven't you been listening? Ben has been studying birds and asked me to bring a kiwi home in my suitcase."

"I'll get Benny a stuffed one."

"He doesn't go by Benny anymore."

The pre-crime area was vast. She decided it included all of

Milford Track between the shelter where Diana was last seen, to the cliff edge. Alexa imagined the killer trailing the doctor like an animal on the hunt, waiting for an opportunity. She scanned the jungle of green.

"Quit doing that," Charlie called. "You're making me nervous."

She shifted her crime sack to her other shoulder and considered the post-crime scene. Alexa suspected the murderer might have tossed Diana's belongings into the river. She would tell Bruce to search downriver. Well, she amended. She'd *suggest* to Bruce that the river be searched. Sometimes she forgot who was boss.

If Diana's backpack was retrieved, it could contain trace evidence. Fingerprints, fiber, hair, or DNA. Killer calling cards. She waited for Charlie to catch up with her. "Are you familiar with Locard's exchange principle?"

"No. What comes next? A lecture?"

She could be patient. Charlie would appreciate Locard's genius. "Locard was a Frenchman. He established the first crime lab in 1912. His principle is that every contact leaves a trace. He'd tested his theory countless times. One time a woman was found strangled at her parents' home. Her boyfriend claimed he had been playing cards with friends—a classic alibi, right?"

"I get it," Charlie said. "Like a computer trail. I can check to see where Ben has been after we've given him laptop time. His digital footprint."

That sounded draconian to Alexa. Her nephew was only seven. Or eight. "When Locard scraped underneath the boyfriend's fingernails, he found pink dust. It matched a custom face powder the dead woman had worn."

"Busted," Charlie said.

"When we get there, I'll secure an area with the twine and look for trace evidence the criminal left behind. Boot prints, for one. They would be the most obvious."

"I hope someone's checking the doctor's computer and cell phone."

"Bruce is seeing to it."

"You're on first-name basis with the guy?"

The throb of rotors stopped Alexa. Her impulse was to dive for cover. She relaxed when she spotted the white underbelly of a copter overhead and watched it disappear beyond the tree canopy. The pilot must be taking Diana to the morgue. Alexa cleared her throat and said, "I'm on a first-name basis with the detective. We're, well, sort of friends."

Charlie made his eyebrows go up and down. Alexa laughed.

The rain and rescue posse last night had most likely destroyed evidence. She wasn't hopeful they'd find prints, but it was worth a try. Diana wore Keens, size eight. If she could find just one imprint, and then a non-matching print behind it, she might kick the killer through footwear impression. She didn't have cast material—it had been jettisoned from her temporary kit because it was bulky—but she could take photographs.

The sound of the waterfall infiltrated her thoughts.

Chapter Twenty-Two

A cloud turned the morning light to silver as the path opened to the clearing. The swing bridge, lifeless and listing, spanned the river like a spiderweb. There was no barricade.

She grabbed Charlie's arm. "Stay back."

"Get real. I'm not going anywhere near that thing."

She imagined Diana crossing the bridge yesterday afternoon, and then taking off her backpack so she could get a photograph of the waterfall. This was the right angle to catch its full height: a plunging spigot thirty or so meters high with three frothy leaps.

But wasn't it raining? It was hard taking pictures in the rain. What about the doctor's yellow raincoat? Why hadn't she been wearing it? And where was her cell phone? Did it have a picture of the murderer on it? Cell phones were key to solving more and more crimes. Myriad questions ricocheted in Alexa's head as she turned her back to the river.

She mentally mapped a crime scene: bridge platform to the path to the cliff edge.

Charlie held one end of the twine as Alexa walked the perimeter. The cliff edge formed one side, which was good because the twine wasn't long enough.

"So this is how it's done?" Charlie called.

"No." A proper crime scene would include inner and outer

cores. She'd be suited up and wearing booties. "But it's all we have for now."

"What should I do?"

Good question. Alexa considered how to keep him occupied and useful, but out of the way. She didn't need more contamination. "Stay on this side of the twine." She gave him her pad and a pencil, and then hung her camera around her neck. "Sketch the scene as best you can."

"Why do you need a sketch? Just take pictures."

Her patience was waning. "A sketch can show where we think Diana fell compared to where the bridge is. You can add a scale. Photographs can distort distances."

"Yes, ma'am."

She turned her camera on. It beeped unhappily and displayed a message: no memory card. *Jeez.* Luckily, the crucial card nestled in her pants pocket. The world in a grain of sand. Her hand shook as she inserted the postage stamp–sized card into the slot.

She leaned forward, eyes on the ground, and began walking in a slow spiral. Her vision narrowed to moss, mud, flattened leaves, and stones. The cloud blocking the sun moved onward, and a glint caught her eye. She bent over and nudged the glint with her index finger. It was crystal sheets of mica.

Near the cliff edge she discovered a full boot impression, the heel a tiny pool of water. She couldn't tell the size, but saw that it was larger than hers. She sucked in her breath, backed up, readied her camera. Wide-angle. Midrange. Close-up. She could see the tread detail better on her screen. The word *vibram*—located in the sole—came into focus.

Diana's boot had Keen stamped into the sole. At first she was disappointed, but then she realized the print could be important if it didn't belong to one of the members of the rescue posse, which had included Charlie.

"What kind of boots do you have on?"

"L.L.Beans. Size twelve," he called.

Dammit. She should have checked Clint, Larry, and Stead's footwear. She'd have to do it when she got back.

She backtracked and cased the scene again. Always check twice, Dr. Winget had advised. This time she spotted pole holes. She knelt and took photos, but wasn't happy with how they looked on the camera screen—too shadowy. She hoped the complete crime kit she told Bruce to bring would arrive before the holes degraded.

She yelled for Charlie to walk the outer border of the twine, checking for a backpack or other belongings. She remembered Stead asking Rosie what color it was. "The backpack is blue. But don't touch anything," she added.

"Does an apple count as a belonging?" he called.

"What?"

"An apple. There are a few bites taken. Maybe it's a poison apple."

She rolled her eyes, but traipsed over to a tiny clearing between two trees. Charlie nudged a speckled half-eaten apple with his boot. "Is it a clue?"

"Maybe." She thought of how Stead had said all trash must be packed out—even apple cores. She took a few photos of the apple and its juxtaposition to the cliff, and then lifted it by the stem and studied the brown-edged bite-marks. Definitely human. Parts of the apple flesh hadn't oxidized. Cool rainy weather probably slowed the process.

She eyed the cliff and bridge, a chill scurrying down her spine. The litterbug might have been hiding out. Was this like a deer stand where a hunter waits to make a kill? "Don't move."

Charlie looked alarmed.

"I need to search for boot prints."

After five minutes she gave up. The leafy debris was unyielding. She adjusted the twine to include the apple area. She fished an evidence bag out of the crime kit and deposited the apple, excited about lifting prints from the skin. Or better yet, analyzing the bite-marks. She had been right to return to the scene. "Good find," she said. "Keep looking while I check out the cliff side."

Heart pounding, she neared the edge and looked down where Diana's body had draped between the boulders, now in the shadow of the cliff. The waterfall drowned all other sound; Diana wouldn't have been able to hear anyone approaching. The hair on Alexa's neck stood. She whipped around.

Poor Diana to suddenly be flying off the cliff, her life about to end. Alexa's gloved hands had gone clammy. She stepped a little closer and looked over. No one could survive this fall. Twenty to twenty-five feet to rock and ruin. Well…maybe if the doctor had been drunk. Sometimes inebriated people survived falls from extreme heights because alcohol relaxes muscles and switches off reflexes.

But Diana hadn't survived.

The water had receded since last night. More bank was exposed. Alexa wanted to step away from the ledge, but forced herself to check the cliff side. Maybe the other pole was there. Or the backpack, lodged in a crevice. Toes inches from the rim, she leaned forward.

Don't fall. Don't fall.

No pole, no backpack. She took a couple photos, then hopped back as a voice penetrated the waterfall racket. For a freaky moment she thought people were crossing the crippled bridge. She turned around. "Charlie?"

"Over here," he yelled.

She saw him waving from the woods.

"Halloo," said a soprano voice.

A ranger in shorts and forest-green pullover walked into the clearing. She tucked a brown curl under her beanie and introduced herself as Tyndall Light, ranger at Mintaro Hut. She patted a coil of yellow rope hanging from her hefty pack. "I'm here to secure the bridge."

"I'm Alexa Glock, a forensics investigator. We spoke on the radio yesterday late afternoon. About the missing hiker, and my brother, and all."

"Ah, yes. I'm sorry to hear about the tramper. She fell off the bridge?"

"No. She, um, fell from the cliff." Alexa pointed in the general direction.

The ranger's eyes widened. "Did the ledge give way?"

The ledge Alexa had just been standing on? Her heart fluttered. "I'm not sure what happened." She pointed to Charlie bushwhacking in their direction. "He's the one who was flipped off the bridge."

"I remember him from the hut. Good as gold, then. He lived to tell the tale."

"Barely. He was able to grab a cable and monkey to the side." The ranger—maybe thirty years old—headed to the bridge.

"Don't cross it," Alexa warned as Charlie joined her. For the first time she wondered if the bridge had been sabotaged.

Had Diana's killer wanted to flip her in the river, and when that hadn't worked, pushed her off the cliff instead, and Charlie was the one who ended up flipped? What would tampering look like?

She followed the ranger to the step platform, and examined the structure. Two thick cables anchored through eyelets into the ground. She nudged one, and wondered if the heavy-duty eyelet was cemented below the dirt. The cables extended upward to a wooden tower, threaded through holes, and extended, sagging toward the middle of the bridge, then upward to towers on the opposite side of the river. *What could go wrong?*

"I'm roping it off," the ranger explained. "The inspector and construction crew are on their way. A chopper will fly them in."

Figures, Alexa thought.

The ranger shouted at them as she worked. "The DOC budget is tight, but luckily most maintenance repairs are minor. Like a rotted-out step or wobbly rail." She looped rope between the handrails of the step platform and pointed to the sign that warned that only three people were allowed on the bridge at a time. "Could be the bridge was over capacity."

"I was the only one on it, so it wasn't overloaded," Charlie said.

"Structural integrity, then. Maybe the giant storm and flooding we had undermined it." She finished tying the rope. "It's all good, then."

"All good?" Charlie's face was grim. "Not as far as I'm concerned. I was almost killed. Did you inspect this one after the storm?"

"Yeah nah, it will be in the records."

"I could sue," he mumbled to Alexa.

"Don't be so American," she responded, and then yelled to the ranger, "What if someone tries to cross from the other side?"

"No one can get through. The track is closed."

Even though she had already known the track was closed, that creepy cut-off feeling made Alexa nervous. *One way only. No return.*

The ranger questioned Charlie as Alexa formulated a plan. She wanted to search below the bridge, but conceded that was a better job for rangers or police. On the other hand, Vince had said rain was forecast. The river would rise again, and suck any beached plunder back. Now was the best time, she justified.

"The bridge blokes will want to speak with you," the ranger told Charlie. "You didn't film the incident, did you?"

"What? Are you out of your mind? I was hanging on for my life."

"The French hikers who were flipped off the North Island bridge happened to catch it all on film, that's all. Even their plunge into the river."

Charlie shook his head in disbelief.

"We're going down next to the river," Alexa told the ranger. "We're looking for the doctor's backpack."

"We are?" Charlie asked.

"You won't get too far. It's a kilometer, at most, to the chute."

Chute? That reminded her of that game Charlie liked when he was little, Chutes and Ladders. You'd get almost to the end, roll a four, and have to start over. Alexa hated it.

They followed the same route as last night, hopping down the steep bank to the river's rocky shoreline as water rushed by. She thought of Gloomy Gus's tale about the hiker who stuck one boot in the water and was sucked away. She vowed to keep her ankle from its clutches.

"What makes a chute?" she asked Charlie. His eyes lit up.

"Erosion, mainly. Chutes form at a curve or loop of a stream. Water wants to take the path of least resistance, and a downhill slope, plus flooding, will encourage it to cut a chute."

"Me too."

"Me too what?" Charlie asked.

"Like taking the path of least resistance."

He laughed.

They reached the boulders Diana had been wedged between. Alexa gloved up and extracted a three-inch hair from the sheen of drying blood. She bagged and tagged it. She also took a swab of the blood-like substance and then photographed the scene in daylight. "Stand next to the boulder," she ordered Charlie. "To give the photo perspective."

"You're not trying to frame me, are you?"

Now she laughed, but the stained rock wiped the smile away.

Charlie didn't have his poles. Alexa used hers to poke through piles of sticks, leaves, and mud disgorged by yesterday's bloated river. Flotsam and jetsam. Types of debris. She could never remember which was which. One was thrown overboard deliberately, to lighten a distressed ship's load. Or a murderer tossing incriminating evidence.

"Feetfirst," Charlie called.

"What? That's how I usually walk."

"If you fall into the river, get into a feetfirst position. It's better for your feet to hit a boulder than your head."

She watched the creek tear past like something terrifying was chasing it.

"Mel and I rafted the Nantahala River once. That's what the guide told us."

She waited for him to elaborate. He didn't.

They walked past where Diana's body was found and stood in the shadow of the swing bridge. The tilt was more visible from below, and the lifeline coil, smeared with Charlie's precious DNA, hung lower than its twin on the opposite side. Ranger Light looked down at them from the cliff side—Alexa thought she was standing too close to the edge—and shouted, maybe another Hallo, but the river stole her words.

"If someone tampered with the bridge, what would it look like?" she asked Charlie.

"You think someone messed with it? You might be able to cut through a support cable with wire cutters or a saw."

Alexa waved to the ranger. "Can you tell if someone did that?"

Charlie picked up a rock and studied it. "Basalt, I think." He chucked it into the rapids and turned his attention to the bridge's underbelly. "It's too high to tell. The bridge inspector will know." Then he turned to the cliff. Alexa followed his gaze to the narrow ledge he had swung to last night. The shelf had saved his life.

"Let's go," Alexa said.

They hiked side by side along Pompolona Creek. Sunlight danced through fluttering leaves. The crunch of rocks under their boots was muffled by the rushing green water. Roots extended sideways from the bank, clawing for survival, reminding Alexa of the skeletal hand on a different riverbank.

Charlie selected another rock and studied it. He showed it to Alexa. "Do you think it's greenstone?"

She shrugged, but his question sidetracked her. She picked up a first-sized stone, glistening and stippled with emerald, rust, and gold. She liked the Māori name for greenstone, *pounamu,* and recalled Gloomy Gus saying that sometimes boulders of it were illegally lifted from rivers by helicopter. Where would you take stolen greenstone?

She craned her neck and searched the strip of sky snaking between the trees. No copter. She tossed the stone into the river.

After ten minutes, the space between the cutbank and river whittled to three or four feet. Why would you even call something a creek when it raged by in Class V rapids? They reverted to single file. She watched Charlie step over a toppled tree that extended into the creek. Water sluiced around the tree's top, trapping a blue object. Partly submerged, large, dark, and nylon, it was stuck in the branches. A whirling eddy of sticks circled like sharks in front of it.

"Charlie," she called.

His plaid flannel shirt blended into the foliage. He kept walking.

She thought she could reach the object. She nosed her left foot three inches in water, mindful of Gloomy Gus's tale, and staked the other on dry ground. She extended her pole and leaned forward. She smacked a circling stick. It broke free and joined the current, racing around the tree's crown. She leaned a little more, causing her left foot to sink in river scree. Another smack, another stick. It made her stomach flip to follow the stick entering the flume. A couple more inches and she could snag the object and reel it in. Icy water flowed over her ankle.

No. Thank. You. She stepped back on dry ground.

The toppled log extended eight or so feet into the twenty-foot-wide river. Could she walk it like a tightrope? The bark was shiny and wet, with knuckles and knots. She visualized herself falling off, riding the river helpless as a stick over the chute. Not. Happening.

Wasn't there such a thing as a human chain? Charlie could hold her by the wrist or hook her elbow so she could lean farther out. She cupped her mouth and screamed his name.

He turned, saw her beckoning, and scrambled back. She pointed to the object. "I think it's the backpack. I can almost reach it with my hiking pole."

"Let me try," he said.

She handed him her pole. He assumed the same position she had, bending forward. His couple extra inches of height allowed him to reach the object with the pole tip. He jabbed, and it submerged. For a terrible second, Alexa thought it was gone.

Then it popped up, flipped over, revealing straps and a side pocket. Maybe a water bottle poking out. Alexa knew that fingerprints could be recovered from objects that had been submerged for days.

On the other hand, the friction of direct water could wash prints away. But even without prints, the backpack might contain other valuable evidence. Bruce would be impressed if she presented it.

"Catch the strap," she yelled.

Charlie stepped in ankle-deep and stretched his arm straight, wielding the pole like a lance. Alexa leaned forward and grabbed his webbed waist belt and wormed her fingers around it, ready to pull back if he fell. He poked the backpack, nudged around for the strap, snagged it.

"You got it," Alexa screamed.

Charlie eased the backpack away from the log, through the churn of sticks, into a flurry of white water. It was smaller than her own backpack, Alexa noticed. But Diana hadn't carried a sleeping bag, food, or cooking equipment. "Come on, come on," Alexa whispered.

The backpack bumped a boulder and broke lose. Charlie lunged for it. Alexa lost her grip on his belt as he smacked the water.

Chapter Twenty-Three

The rapids snatched Charlie in and spun him like a rag doll. She watched in horror as he revolved helplessly. Finally, he came to life and kicked free. A downdraft of current pinned him to the log, and an invisible hand pressed his head below the surface. She saw his pale face through a veil of water, eyes wide, mouth open.

Charlie.

In a single motion she tossed the crime kit and straddled the log. She dug her nails hard into the slimy wood, pulling herself forward, boots dragging on either side. The icy current seized her left foot and tried to pull her into its steel trap. She kicked loose and shinnied to Charlie, grabbing his flailing hand. She leveraged her leg under his body and kicked upward. The suction wouldn't let go. She kicked again, her leg supporting his torso, and leaned sideways. Charlie broke free, thrashing.

"Grab the log," she yelled, backing up.

He groped the log, draped an arm over it, and heaved himself up, almost spilling over the other side. He ended up straddling the log and facing her, his face blanched and bewildered. Alexa slid backward, snagging her pants, until she felt the ground, and clamored off.

Charlie stayed where he was. He leaned forward, nose against bark, his arms hugging the log. She imagined the shock of the icy prison while regrets swirled in his brain. He had so much to lose. Mel. Two boys who needed Daddy.

He straightened and looked for her. She waved wildly. "Come on!"

He pulled himself to the bank, stood, spat water, and sloshed toward her. He wiped his face with his soaked sleeve.

She wanted to hug him. "Dammit, Charlie. How could you do that?"

"Do what?" His voice was hoarse. He coughed and gestured down at his soaked clothes. "Fall in freezing water on purpose?"

"Almost die. Again."

They watched the creek rush past, fast and menacing. The backpack was still there, bobbing and bouncing in the fallen tree's top branches, flaunting itself. They'd never retrieve it.

Finally she asked, "Are you okay?"

"I lost your pole."

"I still have one left." She pointed it at him.

"Oh, shit."

"What?"

Charlie was groping in his front pants pocket. "Never mind. I thought I had my phone on me. It's in the room." He unbuttoned his flannel shirt, jerked it off, and wrung it. "That man was right."

She had no idea who he was talking about.

He grimaced as he struggled back into the sodden sleeves. "The one who said if you looked at the bones, it would unleash danger."

"You said you didn't believe that."

"I do now." His fingers shook as he tried to button his shirt.

"Let me do that." He waited patiently, avoiding her eyes. Her fingers trembled. Why did they make the holes so small? When he was buttoned, she took off her jacket and wrapped it around him. "Let's get back to the lodge."

His eyes widened. "Look."

She followed his gaze. The backpack had broken loose.

"Come on," he cried, and took off.

She grabbed the crime kit, hurdled over the tree trunk, and raced along the narrow riverbank behind him. She watched the backpack twirl and tumble through turbulence, and like a bumper car, hit rocks, bounce back, slide past, taunting them.

She was barely aware of the rocks she hopped in her own path, the scree and grass under her feet, the gnarled roots trying to trip her.

They were in a narrow canyon now. The sound of the rapids reverberated off the walls, pounding in Alexa's brain as she sprinted around a curve. The backpack surged past shoals and under skeletal branches draping from the bank. A weedy island divided the river; Alexa watched the backpack mire on its closer shore, rest, then rush onward.

The roar increased. The pack approached three staircase falls. Drop. Drop. Drop.

Charlie jerked to a stop. "Watch it, Lexi!"

She crashed into him and had to catch him before he stumbled. The earthly strip beneath their feet ended at a precipice that stole her breath like the crest of a roller coaster. They stepped backward. Alexa peered over Charlie's shoulder. The river bottlenecked to a funnel and plummeted over a free fall. She watched the backpack career into the chute, pause, gather its courage, then disappear over the lip. A goner. Like Charlie could have been.

"Crap."

"Got that right," Charlie said.

Evidence was usually lost in more mundane ways: cross-contamination, incorrect packaging, leakage, equipment failure, errors in data entry, transportation issues. Like pressing a sore spot, she thought of her rookie year as a forensics investigator.

She'd driven away from the crime scene with evidence stashed in envelopes on the seat beside her. She gone through the drive-in at Bojangles. Damn if she hadn't spilled sticky, sweet iced tea on one of the envelopes, destroying a wadded tissue that may have contained DNA.

They checked in with Ranger Light at the swing bridge. "We lost some valuable evidence down the chute," Alexa told her. "Where will it end up?"

"The creek hits the Arthur River, then flows into Milford Sound."

She'd have to tell Sergeant Kramer and Bruce to have someone be on lookout. Alexa pointed at the swing bridge. "Do you see any sign of tampering?"

The ranger ignored Alexa and studied Charlie. "What happened to you?"

"Took a swim," he panted.

Her good nature vanished. "You nearly became a statistic, eh? Another tourist underestimating our rivers."

"Something like that."

Alexa reached over and removed a leaf from his hair. He frowned and stepped away.

"Do you need medical attention?"

Charlie looked embarrassed. "No."

"You need to get into dry clothes. Before you get hypothermia. The creek is glacier-fed."

"I never felt anything so cold," Charlie said.

Halfway back to the lodge, he started shivering. Alexa, feeling responsible, picked up her pace. "You can have a hot shower, and use the laundry to dry your clothes," she said brightly. She pointed at his hiking boots. "The fairy will dry those for you. Might as well take advantage of the fancy lodge."

She wanted to lock him in their room and swallow the key.

Charlie pulled her jacket closed. He said through chattering teeth, "Is your job always this exciting?"

She'd had a couple cases when things had been equally "exciting." "No."

As they climbed the steps of Pompolona Lodge porch, they heard the thwapping of another helicopter.

Alexa grabbed Charlie's arm and searched the sky.

Chapter Twenty-Four

A yellow copter hovered overhead, low and loud. "Might be your policeman friend," Charlie said through bluish lips.

"It's too early."

Sergeant Kramer opened the door, his eyes skyward, and stepped onto the porch. They could hear the helicopter landing behind the lodge.

Alexa finally let go of Charlie's arm.

"That's a DOC chopper. It's probably bringing in the bridge inspectors," the sergeant said. He looked at Charlie and frowned. "What happened to you?"

"I had a swim." He gave Alexa her jacket back as the sound of the blades slowed and then ceased. "It could be the pilot who tried to kill you."

"Kill you? What?" Sergeant Kramer's eyes flashed to Alexa's face.

"Didn't you tell him?" Charlie asked.

"Go. You're shaking."

Charlie patted his pocket—Alexa figured he was feeling for the room key. They still had just the one. "Take these with you," she said, giving him her remaining pole and the camera. She debated whether to ask him to drop the apple off in the kitchen so it could be refrigerated, but decided she'd take care of that. She had the safe key and gave it to him. "Lock the camera up, okay?" If she needed to take a photograph, she had her cell phone.

He nodded and left. She watched him through the window as he was stopped by Stead. She wondered what the dripping Charlie told him. She turned her attention to Sergeant Kramer. "Detective Inspector Horne knows already," she began, as if that lent her credibility. Then she told the sergeant about the copter incident.

His thin face peered down at her. "You must be mistaken."

"Four times that bag of rocks whizzed at my head. I'm sure." She felt a draft, but not coming toward her head. It was from the seat of her pants.

"Why didn't you tell me earlier? That's reckless endangerment. It was a yellow copter?"

"Yellow as a school bus."

The sergeant looked puzzled; she remembered school buses in New Zealand weren't yellow.

"What time did this so-called event occur?"

There was nothing so-called about it. "Around three. Maybe later."

The sergeant studied her. "I'll call DOC and get a list of birds in the park yesterday. We keep aircraft activity to a minimum to not interfere with people's Fiordland experience, but what with track repairs and the slip, there has been extra activity."

Bruce had already started a similar inquiry. They could cross-check lists when he arrived. "What about whomever just landed?"

"Right." He adjusted his cap. "I'll check him out, shall I? Did you find anything at the scene?"

"An apple and a boot impression. We saw a backpack in the creek, and followed it, but lost it over the chute. It was probably Dr. Clark's."

"It will end up in Milford Sound."

"Can you get someone to search for it?"

He looked at her strangely. "It's wilderness, lass. No roads. No tracks."

She took that as a "no."

He continued. "The constable and I cleared a few trampers to leave—a Collin and Bill Sloan, from Germany, and the diabetic woman, Emily Wolf, and her partner. They were fine to be fingerprinted and each had a full set of trekking poles, which I photographed."

"Detective Horne asked that I sit in on interviews."

"Then you shouldn't have left this morning, eh?"

Alexa felt the climate of their relationship shifting. She watched the tall sergeant stride down the steps and turn the corner, disappearing toward the landing pad. She entered the lodge and made a beeline for the restroom.

The inseam of her pants was muddy from straddling the tree trunk. Her left boot and sock were wet. She twisted to look at her butt in the mirror. The draft she'd felt came from a tear in the quick-dry fabric. Hello, black undies. She sighed, washed her hands, and removed her scrunchie. Her sable hair sprung to life. *I need it cut.* She reset her ponytail as best she could without a brush. Then she slipped into her jacket. It was damp from Charlie, but long enough to cover the tear.

She filled up a mug in the lounge and took it to an empty table in the dining room, passing huddles of Luxers. Faces were glum. No friendly waves. No laughter. The atmosphere had soured since breakfast.

The taste of stale coffee made her grimace. Larry Salvù, Dr. Clark's anesthesiologist, left the table he was sharing with Cassandra and strode over. "I helped carry Diana's body to the copter. They wouldn't let me or her sister fly out with her."

Alexa nodded. "Would you like to sit down?"

"I'm fine. Why wouldn't they let us go?"

"You should know that an unexpected death needs to be investigated."

"Yes, but I can't be on this hike any longer." He swiped his dark bangs to the side. "It's preposterous to carry on without Diana. Can *you* get me back to Auckland?"

She frowned and moved her chair back a couple inches.

"I need to make arrangements for our patients," he continued. "This is a nightmare. Nine surgeries are scheduled next week."

He was one of three main suspects and wasn't going anywhere. "I don't have anything to do with who leaves." She needed to check his boots and stood to get a look. "What brand of boots are you wearing?"

"My boots? Why?" He scanned the room. "What's going on? Why do we need to be interviewed?"

"For procedure." Alexa hadn't realized he was no taller than she was. He acted taller.

"Maybe you can use the office phone."

He calmed down and let her photograph the muddied soles of his boots—no Vibram logo, size-ten Timberlands.

Sergeant Kramer reappeared at the table. "I was right. It's a DOC guy and a structural engineer to check the bridge. The pilot wasn't in the park yesterday—he flew in from Dunedin."

TMI in front of the anesthesiologist. The sergeant's inexperience was shoving its way through the cracks. "Thanks, Dr. Salvù," she said pointedly. "Why don't you check in with Vince about the phone?"

He ignored Alexa and told the sergeant he needed to get to Auckland.

"All in good time," the sergeant said.

"We aren't prisoners," he snarled.

"He's not a happy camper," Alexa said as Larry stormed away. A few Luxers watched as well, so she lowered her voice. "This helicopter pilot. Is he still here?"

"He's about to check on the swing bridge like I said."

"Maybe I can get him to fly me to the river. I want to check on the bones."

Sergeant Kramer frowned. "I thought you were meant to listen in on interviews? We've got to get going. The trampers have a long hike ahead. Plus, if it's true someone tried to kill you yesterday—"

"It's true."

"Then you could be in danger out there. We won't have the manpower to send with you until my additional officers get here."

The sergeant was right.

"The Willis bloke is out with the DOC fellow and pilot," Sergeant Kramer added.

For a second Alexa didn't know who he was talking about, and then she remembered Stead's last name was Willis.

"He volunteered to help check the bridge, but I said he wasn't to leave. He didn't like it."

"Let's start the interviews with him."

Sergeant Kramer nodded. "I'll fetch him, shall I?"

Chapter Twenty-Five

Alexa was surprised to see Constable Bartlett and Rosie already in the small room that had been commandeered for interviews. Rosie perched on a recliner. Her eyes were red and puffy. The constable grabbed a box of tissues and handed them to her. He then backed against the wall to get out of the way, bumping a framed photo.

Sergeant Kramer gave Bartlett a quizzical look.

"She, well, um, sort of pushed her way in," he stammered.

"Have a seat," Sergeant Kramer said to Stead, pointing to a sofa. "Good morning, Miss Jones."

Rosie blew her nose into a tissue. "Mrs. Jones."

"Married, are you?"

"Yes." She dabbed her eyes. "Twenty-one years. I did marriage better than Diana."

Alexa said hello to Rosie and sat at the dinette. The framed photograph the constable had bumped was of a younger Kathy and Vince and two teen girls. She surmised this was the couple's private quarters. A faint odor of salmon hung in the air.

Stead folded his arms across his chest. "I don't have time for chitchat. I have Mackinnon Pass to climb."

"This won't take a minute. Have a seat," Sergeant Kramer said.

Stead peeked out the room's only window as he slipped off his backpack. His retracted hiking poles, attached to an outer loop on the pack, clanked together. He propped the pack against the wall and sat at the second dinette chair, close to Alexa.

Sergeant Kramer clasped his hands behind his back and looked from Stead to Rosie. "We are conducting an inquiry into Diana Clark's death."

Rosie broke in. "Why wouldn't you let me leave with Di?"

"We don't believe that your sister's death was an accident, that's why," Sergeant Kramer replied.

Alexa dropped her pen.

Stead leaned forward and retrieved it. "Did she take her own life?" His eyelashes were very blond, almost invisible. He handed her the pen.

"That's rubbish," Rosie said. "She didn't kill herself. Diana fell off that awful bridge."

"She didn't fall off the bridge," Stead said. "I recovered her body upriver from it."

Technically, our whole motley crew recovered the body, Alexa silently amended. Not *you* alone.

"Looked to me like she fell off the cliff," Stead continued. "Got too close to the edge. A selfie death maybe. More and more of the search and rescues I lead are related to selfie accidents."

"Very interesting," Sergeant Kramer said. "But Dr. Clark did not fall off the bridge or commit suicide."

The sergeant was divulging classified information. It behooved the investigation that the murderer believed the police thought Diana's death was an accident. Letting this cat out of the bag was a mistake. Bruce would be furious.

Color drained from Rosie's cheeks.

"Now you understand why we need you to remain on the premises," the sergeant said.

"No, I don't," Rosie said.

"What are you saying?" Stead asked.

Sergeant Kramer ignored him. "I'd like you to wait in the lounge, Mrs. Jones. We'll be with you shortly."

The cat would have kittens if Sergeant Kramer let Rosie loose. Alexa sprang up. "Can I have a quick word?" she asked him.

Before the door was shut, Alexa snapped, "What were you thinking? You shouldn't have told them that Dr. Clark's death wasn't an accident." The sergeant clenched his jaw. Alexa saw a shaving nick on his neck. She imagined him up before dawn, nervous and excited about investigating a suspicious death on the Milford Track, and cursing when he cut himself.

"Er, I'm in charge. I'll make the decisions."

"You can't let them tell others. If someone in the lodge had something to do with Diana's death, then they'll react. Try to escape, or, I don't know, lash out."

Kramer's face flushed, but he didn't back down. "I'm in charge until your DI arrives."

Play nice, she told herself. She was here to support the investigation through science, not butting-in advice. "You've been doing a great job. You could get the constable to stay with Rosie while we talk with Stead. Or I could recruit my brother." Charlie the babysitter. That would probably not fly.

The sergeant seemed to consider her recommendation. He cracked the door and called the constable to step out. "Escort Mrs. Jones to the lounge. Stay with her. Don't let her talk with anyone."

"Yes, Senior."

Rosie looked like a fish, Alexa thought. Her mouth kept opening and closing as she followed Constable Bartlett.

Stead had popped up from the table and was looking out the window again when they entered. He left the curtain open and turned. "Are you saying the Clark woman was killed?"

"We're not saying anything," Sergeant Kramer answered. "Have a seat, Mr. Willis." The sergeant sat on the couch and

Alexa back at the dinette. "I'll just record our conversation, shall I?" He turned on his phone's recorder and gave the date and names of people present.

A vein on Stead's temple pulsed. "What's this about?"

"I'll be the one asking the questions," the sergeant clipped.

Stead glanced at Alexa as he sat back down on the matching dinette chair. She kept her face neutral and opened her notebook.

"Your name and address?"

"Steadman Willis." He gave his Greymouth address and occupation.

"What's a piezoelectric engineer do?" Sergeant Kramer asked.

"I work in aviation vibratory reduction. No one likes the noise rotors make."

I do, thought Alexa. *So a copter can't sneak up on me.*

"Where?" Sergeant Kramer asked.

"I told you. Greymouth."

"A Westie, eh? Who do you work for?"

"Anders Aviation. It's a little company going big places."

Sounds like a TV ad, Alexa thought.

Sergeant Kramer asked for, and received, the company's contact info. "What brings you to Milford? We get more foreigners than Kiwis on the Great Walks."

"What brings anyone here? I like the bush, always have. Don't mind fishing while I'm out here, either."

The sergeant chuckled and crossed a long leg at the ankle. "Leave your missus behind?"

"No missus." Stead glanced at Alexa. She looked away. Yesterday morning she had considered him an attractive fish in the man pond, but today he smelled rotten. *Why?*—she wasn't certain.

"Is this your first time doing the Milford Track?"

"No. I've done the walk many times."

Alexa remembered how Charlie offered to take his picture by the Milford Track sign, and Stead declined. It felt like a month ago instead of two days ago.

"How many?" Sergeant Kramer asked.

Stead scratched his light beard. "Six or seven. I'm losing count. First time was when I was twelve."

"A few years back, that was, eh? Always as an independent tramper?"

Stead nodded. "Not that I couldn't afford this, but I'll leave the spots for the Yanks. Huts are good enough for me."

"What brought you to Pompolona Lodge if you're an independent hiker?"

"The ranger at Mintaro Hut told us about a missing tramper." He did a little drumroll on the table. "I'm president of Greymouth Land Search and Rescue. That's what I did. Volunteered my services to look for her." He jerked a thumb at Alexa. "Walked with her brother from Mintaro to Pompolona."

"That would be Charlie Glock, correct?"

Stead looked at Alexa.

"Correct," Alexa said. "Charlie Glock from Asheville, North Carolina."

Sergeant Kramer checked that his phone was still recording. Then he studied Stead, who stared back guilelessly. "Had you ever met Dr. Diana Clark alive?"

"Had I ever met Diana Clark?" He maintained Kramer's gaze. "No. Never."

As an outreach of the North Carolina Bureau of Investigation, Alexa used to offer a lie detection seminar to law enforcement organizations. She'd share the classic signs: avoiding eye contact, long answers, jitters, repeating questions before answering them. "Deception Detection" was the title of her seminar. Newer research debunked those theories. Innocent people fidget as much as guilty ones, and good liars are aware that avoiding eye contact is a red flag, and steel themselves to stare you down. Not that she suspected Stead of lying, but she was alert for discrepancies.

"How did you conduct the search?" Sergeant Kramer asked.

Interview techniques are a better way to reveal deception, she now knew: the verbal dance between cop and suspect with a slow reveal of evidence to give the interviewee time to trip up. Sergeant Kramer had blown the slow reveal. She wished Bruce would hurry up and get here.

Stead explained how they'd broken into three groups and conducted the search. When he crossed his leg, Alexa saw the yellow Vibram logo on his sole. Her heart revved. She scooted her chair closer and made out the brand: CAT was embossed on the side. She never heard of CAT brand boots.

"After Miss Glock and her brother found the body, we transported Dr. Clark to the lodge," Stead said. "I'm sorry the story ended with her death, but I'd like to head on. Before the rain, eh?" He stood and grabbed his backpack, slinging it on one shoulder, the poles clanking.

"If we have further questions, you'll be at Dumpling Hut tonight? That's the next hut for independent hikers, right?"

"Yeah. Among the unwashed." He reached for the door handle.

The sergeant uncrossed his leg. "You must keep the information about Dr. Clark to yourself."

Like that is going to fly, Alexa thought. But really—who would he tell? He wasn't buds with any of the Luxe hikers. He hadn't hung with any of the independent hikers, either, except Charlie and Alexa. He was a loner. But news of a suspicious death was hard to keep bottled. "Sit back down. I have a few more questions," she said.

Stead dropped his hand but remained standing by the door. He sucked in his right cheek.

"What size boot do you wear?" Alexa asked.

Stead looked down. "Twelve and a half. Wide."

It was likely that the boot print she had photographed at the cliff this morning matched Stead's. It didn't prove or disprove anything because he had been at the scene when they retrieved Diana's body, but it would terminate her boot hunt. "Did you know the pilot of the helicopter that landed at Clinton Hut yesterday morning while we were having coffee?"

He looked hurt. "I told you at breakfast I didn't know him."

She wasn't falling for the kicked puppy look. "Did you speak with him?"

"What about?"

"Answer Ms. Glock's question," Sergeant Kramer said.

"I didn't speak to him. I packed up and left."

Alexa hated the thought he might have been following her. "You must have been right behind me on the trail."

"I might have fished a bit more," he admitted.

"For how long?"

"Thirty minutes or so."

So he wasn't right behind her on the trail. She relaxed. "Describe your experience with the landslide."

He weaved his other arm through the backpack and shifted. "When I saw a slip had blocked the track, I poked around a minute, checking to see if anyone needed aid."

Where had she been when he was poking? Wallowing through the river? Examining the bones?

"I headed back to Clinton Hut and told the ranger about the slip. He'll confirm that. A couple Luxers stopped by the hut to use the loo, and he told them to stay. We returned to assess the damage. The track was bloody obliterated. He radioed DOC to fly out and take a look."

"If the slip blocked the track," Sergeant Kramer said, "how is it that you got through?"

"I hitched a ride on one of the copters."

This piqued Sergeant Kramer's interest. "A different pilot from the one Ms. Glock is referring to?"

"I know a few pilots. We use copters in search and rescue, plus I work on helicopters."

"I'll need the name of the pilot who gave you a lift," Sergeant Kramer said.

"I don't want to get him in trouble." He hiked up his pack and buckled the waist belt.

"His name?"

Stead appeared to be chewing his cheek. He ruminated a few moments. "Bill Little."

Alexa thought of yesterday's events. She'd spent over an hour with the bones, then hiked the open valley toward the woods. A helicopter had flown over the landslide. She'd tried to wave it down, but the copter flew off. A few minutes later it was back—or maybe it was a different yellow copter—with the dangling bulk bag. She had only seen one person behind the windshield. She hoped Bruce would have the list of copters in the area. A flight schedule could solve this thing. "What time did you get a lift?" she asked.

"Midafternoon, maybe." He held up his wrist. "I don't wear a watch. Unless you have more questions, I'd like to be on my way."

She retrieved her ink pad from the crime kit. "You don't mind if I take your fingerprints, do you?"

"I'm happy to oblige if you have a warrant."

Chapter Twenty-Six

"Exercising your right, eh?" the sergeant said. "Nothing wrong with that, but I'll make a note that you refused."

"The Crown has too many rights," Stead said. At Alexa's request, he sighed and swung his pack off. He extracted one of his poles and placed it in her gloved hand. It was the same brand as Dr. Clark's, but black instead of blue. The tip had criss-crossed notches. She thought of the wounds on Diana's back, and wished she had modeling clay to take an impression of Stead's pole. She measured the length, width, and thickness of the tip and took photos. She recorded everything in her note-book. Stead reached for the pole.

"I need it for one more minute," Alexa said. "I'll be right back." Before the two men could respond, she left the room with her kit, camera, and the pole.

"Bloody hell," she heard Stead say.

She hurried to the kitchen. She had not met the lodge chef, who indeed wore a chef's hat and a chef's large stomach and looked surprised when she barged in. "What's this, then?"

Alexa introduced herself and her role and explained that the pole she carried might be important evidence in the death of the hiker.

He stopped mincing.

"I need a hunk of cheese."

"What for?"

"A forensic experiment."

He twirled to the stove like a dancer and lifted a lid. "Coconut and lemongrass." He added some of the herb and wiped his hands on the apron.

Alexa tried to concentrate on cheese impressions. "Cheddar would work."

"Cheddar?" The chef stirred his soup and replaced the lid. He opened the double-wide refrigerator and rummaged. "I have Meyer Vintage gouda, Whitestone Farmhouse, and Airedale. Would you like a taste?"

"Isn't Airedale a dog breed?"

"Eh? It melts on your tongue."

"That won't do." Alexa stepped closer. One of the cheeses he unwrapped was partially encased in red wax. The cheese itself—a pale lemony color—looked the right consistency. "I need that one," Alexa pointed.

"Nice choice," he said as if she were going to eat it, which she wished she could. He took a clean knife out of a drawer.

"No," Alexa said. "I need the whole thing." While he watched, Alexa took the cheese and placed it on the kitchen floor. The knife the chef returned to the drawer reminded her that in a knife attack, the blade rarely entered and withdrew from a body at the same angle. The assailant and victim are usually moving. Chop and drag was a common method. So was a sweeping motion. She didn't think this was the case with Diana. The doctor had not seen her assailant coming. Alexa theorized the thrust had been straight in and out.

She stabbed the tip of the pole about one and a half inches into the cheese, stopping short of the plastic basket, and slid it out quickly. The tip came out clean.

"Ack," said Chef. "A waste."

There. She had her impression. She set the pole aside and

put the cheese on the counter. Taking a photo of the indentation would barely show the edge. She needed contrast. "A bit of colored liquid will do. What do you have?"

Chef turned to an open shelf. "Balsamic vinegar."

"Perfect." Proud of her steady hands, Alexa poured a capful of the pungent elixir into the impression. It settled shy of the rim. She drizzled in a drop more and watched as purple-red illuminated the edges of the hole. She had no idea if her experiment would work. She focused the camera and took photos.

"You can pour the liquid out, and store the cheese for me," she told Chef. "I have an apple I need refrigerated as well." She should have gotten the apple to the refrigerator sooner. The room temperature of the lodge would hasten decay. She fished the sealed paper bag out and handed it over. "Do you have a lock on the fridge?"

"A lock? Against midnight raiders? I'm afraid not."

Unlocked evidence would break chain of custody, but these were unusual circumstances. At least the seal was intact. "You're helping with our investigation. Thank you."

She returned the pole to Stead. His release caused her unease—especially since he refused to be fingerprinted—but she couldn't think of a reason to detain him.

"Maybe we could meet up in Auckland," Stead said, hefting his pack on. "Might be moving there soon. A promotion is coming my way."

She hid her distaste—her trail crush was extinguished—and gave him a half-smile. He returned it with a full.

"I'll be back in a minute," she told the sergeant. "I need to check on my brother." She followed Stead out of the interview room, wished him a safe hike, and found Silas vacuuming the dining room. She waved to get his attention and waited until he turned the vacuum off. "Will you send a cup of hot chocolate to my room—for my brother?"

Silas looked harried. "Tauhou, right?"

She was stymied for a second, and then remembered the bird name for her room. "Yep. Thank you." Room-service hot chocolate counted for checking on Charlie, she decided. She returned to find Sergeant Kramer escorting Debbie and Mark into the room. The Pennsylvania couple settled onto the couch, Debbie smiling brightly.

After asking for contact information, Sergeant Kramer established that the couple last saw Diana—along with seven other Luxe hikers—around one thirty at Prairie Shelter.

Debbie said, "Diana left with her anesthesiologist, Larry, shortly after we arrived."

The sergeant leaned forward. "Are you positive they left together?"

Shoulder to shoulder, the couple exchanged glances. Debbie was adamant. "I remember Rosie cleaning up her trash and hurrying after them. She called out, but they didn't even turn around. I felt sorry for her." Then she brightened. "Clint took a group photo of us. Before Diana left."

Alexa underlined this in her notes. Plus the fact that Debbie said Diana and Larry left together.

"We passed Rosie later, but I never saw Diana again," Mark said somberly.

Debbie mentioned seeing another woman after lunch. "Her hood was up so I couldn't get a good look. She wasn't wearing a yellow Luxe raincoat. Her raincoat was gray or black. I said 'hello,' but she didn't answer."

"Debbie never passes up a chance to talk with someone," Mark said. "But didn't she pass us before lunch?"

Debbie seemed to consider. "You're right. It was along the river."

The hooded woman reminded Alexa that there was a whole hut full of independent hikers who might have seen something, and now they were climbing Mackinnon Pass.

After ascertaining that Debbie and Mark had never met

Diana Clark before the hike, Sergeant Kramer said they were free to leave the lodge.

They gave their consent to be fingerprinted and have their poles photographed. "But why?" Mark asked.

"Just procedure." Alexa loved the phrase; people usually did what you asked if you said it was procedure.

Debbie hugged Alexa goodbye as if they were old friends. Alexa tried not to stiffen, but spontaneous acts of touchy-feely left her nervous. Her old boyfriend, Jeb, had complained she must never have been hugged as a kid.

As Sergeant Kramer escorted them out, Alexa stored their prints in envelopes, labeled them, and made a note on her log. Her mind tried to keep track of who saw Diana and when. She turned to a clean page in her pad and made a time line.

Debbie had named seven hikers who had gathered at the shelter: the guide Clint, Rosie, Diana. Cassandra, Larry, and the Fitbit woman and her partner.

According to Debbie, the Fitbit woman—Emily Wolf—and her partner had left first, followed by Diana and Larry, then Rosie. She was about to go see if Charlie got his hot chocolate when Sergeant Kramer entered with Clint Knight, the Luxe Tours guide, his clipboard clutched to his chest, and a camera over his shoulder. He nodded at Alexa.

She settled back in her chair.

"Right, then," Sergeant Kramer said, sitting on the couch and setting up his phone recorder. He mentioned their names, the time, and asked for Clint's contact info. "How long have you been a guide with Luxe Tours?"

Clint perched on the edge of the recliner. His brown hair was pulled into a ponytail, and his face was grave. "This is my fourth season."

Alexa guessed he was in his early thirties. She opened her pad to a fresh page.

"How long is the season?" the sergeant began.

Clint studied his hiking boot. Alexa stared at them, too. They looked about the same size as the footprint by the cliff. "December through April."

"What are your responsibilities?"

"Meet and greet. Explain the schedules. Talk to the guests about flora and fauna. Motivate trampers." He patted the camera. "Take photos. Tell jokes." He smiled as if he thought of one, but then turned serious. "I've just been on the phone with my track operations manager, eh? Shaun. Good bloke."

"How long have you been on duty?" the sergeant asked.

"This is day seven out of nine, and my second back-to-back group."

"What's that like, being at trampers' beck and call for days on end?"

"It's intense. Gotta stay positive, eh? My co-guide for this trek is Ann Kipfer. Yesterday morning I left with the early birds. Ann brought up the rear with the dawdlers. She got stuck at Clinton Hut because of the landslide."

"Was there anything unusual about Dr. Clark's behavior?" the sergeant asked. "Was she worried or afraid?"

Jeez, Alexa thought. Leading questions can distort memory.

"Dr. Clark was right. She didn't act afraid or anything."

"What was she like? Did she get along with the other hikers?" the sergeant asked.

Clint closed his eyes. Maybe he was trying to conjure an image of Dr. Clark. When he opened them, he said, "She acted sort of superior, maybe? She insisted on going ahead of the pace I set. We don't have hard rules about that—and she looked fit. If only I had held her back, maybe I could have prevented what happened."

Sergeant Kramer didn't offer platitudes. "When was the last time you saw her?"

"At Prairie Shelter. Maybe half-past one? I'm not sure."

"One of your clients said you took a group photo at the shelter. May I see it?"

Clint nodded. "Good thing she's all charged." He scrolled through photos. "Here."

Kramer took the camera. He motioned Alexa closer. He tapped the screen and studied the enlarged faces one by one: Diana, Cassandra, Larry, Debbie and Mark, Rosie, the Fitbit woman and her partner.

Alexa wanted to warn Diana her life was in danger. Could one of the people she was surrounded by have killed her?

"I'll need a copy of this," Sergeant Kramer said and gave Clint a card. "Did Dr. Clark leave the shelter alone?"

"Eh, the other doctor—Larry—they left together."

Another witness confirming Larry left with the doctor, Alexa thought. Larry had lied.

"When did you first become worried about Dr. Clark?" the sergeant asked.

"Strange, yeah, that she wasn't at the lodge when the rest of us checked in, given that she'd left the shelter before us. And the doctor man, he was already here and hadn't seen her." Clint swallowed.

The sergeant waited, allowing him time to collect his thoughts.

"After thirty minutes or so, I told the Bergens," Clint continued. "Vince radioed the ranger at Mintaro—that's the independent hut farther up the track. We thought maybe she had missed the turn to Pompolona. She wasn't there. You know the rest, right? We went out searching and all." He looked at Alexa. "She found the doctor by the river. This is bad news for Luxe Tours. I'll probably be let go."

"Feel responsible, do you?" the sergeant asked.

"It happened on my watch, is all. Tramping these mountains is risky."

Alexa remembered one of the Luxers this morning bringing up a lost tramper. "Have you ever lost a hiker before?" she asked.

Clint licked his lips. "It's not keen to say I lost someone, eh?

I'm not a child minder. I generally don't let the faster hikers go ahead, but Dr. Clark was pushy. The alpha dog."

"Have any of your clients gone missing before?" she repeated.

His eyes looked panicked. "Same thing happened last year. What's that word? Déjà vu. We found her. She was fine," Clint said. "So this is totally different."

"Did she go missing in the same area?" Alexa's pen was poised. Maybe that part of the trail was a Bermuda Triangle of sorts.

"It was on the other side of Mackinnon Pass. Her name was Mrs. Nakamura. She never arrived at Quintin Lodge. Her husband was frantic. We backtracked and searched all the way to the shelter. Then we called the police and Te Anau SAR."

"I remember," Sergeant Kramer said. "Last summer, eh?"

Clint jiggled his foot. "March. It was dark by the time the copter arrived. The pilot did a night-vision search. He found her using thermal imaging."

"Wow," Alexa said. "Where was she?"

He continued as if he hadn't heard. "The bush was too thick for a night recovery. They flew back to the lodge and picked up a couple of us, me and the lodge manager, Noel. They lowered us down in tussock. Blimey." He shuddered again. "We hiked to her. When she realized she was lost, she had hunkered down. Otherwise, no telling what would have happened. She could have walked off a cliff."

"Walked off a cliff" ricocheted in Alexa's brain as she took Clint's fingerprints. But Diana hadn't walked off a cliff. She'd been pushed. An approaching helicopter made her smudge his thumbprint. A courtroom judge would toss it.

Chapter Twenty-Seven

She looked out the window. The helicopter dropping from the sky was white, not yellow, and had a pointy nose. Special delivery: Bruce. She quickly finished taking Clint's fingerprints and asked to see his hiking poles.

"Yeah, nah. I don't use poles," he said. "I'll be around the lodge if you have any more questions."

Sergeant Kramer followed her through the lobby. She braced herself for Bruce to stride up the lodge steps, pierce her with his sharp blue eyes—maybe toss her a smile—and assume the reins from Sergeant Kramer. She took a deep breath, tugged her jacket to make sure it covered the tear in her pants, and pushed open the door.

Two uniformed officers rounded the corner of the lodge. No tall resolute detective inspector from Auckland followed them. Alexa was disappointed.

"My colleagues from Te Anau," Sergeant Kramer told her. "Constables. What have you got?"

"Missing person reports, Senior," a female officer answered. Short and skinny, the woman wore a cap that shaded her eyes. All Alexa could see were moving lips.

"There are heaps," the male cop said, holding a sheath of papers. "Three hundred and thirty-three."

Alexa's heart sank. It would take forever to wade through them.

"Some of those are cases from more than twenty years ago, though," he continued. "Haven't had time to weed them out yet. You know, been busy with the regatta. My lad took the dinghy race." He smiled proudly.

"Good on Louie."

"I printed them, since you said there's no connectivity here," he added.

"Used up the paper allotment, did you?" Sergeant Kramer introduced Alexa. "Ms. Glock works for Forensic Service Center in Auckland. This is Constable Daniella Chadwick, and this is Senior Constable L. C. McCain."

The male officer took off his cap and ran a hand through his buzz cut. "You're the one who found the body?"

She didn't know which death he was referring to. "I discovered skeletal remains."

"Who flew you in?" Sergeant Kramer asked the officers.

"Hank," Senior Constable McCain said. "He's waiting for orders."

Sergeant Kramer turned to Alexa. "Do you want to return to the bones?"

If she separated the head from the body, they could transport the skull to the nearest doctor or dental office and take X-rays. That might be a quicker method than wading through missing persons reports. In the U.S., if bones can't be identified, a forensic odontologist performs a dental examination and enters the results into the National Crime Information Center's data system. If the missing person's family contributed their loved one's records—then presto. An identification. New Zealand didn't have a dental data bank, but dentists knew they had a responsibility to help resolve missing persons cases. She could send a mass email to South Island dentists and hope for a match.

But separating a head from a body? That was worse than taking the thumb bone. She was sure the Māori elder she'd met in Wellington would disapprove.

Sergeant Kramer tapped his foot.

It was a temporary separation, and for the greater good. "Yes."

"Let's not keep Hank waiting, then. Constable Chadwick will go with you. I've filled the team here in on your er, helicopter encounter," Sergeant Kramer said.

The sergeant had not wanted her to return to the bones until he could send someone with her, but the tiny constable hardly appeared big enough to serve and protect. Then Alexa decided she was being sexist—Constable Chadwick was probably a kickboxing champ. "I need to grab some things. I'll be right back."

She started to open the door, but stopped. The lodge might harbor a killer. An anxious killer who was a danger to others. Both cases played tug-of-war for her attention. "You have everything under control here, right?" she asked the sergeant.

"Don't you worry."

She couldn't take action on both cases at the same time. Bruce would be arriving soon. She turned her thought to returning to the skeleton. What did she need? She had her pitiful crime kit, and her cell phone. She'd need something to put the skull in. And to tell Charlie.

Silas was collecting discarded coffee mugs in the lounge. "I need a box," she told him.

"Eh?"

"A box." She held her arms out to show how big. "And do you have an old newspaper?"

He looked at her funny. "No paperboy up here. Why?"

"I need to wrap something breakable. I'll be right back." She jogged past Cassandra, who scowled, and into the guest wing. Two rooms past the laundry she knocked. "Charlie?"

There was no answer.

She tried the handle, and the door opened. Charlie's wet

clothes and boots were piled on the floor. So much for using the laundry room. He was burrowed under two duvets, looking like the Michelin man. His eyes were closed and his face, peeking from the duvet, was pale. "Charlie?"

He didn't answer.

She checked to make sure he was breathing and heard a faint whistling of exhale. She tiptoed to the closet and tried the safe, deciding to grab her camera. It was locked, just like she had asked Charlie to do. There was no key on the dresser and night-stand. The safe key was probably in his pocket. She watched the cloud of covers rise and fall, and decided not to wake him. She would continue to use her cell phone camera. She left a note on the nightstand next to the mug of hot chocolate dregs.

In the lounge Silas handed her a box and bubble wrap. "A client sent us cookies wrapped in this."

From box of cookies to box of skull.

She hurried to the helicopter. Sunlight glared off the glass windshield. She went around to the right side, surprised to see the pilot strapped in.

He laughed. "Got your private pilot's license, do you?"

Figures the controls would be on the wrong side. Back-ass-ward. Alexa blushed. She scurried around to the left side, ducking the whole time so she wouldn't be decapitated if he started the rotors. Then she dropped her box and wasn't able to open the door—if it was called a door. The pilot laughed again and opened it from the inside. Constable Chadwick smiled at her from the rear seat. Her teeth were white Chiclets. Alexa stepped on the footplate and pulled herself in. The pilot handed her a headphone and mouthpiece set. "Right-o," he said. "Ever been in a bird before?"

She nodded. Only once, but he didn't need to know that. She studied his profile, suspicious of any helicopter pilot right now, but he looked like any old Joe with silvery hair.

She edged close to the door, but then worried it would come

open and she'd fall out, so she settled in the center. "Been flying in the area lately?" she casually asked.

"Eh?" He pushed some buttons and the rotor blades started turning.

Alexa pressed the headphones tighter to her ears to muffle the ruckus. She glanced at Constable Chadwick. Her cap was on her lap, her fingers tapping its brim. She had big brown eyes and a boyish haircut.

The whirring blades increased in speed and volume.

Hank wore a navy jumpsuit with Police Air Support stitched at the breast. He gave her a grin, and said, "Buckle up." At the click of her belt, the Te Anua Police copter was airborne. She gripped either side of the seat and marveled at the physics of vertical liftoff. The buttons, dials, and screens of the instrument panel teased her with their import. She searched for something familiar. The ENG FIRE light was not on. Check. The gas gauge indicated three-fourths full. Check. The ALT numbers kept rising. Check.

Flying in a copter is probably safer than driving a car, especially in New Zealand. She focused out the window. Pompolona Lodge got smaller and smaller until it was a dollhouse in a fathomless forest. Then she looked up. A wall of mountain filled the windshield. Alexa cowered as they lifted at the last second.

Trees gave way to alpine tundra, granite cliffs, avalanche swaths, and patches of snow. The beauty and enormity of the landscape through the glass bubble was stupefying. A notch was gouged out between jagged mountains. "Mackinnin Pass," the pilot said, steering toward it. "Highest point of the Milford Track."

She didn't dare look at the altimeter.

A thin switchbacking line with sheer drops on one side—the trail, she figured—led to the notch. A lone hiker, his backpack like an orange snail's shell, climbed doggedly. One misstep, and it looked like he, or she, would be a goner. Alexa realized that if it weren't for the murders, she'd be down there, tempting the abyss, and secretly felt glad she wasn't. Some monument marked the summit. A large stone cairn with maybe a cross on top. Was it a grave? A gust of wind buffeted the copter. Alexa yelped. The pilot gave her a thumbs-up, and circled back toward the river.

She relaxed her death grip on the seat. "Dammit," she said, forgetting about the mike.

"What is it?" Hank asked.

"Oh. Sorry. Nothing." She hadn't changed pants. At least her jacket covered the hole. She thought about New Zealand not having a missing persons dental data bank. When she got back to Auckland, she would propose starting one at Forensic Service Center. Her boss, Dan, would like the idea. She couldn't wait to talk with him about it.

Fifteen minutes later she recognized the wide-open Clinton River valley where the helicopter had tried to mow her down. Leaning forward, chest against the seat belt, she peered at the corridor between the range and the river. Everything was exposed. Scrub, grass, rock. Milford Track plowing through it in a straight line. No place to hide. She'd been like a character in a video game being tracked and attacked. She wished she had her water bottle; her mouth had gone dry.

The yellow ribbon would be at the other end of the bowling-alley-like valley. In the brown, gray, and green hues, it would stand out. She strained to catch sight of it. Nothing caught her eye. She found this strange. "Can you fly lower?" she spoke through the mike.

The pilot responded so quickly that her stomach lurched. The shadow of the helicopter passed over the rubble from the rockslide. She traced its tree- and boulder-strewn path from two-thirds up the side of the mountain to the river.

She saw the behemoth boulder, the one she had watched careen down the mountain. It claimed its new spot proudly. They'd flown too far. She poked the pilot's shoulder and twirled her finger. He circled around.

The caution tape should be close to the river, near the lone tree where she had stashed the bird's nest. Life is fragile as egg-shell. She thought of Charlie in the rapids and now a snug bug in their lodge room. Maybe the eggs were safe, too.

She spotted the rock that she'd used to gauge the river's rising. Yesterday it had been swallowed. Today it was spit out from the deceptively charming river. The tree trunk she had climbed over was gone. She homed in on the lone tree. The skeleton had been near it. She had made a little flag with a stick and the last of the tape. She hunted in vain for its fluttering sig-nal. No yellow anywhere. She inhaled deeply, trying to keep panic at bay.

A person could be arrested for interfering with caution tape.

She had tried to rationalize the deadly bulk bag incident after it happened: she was in the pilot's blind spot, low visibility because of the rain, a bored cowboy having tourist fun. Now she tried to rationalize why the ribbon was missing. The wind snatched it was most likely. Or someone had removed it.

"The tape around the skeleton is missing," she said into the mike. She kept her eyes ahead, worried the constable would think this was a wild-goose chase.

No matter. She could find the skeleton without ribbon.

The pilot said, "Where do you want to land?"

She squinted at the squat tree again. The area around it looked different. A jumble of gray rock marked where she thought the skeleton should be. It hadn't been there yesterday. Her mind flew to the gray rock theory in dealing with a socio-path: act uninterested or unresponsive. Show no emotion. Be unresponsive.

To hell with that. "Land over there," she told Hank.

They floated down, landed with a gentle bump thirty yards from the tree. Alexa unbuckled, removed her headset, and grabbed the door latch.

"Eh, hold on there," the pilot said, working the controls.

She could feel vibrations even when the blades stopped. Her body tensed, ready to spring.

When Hank gave her a thumbs-up, Alexa unlatched her door and clambered out. When she was safe from the rotors, she ran toward the tree.

Chapter Twenty-Eight

The pile Alexa stood near was almost as big as a Volkswagen Beetle. The jagged rocks were shades of gray that did not match the brown and tan river rocks. They ranged in size from four to eight inches.

She studied the ground. No footprints. No tire treads. She turned her eyes skyward, gulping oxygen and waited with dread as Constable Chadwick joined her. "Someone dropped rocks on the skeleton."

The constable's mouth opened in an O. She searched the sky, too. "So this heap wasn't here yesterday?"

"That's right."

What would a ton of rock dumped from the sky do to the skeleton? Alexa's mind flew to high school physics class and Mr. Gelt, who had the habit of spontaneously yelling, not out of meanness, but when he sensed the back row nodding off. "Air resistance opposes what?" he'd yell.

"The motion of a falling object," they shouted back.

It had felt good to yell in the middle of a school day. Alexa wanted to yell now. What would Constable Chadwick think if she did? She searched her brain for more physics facts and recalled that as an object falls, it picks up speed until it reaches terminal velocity. Or the ground.

This direct hit probably fractured every bone to pieces. Her knees buckled—yesterday the pilot could have dumped a ton of rock on her, too.

Constable Chadwick noticed. "Are you okay?"

Alexa nodded. They approached the pile warily. It would be daunting to unearth what was left. She took her cell phone out and photographed the rubble. She heard a crunching sound and whirled. Hank, the pilot, was approaching.

"Is Hank a police officer?" she asked.

"No. He's a contract pilot for the Te Anau police. Good bloke."

Hank joined them. "What's this, then?"

Alexa picked up one of the rocks and ran a finger on its sharp edge. She had wanted to ask the constable more about Hank. "What does it look like to you?"

Hank squinted at the mound and then the sky. "A load of rip-rap was dropped."

"How does that work? Aren't bulk bags meant to be set down full?" That's how they'd been at Clinton Hut—still full of rock. "How would you release them from the air?"

She had pelted him with questions.

"Some containers have trapdoors or spouts that are meant to be opened. But the Department of Conservation doesn't use them for moving rock. They use the bulk bags." Hank looked puzzled. "You could retract the hook, and a whole load would drop, bag and all. The bag is probably buried under this rock."

That wasn't all that was buried under the rock, Alexa thought.

Hank walked the perimeter of the pile. "Nah yeah, look here." He'd toed some rocks out of the way to expose a strip of white bulk bag. "I can't make sense of it."

"Me either," Alexa said, pulling her jacket close against a gust of wind.

But really she could. There was a helicopter pilot around who was freaking out. Dangerous. Which probably meant he was connected to the man buried under riprap. Alexa lifted her eyes to the leaden sky and followed a circling hawk. The rocks had in all likelihood destroyed any evidence left years ago by the murderer. She despaired thinking of the striation marks on the ribs, ruined. If she jumped in and began removing rock willy-nilly, she could do further damage. Bone and dirt and rock look alike. Thankfully, she had photographs to prove the skeleton had been whole.

Dr. Luckenbaugh, the archaeologist she'd met in Wellington, would know how to excavate the fragments properly while preserving any remaining evidence.

She bade farewell to her plan to transport the skull to an X-ray machine. Best-laid plans and all that. Her fingers twitched to thumb through those missing persons reports. And maybe, if they had dental records somewhere, the photos she took of the jaw might suffice. "Let's get back to the lodge."

At the lodge she waited for Hank's signal to get out. She would prefer never to ride in a helicopter again. As soon as she rounded the corner of the lodge, she spotted a man in a police ball cap, arms crossed, watching her from the porch. The man removed the cap; her heart revved at the sight of Bruce's handsome face. He would know what to do about everything. The weight on her shoulders lifted.

Then she saw his stony eyes.

"Ms. Glock. I distinctly remember advising you to stay in the lodge."

Her every nerve vibrated as if she was still airborne. This wasn't the greeting she expected. But she realized it should have been. Bruce liked his orders to be followed. Even if they were unreasonable. "Hello, Bruce. It's good to see you."

He looked confused. His eyes softened. "Are you okay?" Then they flickered to Constable Chadwick.

Alexa introduced them, and said, "There's been a disturbing development with the skeleton by the river. Let's go inside, and I'll update you."

Bruce pulled his cap on and picked up his briefcase. They followed him into the lodge. He tried to dodge Cassandra, who planted herself in his path. "Excuse me. Are you in charge?"

Dressed in khaki pants, a light-blue button-down, and a navy police jacket with some type of epaulets on the shoulders, Bruce looked in charge. "DI Bruce Horne. How can I help?"

Cassandra's catty pupils expanded as she looked Bruce over. "Yes. Ta. I'm Cassandra Perry. Dr. Clark, you know, was my friend. I still can't believe she's dead. I don't want to continue my holiday without her, you understand. I'd like to leave, go home to Auckland."

Alexa noted she referred only to herself. No mention of Larry or Rosie.

"Ms. Perry, we will be with you as soon as possible," Bruce said. "Your patience is appreciated."

"But…"

Bruce brushed by and turned to Alexa. "Where's the command center?"

She showed him the way to Vince and Kathy's quarters.

The first thing he said when he entered was, "This won't do. It's too cramped."

The den-cum-interview-room was overstuffed with blue: Sergeant Kramer, Constable Bartlett, and the new senior constable who had arrived with Constable Chadwick—Alexa had forgotten his name. Constable Chadwick went to stand by him.

Sergeant Kramer stood from a dinette chair. "I'll find Mr. Bergen. Ask him for another space."

"Ta," Bruce said, looking at his watch. "And have him round up some sammies, while you're at it. We will think better on full stomachs."

Amen, Alexa thought.

"We'll have a briefing in twenty minutes in the new space. That's all for now." Bruce jerked his head to indicate the officers should leave. He discreetly lifted a hand to Alexa, indicating that she should stay.

Her heart hitched.

When they were alone, Bruce shut the door. He stepped toward her, and then about-faced, and sat on the couch. "Let's have your latest news."

Work first. That was Alexa's philosophy as well. She took off her jacket and sat on the recliner, the crime kit at her feet. "I've just returned from the riverbank where I discovered the bones. A helicopter dumped a load of rock on them. The skeleton is buried."

Under the brim of his cap, Alexa could see one of Bruce's eyebrows rise. This was to be expected, too. Funny how she was beginning to know this man. "The skeleton is gone?"

She hadn't thought about whether the skeleton could be gone. Was she sure it was buried? It would have taken hours to remove every last bone. "I am fairly certain it's buried under a ton of rock. It's good that I took lots of photographs before it was bombarded."

"The pool of suspects who could drop rocks from the sky is small," Bruce said. "Trained helicopter pilots only need apply."

Alexa tucked a wisp of hair back into her ponytail and nodded.

Bruce took a paper out of his briefcase. "I received a list of registration and flight plans of copters who flew in Fiordland yesterday. To our benefit, the airspace is restricted. Four copters from the Department of Conservation, two sightseeing companies, and one Search and Rescue."

Alexa got excited. One of them might be the murderer. "The DOC pilots are the ones who would be moving rock. Can I see the list?" She might recognize the name of the helicopter pilot the Clinton Hut ranger had interacted with yesterday morning. The Danger Zone pilot.

Bruce produced the paper, but the copter registration

numbers didn't list names of the pilots. "I'll get Sergeant Kramer to connect the dots," he said. "How has he been handling things?"

She opened her mouth to tell him of the sergeant's mistakes, then shut it. She wasn't a snitch. "Pretty well."

Bruce's eyes were unwavering.

"The skeleton is probably shattered. You should call in an archaeologist to sift through the rubble." Anger heated her up as she fished through the crime kit for Dr. Luckenbaugh's business card. The skeleton was someone's son. Maybe a brother, husband, and father like Charlie. His bones deserved respect, not demolition.

"The pilot is dangerous," Bruce said. "We need to act on this immediately." He half rose, but then sat again. "And the doctor. What's the latest on her?"

Alexa relished this tête-à-tête as she inhaled his male scent. "Her body was flown to the morgue this morning. Charlie and I..."

Bruce interrupted. "Charlie?"

"My brother. He's in our room. He fell in the creek this morning and got chilled."

"What was he doing?"

"We returned to where I believe Dr. Clark was pushed off the cliff. To see the crime scene in the daylight."

Bruce's eyes went slate. "I told you to stay in the lodge."

Pheromones be damned. "A core principle of nighttime crime-scene investigation is to return to the scene in daylight," she defended. "Evidence can be overlooked at night. And more rain is predicted. I know my job like you know your job. It had to be this morning."

Bruce nodded stiffly. "And?"

"Charlie found an apple, and I photographed a boot impression. Did you bring me a full crime kit?"

Bruce nodded. "It's in my room."

Alexa couldn't wait to see it. The kit, not the room. "We

spotted a blue backpack in the creek." She deliberately said creek, which sounded more benign than the monster river that had tried to spit Charlie over a chute. She was ashamed she had put Charlie at risk and didn't want to face Bruce's scrutiny. "That's how Charlie fell in. He was trying to reach it. The backpack eventually disappeared over a waterfall." She needed to check on Charlie. Make sure he had recovered. She ran through hypothermia treatment: Remove wet clothing. Check. Hot shower. Check. Warm beverage. Check. Cover with blankets. Check. "It was probably Dr. Clark's, and her assailant threw it in the river. I mean the creek."

Bruce stood. He looked down at her like he wanted to say something—their eyes met and held and told a story—but the situation made whatever he wanted to say impossible. They were working a case together. Again. Personal feelings needed to be shelved. That didn't stop her from wanting to grab him by the collar and pull his lips towards hers.

"Team meeting in five," he said, and left the room.

Chapter Twenty-Nine

The rip in her pants split a little more as she stood. She put her jacket back on and slung her crime kit over her shoulder. Time to head back to the room to change into her only other pair of pants. She also wanted to retrieve the camera to show Bruce and the others that the skeleton had existed. She hoped the close-ups of the notches on the ribs were clear. Cause of death in skeletal remains was often hard to determine, but not in this case. Charlie would probably be up. She wondered what it would be like to introduce him to Bruce.

She scurried past the French Luxer making arrangements with Vince to change his accommodations following the hike. "I will be a day late," he was saying. She gathered from this snippet that some Luxers weren't leaving Pompolona Lodge today—probably because of the delayed start. With the landslide and broken bridge, no new batch of Luxers was arriving, so space wasn't a problem.

When she entered their unlocked room, Charlie was still dead to the world under two duvets. Drowsiness was a symptom of hypothermia, but shouldn't he have recovered by now?

She set the crime kit on the chair and took her jacket off. "Charlie? Ready to get up?"

He didn't move.

She flicked on the overhead light and dodged his sodden pile of clothes to open the curtains. She expected him to blink groggily and complain, but his eyes stayed shut. He hadn't changed position since she'd been here an hour ago, reminding Alexa of Savasana at the end of yoga. Flat on back. Hands and feet splayed. Eyes closed.

Corpse pose.

An alarm pealed in her brain.

She hastened to the bedside and stared down. Time stopped as she studied the covers. The double duvet rose and fell, barely perceptible. She touched her brother's face gently and was relived to feel a clammy warmth. "Charlie? Time to get up."

His eyelids flickered, then stilled.

She pulled the duvets off, exposing his ENGINERD T-shirt. The cool air didn't startle him awake. She pressed his shoulder. Nothing. When she jiggled him, he made a snoring sound, but his eyes didn't open. She lifted his hand and used two fingers to press his skin lightly at the wrist, probing for his pulse. She pressed harder and felt the faint beat of life through her fingertips. She was too wound up to count beats per minute and let go. His wedding band glistened on his long pale ring finger, surprising her. When had he slipped it on?

She shook him. "Wake up, Charlie."

When he didn't respond, she shouted his name. This wasn't normal sleep. Charlie needed help.

Alexa ran out the door and into the lounge area. She looked around wildly. Constable Bartlett stood by the Ladies Room. She skidded up to him. "I need a doctor!"

Constable Bartlett jerked his thumb toward the restroom. "Can't leave Mrs…"

Rosie walked out and looked at her, confused. "Now what's happened?"

Alexa ran to the dining room. Bruce and Sergeant Kramer pushed tables together at the far end.

"Bruce," Alexa shouted. "I need help. My brother..."

"What's going on?" he asked.

"He won't wake up!"

Constable Chadwick was dragging chairs out of the way. "I'm an EMT," she said.

"Find Larry," Alexa commanded to Bruce. "He's a doctor." She motioned Constable Chadwick to follow her and sprinted back to the room.

Charlie looked as vulnerable as a slumbering child. Constable Chadwick pulled his eyelids back, checking his pupils. "They're dilated." She put her ear to his mouth and went still.

Alexa held Charlie's listless hand.

"His breathing is shallow, but regular," the constable said. "Help me roll him on his side."

The women pushed him over, his body heavy and compliant. Constable Chadwick set a pillow against his back. "Does your brother take any medications?" Her eyes flitted to the nightstand.

"I don't think so." Alexa surveyed the nightstand, too, confused by Constable Chadwick's question. The note she had left Charlie was crumpled on the floor. Had it angered him?

Larry burst into the room, followed by Bruce and Sergeant Kramer. Alexa was dismayed Larry didn't have a black bag with him. She never went anywhere without her crime kit. Shouldn't Larry act the same?

Constable Chadwick jumped out of the way to let the doctor take over. She must have noticed the lack of medical supplies as well. "I'll run get my kit."

Bruce looked at Alexa accusingly. "What happened?"

His look was a gut punch. "I found him like this. He won't wake up. It's got to be hypothermia."

Larry had returned Charlie to a prone position and was taking his pulse. "Why do you say that?"

"He fell in the creek about ninety minutes ago." She toed

the pile of Charlie's wet clothes and thought of him spinning like a doll in the cruel river. Even as she thought this, she knew the river wasn't cruel. Just indifferent. "He seemed fine. He ran along the bank right afterwards." She looked at Bruce. "To chase Dr. Clark's backpack."

"Ran?" Larry's brows knit together. "While he was wet?"

"For a little bit." Running always warmed her up, so why was everyone frowning at her? "I gave him my jacket and we walked back here." She looked at Sergeant Kramer. "You saw him. He was okay, wasn't he?"

"His lips were blue, lass. But he was cognizant."

Charlie's slightly parted lips were colorless now.

"What happened to his palm?" Larry asked. He was examining the raw abrasions.

"They're both like that. It's from the wire coil under the swing bridge. He had to..." She swallowed, afraid she would cry.

Larry set Charlie's palm down and softly slapped his cheeks. "Mr. Glock? Can you hear me?"

Alexa skirted Bruce and went to the bathroom door. She touched the towel draped from the knob; it was damp. "He had a hot shower." She should have stayed with him and not been indifferent like the river. She should have recognized what was most precious—her brother—not stupid interviews. "I sent him a cup of hot chocolate." She gestured to the mug on the nightstand. "He should be okay. What's wrong with him?"

Larry asked for a flashlight.

Constable Chadwick returned with a large first aid kit and set it on the dresser. "We've notified Lakes District Hospital. Medi-flight is on standby."

Bruce gave Larry his Maglite. Larry shone it in Charlie's eyes. "His pupil is responsive. That's good. If you'll all clear the room, please. I'll examine him more fully."

"I'm not leaving," Alexa said. No way in hell.

Sergeant Kramer and Constable Chadwick filed out. Bruce hesitated, his concerned eyes searching hers.

She felt acquitted—he cares—but redemption turned to horror when she noticed the closet behind him. The safe was open. "Wait!"

Bruce looked confused.

Alexa flew to the gaping safe. She ran her hand all the way to the back and up the sides. Empty.

"What's wrong?" Bruce asked.

"I told Charlie to lock my camera in the safe. It's gone."

"Maybe he forgot."

"When I came in earlier, the safe was locked."

"When was this?"

"Just before I rode in the helicopter. Charlie was sleeping. I thought he was okay. I left him a note." She was rambling.

Charlie's backpack was stuffed in the closet next to the safe. She rooted through it—tossing a guidebook and rain gear aside—but didn't find the camera. The one shelf in the closet held an extra blanket. Alexa shook it. She pushed past Bruce to the dresser and yanked open the three drawers. Empty. Empty. Empty.

"Is the camera important?" Bruce asked calmly.

"I told you. It has pictures of the skeleton, the ribs, and Dr. Clark." Now she had no proof. She stood there, helpless.

"Was the room locked?" Bruce asked.

They only had one key. Charlie had left it open so she could come in. She and whoever else. "No," she mumbled. "I..."

Larry interrupted. "What's important is this man's health. Take your concerns into the hallway."

Charlie moaned.

Alexa forgot about the camera. She dove at her brother. "Charlie? Can you hear me?"

His eyes flickered. He tried to sit up, but fell back. "Mel," he said.

"No, I'm Lexi. It's me."

"I'll leave," Bruce said. "Come find me when you can."

His words barely registered. Alexa looked at Larry. "What's going on?"

"See if there's a thermometer in that kit."

Alexa found one.

Larry placed it in Charlie's ear until there was a beep, and then peered at the little screen. "Thirty-seven. Normal. This isn't hypothermia." He set the thermometer on the nightstand and brushed his dark bangs to the side. "He's exhibiting symptoms of an overdose. A sedative of some type. Sleeping aids, perhaps. What medications does he take?"

"An overdose? I'm sure he doesn't take sleeping pills."

Larry's eyebrows knit together as he rummaged through the first aid box. "Check his toiletries."

Charlie's kit hung in the bathroom. It contained bare essentials: comb, mini toothbrush, floss, and toothpaste. A tiny shampoo, bar of soap, plastic razor blade. A card from Mel: *I love you. I'm sorry.*

She ran back. "No pills."

Charlie moaned and tried to sit again.

"It's all right, lad," Larry said. He looked at Alexa. "Do you have any medications he could have taken?"

"Only over-the-counter pain meds. Ibuprofen." In New Zealand, the tablets came individually wrapped, which drove her crazy when she wanted to pop a couple.

Larry spoke to Charlie. "Did you take some pills?"

Charlie shook his head slowly.

"I found activated charcoal in the first aid kit," Larry said. "It will absorb some of the drug in his system. Help him come round quicker." He looked at Alexa, waiting for the okay.

"I don't know." She looked at Charlie. His color was better. "Charlie? Can you hear me? What happened?"

Charlie blinked his eyes open. They were slightly glazed. "Call 911."

"It's okay. Larry is a doctor."

His hazel eyes were beseeching. "Call 911. That's what she told me." His voice was weak. "We practiced in Cub Scouts, but I forgot the numbers."

Her breath caught. Charlie wasn't making sense. "We have an air ambulance on standby. You're going to be okay."

"*911,*" he slurred.

Alexa looked at Larry. "Will that charcoal pill hurt him?"

"It's safe."

Alexa nodded, a tear tickling her cheek.

Larry emptied two of the pills into a glass of water. She helped Charlie sit up, stuffing a pillow behind him. He shivered; she pulled one of the duvets up to his chest. When Larry handed her the half-full glass, she held it to Charlie's lips. "Drink."

Chapter Thirty

A half hour later Charlie was lucid. "I swear I didn't take anything."

Larry shrugged and checked Charlie's pulse and reflexes. "Good to go, lad. Like you've come out of general anesthetic. No operating machinery or driving a car for twenty-four hours."

Alexa laughed at the ridiculous instructions, but then sobered. She had entrusted her brother's care to one of the main suspects. She waited until Larry left the room and then turned to Charlie. "Tell me what happened."

Charlie swung his legs around and sat up. "I feel woozy."

She was trying to be patient. "Did you lock up my camera?"

He rubbed his eyes. "I think so."

"If you locked it up, what did you do with the key?"

He snaked a hand in his pants pocket, came up empty, and tried the other. "It's gone."

She pointed to the safe. "It's open."

Charlie looked mystified.

"What do you remember?" Her voice was shrill.

"I remember taking a shower. I was so cold."

She plopped on the other bed. "Then what?"

He rubbed his eyes so hard Alexa wanted to stop him. "I got under the covers."

"But did you drink hot chocolate first?"

The mug on the nightstand bore witness. Charlie eyed it. "I remember now. Someone knocked. I opened the door and there was a tray with hot chocolate and cookies on it."

"No person?"

"Just the tray. On the mat. I figured it was from you, but that you didn't have time to come in."

Actually, she thought guiltily, she hadn't even taken the time to deliver it. "It wasn't me. I asked Silas—the bartender guy—to deliver it to your room." She'd track down Silas and get to the bottom of this. "Didn't you think that was strange that no one was there when you opened the door?"

"Everything in New Zealand is strange. You're strange."

His words hurt. Alexa choked back a rebuttal.

"I drank the frickin' cocoa, ate a cookie, then crawled into bed to get warm."

Alexa retrieved gloves from her kit and picked up the mug. "I think someone mixed sleeping pills into it and waited for you to conk out, then came in, found the key, opened the safe, and stole my camera."

"For real?" He looked like he might be sick. "Some dude put his hand in my pocket?"

"Or dudette." She noted the crumpled paper on the floor. "Did you read my note?"

"What note?" Charlie looked back at the closet. "Why is my stuff all over the place?"

"Sorry about that. I was looking for the camera."

Proving someone's drink had been doped was hard. Date rape drugs like roofies and ketamine leave the bloodstream quickly. Maybe sleeping pills did, too. If she took a sample of the leftover cocoa and matched its contents to a drug in Charlie's system, that would provide the evidence. She dashed into the bathroom and grabbed a water glass. "I need you to pee in this."

"Like I said. Strange." He heaved himself out of the bed and walked to the bathroom like he was on a rolling ship. Alexa carefully wrapped the mug. She would dust the slick surface for prints and take a swab of the cocoa slurry. But she was stuck in La La Land without a lab to process the results.

She quickly changed into her other pants—the pair without a hole—and grimaced pulling them on; they were damp from yesterday's rain.

When Charlie returned she said, "I'll refrigerate the, um, sample. Then I have to check in with the police. Do you feel strong enough to come with me?" She bagged the crumpled note—paper was easy to lift prints from—and wrinkled her nose as Charlie handed her his sample.

"My legs are shaking."

"Stay here. Lock the door when I leave. There are five cops in the lodge, so you're safe."

His hazel eyes bore into hers. "Are *you?*"

Chapter Thirty-One

Chef found a little Tupperware-like container for Alexa's sample. "I'll hide it behind the cheese and apple, shall I? Like wine to go with a picnic."

She appreciated Chef's humor, but this wasn't a laughing matter.

Bruce stood at the far end of the dining room at an easel, Sergeant Kramer by his side. Alexa thought of her stolen camera and had an urge to yell, "Start searching the lodge."

Get a grip, she told herself.

A giant memo pad, divided down the middle with a straight black line, rested on the easel. DR. DIANA CLARK was at the top left. A photo of the doctor was taped next to the name. Bruce wrote JOHN DOE on the top right as Alexa watched.

John Doe must be her crushed skeleton. The use of John Doe as a stand-in for an unidentified male was hundreds of years old and came from England. Two names were needed on legal eviction notices—for a defendant and a plaintiff. John Doe and Richard Roe were picked. Alexa didn't know when police started using John Doe, but seeing it printed on the pad made the skeleton come alive. A proper toe tag waited for him, maybe in the stack of missing persons reports. Who was he? Who mourned him? Was someone still praying his name?

A big map of Milford Track was tacked to the wall behind the easel. Apparently, the dining room was the new command center.

Constable Chadwick and the senior constable—What's His Name—sat catty-corner at the tables that had been pushed together. A tray with a couple sandwiches sat in the middle of the table.

Bruce saw her. "Join us over here. How is Charlie?"

She strode to the table and decided to speak frankly in front of everyone. "He's better. Larry—Dr. Salvú—thinks he was on sleeping pills." That hadn't come out right. "I think someone drugged him," she clarified. "Maybe in his cocoa."

"To take your camera?" Sergeant Kramer asked.

She was surprised at first, but then remembered he had been in the room—or hallway—when she discovered the camera was gone. "It has lots of evidence on it. From both cases. We need to search the lodge."

"Have a seat," Bruce said. "Events are evolving and we need to establish a plan."

She wanted him to form a posse and head out immediately. "Whoever took the camera could be getting away. And I know who was supposed to deliver the hot chocolate. Silas. He's a server."

One of Bruce's eyebrows rose.

Alexa huffed and took a seat. She felt like she'd downed eight cups of coffee.

Bruce looked around. "Is this everyone?"

"Constable Bartlett is with Dr. Clark's sister," Sergeant Kramer said.

To keep Rosie from spreading the news that Dr. Clark had been pushed, Alexa thought.

"Get him in here," Bruce said.

Constable Chadwick hurried out of the room. Alexa forced her shoulders to detach from her neck and practiced some yoga breaths. In less than two minutes, the tiny constable returned with her colleague. They slid into chairs.

Bruce said something softly to Sergeant Kramer and stepped aside.

Sergeant Kramer clasped his hands behind his back. He nodded at Bruce and Alexa. Then he addressed the Te Anau officers. "You all know I'm Sergeant Adrian Kramer." He cleared his throat. "You know as well that in murder investigations, higher-ranked officers are called in to assume control." He remained standing tall. "Only five percent of New Zealand police officers have the rank of detective inspector, so it's an honor and privilege for us to collaborate with Detective Inspector Bruce Horne from Auckland."

Bruce stepped forward. "Thank you, Sergeant Kramer. From all accounts you've handled the initial investigation with competence and skill."

The sergeant smiled stiffly. Alexa thought it was very civilized and wished the world operated this way more often. She reviewed rank in the room in descending order: detective inspector—Bruce, sergeant—Kramer, senior constable—she couldn't remember the man's name. His kid won a sailing race that morning, and the two constables—Bartlett with buzzed hair, and Chadwick, the woman. There were a lot of new people to keep straight.

"...to introduce Ms. Alexa Glock,"

She looked up.

"...a Forensic Service Center investigator, with a specialty in teeth. I've worked several cases with her. She is not a sworn officer but provides support and valuable input. We are fortunate you were in the area, Ms. Glock."

Constable Bartlett laughed. "Some vacay, eh?"

Alexa flushed. She hadn't expected Bruce's endorsement.

Constable Chadwick google-eyed Alexa like she was a celebrity.

"Look at the people around you," Bruce commanded. "We are now a team, 24/7, until these two cases are closed. Is that clear?"

"Aye, Senior," Constable Bartlett said.

Constable Chadwick nodded solemnly. Alexa leaned forward to read the other guy's name tag: Senior Constable L. C. McCain.

"Events are unfolding—dangerously—as Ms. Glock pointed out. We have two cases," Bruce said, pointing to the easel. "A quick rundown on case one. We'll call it Black Diamond. That's after the hiking pole Ms. Glock found at the scene where Dr. Diana Clark's body was discovered."

Sergeant Kramer sat next to Alexa.

"I had time before leaving for the airport to look into Dr. Diana Clark," Bruce continued. "This is her photograph." He passed copies to everyone.

Alexa studied hers. Diana wore diamond studs and a pink button-down, collar upturned. Her blond hair looked artfully highlighted.

"Dr. Clark practiced orthopedic medicine in Auckland." He reached into his briefcase for some papers. "Our victim resided at 8708 Payne's Way, Parnell." He went quiet for a second, perhaps waiting for a reaction. None came. "That's a fashionable neighborhood, with views of Waitemata Harbor."

This didn't surprise Alexa. Orthopedic surgeons in the U.S. raked in the big bucks, so it stands to reason Diana lived in a fancy area.

"I have a team searching her premises today."

This was typical in a murder case, Alexa knew. Didn't even need a warrant.

"She had a stand-alone practice, Quay Park Orthopedic on Six Kings Avenue, and specialized in hip and knee replacements. She served mostly private healthcare patients and used Owens Hospital—a private care facility—to perform her surgeries."

"That hospital is more like a posh hotel," Constable Bartlett said. "My aunt…"

"Yes." Bruce cut in. "My officer in Auckland is digging into Dr. Clark's computer, phone records, and finances. The only red flag she's uncovered is a warning from the Health Practitioners Disciplinary Tribunal in July for overprescribing medication."

Alexa thought of Charlie, drugged. *Was there a connection?*

"Sergeant Kramer—I'll turn the this over to you for a quick review of current events."

Sergeant Kramer stood but stayed where he was. "When Dr. Clark failed to arrive here—Pompolona Lodge—yesterday afternoon, a search party was convened." He described the events leading to the discovery and retrieval of the body. "When Ms. Glock examined Dr. Clark, she discovered puncture wounds on her back that match trekking pole tips. She concluded that Dr. Clark was pushed to her death. Constable Bartlett and I were called in on another matter—the bones by the river—and arrived at six thirty this morning."

"Had to get up at cock's crow," Sergeant Bartlett added while Sergeant Kramer sat.

"Let's consider who had the opportunity to kill her," Bruce said. "Who had the ability to push Dr. Clark off the cliff? Most trampers use hiking poles, right?"

No one answered.

"Right?" Bruce demanded.

"Yes," Alexa said.

"With a running start, as Ms. Glock suggests, our attacker could be male or female."

Bruce faced the team. "Motive. The usual: greed, jealousy, revenge, or power. What else?"

"Drugs, maybe," said Constable Chadwick.

"Right." Bruce made a list in the corner of the big pad. "She is a physician, and there is that warning for overprescribing drugs. Hopefully, one of these motives will resonate as we dive deeper into her background. What suspects do we have?"

Sergeant Kramer looked at his notes. "The sister, Rosie Jones. She had an argument with Diana Saturday morning that Ms. Glock overheard. She, ah, well, I told her that her sister's death was not an accident."

Bruce stayed calm. "I'm sure you had your reasons. How did she react?"

The reason being inexperience, Alexa thought.

"She didn't believe it," the sergeant said. "She insists Diana fell off the swing bridge."

"Who else knows the death wasn't accidental?"

Sergeant Kramer colored. "A tramper named Steadman Willis. He helped retrieve her body. He's a Search and Rescue volunteer. I cleared him to leave the lodge."

Bruce frowned. "He's gone?"

The sergeant nodded. "Other suspects are her traveling companions Dr. Salvú—her anesthesiologist—and her drug rep, Cassandra Perry."

"I met Ms. Perry on my way in here." Bruce wrote the suspects' names on the pad. "Neither Salvú or Perry has a record. I checked. Anyone else as a possible suspect?"

The team stayed quiet.

"Is there a disgruntled lover or patient at the lodge?" Bruce probed.

"We've talked with all Luxe trampers," Sergeant Kramer said, "and no one else knew Dr. Clark before the hike."

"Staff? Guides?"

"The guide from Luxe Tours, Clint Knight, had never met Dr. Clark before the tramp. Neither had the lodge managers. We haven't had time to talk with the other staff yet."

"I'll do it, boss," Sergeant Bartlett said.

There was a knock, and Vince stepped in. His eyes landed on the platter of sandwiches on the table. "Checking to make sure you had enough to eat."

"Ta," said Bruce. "We have plenty."

The scent of roast beef and horseradish got to Alexa. She grabbed half a sandwich and a napkin.

Bruce capped the marker. "Mr. Bergen, how many guests are left?"

Vince counted on his fingers. "Eleven, plus all of you. And Ms. Glock's brother. I've allotted Kotare, Tuke, and Toutouwai for your rooms."

Bruce looked puzzled.

"The rooms are named after birds," Alexa explained.

"All the rest of the current guests must remain," Bruce told Vince. "We need the satellite phone and radio in here. That's all."

Vince nodded solemnly. He walked over to a door, unfastened a bolt, and ducked into a little pantry. In a second he backed out with a case of bottled water and set it on the table. "I'll have Clint tell the Luxers they must stay—it's too late to tackle Mackinnon Pass at this point anyway."

It hit Alexa that the situation, with its isolation and small pool of suspects, was like a locked-room-manor mystery. A distant rumble made them look out the windows. Far off, a dervish of rocks tumbled down the mountainside.

"A slide," Senior Constable McCain murmured.

"Mount Elliot is acting up," Vince commented.

Alexa choked on her bite of sandwich. Then she remembered the waitress said the lodge was too far from the mountain to be in the path of landslides. She swallowed and asked Vince to find Silas. She wanted to ask him how Charlie's hot chocolate had gotten drugged, even if no one else felt rushed to do so. She glanced at Bruce to see if this was okay. He gave a curt nod.

"Right," Vince said. "I'll leave you to it."

"Back to Black Diamond," Bruce said after the door shut. "We have a small pool of suspects. Who else knew Dr. Clark?"

"There are thirty-five independent hikers in the area," Alexa said. She realized that included Charlie, Stead, and herself. "Well, thirty-two. Maybe one of them knew her."

244   *Sara E. Johnson*

"Independent hikers? What do you mean?"

"You can hike Milford Track two ways." Stead Willis had explained this to her and Charlie at the beginning of the hike. "Everyone starts at the same place—Glade Wharf. You can hike with a guide and stay in lodges like here, or hike on your own and stay in the DOC huts."

"Locals call them freedom hikers," Constable Bartlett said.

"Charlie and I are independent hikers."

"Why does that not surprise me?" Bruce asked.

The team stared at her.

Alexa wondered what Bruce's comment meant. "Charlie and I were supposed to be staying at Mintaro Hut last night. Until this happened." She wiped her mouth with the napkin and walked to the map, tapping Mintaro Hut with her finger. "But the independent hikers..." She pictured the ones she could remember: the loud nurses, the rushing businessmen, the woman who dropped the postcard at the ranger station, the mother who told her to take her boots off, the card-playing Germans. "They wouldn't be there anymore. They'd be hiking over Mackinnon Pass and onto the next hut."

"Dumpling Hut," Constable Chadwick said.

Bruce was suddenly beside her, circling the huts with his marker. "Has anyone talked to these independent trampers?"

Sergeant Kramer tugged at his collar. "No, Senior."

Bruce's eyes were like a mood ring and deepened to angry. "That's an oversight. Our killer could be bush-bashing out of the woods as we speak. Call DOC and get a list of people staying in the huts. They had to register, right?"

"Yes," Sergeant Kramer said.

"Tell the rangers at Mintaro and Dumpling to hold all trampers until further notice," he ordered. "And get that phone in here."

So much for a locked-room-manor mystery, Alexa realized. The door was flung open.

Chapter Thirty-Two

Bruce gestured to the easel pad and didn't miss a beat. "Let's move to case two before we form a plan. We'll call it Bone Track." He tapped on the right-hand side of the pad. "John Doe is a skeleton Ms. Glock found near the river. Normally I would consider this a cold case, with less urgency than Dr. Clark's death." He paused. "However, shortly after Ms. Glock discovered the bones, her life was threatened. A helicopter pilot came after her with a bulk bag."

Constable Bartlett appeared to be the only one who hadn't heard this news. "Aw stink," he said, mouth open.

"Ms. Glock—show us where you found the bones."

Alexa returned to the map and trailed her finger along the Clinton River. "Here, I think."

Bruce uncapped his marker and circled the area. "Describe the condition of the bones and why you suspect foul play."

She tried to be concise. "The bones were in decent shape. I believe the skeleton to be an adult male, with fillings in his teeth consistent with modern dentistry. I examined the rib cage and noted notches consistent with a knife attack. That's why I suspect foul play."

"But for how long has he been buried?" Constable Bartlett asked.

"I can't tell," Alexa answered. She thought of the dental work. "I'd say twenty years or less—but it's just a guess. Constable Chadwick and I returned to the scene ninety minutes ago. Someone dropped a ton of rock on the skeleton. One of those bulk bags. It's now buried and most likely smashed to pieces."

"Sod all," Constable Bartlett said.

"Ms. Glock has an acquaintance who is an archaeologist and trained to recover bone fragments," Bruce said. "I've placed a call for her to join us, but I don't know when she'll arrive."

"Her name is Dr. Luckenbaugh. She'll confirm my findings." Alexa hated a my-word-against-your-word situation, but no one seemed to question her story. She was grateful.

"Do you think your camera was stolen because of the skeleton or because of Dr. Clark?" Constable Bartlett asked.

"There were crucial photographs for both cases on it," Alexa said.

"The two cases—though years apart—could be related," Bruce said.

"Not likely though, right, Senior?" Constable Bartlett said.

"We can't discount the possibility," Bruce said. "I contacted Southern Lakes Aerodrome this morning. They immediately suspended all local helicopter trips. I'm waiting on a list of pilots who were in Fiordland the past two days. If there is a connection between pilots and the death of John Doe, our pool of suspects is small."

Constable Bartlett raised his hand.

"This isn't a classroom," Bruce said. "When you have something to offer other than offhand comments, jump in."

Constable Bartlett gave a nervous cough. "Who will track down the pilots? Who will interview them?"

"Good question, Constable," Bruce said. "We may be top-heavy here at the lodge. How many officers do you have left in Te Anau?"

"One," Sergeant Chadwick answered. "Jaiden Sprunt is holding down the fort."

"That's a start. What have we got from the missing persons reports?"

Senior Constable McCain sat straight. "I've been working on them for the past hour, sir. I've whittled the stack to the South Island over the past twenty years, yeah? There are forty-six."

"Are any of them Māori?" Alexa asked. She retrieved her phone and found the picture of the belt buckle, with its eel-like creatures. "I found this on the body."

McCain looked at her phone. "Looks Māori. Can you send that to me?"

"There's no internet," Constable Bartlett reminded him. "Take a picture of the picture. It could be a tourist bought the buckle in a shop. Sometimes they go home looking more Māori than the Māori."

Bruce didn't laugh. "We don't know who our victim is, but let's speculate means, motive, and opportunity. Means?"

"The perpetrator had a knife," Alexa said. "It wasn't a surprise attack. They were standing face-to-face." In the U.S., the most common situations resulting in knife attacks were arguments. "He might have been arguing with someone he knew."

"What was the argument about?" Bruce asked.

"Don't see how guesswork gets us anywhere," Constable Bartlett mumbled.

Bruce was unflappable. "Think of the scene. Two people arguing along a wilderness river. About what?"

The dining room darkened. Out the window, gray clouds smothered Mount Elliot.

"Could have been trampers. Like all the people staying here," Constable Bartlett said.

"If he'd been expected at a lodge or hut, there would have been a massive search," Senior Constable McCain said. "Like the missing tourist last summer. Would have made the news."

Constable Chadwick cleared her throat. "Sir?"

Bruce nodded.

"The river is a source of *pounamu*."

"Greenstone. Go on."

"We've had complaints over the years from the chairperson of the Ngai Tahu. About *Pakeha* stealing greenstone."

Pakeha were non-Māoris, Alexa knew. And Ngai Tahu was the main Māori tribe of the South Island.

"The Māori call the greenstone trails blood arteries," Constable Chadwick added. She looked elfin next to Senior Constable McCain. "The chairperson, Sherman Tumuha, claims people are stealing it right out of the river. He says they're using helicopters. All it would take is for someone to identify a boulder of *pounamu* and use a copter and a winch to lift it out."

"Two years ago a greenstone boulder the size of a Fiat was found in the Greymouth River," Constable Bartlett said. "They used a copter to move it."

"Well done, Constable Chadwick," Bruce said. "There's our connection with helicopter pilots. Could be John Doe was killed over greenstone. What follow-up have you taken?"

"We nosed around, but didn't find anything," Senior Constable McCain said. "None of the locals know anything."

"Or if they did, they wouldn't talk," Constable Chadwick said, staring at McCain. "Ngai Tahu have started private investigations since we've been no help."

Something flashed between the senior constable and Chadwick. Alexa suspected the female constable wasn't satisfied with the nosing around.

Sergeant Kramer rushed in with the satellite phone. Bruce brought him up to date. "Let's list our motive as greed," Bruce said. "Get that chairperson on the phone. I want to hear what he has to say and what his investigation has found." Bruce looked out the window, now spattered with raindrops. "I'm splitting our group into teams. Sergeant Kramer and Constable Bartlett will work on Black Diamond. Senior Constable McCain and

Constable Chadwick will be on Bone Track. Ms. Glock—you'll float as needed. All of you report to me. Any questions?"

"No, Senior," Constable Bartlett said.

Silas knocked on the door.

Chapter Thirty-Three

Alexa beckoned Silas to follow her past the lounge where remaining Luxers were camped out. She wanted to question him in private. The French man, playing backgammon with the teen son of the Israeli couple, sprang up at the sight of Alexa. "We know why we are being kept here. *Le crime de meurtre.*"

The teenager's eyes got big.

The cat had escaped. She wasn't surprised.

They found grim-faced Kathy emerging from the office. "I've been dealing with cancellations," she said.

"Can we use your private quarters to talk?" Alexa asked.

Kathy frowned at Silas. "Is everything all right, then?"

"We're questioning everyone," Alexa said vaguely.

Kathy opened the door and stood back. "I heard that DOC is working to repair the rockslide damage. Do you know when the trail will reopen?"

"No," Alexa said.

Silas followed Alexa in and stared at the framed photo of Kathy, Vince, and their daughters. "Have a seat," she said.

He picked the recliner.

Alexa sat on the sofa and took out her pad and pen. "I need some information. Let's start with your full name."

"Silas Monroe Cannon."

She took down his age and contact information. He added that this was his second season at the lodge. "I'm taking time off from uni."

Alexa wondered what brought a nineteen-year-old to work at a remote lodge. A Neil Young song her old boyfriend Jeb had liked popped into her head: "Everybody Knows This is Nowhere." Pompolona Lodge fit the lyric.

"Had you ever met Dr. Clark?" She showed him the photo Bruce had passed around.

Silas shook his head.

"Around ten a.m., when you were vacuuming the dining room, I asked you to take a cup of hot chocolate to my brother. In our room."

"You're staying in Tauhou."

"That's right. Did you deliver the cocoa?"

Silas fidgeted. "I had to finish the tidy up, yeah?" His eyes darted around the room. "Then I popped into the kitchen and made the hot choc myself. We use instant."

He colored as if instant was bad. Alexa didn't think so. "Then what?"

"Well, see," he rubbed his hands on his black jeans, "that was, um, the thing. I arranged the mug on a tray, added biscuits—is that important?"

Alexa was poised to write whatever came next.

"When I left the kitchen, your friend was waiting. He offered to deliver the hot choc to your brother."

She almost dropped the pen. "What friend?"

"The search and rescue bloke. You had brekkie with him."

"Stead Willis?"

"I'm not sure his name. He wasn't a proper guest." Silas colored again, probably realizing she wasn't a proper guest, either. "He knew your room, so I thought it was okay?"

After she and Sergeant Kramer had interviewed Stead, she had walked out with him and practically shouted to Silas to send hot chocolate to Charlie. Silas had shouted back, "Tauhou, right?" Stead had to have overheard.

Her heart skipped a beat. "We need to report this."

Silas followed her obediently. Alexa scanned the dining room, found Bruce bellowing into the satellite phone, and hurried over. "I know who drugged Charlie!"

Bruce raised a finger and turned his back.

Alexa told Silas to have a seat, and joined Senior Constable McCain, who pushed some papers her way. "These four blokes are Māori."

They were missing persons reports. She switched her brain to the bones by the river and scanned the top one: Michael Eugene Wilson, DOB: 06/06/1987.

Michael Wilson was listed as Māori and five feet, eleven inches (180 cm.). He was last seen in April 2015 in the Dunedin area with the intention to take the bus to Palmerston. She studied his photo; his eyes seemed to plead for help. She scanned the other reports. No one was last seen in Fiordland or even Te Anau. The general description included clothing. She checked the four forms, looking for mention of a belt buckle. Wilson had been wearing a short-sleeved striped shirt, sweatpants, and jandals, which Alexa knew were flip-flops. No one wore a belt with sweatpants.

The other missing men had been wearing shorts, jeans, or cargo pants, all belt-worthy, and had last been seen in the South Island towns of Hokitika, Queenstown, and Wanaka.

"Can you call the contact numbers on these three and ask about a belt buckle?"

The senior constable reached into his pocket for his phone. "Oops, eh? No service. I'll do it when Senior is finished using the satellite phone."

"Check the other South Island forms to see if anyone was last seen in Milford or if there's any mention of a belt buckle."

"On it," he said.

Bruce hung up. Alexa introduced him to Silas, who sprang from his chair. "Tell the detective inspector what you told me."

When Silas finished, he added that he'd watched Willis leave the lodge with his backpack on. Bruce asked which way he went.

"There's only one trail out. It splits after a ways, but you can't see the fork from the porch."

Alexa could visualize the fork. One way led to the evil swing bridge and the landslide. The other way led to Mackinnon Pass and Dumpling Hut. Alexa assumed Stead, with her camera in his pack, was heading toward Mackinnon.

"How long ago did he leave?" Bruce asked.

Silas scrunched his brow. "Ninety minutes, maybe?"

"How long does it take to trek to the next lodge?"

"He'd be headed to the hut, not the lodge," Alexa reminded him.

"Dumpling Hut is eleven kilometers from here," Silas said.

"Thank you, Mr. Cannon. That's all for now." After Silas left, Bruce said, "It was a mistake to let this Mr. Willis leave the lodge. That's on me. I'll get that officer in Te Anau to dive into his background, and remind the ranger of Dumpling Hut to detain all guests."

"Sergeant Kramer has a recording of our interview with Stead," Alexa said.

"I'll take a listen. What are your thoughts on the man?"

Alexa couldn't admit she had had a trail crush on Stead. "He knows search and rescue. He's been to this area six or seven times."

Bruce looked down at her, and she met his eyes. "That makes me think he's involved with the skeleton rather than the doctor," he said.

His theory made sense. Maybe Stead returned yearly to check on the grave. Add a few more rocks to the pile. "He got a helicopter ride yesterday over the landslide to Mintaro Hut. That might provide an alibi around the time of Diana's death. It should be easy to check." She got out her notepad and flipped through the pages. "A DOC guy name Bill Little. He'll be on the list."

"The fact that Mr. Willis knows pilots further points to him being involved with the skeleton," Bruce said.

Alexa thought of having been alone with Stead when she had returned for her forgotten hiking poles. His stuff had been spread on the table in the hut. The tableau flashed in her mind: coffee mug, fishing pole, map, trowel, a baggie of sandpaper. And a knife. "Stead Willis carries a knife. He said he used it to gut fish."

Their eyes met.

"He refused to be fingerprinted." She angered as she thought of Charlie, drugged. "Are you going to chase him down?"

Bruce blew air out of his mouth. "I'll call in a chopper from Queenstown so I can get to Dumpling Hut."

A loud boom made Alexa jump. Thunder.

Bruce touched her arm. "I don't sense drugging your brother was premeditated. Find out if any of the guests are missing sleeping tablets. Be careful." He handed her a list of guest names and their room numbers. Their fingers brushed. "Start with Ms. Perry, Dr. Salvú, and Mrs. Jones."

Chapter Thirty-Four

Back in their room, Charlie sat on the edge of the bed and listened as she told him what Bruce asked her to do. "I'll come with you," he said.

"Do you feel okay?"

"That Larry guy came back and checked me. He said I was fine."

Alexa walked into the bathroom. The last thing she wanted was to put Charlie in more danger, but Bruce's "be careful" echoed in her head. Having Charlie with her was protection, and a second set of eyes and ears. She looked through the open door. "When you were coming to, you called me Mel."

Charlie grunted.

She spoke louder. "I noticed you're wearing your wedding ring." She watched him look at his hand.

"I got weirded out after falling in the river. Like what if I had died? Mel says she's sorry. That she made a mistake."

Cheating on Charlie was unforgivable, wasn't it? But clearly—with the wedding band back on his finger—Charlie didn't think so. "What are you going to do?"

"I don't know. I just want my family back."

Growing up, that's all she had ever wanted: Mom, Dad, Lexi, and Charlie, together again. She scowled. Maybe the construct of family was fluid, and her concept—father, mother, two children—was as outdated as her penchant for canvas Keds. In Auckland, Charlie had called her favorite pair "old lady shoes."

She gazed at Charlie, head down, hands on his knees. His hair was thinning at the crown; the sight made her heart swell. *We're getting older, and this is our one chance at life.*

"When we get out of here, let's call Dad and Rita. And the boys." She couldn't meet his eyes. "Come on. Let's go."

Cassandra Perry, Dr. Clark's drug rep, was staying in Kiwi.

"I bet everyone wants Kiwi," Charlie said. "No one can pronounce the other rooms."

"You probably could if you were a Kiwi."

He looked at her quizzically. She decided it wasn't worth explaining kiwi bird and Kiwi person. Let him think she was cuckoo. Alexa rapped on the door. They waited, and then she rapped again. No answer. Dr. Larry Salvú's room, Weka, was across the hall. Clean Timberland boots waited on the mat. He opened his door promptly and swiped his bangs from his forehead. "What wrong?" he asked Charlie.

"He's good," Alexa said quickly. "Thanks for helping."

Larry picked up the boots, scrutinizing the tread. "The bill is in the mail."

She figured he wasn't kidding. His tight, short-sleeved T-shirt emphasized his muscular arms. *Gym arms,* Alexa thought. "Can we come in?"

He acted like they were old buds and waved them in. His room was similar to Charlie and Alexa's but with a queen bed instead of twins. The queen was neatly made except for pillows leaning against the headboard. A Lee Child thriller was on the nightstand. "Sit, sit," he said.

Alexa remained standing. "This won't take long."

Charlie sat on the bed. Larry leaned against the dresser, arms crossed, no visible tattoos, and gestured with his sharp chin to the window. "I'm glad I'm not hiking."

She gazed out. Rain pummeled the earth; trees drooped in misery. She thought of Debbie and Mark, zigzagging up the pass, exposed and guide-less. She hoped they'd be okay.

Larry looked at Charlie. "Any dizziness?"

"A little groggy. Some coffee would…"

Alexa interrupted. "Since we believe Charlie was drugged, we're trying to locate the source. Do you carry sleeping pills?"

Larry's eyes hardened. "What are you implying?"

"Just answer."

His voice rose a couple decibels. "I don't carry sleeping aid. I certainly wouldn't risk my medical license by doping your brother." He looked to the door. "Talk to Cassandra. At breakfast she mentioned how well she slept last night. I found that peculiar, given Diana had passed away."

"Thanks for your time," Alexa said.

In the hallway Charlie said, "I don't trust him."

Alexa shrugged noncommittally. She tried Cassandra's door. Still no answer.

Rosie wasn't in her room, either. They found her in the lounge, sitting on a couch next to a Luxer woman with a British accent. "It's a bit wet out," the Luxer was saying, "so all's well to be cozy and safe."

Cozy maybe, Alexa thought. *Safe? Not so sure.* The Luxer offered to get Rosie a cuppa. Alexa took her place on the couch. Rosie responded to her questions dully and dutifully. She didn't have or use sleeping pills.

They intercepted Cassandra coming out of the restroom. She was hard to miss in her bright red sweater. Alexa was direct. "Do you have sleeping pills in your possession?"

Cassandra flicked a speck off her sweater. Her black onyx ring looked like a spider clinging to her finger. "I carry samples everywhere. Habit from being a pharmaceutical sales rep."

"Did you share any medication with anyone?"

She hesitated. "Diana asked for a little something on our first night. She had a headache. I gave her an ibuprofen." Her honey-colored eyes pinged from Alexa's to Charlie's. "I know you're with the police. What's happening?"

"Can we see your samples?" Alexa marched off without waiting for an answer. She was relieved Cassandra followed.

She entered Kiwi without a key.

"Don't you lock your door?" Alexa asked.

Cassandra turned on the light. "This is New Zealand, not America, where the crime is."

Charlie looked like he was about to say something. Alexa made a face at him.

Toiletries were strewn across the dresser top. Cassandra rummaged through them, her red nails poking a brush, moving lipstick and lotion, knocking a small bottle to the floor. Alexa picked it up, surprised to see eau de toilette on the label. Perfume? On a hiking trip? Diana Clark had worn perfume, too. She set the bottle back on the dresser.

Cassandra hurried to the bathroom, flicking on the light. She looked around, her face pinched. "My pills are gone. What's this about?"

"My brother was drugged. Larry thinks it was sleeping pills."

Cassandra whipped around to face her. "You aren't suggesting I drugged him?"

"Did you?"

Cassandra's nose flared. "Of course not." Her voice lowered as if she didn't want someone to overhear. "Are you saying someone came into my room?"

Alexa shrugged.

"I felt like a zombie," Charlie said.

"I only had a couple sleeping pills. You're lucky Ambien is short-acting."

What if she had had a whole bottle? Alexa thought. *Would Charlie be dead?*

"Men metabolize the effects faster than women," Cassandra

was regaining her footing. "Probably because of your testosterone."

Charlie blushed. "Whatever."

"Come with us," Alexa said.

She could hear Bruce's loud voice before they entered the dining room. "We have too many people here when we need them elsewhere. Milford Sound Airport, for instance," he said to Sergeant Kramer. "Get talking to those pilots."

"Yes, Senior," Kramer said.

They hushed as Alexa and her entourage approached.

Alexa was nervous as she introduced Charlie to Bruce. It felt like a big deal.

"Bruce Horne. Glad to see you up and about." He held out his hand. "One of our officers will need to take a statement about your incident."

Charlie and Bruce shook.

"Been a rough morning for you," Sergeant Kramer said to Charlie. "At least your lips aren't blue anymore. Come with me. I'll get Constable Chadwick to take your statement."

Charlie followed Kramer.

Cassandra stepped around Alexa. "I need to make a statement as well."

"This is Dr. Clark's pharmaceutical rep," Alexa explained. "She had sleeping pills and says they're missing."

"*All* my samples are missing, not just the Ambien," Cassandra huffed.

"Ms. Perry. We spoke earlier." Bruce's voice had calmed. "I'm sorry to hear about your missing medication. I've been wanting to talk with you about Dr. Clark."

Alexa watched the interaction with interest. She supposed Bruce found Cassandra attractive.

"I don't like the thought of someone entering my room and pinching my medication."

"I agree," Bruce said. "Was your door locked?"

She smiled demurely, showing perfectly aligned teeth. "No. I've a trusting nature."

"Ms. Glock, will you join me as I interview Ms. Perry?"

Bruce chatted with Cassandra on the way to Vince and Kathy's private quarters. Alexa supposed he was establishing rapport. *Or is he flirting?*

Cassandra arranged herself on the couch close to Bruce in the recliner. Alexa sat on a dinette chair and got out her pad and pen.

"I'm recording our talk." Bruce set up his phone as a tape recorder.

"Is it true that someone pushed Diana off the bridge?" Cassandra asked.

"The circumstances of her death are suspicious." He asked for Cassandra's address and phone number. "When did you last see Dr. Clark alive?"

"Yesterday. At lunch. She left before I finished. Diana liked to be first."

"And this was what time?"

"Around one o'clock. Our Luxe guide would know. He was there. So was Larry. Diana and Larry left together."

That's not what Larry said, Alexa thought.

Bruce asked Cassandra about her job.

"I'm a sales rep for Lunar Pharmaceuticals." She assessed her painted nails. "I promote and sell Lunar products."

"To whom?"

"To doctors, pharmacies, and health stores."

"What are your biggest sellers?"

She didn't hesitate. "Drugs, of course. It's silly to spend time pushing beauty products. The profit is in pharmaceuticals."

"What drugs did you supply to Dr. Clark's practice?"

Cassandra wrinkled her nose. "I don't provide drugs directly, of course. My job is to educate physicians about our newest products, sell them, and schedule orders."

"Answer the question," Bruce said.

"I'd have to check my records."

"I'm having them checked as we speak."

Cassandra absorbed this information slowly. She shifted a little farther from Bruce and chewed her bottom lip. "Meperidine and oxycodone are big sellers," she finally said. "Diana deals with people who are in pain."

Bruce studied Cassandra. "Did you know Dr. Clark was warned by the medical tribunal for overprescribing painkillers?"

"Prescribing medication to help people deal with pain is justified. It's not Diana's fault if someone hoards pills or doubles the dosage or gets prescriptions from more than one doctor. That's what happens, and then people blame the doctor."

Bruce sat back. "Who paid for this trip?"

"Diana was treating."

Alexa thought it was usually pharmas that gifted the docs. This was backward, like the seasons in New Zealand. She wondered if Bruce would follow up.

"Is it ethical to accept a trip?" Bruce asked.

"We're also friends. I can't believe she's dead. Was she really murdered?"

Bruce assumed a sympathetic expression. "I'm not at liberty to say. What was Dr. Clark's relationship with Dr. Salvú?"

"Larry? Well, a little tense. I heard them arguing about patient volume."

Alexa doodled a mute button in her notes but scratched it out. Cassandra must be referring to number, not loud patients. She remembered something Cassandra had said at dinner and interrupted Bruce. "Last night you mentioned you saw someone out the window the first night of the Milford Track. Is that right?"

A blotch of lipstick marred one of Cassandra's incisors. "Yes. Standing in the bushes, peering in. Eerie, I must say. I dropped my phone. When I picked it up and looked again, he was gone."

"A man?" Bruce asked.

"Might have been. It could have been a caretaker. I didn't report it, silly of me, I know. Are we done? When can I leave the lodge?"

"We need you to sit tight for a while longer," Bruce said.

Alexa anticipated the final question. She didn't have to wait long.

"Do you know of anyone who wanted to harm Dr. Clark?"

Cassandra contemplated her bloodred thumbnail, frowning perhaps because it was chipped. "She didn't get along with her sister. You might look there."

Chapter Thirty-Five

Cassandra's eau de toilette lingered like a ghost after she left.

"What do you think?" Bruce asked.

Alexa pulled her chair closer. "If Cassandra pushed Diana, what would her motive be?"

"What if Cassandra is running a pill mill, and Diana threatened to turn her in? I'll have Constable Cooper in Auckland check her out."

Alexa nodded. "Put Larry Salvú on your list, too. He claims Diana left the shelter alone, but Cassandra and Rosie both say Larry and Diana left together." She ripped out the time line she had made earlier and gave it to him.

Bruce thanked her. "Sergeant Kramer interviewed Rosie. Take a listen." He fiddled with his phone, frowned, pressed start. "This is about halfway through."

"*She never cared about coming home for the hollies, never visited Mum. Sent a box of pears and chocolates at Christmas is all, and Mum is diabetic! Di wanted to escape her roots.*"

"*She was quite accomplished, eh?*"

Alexa identified Sergeant Kramer's voice.

"*Yes, sure, she worked hard in school, even though we moved a lot. She was on a mission for the highest grade, no matter where we lived.*"

"*What was your childhood like?*"

Rosie's voice got soft. Alexa had to lean in to hear.

"*We grew up picking coins up from the parking lot? Didn't have enough for the pot sometimes. After Dad left, Mum had to use the Salvation Army for food parcels.*"

"*No shame in that, eh? Your Mum must be proud. You became a schoolteacher and your sister a doctor. What about a partner? Was Dr. Clark involved with someone?*"

"*Di had all sorts of boyfriends but they never lasted like my Roy.*"

"*Your husband, eh?*"

"*All she had was a cat. Panther. Who will look after Panther?*" Rosie's voice faltered. "*I suppose I could. She went on about Paul, her new office manager. I never met him. He might be the reason she planned this trip. But Paul canceled too late for a refund, and she asked me to come instead. Roy said to take advantage of a free trip with all the trimmings, even though he knows we're oil and water.*"

Alexa heard Sergeant Kramer chuckle.

"*We were at a pub in Queenstown the night before we started. Steamer's Wharf by the lake. When I left she was chatting up some bloke twenty years her junior. He had his hands all over her. Sad, really.*"

Bruce paused the tape. "Something to follow up."

Alexa nodded. "There was a slip of paper in Diana's pants pocket, with a name and number. Maybe it's from this guy. I couldn't make it out. It's at the lab."

They listened to the rest of the interview. Sergeant Kramer told Rosie one of his colleagues had overheard an argument she'd had with Diana on the riverbank. Alexa realized he was talking about her and Charlie the first day of the hike.

"'*We argued all the time. It's the only way we know.*"

"*What did you mean that she was free with her prescription pad?*"

"*She was. When Roy hurt his back, Diana called him in some meds. Same with Mum. Anything she wanted.*"

Alexa heard Rosie hiccup.

"Di wanted to be admired. To be loved. She showed it with her prescription pad."

When the interview ended, Bruce stayed quiet, twiddling his thumbs, and finally cleared his throat. "I hope Sammie and Denise get along better than that."

Those were Bruce's teen daughters. The thought of them terrified Alexa.

"How do you and Charlie get along?"

His question surprised her. She tried to be honest. "I think now—since this trip—we're starting to get along. Even understand each other. He's a nice guy." She almost told Bruce about Mel, but held back. "Do you have siblings?"

There was an ocean of information she didn't know about Bruce.

"Two. I'm the youngest." He colored as if this embarrassed him. "William is a barrister in Wellie, and Tracy is an intermediate school principal in Hamilton. Rosie most likely resented her sister's success. This could be a sororicide case, though I'm not inclined to think so. That last part of the interview showed compassion."

Compassion can be faked, Alexa thought. She stood. "Where's that crime kit you brought? I have a date with an apple."

Bruce laughed. "It's in my room."

"Lead the way."

Bruce put the tape recorder in his briefcase, snapped it shut, and appeared to be on a mission striding through the lobby. She imagined he had a "don't bother me" look on his face as she hustled to keep up. He turned down her wing of the lodge and stopped next door to Tauhou. Now she laughed. Bruce's eyebrow went up.

"That's mine." She pointed. "I was just thinking we were next door to each other on the Stewart Island case, too," she said. "Remember the Island Inn?" She'd hoped to hear a come-hither knock on the adjoining wall in the middle of the night. "You probably didn't notice."

He stepped aside so she could enter. She checked to see that the hall was clear and stepped in. Bruce followed quickly, shut the door, and tossed his briefcase on the bed. She turned to him; his smile jackknifed straight to her heart.

"I noticed."

Alexa held on to a lot of things—scientific facts, old griefs, curses, love for Charlie—but when Bruce took her face in his warm hands and kissed her, she let them tumble away, let sensation and desire and need fill the void. Bruce angled her against the door, which was good because her knees wobbled. The texture of his lips, the probing of his tongue, his stubble against her cheek, carried her away.

Footsteps in the hallway jolted her. She pulled away. "We shouldn't."

Bruce's irises were sapphire in the dimness. His pupils had expanded, searching for light. He took an escaped lock of her hair between his fingers and tucked it behind her ear, melting her reserve. "I know," he said, and bent forward.

Alexa met him halfway, eager for more, giving more.

A knock made them both jump back. Alexa sidestepped Bruce, tripped on his leg, regained her balance, and dashed to the bathroom. She hid behind the door, heart racing, embarrassed at being forced to act like a busted teenager. This was absurd. She heard Bruce open the door, and heard Sergeant Kramer's voice.

"Urgent phone call for you, Senior."

"Right."

She heard the door shut and held her breath. After ten seconds, she cracked the bathroom door; the room was empty. She looked at herself in the mirror, startled that her eyes were luminous, her pupils dilated. Her knee-jerk reaction was to be angry at Bruce for this ridiculous predicament, but she was as much to blame, mixing their tenuous professional relationship with personal feelings. *That* was a danger zone. On the sink ledge was a leather bath kit and a roll-on Black Spruce natural deodorant. She uncapped the deodorant and rubbed some on her wrist. A whiff of outdoors. Woods and holidays. Bruce. She wanted a relationship with him outside the confines of a work zone. She left the bathroom and brightened when she saw the full crime kit on the dresser. Her mini-kit supplies were almost depleted. She hefted it up—hoped no one was coming down the hall—and left.

Chapter Thirty-Six

She opened the door to Tauhau and wondered if Charlie had heard what went on next door. He was stretched on his bed, reading a New Zealand bird guide and scratching his almost-beard. "Where did you go?"

"Bruce asked me to listen in while he interviewed Cassandra."

"So he's the guy you have the hots for?"

"No," she lied and set the new kit down. It was heavy. "Yes, I guess. But not during a case." Ha. She looked at the hot chocolate mug that she had protected with an evidence bag. "I've got some work to do."

As Charlie watched, she took a sample of the cocoa slurry from the bottom of the mug and inserted it into her last evidence tube. Then she dusted the mug for latent prints, the familiar feel of the brush in her hand lowering her heart rate, swirling Bruce out of her head. If Stead's prints were on the mug, she didn't have a comparison. *Damn him for exercising his rights.*

"Don't you need a sterile environment?"

She laughed. "Since when are crime scenes sterile? I'll need your prints now, to compare."

"They'll be all over the mug, right?" He held out his hand. The torn flesh on his palms from monkeying across the cable reminded her of everything he'd been through. "You must wish you had never come." She pressed his thumb into the ink. "When you were under the influence of those pills, you kept telling me to call 911."

"I did?"

She pressed his pointer finger onto the ink and rolled it on the backing card. "You said you learned to dial 911 in Cub Scouts."

Charlie jerked his hand away. "Don't you remember?"

Alexa didn't know what he was talking about.

"When you had the accident, Mom yelled for me to call an ambulance. She was trying to get your shirt off while you thrashed on the floor. I ran upstairs to the phone, but I couldn't do it."

Her scars tightened.

His eyes teared. "I forgot the numbers, Lexi. They just disappeared from my head. I'm sorry."

"I don't get what you're saying. Besides, you were a little kid."

"I was nine. Old enough to remember three damn numbers. Ben and Noah do. I test them all the time."

Alexa shook her head.

"I had to go tell Mom, Rita. You were screaming, and she couldn't hear me. The phone in the kitchen was broken, remember? She finally ran upstairs to call."

The boiled water worked its way through her epidermis, dermis, and into the subcutis. By the time the ambulance had arrived, she had gone into shock.

Charlie looked like a trapped animal. "You should hate me, not Rita."

She was spinning in space. She took a deep breath, felt something shift, felt her scars relax. All these years she had thought Rita deliberately delayed getting help. "It's okay. You were a kid. A few minutes didn't matter."

But the doctor had said they did. That every minute had counted.

Her hands shook as she finished taking Charlie's finger-prints, using supplies from her mini-kit. When she was done, he stared at his black fingertips. "Next time you visit, bring your print supplies. The boys will love it."

"I will. Visit, I mean. And bring my kit." She labeled Charlie's prints and tucked them, and his 911 confession, away. "Wash your hands. I'll be back with the apple you found."

There was a scientist in Scotland—Dennis Something—she had a professional crush on, not that they had ever met. One of his *Science & Justice* articles had taught her the process of lifting fingerprints from bird feathers. He had also published an article on a method for recovering fingerprints from fruit. She racked her brain for the facts as she entered the kitchen.

The chef painted horror on his face. "Now what have you brought?"

"Nothing. I need the apple." She was nervous that the apple had not been under lock and key, but the tamper-evident seal was intact on the bag, so that calmed her. "Thanks," she told Chef.

The Scottish scientist's procedure was a modification of an existing technique used for lifting prints from the sticky side of tape, even though tape glue and apple surfaces are totally different.

The magic of science, Alexa reminded herself. *What's not to love?*

It wasn't unusual for criminals to leave food at crime scenes: in her career she had bagged pizza crusts, a half-eaten Wendy's burger, a partial Lindt chocolate bar—though why someone would only eat part of the chocolate had always puzzled her. The apple Charlie found could prove who had been in the woods. Alexa smiled. Then she reminded herself of the evil prowling the edges of the lodge.

She hurried through the lobby, alert for Bruce's voice, anxious to find out what supplies the new kit held. What was it Dennis

Somebody used to lift the fingerprints from fruit peel? Powder suspension—a thick gooey substance—and a soft brush. That was it. Dip, paint, wait ten seconds, wash off. Voilà: a print is left behind on the peel. The trick was to dilute the powder suspension to the right consistency.

Back in their room, Charlie had gone back to reading his bird book. Alexa set down the bag and rummaged through the kit like a kid tearing wrapping paper until she found the prints pouch. She unzipped it. Standard black powder, magnetic black powder, magnetic white powder, fiber brush, magnetic applicator. Lifting tape. Backing cards. That was it: a bare-bones collection. No powder suspension.

She considered making her own using powder and liquid soap, but decided on Plan B: DNA. She broke the seal, jotted this down on the log, and peeked at the lunchbox-sized pink-red speckled fruit.

Charlie put down his book. "Now what are you doing?"

"I'm going to swab the apple." She had doubts; DNA left on food was vulnerable. Bacteria and fungus party hardy. *The sooner the sample is taken the better.* She hoped the cool weather and refrigeration had preserved the deoxyribonucleic acid and kept the marauding pathogens at bay.

She readied the supplies, slipped on gloves, and took the apple out of the bag, setting it on a backing card on the dresser. Then she removed a swab from its wrapper and wet it with a single drop of distilled water, proud of her steady hands.

Charlie swung his feet around, sat up, and watched like she was performing a magic trick.

The DNA would be at the bite-mark. She rubbed the swab where the central incisors pierced the peel. She rotated the swab one time only to ensure the entire tip made contact with the sample. Then she held the swab up, allowing it to air dry.

"That's it?" Charlie asked.

She frowned. Didn't Charlie realize DNA had changed the

world of forensics forever? She inserted the swab into the transport tube and labeled it. Then she studied the apple.

The oxidation process had progressed. The flesh had browned. She needed to take good-quality photographs before there was more decay. Her cell phone wouldn't do. "Go find Clint and ask if I can borrow his camera," Alexa told Charlie.

While Charlie was gone, Alexa considered how she ate an apple. She liked twisting off the stem. When she was young, she'd recite the alphabet while twisting. When the stem broke off, the letter she was on would be the first letter of her future husband's name. *The mindless rituals of youth,* she mused. Then she'd hold the apple in the top and bottom indentations, and take a random midrange bite through the peel. This virgin bite led to the next, as she rotated the apple. She avoided biting deep enough to reveal the seeds.

The owner of this apple had ignored the stem and had a top-down approach. The bites were so deep that little seeds were visible. Almost like the biter had attacked the apple.

Examining the bite-mark pattern on the apple was the best part.

She retrieved her magnifying glass, ruler, and dental probe. The beauty of bite-marks on food was that they offered width, breadth, *and* depth impressions. She longed for her Auckland lab with workstations, microscopes, and fume hoods. If she were there, she'd fill her plastic gun with silicone and inject it into the deepest bite-mark. Then she would take that impression and place it in die stone to obtain a positive replica of the bite.

Of course, to prove anything, she'd have to have the suspect's dental impression to compare it with.

She sighed and maneuvered the apple to the bite with the cleanest edge, propped it against the fingerprint pouch to keep it stable, and got to work. She measured the curve of the biting edges, the distance between canines and distance between incisors. She had taken half a page of notes when Charlie returned with the camera.

"It belongs to Luxe Tours. Clint said it's fully charged."

She placed the ruler next to the apple for scale and took photos from several angles. Then she placed the apple in a clear plastic bag instead of paper, labeled and sealed it, and recorded it on her log.

She removed her gloves and reviewed the photos on the screen. When she tapped one photo to enlarge it, scrape marks left by the teeth were clear. A ridge between the teeth was visible. The photo was evidence of a diastema. The apple-biter had a gap between the upper front teeth. That excited her. Someone she'd seen had a gap, but she couldn't remember who.

Chapter Thirty-Seven

Alexa was suspicious of people who smiled with their mouths closed. They were hiding something: an overbite, crowding, a missing tooth. Shyness. Insecurity.

Or a secret.

To test her theory, she and Charlie entered the lounge, and she smiled brightly at the Israeli father and son playing cards. Charlie had befriended them and told her that the son, Eitan, was about to turn eighteen, and that this was his farewell trip before his mandatory military service. Eitan returned the smile. A brief flash of white so quick that Alexa couldn't check for a gap. Not that he was a suspect, anyway.

Charlie introduced Alexa.

"I em heppy to mit you," Eitan said. "Want to play?" He held his hand so Alexa could see three jacks, a run of spades, and some mismatches. She wanted to tell him to hold his cards close.

Charlie looked at Alexa. "Go ahead," she said. "I'll find you later."

Clint's camera hung off her shoulder; she wasn't going to let it out of her sight. In the dining room, Sergeant Kramer was on the phone and Constable Bartlett was ushering Rosie out of the room. The other two constables were missing.

Bruce stood with two men in bright rain slickers—one

orange, the other yellow—and muddy boots. He motioned her over. She met his eyes, trying to convey a professional demeanor, ignoring, mostly, the butterflies in her stomach.

He introduced her. "Ms. Glock is our forensic investigator." The men nodded. "Mr. Ferguson is a construction manager with DOC and Mr. Maunga is a structural engineer. They've checked out the swing bridge. It was Ms. Glock's brother who was flipped off the bridge."

"Crikey," Mr. Ferguson said.

Mr. Maunga, who had dark hair and eyes, said, "It was cable failure. We are extremely concerned, and it's a huge relief your brother wasn't harmed."

"Is there any sign of human tampering?"

He looked at her curiously. "No sign."

She could let go of her sabotage theory. "What caused the cable to fail?"

Mr. Maunga rubbed his hands together as if he were warming them up. "The big rainstorm a couple weeks ago. Fifty millimeters in one day, eh, and then some. It undermined the rock bolt and upset the bridge's stability. As a precaution, we're closing the entire track so all bridges can be rechecked. There are three more between here and Sandfly Point."

Sandfly Point was the terminus of the Milford Track. Funny to think two days ago she had believed the biggest danger on the Milford Track was sandfly bites.

Mr. Ferguson jumped in. "Repairs to the Pompolona Creek bridge should take three or four days. Probably the same amount of time it will take to clear the track from the slip anyway. Current guests, here and at Dumpling Hut, will need to be evacuated."

"No evacuations until I say so," Bruce said firmly. "Mr. Ferguson has offered me a lift to Dumpling Hut." He looked at his watch. "Mr. Willis would still be a couple hours from arriving."

Alexa hadn't realized Mr. Ferguson was a helicopter pilot. She conveyed her suspicion to Bruce by widening her eyes.

Bruce got the message. "These gentlemen flew in from Dunedin."

"We should be ready to go in two hours," Mr. Ferguson told Bruce. He and Mr. Maunga walked toward the door.

Bruce ushered Alexa to a corner and lowered his voice. "Sorry I had to rush off."

She blushed. "Me too."

"I'm putting you on the back burner only until we get home." She could feel the heat.

"Constable Cooper called from Auckland with a list of Dr. Clark's recent patients." His voice returned to loud and clear. "Sergeant Kramer is speaking with DOC, comparing the patient list with registered trampers. He'll do the same with lodge guests."

"Where are the other constables?"

"Constable Chadwick is fetching Dr. Salvú for a second interview. Your time line differs from a statement Dr. Salvú made in an earlier interview."

She nodded.

"Hank flew Senior Constable McCain to the aerodrome in Milford."

Hank was the pilot who flew her to see the bones—or rather the rock pile now covering them.

"McCain will round up the helicopter pilots who have flown in the area since Sunday. We've got the latest list with names to match registration numbers."

"Can I see it? I might recognize the name of the pilot Ranger Harker admonished about flying in the danger zone."

Bruce walked to the head of the table and pointed to two side-by-side sheets. One was a printout of helicopter identifiers—the sheet she'd seen before—and the other had a list of names, dates, times, and registration numbers scrawled in Bruce's handwriting. "The registration digits are the link. They're on both lists."

She took the list with names and started at the top. Her eyes stopped three names down. "Damien Riggs. Damien is what the ranger called the pilot." The scene came back clearly and her breath hitched. "There were bulk bags lined up around the helicopter pad."

"Do the times match when you saw him?"

Alexa checked. "Yes."

Bruce looked at the other list. "The registration number is for a Southland Helicopter. A DOC copter."

"Yellow, right?"

Bruce nodded. "I'll get McCain to check Riggs's records and find out if there's a connection between him and Stead Willis. If they're involved in greenstone thievery, maybe Stead is the hunter and Riggs the gatherer, using a chopper."

Alexa noticed something. "Riggs's name is on the list twice. Here, at the bottom."

Bruce squinted at his writing like he needed reading glasses. "He must moonlight for Queenstown Limited. They're for-hire copters. Like a taxi. It's dated today. Must have lifted off before we halted local traffic."

Alexa flashed to the man in the red jumpsuit who flew in Sergeant Kramer and Constable Bartlett at the crack of dawn.

Red equals danger.

Vince had invited Riggs for breakfast. Maybe the same man who tried to kill her yesterday enjoyed sunny-sides-up today. "I saw him this morning. He brought in Sergeant Kramer and Constable Bartlett and then transported Dr. Clark's body to the morgue."

They stared at each other, trying to absorb what Riggs's name twice on the list meant. Constable Chadwick broke their stare fest. "Dr. Salvú for you, Senior."

Bruce nodded at the anesthesiologist. "I need to make a

phone call. Ms. Glock, will you escort Dr. Salvú to the interview room?"

Larry walked beside Alexa. "What's this about? I already gave an interview. I told you I didn't have any sedatives."

Charlie was still playing cards. He and the Israeli father sipped from cans of beer. She hadn't had time to process his story about botching the 911 call. She ignored Larry's entreaties. Vince and Kathy's private quarters were locked. "Wait here," she told Larry.

Vince, harried and rumpled, was across the hall in his office. "I need to get into the other room," she said. "But I have a question."

"Yes?"

"Do you know that helicopter pilot who dropped off Sergeant Kramer and Constable Bartlett this morning?"

"Know him? I've seen him before. He makes occasional deliveries. I always feed the pilots."

"Do you know his name?"

"No, but we keep a log of all copters that land on our pad. I had him sign it." He took a clipboard off a hook and handed it to Alexa.

Damien Riggs had signed his name, proof he had been at the lodge. She fumbled with Clint's camera and took a photo of the signature. "I'll need to keep this."

Across the hall she ignored Larry as he harped. She was having trouble keeping the cases separated. Black Diamond and Bone Track. Dr. Diana Clark and John Doe. Bruce walked into the room.

"Thank you for your patience, Dr. Salvú . Have a seat."

Alexa decided to wait until after the interview to show the log. She sat at the dinette; Larry sat in the middle of the sofa. "What's up?" he asked. "I've already answered questions."

Bruce ignored him and fiddled with his phone, played a section aloud, rewound, pressed stop. He looked down at Larry, who shied back into the cushion, and set the phone on the coffee table. "Have a listen to our earlier conversation." He pressed play and the recording started mid-sentence.

"...*group of us eating our sammies out of the rain.*"

Alexa identified Larry's voice.

"*When did you last see Dr. Clark?*"

That was Bruce.

"*She left the shelter before me. That was the last time I saw her.*"

Bruce stopped the tape and studied Larry. "Let's go over yesterday's events again, shall we?" He sat on the recliner. "What time did you arrive at Prairie Shelter?"

"I already told you everything."

"Please do so again."

"I'm not sure I checked my watch. It was around one. There was a group of us. You could ask the others. Ask Clint, our guide."

"Yes, I have," Bruce said. "Who were you with?"

"It's all on the tape."

Bruce waited patiently.

Larry swiped at his bangs. "I shared a bench with Diana and Cassandra. Rosie came up, but there wasn't room. She sat across from us."

Alexa imagined they could have made room. She studied Larry's teeth—a flash here, a grimace there. He did not have a gap.

Bruce stayed quiet.

"We ate lunch, that's what. Do you want to know what we had in our sacks?"

"In what order did people leave the shelter?" Bruce asked in monotone.

"Diana left first. Took off like the rest of us were sloths." His jaw thrust forward. "I don't remember who left next. I wasn't paying attention."

Bruce fiddled with his phone again. "Listen. This is Ms. Perry. I asked her when she last saw Dr. Clark alive."

"*Yesterday. At lunch. She left before I finished. Diana liked to be first.*"

"*And this was what time?*" Bruce asked.

"*Around one o'clock. Clint would know. He was there. Diana and Larry left together.*"

Bruce turned his phone off.

Larry swiped his hair again. "You think I pushed Diana off that cliff?"

"That's rather jumping to conclusions," Bruce said. "Tell us what happened."

Larry's forehead had a sheen of sweat. "I did not kill Diana."

Kathy and Vince's quarters were earth-toned, the sofa and recliner forest green, the floor burnished wood, the drapes mossy. Like the outdoors, Alexa realized, as she waited for Larry to spill.

"Okay, if that's what you want. I tramped off with Diana."

Bruce pressed the record button. "Please repeat what you just said."

"I left the shelter with Diana. We had to scamper away so Rosie didn't catch up. She's so needy, and Diana wanted privacy. I knew that would make me a suspect. I had to protect my reputation."

Lying never protected anyone's reputation, Alexa wanted to say.

"Diana was driven. I don't know why. She had issues. She said in order for Quay Park to make a profit, to stay afloat financially, we had to increase our number of patients." His wiry arms pressed against his kneecaps as if he might spring up.

"Was the practice in financial difficulty?" Bruce asked.

"No. I think it was Diana who had trouble. Lousy investments. Plus she had the fancy house and car, and the premium rent on our office. Then she takes us on this trip." He shook his head.

Bruce jotted in his notebook.

"She harped that we had to bring in more patients. She became unreasonable."

"Go on," Bruce said.

"She would rather bring in new patients, get the ball rolling again, before we provided follow-up care for existing patients. Send them home with prescriptions and say ta-ta. She wanted to start Saturday clinics. I said no." He sniggered. "She didn't like hearing no. She stomped off like a spoiled child." He studied his knees. "But I didn't wish her harm."

"So you never caught up with her or passed her?"

"No."

"After Dr. Clark left the shelter, did you see any other trampers? Luxers or independents?"

"No."

"What about when you crossed that swing bridge? Did you look around? See anyone?"

"That bridge scared the daylights out of me. I wasn't about to stand there and look around. Besides, it was raining hard."

"Did you know Dr. Clark received a warning from the medical tribunal for overprescribing medication?"

Larry scoffed. "One complaint. Not even the patient. The patient's angry mum."

"Was Dr. Clark overprescribing medication?" Bruce asked plainly.

Larry avoided Bruce's eyes. "I can't speak to her prescribing habits."

There was a knock at the door.

"A minute, please." Bruce stood, gave the date and time, and stopped recording. "Making a false statement to the police is an offense. Don't make it a habit."

Sergeant Kramer popped in as soon as Larry left and thrust papers at Bruce. "This not having internet is hard on my hands. I had to write everything with a pen."

"What am I holding?"

"Your lass in Auckland called with the doctor's most recent bank statements." He wrung his fingers. "Here today, gone tomorrow—just like my wife says, Senior."

Alexa laughed and walked over next to Bruce.

"What about her phone records?"

"Nothing in yet, sir."

Bruce read aloud from the papers. "Diana Clark. Primary checking, 03 January to 03 February, beginning balance: $18,234.48, ending balance: $623.11. You're right, Sergeant. Money in, money out. Let's see. Debts include automatic payment of $6,550 for mortgage,: $3,200 for Mercedes, gas/electric at $287.75. What's this? Can't read your writing."

Sergeant Kramer squinted. "Fitness club, sir."

Bruce continued. "Lots of EFTPOS transactions. Restaurants, hair salon, Remedy Coffee."

Alexa knew EFTPOS was the New Zealand debit card.

"Luxe Tours nearly sank her. Balance due was $5,767.12. And here's $1,589.44 for Air New Zealand. Four flights from Auckland to Queenstown."

Diana had lived large, spent hard, Alexa thought.

"I don't see anything about the student loans Dr. Salvú mentioned," Bruce said.

"You wouldn't," Sergeant Kramer said. "Student loans are deducted straight from base pay. Look what she had coming in."

Alexa leaned over Bruce's shoulder to see. The scent of spruce was distracting.

"Credit: $4,000 from Lunar Pharmaceutical. Odd," Bruce said. "Why not deposit this in the business account? I'll need to speak to Ms. Perry again and see if she can explain. Did you receive anything about her business finances?"

"According to your Constable Cooper, Dr. Clark's office manager, Paul Worthy, says we need a warrant or death certificate. But your lass found out a little more."

Bruce's forehead crinkled as he waited for the sergeant to continue.

"Mr. Worthy backed out of the group jolly because he didn't feel comfortable around Dr. Clark." He cleared his throat. "Mr.

Worthy alleges that the doctor made sexual advances. Said he was looking for another position."

Bruce looked surprised. "Had he filed a complaint?"

If Mr. Worthy was telling the truth, Alexa knew Diana's behavior was unlawful and unethical.

"No complaint. Mr. Worthy said he wanted to handle it himself." Sergeant Kramer cleared his throat again. "There's another sheet. The doctor's investment statement."

Alexa and Bruce studied the second handwritten sheet as Kramer went to fetch Cassandra Perry. Dr. Clark's beginning portfolio balance was $7,114.92 and the ending balance was $6,768.14. "Makes my portfolio glisten," Bruce said. "Whatever she was investing in wasn't returning. Cash flow was an issue for Dr. Clark. She wasn't in arrears, but she would have been without that infusion from Lunar." He looked grave. "Money appeared to be her master, not her servant. And she acted unprofessionally to a subordinate. How does this information help us find who killed her?"

Alexa hoped this was a rhetorical question. She was just here to support the team with science. "I have two things to offer."

Bruce raised an eyebrow.

"Remember I told you I lifted fingerprints from the hiking pole found near Dr. Clark's body? A few prints on the pole don't match hers." He waited.

"If Dr. Clark set her backpack and poles down, and went to take a photograph of the waterfall, someone could have snatched her poles and used them to push her off the cliff."

"That's speculation."

"I know."

"And how is it that no one saw her body on the riverbank? Your whole list of Luxers from the shelter crossed that bridge after Dr. Clark did."

"I did, too." Her mouth dried thinking about it. "All I can say is that it was, well, terrifying. No way I was going to stop in the middle and look down. That...that creek was raging. The rain made it hard to see anyway."

Bruce studied her.

She took a step back. "The lab will have to confirm whether the tip of the pole matches a wound in Dr. Clark's back. But let's say it does. I need to keep taking fingerprints, including the guests.'"

"Agreed. What about the independent hikers?"

"Them, too. The second thing. I examined the apple found at the crime scene. The apple-biter has a space between his or her upper front teeth."

"But you don't know whose apple it is, right?" He didn't wait for an answer. "I'd like you to come with me to the independent hut. Take fingerprints there, too."

She nodded and showed Bruce the clipboard. "Damien Riggs signed this at 7:01 this morning. It's a link to Bone Track."

Cassandra's indignant voice came from the hallway.

"This morning when that helicopter pilot Riggs came into the lodge—before he signed the log—he made a beeline to the coffee station. I thought he was excited about caffeine, but guess who was already there?"

"Enlighten me."

"Stead Willis."

"Ships passing in the morning light," Bruce said.

When Alexa returned to the interview room with the crime kit, she could tell Cassandra Perry was not happy to be back in the hot seat. Her shapely nose flared. "It's probably a simple accounting mistake. Diana meant to deposit it into her business account."

"It's a large sum of money," Bruce said, adjusting his phone's recorder. "Shouldn't the doctor be paying Lunar for pharmaceuticals, and not Lunar paying the doctor?"

Cassandra flipped her hair off her shoulder and didn't answer.

Alexa took out the fingerprinting supplies.

"What's she doing?" Cassandra asked.

"Answer the question, please," Bruce answered.

"Honoraria are common." She had fixed her lipstick, and her central incisor was no longer blotched. "We rewarded Diana for speaking and consulting engagements. It's common practice in our industry to use the smartest doctors as educators."

"What did she speak about?"

"She's a recognized authority on knee and hip pain-management."

"Using drugs?"

Cassandra rubbed her right kneecap. "In conjunction with surgery, yes."

"To whom does she speak?"

"Mostly to other doctors."

"Surely there's a correlation between honorarium checks and an increase in sales of your biggest sellers?" Bruce checked his notes.

"Opioids are an important part of managing pain. When prescribed in moderation."

Alexa removed her ink pad and a clean backing card.

"From what you observed, what was Dr. Clark's relationship with her staff?" Bruce asked.

"Fine. I don't know. She's treating them to this trip."

"What about with her new office manager, Mr. Paul Worthy?"

"She adored him. She went on and on about how smart he was."

"Evacuations will begin first thing in the morning," Bruce said, stopping the recording and standing. "Ms. Glock needs to take your fingerprints now."

Chapter Thirty-Eight

Alexa set up a station in the lounge and fingerprinted the remaining guests—all of whom cooperated with curiosity. The teenaged Israeli boy rubbed his eye before washing the ink off his hands and looked like he had a shiner. The problem was that the prints she extracted from the hiking pole were at the lab. She had nothing to compare with this new batch.

She cleaned up and walked into the dining room. All the police officers were accounted for except Senior Constable McCain, who was at the Milford Airport.

There was a blank page on the easel. The previous page was taped to the wall.

Sergeant Kramer waved her over, but with prints on her mind, she held up a finger and headed to the satellite phone so she could call the lab in Christchurch. She wanted to know if the scant collection of evidence had arrived. Bruce would want updates.

Someone picked up after one ring. "South Island Forensic Service Center. How may I direct your call?"

Alexa turned her back, identified herself, and gave her Forensic Service ID number and the case number. "I am working a homicide in the Milford Track area. Can you see if the initial shipment of evidence has arrived?" Murder cases take priority; if it had arrived, the crime scene investigators would set aside less urgent work and jump on it.

"It has. I'll connect you with CSI Pippa Day."

When Day picked up, Alexa introduced herself again and inquired about the evidence.

"I was taking a look-see," Day said. "Let me go through it with you."

Alexa glanced out the window. Mount Elliot was draped in fog.

"These prints were lifted from this trekking pole?" Day asked.

"Yes."

"What do you need?"

"Run the prints through the database and see if there are any matches." She doubted there would be. None of the main suspects had criminal records. "Photograph the tip of the pole and compare it with a photograph of the wounds on the deceased's back. See if they match."

"Are you sending photographs of the wound?"

"I would if I could. There's no internet." *And all my photos were stolen.* "Call the morgue in Queenstown and get them to send you pictures. It's really important."

"I'll jump on it."

"There's trace I extracted from the wound—maybe organic—and a belt buckle, too." Alexa could hear rummaging.

"No belt."

"Belt *buckle*. Maybe Māori. There are squiggly things on it—like eels."

"It's not here," Day insisted.

"Find out who has it. Send the DNA off." She thought of the additional DNA sample she had taken from the apple bite and wished she could teleport it to Christchurch. "There was a note with the body. Can you see what the status is?"

"I've already sent it to John Weiner. He's our forgery and handwriting examiner. I'm putting you on hold."

As she waited, Alexa twirled around and waved Sergeant Kramer over. "What's up?"

"I found some information about your fellow."

For a horrible second she thought the sergeant was talking about Bruce.

"Mr. Willis is married and has a couple wee ones. He's not who he says he is."

Alexa's stomach clenched. She was about to ask for details when a voice came on the line. She put a finger up and turned her back.

"This is John Weiner. I have your paper specimen here. Been taking a look."

Alexa's heart skipped a beat as she thought of the note she'd extracted from the doctor's pants pocket. "Can you make out the name and number?"

"Dampness obliterated some of it, eh? But I've retrieved the text using EDD."

"EDD?"

"Electrostatic Detection Device. Applied charges and toner against the indentations…"

"Yes. Good." She'd research EDD later. "I have a meeting. What did you make out?"

She could hear her brusqueness disappointed him. "The letters are D-E-A-N, space, J-A-C-O-B-I, and the number is 03-428-3299."

Alexa made Weiner repeat as she wrote it down. "You're genius. Thank you. I'll be in touch." She hung up, slipped into a chair, and turned her attention to Bruce.

He stood by the easel, a pillar of order, ready with marker and blank page. "We'll start our initial reports on Bone Track—the skeleton by the river. Sergeant Kramer, what do you have?"

Sergeant Kramer checked his notes and stood. "Our man Constable Sprunt in Te Anau has been busy. He found out about this independent tramper Stead Willis, the bloke who refused to be fingerprinted."

Bruce nodded.

"In our interview, Willis said he wasn't married—well, to be clear, he said he didn't have a missus—but turns out he does have a wife—Sue Willis—and two children."

Bruce wrote STEAD WILLIS in bold black letters. He added a bullet point and wrote "wife/kids."

"He works for Anders Helicopters in Greymouth, but not as a pi-zo engineer. He's a mechanic."

He inflated his resume, Alexa realized.

Bruce added this information to the page. "What about his search-and-rescue claim?"

"Half-truth. He's not president of Greymouth SAR, but he volunteers with them."

"Anything else?"

"His wife says he's staying at his bach on the Grey River."

Bruce's blue eyes skipped from person to person. "How does this information help?"

"He lies and has connections with helicopter pilots," Sergeant Kramer said.

Constable Chadwick popped up from her seat. "I have an update. Senior Constable McCain spoke to William Little, a DOC pilot who flew over Milford Track yesterday to assess the landslide. Little confirms he gave Mr. Willis a lift from Clinton Hut to Mintaro Hut. They flew over the slide, natch—and..." she checked her notebook, "this was at three fifteen p.m."

Bruce slapped the marker against his palm. "Ms. Glock has established that Mr. Willis crossed paths with another pilot— Damien Riggs—while he was here this morning." He wrote RIGGS on the paper and pointed to Sergeant Kramer and Constable Bartlett. "Riggs flew you in this morning, gentlemen, and then flew Dr. Clark to Queenstown."

"Blimey. Didn't know he was a suspect," Constable Bartlett said. "I talked with him, even. He wants to buy his own bird and start his own company—fly tourists to glaciers and volcanoes, yeah? Like Over the Top Helicopters."

"Raising capital might be his motive for dealing in *pounamu*," Bruce said. "He was in the park Sunday morning, witnessed by the Clinton Hut ranger Beckett Harker. Ms. Glock saw him, too. Ranger Harker said Riggs is being investigated by DOC for landing in an avalanche zone."

"Why is he still flying, sir?" Constable Chadwick asked.

"Find out. Riggs could have attacked Ms. Glock with the bulk bag and dumped rock on the skeleton after she left. He is a person of interest." He underlined Riggs's name for emphasis. "What's the status on the Ngai Tahu chairperson?"

"Nothing yet, Senior," Constable Chadwick said.

Bruce looked frustrated. "There's only so much we can do at Pompolona. The engineers who are checking bridges will be returning soon. They will give me and Constable Chadwick a lift to Dumpling Hut, where we'll speak with Mr. Willis about Bone Track, and the trampers about Black Diamond. Ms. Glock will accompany us so that she can continue to take fingerprints."

"What is the point of that, sir?" Sergeant Kramer asked.

Alexa spoke up. "The hiking pole I found near Dr. Clark's body may be the murder weapon. It has Dr. Clark's fingerprints on it, of course, but also some other prints that might match the killer's."

"Why wouldn't the perp use his own poles?"

"Not everyone has poles, or if they do—sometimes they're clipped to the pack, and hard to get to," she said. "I just got off the phone with the lab. They'll compare the hiking pole with the wounds in Diana's back. We should know soon if they match."

"We're making progress," Bruce said. "Anything else?"

"The handwriting expert was able to decipher the note found in Dr. Clark's pocket." She repeated the name and number.

"The note was found during your examination of the body, right?" Bruce asked.

"Yes. In Dr. Clark's pants pocket."

"Have you called?"

"Not yet."

"I'll ring him now, Senior," Sergeant Kramer offered.

Bruce nodded his okay. The team went quiet as Kramer dialed. Alexa checked her watch and was startled to find it was after five. The day was waning. Would she and Bruce and Constable Chadwick spend the night at Dumpling Hut? What about Charlie? She felt a jolt of panic at leaving Charlie, then forced herself to focus.

"Hello? This is Sergeant Adrian Kramer of Te Anau PD. Is this Mr. Dean Jacobi?"

Silence. Then the sergeant gave a thumbs-up. "I am working an investigation involving a deceased person, and your name and number were found in her pocket. May I have your address please?"

A panicky voice emanated from the phone.

"No sir, no sir. The woman's name is Dr. Diana Clark. Your address and occupation?"

The sergeant covered the mouthpiece and whispered, "Queenstown, graduate student." He took some notes. "Dr. Clark had an accident. Can you explain why your name and number were found in her pocket?"

Sergeant Kramer listened some more. "In her forties. Blond hair. From Auckland." He listened, scratched his neck. "Steamer Wharf Pub? What time?" The sergeant took a few notes, thanked Mr. Jacobi, and hung up. He scribbled another line in his notebook. "Sounds like a pub hookup, Senior."

"Dr. Clark's sister said something about a Queenstown pub the night before they left for Milford Track, remember?" Bruce asked.

"Yes," Sergeant Kramer said. "Mrs. Jones mentioned a young

bloke and Dr. Clark getting frisky. Our victim might have been a cougar."

Alexa's hackles stood. "There's nothing wrong with a successful woman seeing whomever she wants," she snapped. "Let's not demean the victim." *Making unwanted sexual advances toward her employee was another matter.*

Bruce looked surprised. "Right. Have you heard anything from the autopsy?"

"I haven't checked. Do you know who is standing in?" It was customary to have a law officer—usually a higher-up—attend the autopsy.

Bruce opened his notebook. "Tell the team about your date with the apple while I look."

Alexa blushed, thinking of her "date" with Bruce. "My brother found an apple at the scene. I examined it. If the apple belongs to Dr. Clark's killer, we're looking for someone with a slight gap between their top teeth."

Constable Bartlett bared his teeth to Constable Chadwick, who rolled her eyes.

Bruce gave her the name and number of a Queenstown police officer attending the postmortem. "Let's review our suspect list. Dr. Salvú admits he lied. He left with Dr. Clark after lunch like several witnesses reported, therefore he is the last known person to see her alive. They argued and the doctor hiked off."

"What did they argue about?" Constable Chadwick asked.

"Whether to expand the practice. Dr. Clark wanted to bring in more patients without hiring another physician. She was a hard driver. Dr. Salvú was against it, although I don't see this as a motive for murder. She was his bread and butter. Let's move to Cassandra Perry, the drug rep," Bruce said. "There's a large deposit from Lunar Pharmaceuticals in Dr. Clark's personal checking account that I don't like."

"Was Dr. Clark blackmailing Perry?" Constable Chadwick said.

"Over what?" Bruce countered.

"Drug related?" she offered. "Perry paying Dr. Clark to be quiet about her pill mill?"

"Call Constable Cooper in Auckland, and get her to dive deeper into Lunar Pharmaceuticals and into Perry," Bruce ordered.

"Perry admitted that she had drugs that are now missing," Bruce continued. "Maybe it wasn't Stead Willis who drugged Charlie's hot chocolate."

"I've already talked with your Auckland lass," Sergeant Kramer said. "She called with a list of Dr. Clark's patients. We compared them with our list of Luxe guests. There isn't a match. I'm waiting on DOC for a list of registered independent trampers."

Bruce scowled. "Get it."

"There's more, sir. She gave me the name of the patient whose parent made the complaint against Dr. Clark. Jerry Nelson, aged twenty-one. He died of an overdose last year."

Chapter Thirty-Nine

The plan was that Sergeant Kramer and Constable Bartlett would stay at Pompolona Lodge to interrogate Cassandra Perry and dig deeper into Perry's background via Constable Cooper in Auckland. "Keep it light," Bruce warned. "If Perry is guilty and feels cornered, she could be dangerous. Don't let your guard down. If Perry isn't guilty, someone else nearby is. This murderer hasn't left the park."

Alexa wrapped her arms around herself.

Bruce, Constable Chadwick, and she would spend the night at Dumpling Hut. Bruce and Chadwick would interview the independent hikers to see if any of them had connections with Dr. Clark or had run into her between the shelter and Pompolona Creek on Saturday. Alexa would take fingerprints and examine trekking poles.

Most important, they'd home in on Stead Willis. "He could be dangerous," Bruce said. "We'll let him think we are at the hut only to investigate Dr. Clark's death."

The team, plus Charlie, had a meal together. Chef and Silas hovered like mothers, making sure they had enough lemongrass soup, merino lamb rump, and crispy sweetbread. Alexa had seconds; the calories would keep her going. Sergeant Kramer took a phone call during the meal and wrote down the list of registered independent hikers. Bruce tucked it in his pocket.

Charlie didn't want Alexa to leave. "We'll be back at eight a.m.," Bruce told him. "I'll make sure Lexi is safe."

Lexi? How had Bruce picked up on that?

They were walking to the waiting helicopter when Sergeant Kramer ran after her. "Urgent phone call," he said.

"We'll have the pilot wait," Bruce said.

In the command room Constable Bartlett handed her the phone. "It's the lab. They said it was…"

"Hello?"

"Ms. Glock, it's Pippa Day. I have some results for you. I did an overlay of the hiking pole tip with photographs of the puncture wounds. The serrations match the spacing and distribution of the victim's left puncture wound. Also, the trace you extracted from the wound wasn't organic. It's carbide steel and matches the pole tip."

"Is it a direct match to the pole you have there, or could it be another Black Diamond tip?"

"It's a direct match. I can see where the fragment broke off."

The pole she had retrieved from the cliff bank was the murder weapon. One of them, anyway. When she could speak, Alexa asked, "Have you had time to run the fingerprints?"

"I knew you'd ask, but you didn't have much, eh? A couple partials I couldn't work with, but there were two almost completes. I ran them. There are no matches in the National Fingerprint Database."

The helicopter rotors were spinning. Alexa didn't know if she could do it, but the pilot motioned for her. She ducked and ran. Bruce extended a hand to pull her in. Alexa adjusted her headphone set as the copter lifted. She hoped her sharp intake of breath hadn't been noticeable. She would share her news when they landed.

Rain smeared the glass. Alexa pushed back against vibrating

vinyl and closed her eyes. Her endless day had started with breaking the rigor mortis of Diana Clark's fingers and going back to the scene of the crime. Charlie swirling in the rapids, a return to the skeleton to find the bones buried by rock. She opened her eyes and looked past Constable Chadwick's profile, startled to be flying in a sea of azure above a cloud duvet. She was so struck by such hidden beauty that her mouth opened. She expected a mountain peak to cut through the cloud cover like a shark fin. Wind buffeted the thin metal cocoon. She gripped the seat.

Bruce covered her hand with his, gave a squeeze, let go. He took the papers Sergeant Kramer had given him and showed Alexa. Together they perused the list of Dr. Clark's patients and compared them to the registered hut guests. Alexa was startled to see her own name. It made her dizzy, thinking of herself down there when she was up here.

There were no matches. Dr. Clark's patients probably couldn't hike anyway, with their injured knees and arthritic hips.

After ten minutes of grazing the clouds, the helicopter punched a hole through them, making Alexa feel slightly sick, and slowed above a canopy of trees, rain again pelting the glass. A meadow appeared. The copter hovered over a barracks-style building with a metal roof, and veered to a helipad behind it.

Dumpling Hut was a single building instead of three separate ones like Clinton Hut. When they set down, Alexa grabbed her things and clambered out behind Bruce, her legs shaky. Behind her, Constable Chadwick's poncho whipped in a frenzy of rotor draft. They watched the yellow bird lift off into the clouds.

Alexa explained to Bruce and Constable Chadwick that they had a murder weapon.

"Good work, Ms. Glock," Bruce said. "How does this change things?"

She had been pondering the same. "I can quit examining hiking poles, but I need to keep taking fingerprints. They could be key to finding the murderer."

Bruce nodded. Constable Chadwick's eyes gleamed.

They sloshed through spongy meadow, trampling small, white flowers, and rounded a bathhouse to the front of the hut. A wraparound veranda offered shelter. Bruce took a radio out of his backpack and turned it on. "Check, check," he said. "Over?"

Hiking poles and a few raincoats hung from hooks. Waterlogged boots and a set of pink Crocs nudged the wall. Alexa counted: thirty-one pairs. There had been thirty-five independent hikers, including her and Charlie. So two hikers hadn't left their shoes here. None of the boots were Stead Willis's CAT brand. She checked her watch: seven thirty. Even with his delayed start, he should have been here by now. "Willis's boots aren't here," she said.

"We should go looking for him, sir," Constable Chadwick said.

Bruce frowned. "Ms. Glock—pop in and double-check he's not here."

Through steamy windows, forms moved about. She struggled out of her boots and pulled on her Tevas. Inside, people gathered at metal-topped tables. The cooking area was empty, as if everyone had already eaten. A lingering scent of curry mingled with damp clothes and unwashed bodies. She recognized the German women poring over a map. A bearded man laughed over something another man said. One of the American nurses, dressed in bright floral tights, arranged drooping socks on a drying rack near a blazing woodstove. Alexa set her belongings down, unzipped her raincoat, and headed toward a staircase. The mother who had yelled at her at Clinton Hut clomped down in clogs. Alexa let her pass and climbed to a musty-smelling bunk room. The woman's two children read books in their bunks. The father struggled to open a window. "This room is full," he said.

She returned to the main level and asked the nurse by the fire where the ranger was. "I haven't seen him. Did you take the side trail to Sutherland Falls? Wasn't it awesome?"

Alexa remembered the nurse's thick braid and glasses, but couldn't remember her name. "Yeah, great." It appeared as if no one had noticed she had disappeared for a day.

At the other end of the common area was a room with skylights, and puddles on the floor. Three older men in flip-flops conversed in low tones. A small hallway led to two more bunk rooms, each messy with backpacks and hanging clothes. She returned to the porch. Constable Chadwick waited alone.

"Did you see Willis?" she asked.

Alexa shook her head.

"Detective Inspector is at the ranger's quarters," Constable Chadwick said, pointing.

A small square cabin was hidden in the trees. Bruce and a male ranger exited the door.

"The DI decided we shouldn't go into the woods to find Mr. Willis," Constable Chadwick said. "We'll wait for him to come to us."

Bruce crossed the grass briskly and introduced them to a gangly young ranger, Nick Llano. "Ranger Llano will take the lead inside," he said, removing his ball cap.

"Time to collect tickets," the ranger said, tapping a clipboard.

Alexa decided it wasn't her business to tell Bruce or Chadwick to take their boots off. The ranger kept his on, too. People looked up as they entered.

"*Kia ora*, welcome to Dumpling Hut," the ranger said loudly. "I'm Ranger Llano. Fine day, eh? Once you climbed out of the rain? What did you think of Mackinnon Pass?"

"Epic," a man shouted.

"Ve popped out of the clouds, and it was sunny," one German woman said.

Ranger Llano called up the stairs, "Hallo? Meeting. Come down." He made his way to the back rooms. "Meeting, meeting," he called. "Bring your hut tickets."

Hikers at the tables hopped up, presumably to fetch their

tickets. There was commotion as other hikers arrived from the bunk rooms. Alexa realized she had hut tickets, too, somewhere in her pack. They made her miss Charlie and the Milford experience that would never be.

The door opened. Alexa expected Stead, but it was the heavy-set woman from the ranger station, the one who had dropped a postcard. Postcard Woman lowered her head and plodded through, her raincoat dripping on the floor.

"A straggler," Ranger Llano said. "Welcome."

"Hang your coat up outside," the bossy boot woman said. Postcard Woman ignored her. Alexa remembered she had arrived at Clinton Hut late, too. A tortoise, not a hare. She made thirty-three, and Charlie would have been thirty-four.

Only Stead was AWOL.

Chapter Forty

With the ranger occupied, Bruce and Constable Chadwick explored the hut. The petite constable disappeared in the back, and Bruce climbed the stairs. Alexa skirted the crowd and stood by the woodstove, its flames a primal refuge.

The ranger checked his clipboard and called, "Mr. and Mrs. Glock here? Mr. Willis?"

Alexa waved him over. "I'm Ms. Glock, remember? My brother, Charlie Glock, won't be coming. He's at the lodge."

"Right, then." The ranger had deep-set eyes. "What about this Mr. Willis? He at the lodge, too?"

Alexa lowered her voice. "I don't know why he's not here. We need to talk with him." She didn't know how much Bruce had told him. "He left Pompolona around ten. Maybe a little later."

The ranger looked concerned. "It takes six or seven hours to trek here, and another ninety minutes if he detoured to Sutherland Falls. He should be along, but I'll head out, have a look around."

Alexa wondered if she should warn him that Stead might be dangerous.

Ranger Llano stuffed in another log. Alexa backed away from the flurry of sparks as Bruce descended the stairs. "Folks, our guest here has an announcement," the ranger said loudly.

Bruce strode to the counter as the gathered hikers watched. Constable Chadwick joined him. Bruce introduced himself and the constable. "I am here to share some bad news. One of the Luxe Tours trampers, a woman, has died. We are investigating the circumstances." He searched the shocked faces.

"How did she die?" one nurse asked.

"I'm unable to say," Bruce said. "Constable Chadwick and I will speak with you individually. Maybe you have information that will shed light on the investigation. That's why we are here."

The trampers stayed quiet, solemn.

"Ms. Glock," he pointed to her, "will take your fingerprints. This is voluntary."

"Why?" a man asked.

"Process of elimination," Bruce said.

Alexa watched the hikers' faces as they turned to one another, asking silently if it was okay to give their prints. A couple of people shrugged; one of the Middle Eastern men looked afraid; a few people whispered.

Bruce cleared his throat. "Before we begin, I have another announcement. All bridges on the Milford Track are closed until they can be checked for safety. That means you'll be evacuated from Dumpling Hut tomorrow morning. The track is closed."

"Wait. Tomorrow is the last day," a man said. "Why can't we just hike out?"

Ranger Llano joined them. "Safety first," he said. "There are two swing bridges between here and Milford Sound, and we want to test them."

"Are zee bridges not safe?" the German woman asked.

"How will we get evacuated?" a nurse asked.

"By helicopter," Bruce said.

Voices rose. Bruce ignored the clamor and motioned Alexa and Constable Chadwick to follow him into the skylight room. "We'll work in here." He set his briefcase and backpack on a chair and pulled a wooden table in front of it. "Constable Chadwick and I will talk to each tramper in this corner and then send them to you in that corner."

Alexa set up a fingerprint station across the room. The lowness of the bench wasn't ideal, but she was grateful for the overhead solar light. Movement through the window made her start. Someone on the way to the bathhouse, probably. She reviewed her purpose: fingerprint each hiker so that she could compare them with the murder-weapon prints later.

Bossy Boot Woman was first. Her two tween boys shadowed her, which Bruce allowed, but he motioned for her husband to wait in the other room.

"Your name, please, and where are you from?"

"Naomi Crew," the mother said. "Perth." The children introduced themselves, too. No, they hadn't met or passed any Luxe hikers. "We choof off early," the mother explained.

Alexa wondered what *choof* meant.

"Too early," one kid said.

Bruce showed them a photo of Dr. Clark. The boys' eyes got big. "She's dead?"

"Did you see her on the hike?"

"No," the mother answered.

"Think hard," Bruce commanded. "What about between Prairie Shelter and Pompolona Creek?"

"No. I told you."

Constable Chadwick checked them off on the list and went to retrieve the father.

Alexa fingerprinted the kids first. After three days of no baths, their fingers were dirty. She tried not to recoil. A clear print needed to be free of dirt or other particles. She was happy the new kit came with alcohol wipes and gave one to each boy. When they were clean, she proceeded. "Loops. You both have loops."

"Is that good?" the shorter one asked.

They weren't good or bad; sixty to sixty-five percent of people had loops. Diana Clark had loops. "They're the best."

The boys were crestfallen when she kept the cards, so she took their prints again so they could keep a set. "Are you sure you didn't see that woman in the photo?"

They shook their heads in unison. "Did she blow up?" the short one asked.

"Did she get shot?" the other asked.

Video games, Alexa decided.

The father shared strong opinions about aborting the hike. "I'll expect a partial refund," he told Alexa, pressing so hard she had to repeat to get a clear print.

The nurse who made Alexa jokes told Bruce she didn't remember seeing Dr. Clark. When she straddled Alexa's bench, she said, "I remember your brother is from Asheville. I don't see him."

"He's at the Luxe lodge." Alexa took the young woman's hand and pressed her pinkie—not too hard—into the ink. "It's a long story."

"What happened to the woman who died?" she asked.

"I can't say."

The other two nurses didn't remember seeing Dr. Clark, either. Alexa took their prints and then listened as Bruce showed Diana's photos to one of the Germans.

"She pass us on zee first day."

Bruce looked alert. "Did you see her on Sunday?"

"*Nein.*"

Each time Alexa took a hiker's fingerprints, she labeled the card with name, date, and case number. As a backup, she photographed each card with Clint's camera. Outside the window, darkness gobbled the last light. She pulled her NC State sweatshirt over her T-shirt and cussed when she got ink on the sleeve. Postcard Woman was last. She sat heavily across from Bruce, as if exhausted. Bruce asked her name and where she was from.

She mumbled something.

"What?"

"Gina. Granger."

Bruce waited.

"From Burswood."

Bruce looked interested. "That's the Auckland area, right?"

"She's not on my list here," Constable Chadwick interrupted.

"Why aren't you on the registration list?" Bruce asked.

Ms. Granger mumbled something about cancellations.

"Who are you hiking with?" Bruce asked.

"On my own."

"Brave, that. Did you see this woman on the hike?" Bruce smoothed the photo of Dr. Clark and set it in front of her.

Her clumpy hair hid her face as she mumbled no.

"What about yesterday, between Prairie Shelter and the swing bridge?"

She shook her head dully.

"Did you ever meet Dr. Diana Clark or visit Quay Park Orthopedics in Auckland?"

She said no, and Bruce thanked her.

The woman's chunky fingers were dirt-caked. Alexa handed her a wipe and watched Ms. Granger rub half-heartedly.

"Long day, right?"

Ms. Granger shrugged, and Alexa got to business.

When Ms. Granger left, Bruce sent Constable Chadwick to ask the ranger about how the cancellation list works. Then he turned to Alexa. "How is it that they shared the same track but nobody saw her? See no evil, hear no evil, speak no evil?"

Alexa shivered. "The huts and lodges are staggered. Except for the first day when everyone started at the same place, the independent hikers have a head start."

"Just because they had a head start doesn't mean one of them didn't backtrack and wait."

He had a point.

Bruce closed his notebook and stood. "Constable Chadwick and I will join Ranger Llano to look for Mr. Willis."

"In the dark?"

"I have a VHF radio. If you need to get in touch, there's one in the ranger's hut. Make sure no one leaves."

Alexa was not happy with "make sure no one leaves." Was she supposed to act as a guard? Who would leave, anyway? She decided to act like she was a regular hiker. She cleaned up, collected her belongings, went into a back room, the darkness a surprise. The only lights were in the common area and skylight room. She fumbled for her flashlight and clicked it on. A set of bunk beds toward the back wall was unclaimed. She picked the bottom bunk, unpacked her sleeping bag, and spread it out. Where would Bruce sleep, she wondered? Would he find Stead Willis?

Two figures came into the room, their flashlight beams bouncing around. Alexa shone her light at the first one. The German woman squinted. "Sorry," Alexa said.

"*Das ist* okay."

They zipped their belongings into their packs and climbed into their sleeping bags, whispering softly to each other. Alexa found her travel mug and a tea bag. She'd hang out in the common room. Then she realized she wouldn't be able to heat water; Charlie had their little stove. She checked her watch: nine thirty. What the heck. Tea would make her need to pee in the middle of the night, and that hadn't gone well last time. She collected her toiletries, tiny towel, and crime kit—to keep it secure—and left through the rear door.

The bathhouse was connected to the hut by a covered walkway. Rain blew sideways, getting her damp.

The boys and their mom were using three of the sinks, their faces disembodied in the glow of Mom's flashlight. Alexa stuffed her flashlight in her pocket, pushed up her sleeves, and washed her hands at the remaining sink, wincing at the cold water.

The boy next to her smiled shyly and showed her how he was keeping his inky thumb dry. She laughed—*sneaky imp*—as she readied her toothbrush.

Teeth clean, she followed the family out to the porch. They headed right, she headed left to the back of the building. A figure in a long raincoat slipped out of the bunk room as she approached. Alexa stepped against the building, expecting the person to pass on his or her way to the bathhouse. Instead, the person walked to the end of the porch and stepped into the rainy night.

Chapter Forty-One

Alarms went off in Alexa's head. "Stop!" she shouted.

The figure neither slowed nor hastened.

Alexa pulled up her hood, hiked the crime kit to her shoulder, and followed, intent on confronting whoever it was. As she stepped off the porch, her Teva slipped on the wet wood, and she landed on her butt.

"Dammit."

She hopped up, untangled her kit, and took a couple steps to see if she was okay.

Wet ass, but everything worked. She reached into her pockets to check for her toiletry kit and Maglite. The flashlight was gone. A ripple of panic; the Maglite was her lifeline. She groped left and right, reached under the bottom step, felt its cool slim cylinder. She pressed it on, and directed its lumens toward the trail. The beam could penetrate a football field's distance, but it didn't land on a retreating form, only slanting rain as if the figure had parted the veil of a waterfall and stepped through.

Alexa's fall knocked sense into her. She adjusted her hood and took a deep breath, thinking of Bruce. She changed course, hurried to the ranger hut, and rapped on the door.

No answer.

She turned the knob; the door opened. The single-roomed

hut was dark and fusty. Alexa illuminated a messy desktop with paraphernalia—radio, mug, twine, scissors, a fern frond, logbook. She set her crime kit on the chair and grabbed the radio. She pressed a button. "Hello? Hello? Over?"

There was static, and then, "Eh? Pompolona Lodge?"

Alexa was confused. "Who?"

"Constable Joel Bartlett, Te Anau Police at Pompolona Lodge."

"This is Alexa Glock at Dumpling Hut. I'm trying to reach Bruce. I mean DI Horne." She turned her Maglite off to conserve its battery. The dark settled on her like a weighted blanket.

There was a squelch. "Senior? DI Horne?"

"Yes. I need to speak to him."

"He has a handie-talkie?"

"A what?"

"A radio with him?"

"Yes."

"DI Horne? Over?"

This conversation was a Who's on First. "Yes. I'm trying to contact DI Horne."

"I'm communicating with him, if he's out there," Constable Bartlett said. "VHF channels can be heard by numerous people at once. Hello?" he said again. "Senior?"

Alexa finally understood and listened for Bruce's response.

After a few moments, Constable Bartlett said, "He must be in a dead zone."

Alexa didn't like the sound of that. "Keep trying. Someone left the lodge. I'll follow a short ways. DI Horne and Constable Chadwick are still out looking for Willis."

"Willis not there yet?"

"No."

"I'll try the DI at intervals."

Alexa felt marginally better as she set the radio down. She'd walk fifteen minutes, might bump into Bruce on the way, and then turn around. Maybe the mystery person was looking for glowworms. Did glowworms glow in the rain? When a light blinded her, she felt confused. She held her hand to block the beam. "Ranger Llano?"

The beam left her face and traveled to her Tevas and back up again, fast. The cabin door had not opened. Whoever this was had been here the whole time. The thought chilled Alexa to the marrow. "Who are you?"

The beam didn't waver. Alexa could feel her irises close up, protecting her. She dropped her hand slowly and felt for her Maglite, clicking it on. When her beam hit the intruder's wide white face, Postcard Woman didn't flinch, but her mouth began to move. "I'm leaving. You'll come with me." She said this matter-of-factly, and quick as a snake flicked Alexa's flashlight out of her hand. It clattered to the floor, going dark.

Alexa's knees almost gave out. In the brief illumination, she saw that Postcard Woman had a gap between her top teeth. The apple-biter stood before her.

Bad apple. Rotten apple. Poison apple.

Alexa didn't turn her head but glanced sideways, out the single window. Blank, black abyss. Oh, God.

The name came to her: Gina Granger.

Gina floated closer and turned off her light. Alexa smelled her smoker's breath, and edged back, into the desk, gears spinning. Gina Granger and Diana Clark. What was their link?

"Hand me the radio," Gina said.

The desk pressed into Alexa's butt; she was trapped. She groped behind her, found the radio, pressed the button, and yelled into it, "I'm not going anywhere with you."

Gina pounced, clamping onto Alexa's arm and swinging it like a rope so the radio flew from her fingers. As Gina dashed after it, Alexa sprang toward the door. Gina turned and tackled her. They fell hard. Alexa's chin bounced off the hardwood, her mouth filled with blood. She turned her head, spat, and tried to breathe. Gina was as heavy as a sack of sand on her back.

The radio screeched. "Eh, hello? Constable Bartlett here. Miss Glock? Over?"

Alexa tried to scream but the weight pressed on her diaphragm.

Gina pushed on Alexa's shoulder blades to heave herself up. The floor shuddered under her staggering lunges toward the radio. Alexa swallowed, gagging on warm, salty blood, and rose to her hands and knees, remembering that she had walked across a swing bridge with this woman behind her. She crawled to the ranger's cot. Instead of rising, she sat against it, pulling her knees into her stomach, circling them with her arms, making herself a harmless ball.

The radio bleeped. "Pompolona Lodge checking in with Miss Glock. Over?"

She sensed rather than saw Gina pick up the radio.

"Nothing heard. Over." Constable Bartlett signed out.

In the pitch dark, Gina's breath came louder than the rain assaulting the roof. Alexa squeezed her knees tighter to her chest, felt her back scars protest. She heard something dragging across the floor. A chair maybe. Then a rustling. A creak from the cabin entrance. She guessed Gina had barricaded the door.

Alexa's tongue throbbed where she had bit it. She took a deep breath and straightened up. "How did you know Dr. Clark?"

No answer. A whoosh of wind rattled the window.

She tried again. "Were you Dr. Clark's patient?"

A hollow reply: "Jerry was."

Something scurried over Alexa's foot. She screamed and jumped up. Gina was on her in a flash, pushing her onto the cot, smashing her face against scratchy wool.

Alexa rolled out from under her and lunged for the door, but Gina clamped her arm again and jerked her back, her strength like a mother lifting a car. "Okay, okay. I'll just stay here," Alexa said, sitting on the cot.

Gina blinded her with light again.

Alexa shielded her eyes. "Who is Jerry?"

The beam spun away, pointed to the floor, the ceiling. Gina backed up six feet and stumble-sat in the chair propped against the door. "My son, my lad," she mumbled.

The gears in Alexa's brain turned sluggishly. She shook her head, trying to make sense. "Was Jerry a patient of Dr. Clark?"

"Dr. Clark killed Jerry."

The woman's reply was robotic, terrifying. Alexa dug into her memory. There had been no malpractice suit filed against Dr. Clark that she was aware of, just that warning from the medical tribunal. "What happened?"

Silence stretched like a bungee cord, ready to whip back. Alexa placed her feet on the floor, rodent be damned, the better to spring up and protect herself. She felt like she'd been in the cabin for hours. Bruce or the ranger would come back soon. She tried again. "How did Dr. Clark kill your son?"

"He turned blue. He wasn't breathing."

The flashlight lay across Gina's lap, casting a full moon on the cabin wall. Maybe someone from the hut would notice the glow and investigate.

"I shook him and slapped him and gave him Narcan. Nothing worked. I called an ambulance, but they couldn't get him breathing. They shocked him. Shocked his heart." She said all this in monotone.

Alexa remembered Sergeant Kramer saying one of Dr. Clark's patients died of an overdose. But his last name was different.

The radio squelched. "Sergeant Kramer here. Over? Senior? Dumpling Hut?"

Alexa looked around furtively, straining to see a back door, an escape hatch.

Gina ignored the radio. "He barely came home for months. Only when I was at work. He took my phone. My computer. My car. He needed money to buy the drugs. I lost my job to help him." Her voice stayed expressionless. "He had headaches and cold sweats. I took him to rehab, and he walked out. No one could help him, my Jerry."

That last bit, "my Jerry," was when Alexa heard Gina's voice crack. She quickly said, "I'm sorry."

"Dr. Clark did it," she said as if Alexa hadn't spoken. "She gave him the pills. Again. And again."

The death of a child must be the worst loss. Worse than losing a mother, a hollow never filled. Alexa flared with anger at Diana's recklessness.

"Calling DI Horne? Over?" Sergeant Kramer's voice barked from the radio. "Sir? New information about Mr. Willis. Sir?"

Stead Willis and the skeleton were far from Alexa's mind.

"Senior? The police in Greymouth discovered a whole rock garden of *pounamu* at his bach, like a private Stonehenge."

Alexa scooted to the edge of the cot. The radio transmission came from the floor near Gina's feet. Where was Bruce? Why didn't he or that ranger answer?

"Eh? Eh? Pompolona Lodge, over?"

The radio went dead. Dead zone. Danger zone.

"Thirty-day supply, then sixty days and a refill," Gina said. "Then she cut him off. He tried other things. Cheaper things. Powder. Heroin, maybe. Or worse. Skin and bone, less than seventy kilograms, he wore long sleeves to hide his arms, and I couldn't help him." She grabbed the flashlight and shone it on Alexa. "No one is sorry. She wasn't sorry. She didn't care."

Alexa blinked in the glare. "*I'm* sorry."

Gina lowered the light and flung the chair. It crashed into the desk.

Alexa jumped up. Fight or flight.

"I called her for weeks to tell her. She never called back. She never answered her door. She never apologized." Still Gina's voice was flat. "I went to her clinic to warn the people in her waiting room. They had to know. She screamed at me to leave. Said she would call the police."

Crisis de-escalation was beyond Alexa's purview. What would Bruce do? Stay calm, show sympathy. "That must have been awful," she said. "Dr. Clark should have listened to you."

Gina paced in front of the door, her beam of light erratic. "Nothing happened when I reported her. I told them she killed my son, and they didn't do a thing."

"Detective Inspector Horne will be back any minute," Alexa ventured. "You can tell him what you told me. He'll understand."

Gina turned off the flashlight. "It wasn't hard to kill her." Her voice floated through the dark. "I just had to wait for the right time. I followed her and passed her, hid in the woods, watched her in the lodge—laughing, drinking while my Jerry is gone."

Gina had stalked Diana. And like a mountain lion, when she attacked, Diana had probably not seen her coming. Alexa could make out her cat eyes across the small room, watching her for reaction. Fear extinguished any sympathy Alexa felt.

"I planned to jump off the cliff right after, but then that other doctor crossed the bridge."

Alexa sensed movement and shrank back against the cot. She could smell Gina's tobacco breath.

"I changed my mind. No one saw me. I decided to live, to walk out of here and go after that pharma lady and drug companies. Make them pay."

Her tenor was infused with malevolence. Alexa sidled to the wall. Gina followed like a shadow.

"Then you show up. With your fingerprints and closing the trail." Gina's cold fingers probed Alexa's cheek, chin.

Alexa jerked away. "The police have the fingerprints. They know you killed Dr. Clark."

A strobe of lightning lit the room; the women locked eyes. Something flickered in Gina's. The room went black as thunder boomed. Alexa held her breath as Gina moved away. Something fell off the desk. There was rummaging, and then Alexa heard heavy footsteps. The cabin door opened. A gust of wind slammed it against the wall.

Then she was alone. Gina had left. She crept toward the lighter shade of gray, the louder sound of rain, the trail of tobacco. She peered beyond the threshold and watched Gina trudge toward the trail.

Going. Going. Gone.

Relief flooded Alexa's veins. She was unhurt, and Gina was gone. She twirled and groped the floor for the radio, grabbed it, smashed the button. "Hello? Hello? Bruce? Sergeant Kramer? Anyone?"

After twenty eternal seconds of static she heard, "Sergeant Kramer, Pompolona Lodge, over."

"Alexa Glock here. This is urgent. I know who killed Dr. Clark."

"Eh? What?"

Alexa wanted to scream. "Listen! Gina Granger killed Dr. Clark. Now she's getting away."

"Who is Gina Granger?"

Progress. "She is the mother of Dr. Clark's patient. The one who died. Jerry. She blames Dr. Clark."

"Bugger all. What's your current situation?"

"I'm in the ranger's cabin. Gina is headed into the woods. DI Horne, Constable Chadwick, and the ranger are still out there looking for Stead Willis. Why don't they answer the radio?"

"Can't say. Is the suspect armed?" Sergeant Kramer asked.

Alexa dashed to the desk and flailed around. Mug. Twine. Radio dock. Fern. Damn. "She has scissors."

"Snips?"

"You know. Tools for cutting. Scissors. Should I follow her?"

"Go to the main hut. Take the radio. Wait for further instruction."

For a change, Alexa didn't mind taking orders. She groped around the floor for her Maglite, turned it on, double-checked the desktop to make sure that the scissors were missing, grabbed her crime kit, and got the hell out of hell. The beam was an old friend, pointing her to Dumpling Hut.

Just the same, she ran.

Chapter Forty-Two

The three nurses were alone in the darkened common room, huddled around the woodstove. Their eyes went owl-wide as Alexa dashed in.

"Have you seen the ranger or the police officers?" Alexa panted.

Nurse Hannah hopped up. "Are you okay?"

Alexa wanted to cave, confess how scared she'd been, yell about a killer on the loose, but breaking down or causing panic would be counterproductive. "I'm fine."

"Your lip is bleeding," Hannah said.

Alexa licked her bottom lip, tasted blood. "Occupational hazard."

"The police and the ranger aren't here," the nurse with the thick braid said. "We wondered where they were. What's going on?"

Alexa squelched close to the woodstove; her Tevas and socks were wet from dashing through puddles. "Have you met that hiker who came in late tonight? Brown hair. Heavyset. She's a Kiwi."

"We call her Snail," Hannah said. "She's not the least bit friendly."

"Her stuff is in our bunk room," the third nurse said. "I hope she's not a snorer."

Gina had hiked off with nothing but a flashlight. And scissors. "Show me."

They tiptoed in. It was the same bunk room where Alexa had spread her bag and left her pack. The German women and another hiker were inert lumps in their sleeping bags. Alexa shone her Maglite where Hannah pointed. She half expected to see Gina, but the bottom bunk mattress was bare. A pack leaned against the bunk. Alexa hefted it by the strap and backed out of the room. Under the circumstances, she believed searching the backpack was justified. She pulled on gloves and opened the pack as Hannah watched. "Where did she go?"

"She's gone walkabout," tumbled out of Alexa's mouth like she was Crocodile Dundee.

"That's not a good idea," Hannah said. "It's dark and dangerous out there."

Alexa nodded and spread items on the metal-topped table: a dry bag full of clean clothes, as if Gina had never changed. Two water bottles. Pack of Pall Mall cigarettes, half empty. Matches. Trash bag. Toiletry bag with a tiny bar of soap, toothbrush, and toothpaste, Band-Aids. No sunscreen or bug spray. No cooking pot. This was minimalist packing. A final dry bag held three trail bars and two apples. Alexa examined the apples; they looked similar to the one Charlie had found.

The hut door burst open, and Bruce barreled in, directing a spotlight on Alexa. "Are you okay?"

Constable Chadwick and Ranger Llano crowded behind him.

Alexa blinked. "Why didn't you answer the radio?"

Bruce lowered the light. "We could hear transmissions, but we couldn't send them."

"A busted mike or loose connection," Constable Chadwick said, swiping off her poncho hood.

"Did you hear everything I told Sergeant Kramer? About Gina Granger?" Alexa asked.

Bruce nodded. "How did you know it was her?"

"She has a gap in her upper teeth. The bite-marks in the apple Charlie found at the crime scene probably match it." She took a breath. "But then she told me everything. You must have passed right by her. Didn't you see her?"

"No sign of Stead Willis or Ms. Granger." Bruce noticed the nurses. "Ladies, will you excuse us?"

The nurses reluctantly gathered their belongings and headed to the back. Ranger Llano turned on the overhead light.

"What can you tell us?" Bruce asked.

"She said she tracked Diana and waited for the right time to kill her. She admitted it. She said Diana got her son hooked on opioids. Jerry. That's his name. He died."

"Mother of God." Bruce stepped close to Alexa and took her chin in his thumb and forefinger. "Did she hurt you?"

She longed to burrow into his arms. "She tackled me a couple times. The worst was the way she talked. Like she was reporting the weather when she talked about how her son died."

He dropped his finger, studied her. "Is she a danger to herself or others?"

Alexa stepped away from him. "Yes! She's got scissors. She said she was never going back."

Ranger Llano took the radio from her. "I'll notify SAR. They'll send a copter. We'll use thermal imaging to find her."

"I don't think she'll go far in the rain and dark," Bruce said, looking at Constable Chadwick. "Fancy going back out?"

"I don't recommend it, sir," Ranger Llano said. "We can get a helicopter crew here within a couple hours."

"We'll contain our search to around the premises."

Alexa, in a chair by the dying fire, started awake when Bruce and Constable Chadwick returned. She could tell by the look on Bruce's drawn face that he was empty-handed. He added another log to the stove and settled in to wait for the SAR helicopter.

TUESDAY

Chapter Forty-Three

A sense of failure numbed Alexa in the morning. The gruesome facts—Gina's body in a copse of trees a half mile from the hut, her wrists shredded by Ranger Llano's shears, her blood saturating the ancient soil—were blocked by her sense of inadequacy, her botched attempt at cabin psychology: *I'm sorry. That must have been awful.*

I should have kept her in the cabin.

There had been a moment—Gina's fingers probing her face, so near her throat—when she believed Gina was deciding whether or not to kill her. The bolt of lightning had saved her. She was lucky, she supposed.

At three a.m. Bruce had radioed from the SAR copter to relay the news. "We saw Ms. Granger's image near the twenty-two-mile peg. Had to land at Racecourse Flat and hike back. She wasn't breathing when we got to her."

Alexa argued. "She can't be dead. The thermal imaging wouldn't have worked."

"She's dead," Bruce replied curtly.

After Bruce ended the call, Constable Chadwick explained that thermal patterns emitted from a body don't dissipate completely for twenty-four hours. "It's not like a flick of a switch," she said.

Alexa, who had been catnapping in a chair by the woodstove, wondered if the thermal-imaging camera could detect Gina's soul departing like a spark to the heavens.

Or hell.

Grumpy hikers were now gathered in the common area waiting to be evacuated, unaware—except for the nurses—of the night's calamity. All they knew was that their Milford Track experience was being cut short. Bruce hadn't returned to the hut. He had flown with Gina's body to Queenstown. Alexa didn't like the sense of abandonment this caused her. At the end of their last case—in Stewart Island—he had done the same thing. Left without a goodbye. She knew it was because he was following procedure. But still.

"Six more trampers, let's go," Constable Chadwick said at the sound of chopper blades.

What if she gave her heart to Bruce and he left her? Would she ever overcome Mom's death? Little girl left behind syndrome, that's what she had. She didn't know if loving Bruce was worth the risk.

The cabin quieted as more hikers left. The nurses hung back, flitting like moths to misfortune. They heated water for Alexa's oatmeal, poured her coffee, and fired questions. The news would soon be in the papers. Alexa envisioned the headline: MURDER ON MILFORD. She probed her sore chin and let the story tumble out: Gina's loss, her fierce grip, her emotionless voice, throwing the chair, grabbing the scissors. Hannah surprised her by saying she was a psychiatric nurse. She said Gina's flat affect and erratic behavior sounded like a bereavement disorder. "Some people can't get past their grief after someone they're close to—like her son, Jerry—dies. They let go of reality and wish they were dead, too."

"I bet when you and the police showed up, she panicked," the nurse with the braid said. "That's why she left at night."

Alexa considered the bereavement theory. Maybe it applied,

but Gina Granger had been stable enough to execute her malicious attack. Then she suddenly had the will to live and exact more revenge.

Waving the nurses off was sad. She had judged them as silly annoyances, but they'd been smart, insightful women.

She and Constable Chadwick had been ordered back to Pompolona Lodge. "Lots going on with Bone Track. We need all hands on deck," Sergeant Kramer said by radio.

The flight over the slumbering mountains didn't faze Alexa. The worst had already happened. Shortly after liftoff, she stared down at a tiny turquoise lake, unmoved by its beauty, and then over at Constable Chadwick, who looked straight ahead, her tiny chin quivering with the vibrations of the engine. Alexa imagined she, as well, was shaken by the events.

The thought of the crushed bones by the river was a jolt of adrenaline. They deserved her full attention. And Stead Willis was at large. Where was he? She thought of Charlie. Charlie was waiting. Suddenly, the flight was taking too long.

At the lodge, Luxers, their belongings at their feet, awaited evacuations. Everyone seemed focused on leaving the woods. Clint was passing out hotel vouchers. "For when you get to Queenstown," he said in false-cheery voice. Cassandra and Larry sat at the bar. Rosie sat on a sofa, head down. Alexa was glad it hadn't been her job to inform them about Gina.

Sergeant Kramer scurried to meet them. "We've got lots of updates. I'll see you in the meeting room after I get this lot sorted." He gestured to the Luxers.

Alexa's mind had already slipped into gear. "I have evidence. I need it transferred to the lab ASAP."

Sergeant Kramer nodded. "Round it up and get it to me."

After gathering the evidence from the lodge refrigerator (she threw out the cheese experiment) and crime kit, Alexa found Charlie in their bathroom shaving away his Milford Track beard.

"You okay?" he asked mid razor swipe.

324   Sara E. Johnson

She nodded and dropped her backpack to the floor. "I need to turn over evidence to Sergeant Kramer." She unlocked the safe and checked that everything was logged correctly. "I'll be right back."

She found the sergeant and turned everything over to him with relief. The apple, DNA, fingerprints. It all would point to Gina. "I need to update my brother."

In Tahu, she told Charlie the team had identified Gina Granger as Dr. Clark's murderer. He didn't need the grim details now. Or maybe ever.

"What about my apple?"

"The apple helped."

"So that woman from the ranger station is a murderer? You picked up the postcard she dropped. Remember?" He set down the razor and grabbed a towel. "What happened to your face?"

Her lip was swollen, and her chin was cut. "I fell."

Charlie snorted, but then stared at her. "Right. So that Larry dude isn't guilty?"

"No."

Charlie swung the towel over his shoulder and walked to the window. "Is your job done?"

"One down, one to go." She closed her eyes. Saw Gina's face.

"If we're staying around, I might hike up Mackinnon Pass. To come this close and not see it is a waste."

She rubbed her eyes to make Gina disappear. "That's not safe. Stead Willis is still out there. Plus the bridges haven't been checked."

Charlie flicked the towel at her. "Old lady. I'm telling you."

Constable Bartlett fetched Alexa a few minutes later. "Meeting," he said. He peppered her with questions on the way through the empty lodge. "So, you yelling into the radio 'I'm not going anywhere with you' was code, right? Like an SOS?"

Alexa had forgotten she had done that and shrugged.

"I knew it!"

As they entered the command center, Sergeant Kramer turned to a fresh sheet of paper on the easel and wrote JOHN DOE at the top. Alexa sat down next to Constable Chadwick.

He turned to face them. "Job well done at Dumpling Hut, Ms. Glock and Constable Chadwick. Senior asked me to stand in until he gets back from Queenstown. He'll return this afternoon."

Alexa sat taller. Bruce was coming back.

The sergeant scratched his shaving nick from yesterday. "The Luxe hikers and the lodge staff have been evacuated. Remaining at the lodge are Vince Bergen, Ms. Glock's brother, and the four of us."

A skeleton crew, Alexa realized. She glanced out the window, half-expecting Stead Willis's face pressed to the glass.

As if Kramer had read her thoughts, he said, "If Stead Willis doesn't turn up by night, there will be another SAR search. We consider Black Diamond closed, pending lab work, eh Ms. Glock? An apple a day?"

Alexa grimaced.

"For now, we are working solely on Bone Track," the sergeant continued. "A lot had been going on in Greymouth, Willis's hometown. After interviewing Stead Willis's wife, Sue Willis, the town police went to his bach on the Grey River and discovered a veritable rock garden of uncut greenstone." He wrote SUE WILLIS on the pad, followed by an arrow pointing to *bach* and *greenstone garden.*

"How much is it worth, Sarge?" Constable Bartlett asked.

"Don't know."

"Greenstone has both economic and spiritual worth," Constable Chadwick said.

"The wife says greenstone belongs to everyone, not just the Māori, and that Willis and Damien Riggs went to flight school together years ago." The sergeant wrote this on the pad. "Willis flunked out. Couldn't do the math. The garden indicates Willis and Riggs have been going at greenstone theft for years."

326 Sara E. Johnson

"Riggs is the dodgy Ace who flew us in, eh?" Constable Bartlett asked.

"Yes. Our lad in Te Anau has been looking into him." Sergeant Kramer shuffled through a stack of papers and pulled one out. "Damien Riggs lives in Queenstown. Divorced twice, currently single. Started as a jet boat pilot. Got trained as a pilot in 2013. Did aerial flying for the movie industry. *Pete's Dragon*, it says here. Currently works as a contract pilot for DOC and Queenstown Limited. He has a citation for flying in a Fiordland danger zone and is on probation with DOC." He drew an arrow from Stead Willis's name and wrote DAMIEN RIGGS.

"Why was he flying if he has a citation?" Alexa asked.

"We'll have to ask the DOC supervisor that question. No telling how much illegally harvested stone he and Willis have sold that will never be recovered. All you have to do is look on Trade Me. People selling," he made quote marks with his hands, "'authentic *pounamu*.' It's right in the open. Chairperson Sherman Tumuha has been notified. He'll work with police to suss out the thievery ring."

"Stealing the stuff is hardly the same as murder, though," Constable Bartlett said. "How does the skeleton factor in?"

"The threat made on Ms. Glock's life and the rocks dropped on the bones connect John Doe to Riggs." He drew an arrow from Riggs's name to JOHN DOE. "Riggs is on the defensive, but we still don't know who John Doe is or what their connection is."

"Is Riggs in custody?" Alexa asked.

"He is at large. Two nights ago he was spotted in a Te Anau pub, drunk," the sergeant said. "The next morning, he delivers us to the lodge. That's the last sighting. His supervisors at DOC and Queenstown Limited are notified. He's banned from flying. They'll contact us if he shows. We've a warrant for his arrest."

"What's next, boss?" Constable Bartlett asked.

"Get back to the missing persons reports. Senior Constable

McCain made a good start. Whittled the pile down. We have to find who John Doe is so we can find a link with Riggs or Willis." He turned to Constable Chadwick. "You and I will search the premises and surrounding area for Mr. Willis."

"The premises?" Alexa asked.

"There's been coming and going. What if Willis hasn't strayed far and slipped back in?"

That gave Alexa chills.

"Your archaeologist friend will arrive any moment. She requested that you accompany her to the scene to begin uncovering the remains."

Alexa was heartened to hear Dr. Luckenbaugh was on her way. A single tooth would yield DNA, and a partial notched rib would be enough to indicate the man had been stabbed. Plus, she could hire Charlie to lift rocks. Keep him busy.

After Sergeant Kramer dismissed the meeting, she called the lab and was able to speak to the same investigator, Pippa Day. Her voice was animated. "I found the belt buckle. It's made of zinc. After taking photos, I cleaned it with Wattie's tomato sauce. There's a mark. It's made by Māori artist Malcolm Solomon and sold in Hokitika."

Hokitika rang a bell. Alexa thanked Day and told her more evidence was on its way. After hanging up, she told Constable Bartlett about the buckle being from Hokitika. He stabbed one of the missing persons reports with his finger. "This bloke is from there."

Alexa began reading. Karl Atul was of Māori descent, fifty-three years old at disappearance, five feet, nine inches (175 cm.), and last seen March, five years ago, in Hokitika—long enough ago for his clothes to disintegrate in the relentless Fiordland rains. She studied his photo: balding, brows shading shy eyes, a straggly beard, tattooed arms folded high on his chest as if to guard his heart. There was a large bird—a hawk, she thought—on a perch beside him.

328 *Sara E. Johnson*

She hadn't remembered until this moment that a giant hawk had dive-bombed her head when she discovered the skeleton.

She thought back and tried to flesh out the skull, with its prominent forehead, eye sockets packed with soil, the square jaw. Add clay, like a reconstruction artist. Press, pinch, sculpt.

She read further. Karl Atul had last been seen wearing a gray polo and jeans. He told the people he was staying with that he was going fossicking.

"Fossicking. Does that have something to do with green-stone?" she asked Constable Bartlett.

"Yeah. Hokitika is *pounamu* country, like we are."

"Where is Hokitika?"

"Up the west coast. This side of Greymouth."

"So is it nearby?"

"Yeah nah. Nine-hour drive."

Her heart sank. In North Carolina, you could drive to Florida in nine hours. When she heard how far Hokitika was, she doubted Karl Atul was John Doe. "Did Senior Constable McCain call the reference number to ask about the belt buckle?"

"I don't know. I'll do it now."

Dr. Luckenbaugh hadn't arrived, so she sat next to him. "Does the satellite phone have speaker mode?"

Constable Bartlett crossed his eyes at her as he dialed and gave the reference number to the person who answered. Alexa leaned close. A tinny voice said, "Twelve-zero-seven, Karl Arthur Atul, is still missing. Let me pull out his file."

Constable Bartlett drummed his fingers nervously. "What should I ask first?"

"If there's any mention of a belt buckle. Then about dental records. Then…"

He handed her the phone.

"This is Nadine Charlsen, missing persons coordinator. How can I help you?"

Alexa identified herself and explained about the remains. "The deceased was wearing a distinctive Māori belt buckle made in Hokitika. That's why we are inquiring about Karl Atul."

"I see." The woman went quiet for a moment. "He was last seen wearing jeans and a polo shirt. There's nothing about a belt buckle. I can ask his mother, Ngaio Atul. She is listed as next of kin. Shall I send you the additional information we have here?"

"We don't have internet. Can you read it to me?"

Alexa grabbed Constable Bartlett's legal pad and pen.

"Certainly. Let me find my glasses. There now. Yes. Mr. Atul is single, no children, referred to as a loner. His address is listed as 19 Terrace Street, Hokitika, which is a studio, not a residence."

Alexa stopped scribbling. "What type of studio?"

"Mr. Atul is a registered *pounamu* carver. It says he applies his craft with a heartfelt *karakia* to his ancestors of Ngai Tahu. That's what it says."

Alexa stared at Constable Bartlett.

"His mother said Kahu—that's his nickname—stayed at the studio when he had birds."

Goose bumps broke out on Alexa's arms. "Birds?"

"Mr. Atul is a volunteer with Hokitika Wildlife Rescue. It says here that he helps injured and sick birds."

The woman spoke in present tense.

"Are there dental records with his file?"

After a silence, Ms. Charlsen said no. Alexa told her to call Mr. Atul's mother at once and ask about the belt buckle. "Forensic Service Center in Christchurch has it. They can send you a photo. And track down his dental records. Are you writing this all down?"

"Hold on." There was silence. "Okay. Caught up now."

"Ask if Karl knew a Steadman Willis or Damien Riggs. And where he went fossicking. Call back as soon as possible. This is an active case."

"Might have a winner there," Constable Bartlett said when she hung up.

The connection to greenstone ignited Alexa's energy. The remains might be the bird man from Hokitika.

There was still no sign of a helicopter. Alexa returned to her room to talk Charlie into rock duty. His "Hiking Mackinnon. See you later" note made her fume. She looked out the window, angry at the enticing swath of blue sky. The throttle of rotors made her flinch. Dr. Luckenbaugh had arrived. There was nothing she could do about Charlie. She doused herself with bug spray and collected her raincoat, water bottle, fishing hat, crime kit, and Clint's camera.

Dr. Luckenbaugh met her in the lobby. She waved and said she needed the restroom. Her dark hair was in a messy braid, her work boots were muddy, and the oversized pockets of her safari vest sagged. Alexa ducked into the dining room to tell Constable Bartlett she was leaving. He was on the phone and covered the mouthpiece. "I'm on hold. Senior Constable McCain says there's shenanigans at the aerodrome."

What next? Alexa thought. "I'm off with the archaeologist to the river. My brother is hiking up Mackinnon Pass."

"Is that a good idea?"

"No. Let the sergeant know when he gets back."

Dr. Luckenbaugh appeared. "Ready, then? You can tell me what it's all about on the way."

Alexa introduced her to the constable, and asked if Dr. Luckenbaugh had a radio. "The heli-copper does," she said.

They left the lodge and circled around the side to the helipad. The copter was white. Alexa glanced at the pilot as she pulled herself in. It was Hank, from Police Air Support. Now she understood the heli-copper remark. Before slipping on the headset like a pro, she told Dr. Luckenbaugh about the bones.

"You know exactly where they are?"

"A load of rock marks the spot."

"How was the body positioned?"

She yelled over the sound of the rotors. "On his back, arms at his side."

"Extended supine, arranged then, by someone else. Was it buried in the earth?"

"Shallowly. The rockslide uncovered it." Alexa wiggled in her seat remembering the thumb bone she lost.

Chapter Forty-Four

Hank flew low, skimming the trees, no commentary. Alexa searched for Stead or Charlie, but the bright green canopy was impenetrable. She marveled when the trees ceded to the wide Clinton River Valley, the emerald river sparkling benignly. Only the raw rockslide marred the landscape.

"Set down at the same spot?" Hank asked.

Alexa nodded. After they bumped down, she waited until he gave the okay to hop out.

"Call me Ana," Dr. Luckenbaugh said as they walked to the mound. She handed Alexa work gloves. "You'll need these. I keep spare."

Hank, also gloved, carried Ana's trowels and buckets.

The mound looked the same as it did yesterday: a heap where there shouldn't be one. Ana, hands akimbo, studied it. "The rocks weren't dropped from tremendous height. There would be more spread if they had been. Some of the bones might not be fragmented."

Hank set the buckets and trowels down nearby. "There's a scrap of bulk bag. See there?"

The patch of white polypropylene fabric gleamed through the rocks. It reminded Alexa that she had covered part of the skeleton with her green ground cloth. She told Ana. "That's good," Ana said. "It will help us locate the bones."

Alexa scanned the sky for hawks or stealth helicopters, but it was vacant even of clouds. Cold air skipped off the river, chilling her cheeks. She pulled her hat down to warm her ears.

Ana marked off a big square ten feet from the mound by dragging her boot in the soft ground. "This will be our spoil area. Examine the rock, determine that it *is* rock, and drop it here. Place scraps of bulk bag in this bucket. Anything else, show me. Our goal is to expose bone."

"How do I tell the difference between bone and rock?" Hank asked.

Ana seemed to respect his question. "The first way is to compare the specimen to other rock in the area." She picked up a rock. "Since this load of rock didn't come from here, compare it to other riprap." She picked up another rock and held them side by side. "Note any obvious difference?"

"No."

"If the object is fragmented..." She showed the rough edge of the first rock. "Remember that rock is solid throughout, but bone is porous."

The pilot nodded. Alexa could tell Ana was enjoying the lecture.

"You can also try the tongue test," Ana said. "If you lick a rock, it just tastes like dirt or mineral, right?"

Hank shrugged. "I had a dog who ate rocks."

"If you lick a bone, it sticks slightly to your tongue."

Alexa wondered if this was true.

The rocks weren't heavy, but there were so many. One by one, rock by rock, Alexa warmed up. After an hour, she removed her jacket and sipped water, glad for the rote exercise. She kept her hat on, knowing her fair skin would burn if she didn't. Physical labor helped dilute the failure she felt at Gina's death and strengthened the resolve she felt to bring justice to the man buried beneath the rubble.

"How's your daughter?" she asked Ana.

"She's cheeky, telling everyone it's her birthday, when it's not." Ana examined a clump of mud, a smile tugging her lips. "My mum will spoil her. Give Shelby sweets and let her stay up late. She'll be feral when I get back."

Proud she had remembered to ask, Alexa scrutinized the rock in her hand, noting its sharp edge and dull color. Another ugly duckling rock. She tossed it in the growing spoil pile and leaned to pick another, her back aching. Rock by rock. On the rocks. Rock-bottom. Half the riprap had been moved.

Ana offered them energy bars. "Let's sit in the shade, take a break," she suggested.

Alexa pulled off her gloves and flexed her fingers. A bead of sweat ran down her cheek. For the first time on Milford Track she was hot.

The only shade was the small tree where she'd stashed the bird nest. As Hank and Ana sat in its shade, she poked under the tree's low branches to check on it. It nestled where she had left it only two days ago, sheltered from rain, the three eggs like malted milk ball treats. No mama bird scolded her. Sometimes things worked out, sometimes they didn't, like moving nests or keeping Gina alive to face consequences.

Another hour passed. Hank made chain gang jokes. He's the one who noticed the circling bird and pointed it out. "The harrier is watching us."

"Harrier?" Alexa asked, taking off her hat and wiping her brow. "Is that a type of hawk?"

"That's right. I wonder what it's looking for?" Fifteen minutes later Alexa saw a scrap of green material—a piece of her tattered ground cloth—followed by an inch-sized bone fragment. Her tongue twitched. She almost bit it when she heard the drone of rotors and looked up at a helicopter buzzing low, headed straight for them.

"Duck!" Alexa yelled. She smashed her face into the muddy earth, and put her hands over her head. It was happening again.

Ana pitched herself beside Alexa. The engine and rotor noise intensified. There was no place to hide. Alexa put an arm over Ana. Tasted dirt and fear. Needed to see what was coming and lifted her head, whipped her hat off. The chopper was military green, not yellow. Hank walked toward it as it landed. Alexa felt foolish and struggled to her feet. "I think we're okay," she told Ana.

Bruce climbed out before the rotors stopped. He ducked and ran toward her.

Chapter Forty-Five

His eyes were gunmetal blue. "Riggs stole a DOC copter. He's in the air. It's not safe to be here."

Fear compressed her lungs. She searched the sky. The hawk circled slowly, watching them. It flew close to the mound and dropped a stick or stone from its talons. Alexa shook her head as if seeing things.

"You must be Dr. Luckenbaugh," Bruce said to Ana, helping her up. "I'm DI Bruce Horne. Get your gear gathered."

Ana paled. "But we've just reached the skeleton."

"We'll get you back here as soon as the area is secure."

Hank helped Ana gather equipment. "Take the women to Queenstown," Bruce told him. "If you spot a yellow Hughes 500, report to air traffic control, but do not engage. Riggs disabled the radar, so it's sight only."

Alexa's mouth dropped. "I'm not going to Queenstown. Charlie is out there."

Bruce frowned "Out where?"

"He's climbing Mackinnon Pass. We need to search for him."

"What time did he leave?" Bruce asked.

"I don't know. Around eight thirty, maybe."

"He'd be headed back," Hank said. "Let's get moving."

Alexa thought of the razor-slash switchbacks on the

mountain's flank, exposed from air. "I'm not leaving without Charlie."

Bruce took her hand, squeezed it. "I can't force you to evacuate, but Charlie would want you to be safe."

She jerked it away. "I'm not leaving my brother. I'll walk back to the lodge if you won't take me."

"With the bridge out?"

They locked eyes.

Bruce sighed. "Right, then. We'll get you to the lodge."

She grabbed her things and glanced at the flattened mound and abandoned bones. The hawk circled protectively.

An unfamiliar pilot and a police officer nodded to her as she climbed up two footplates and pulled herself in. The bay was large, with two benches facing each other and a cargo area. Bruce sat next to her and told the pilot to drop her off at Pompolona Lodge.

Alexa tried to still her heart as she watched Hank and Ana climb in the other copter, and saw its blades begin to whirl. The copters lifted in unison and parted in synchronicity. The pilot spoke softly to what sounded like air traffic control. "Milford Sound Airport, Bell 429, request Fiordland vicinity traffic, over."

She glued her eyes out the window. She had no idea what would happen if the yellow copter came into view. Would they chase it? Could one helicopter force another helicopter to land? Maybe Riggs had already landed, and they were searching for a yellow bird on the ground.

In fifteen minutes, Pompolona Lodge's metal roof, silvery in the sunshine, came into view. Alexa wanted a moment alone with Bruce, to find out what the plan was, but he didn't unfasten his seat belt. "Don't leave the lodge," he ordered.

She watched the chopper lift, fighting the familiar feeling of abandonment. Bruce had done what she'd asked. Maybe Charlie was already back. Rounding the side of the lodge, she saw Vince Bergen clipping one of the unruly bushes flanking the steps.

"Doing some maintenance," he said, lopping a branch. "What's the latest?"

"I'm not sure. Have you seen my brother?"

Vince attacked another offshoot, the steel blades cutting cleanly. "I thought he was evacuated."

"No. He hiked to Mackinnon Pass."

He pointed the clippers at the sky. "Nice day for it."

She went inside. No excited hikers roamed the lounge, no aroma of scones filled the air. Alexa thought of Sergeant Kramer's theory that Stead Willis may have reentered the lodge. Good thing it had been searched. She hustled to her room; Charlie wasn't back. She crumpled his damn note, tossed the crime kit onto the bed, and paced. *Calm down and think*, she told herself. There is no reason to believe Charlie is in danger. He's probably making his way back, feeling all HeDaMan about conquering Mackinnon Pass.

But still.

In the dining room, Constable Chadwick was standing at the windows, looking toward the sky. She jumped when Alexa said hi. Her face scrunched. "Did you hear Riggs flogged a helicopter?"

Alexa nodded. "That's why we called off the excavation."

"It's my turn to stay here. Sarge and Bart, I mean Constable Bartlett, are searching the track for Willis." Her elfin face brightened, and she walked to the easel. "We have updates."

Alexa forced herself to pay attention.

"The missing persons coordinator rang us back. Karl Atul's mother recognized the belt buckle. Karl wore it all the time. She said he followed the *pounamu* trails once or twice a year. He was after the rarest of all *pounamu*, she said. A kind only found in Fiordland."

KARL ATUL was written next to JOHN DOE. The tale of his hunts for treasure made Alexa sad. "I'm glad we know who he is." Dentals or DNA would confirm it, if they could get back to excavating the bones. "I'm going out to meet my brother. He's walking back from Mackinnon Pass."

"But Willis is out there. And that pilot."

"It's a big park. I'll be fine."

"Don't know about that," a voice said.

Alexa twirled and did a double take.

Stead Willis stood in the doorway. His eyes were wide and glassy. His left hand rested on a pouch hanging from his belt.

Alexa snapped to attention. "Where have you been, Stead? You didn't show up at Dumpling Hut. People are worried."

"You weren't worried when I left yesterday." He stepped into the room and jerked his thumb. "Who's the little lady?"

The constable had quietly drifted to the head of the table, near the satellite phone.

Alexa looked beyond Stead, toward the lounge, hoping to see Vince or Sergeant Kramer. Anyone. She spotted Stead's pack, leaning against a chair. "Constable Chadwick is investigating Dr. Clark's death."

"My name is Daniella," Constable Chadwick said calmly. "I'm glad you're safe."

Stead ignored her. When he said, "She needs to come this way. Now," Alexa knew they had a situation.

The constable scurried next to Alexa. Her breath came in quick little bursts.

Stead noticed the easel. His brown-gold eyes flitted back and forth. "Who's Karl Atul?"

Alexa's mouth went on autopilot, while her brain tried to make a plan. "I found a skeleton by the river the day of the rockslide. Remember the caution tape I asked you about while we ate breakfast with my brother, Charlie? It marked where I found the skeleton. We think it's Karl. He's been missing five years."

Stead's brow furrowed. "Why is there an arrow connecting his name to Riggs?"

"Someone dropped a load of rock on the bones. We think Damien Riggs did it."

"I don't know anything about bones or rocks."

"That's good. I mean, we didn't think you did." Maybe trail-talk would fix things. "Have you caught any fish?"

Stead sucked in his right cheek. "Did you take pictures of the bones?"

She wanted to say, "You should know. You stole my camera," but she played dumb. "Yes. Lots of them to help the police figure out what happened."

Constable Chadwick glided closer to the phone.

"Charlie is in the lodge," Alexa said to distract Stead. "He'll be glad to see you."

His eyes narrowed. "I watched him leave this morning. Followed him for a while. He's not here."

The hair on Alexa's neck stood.

Stead's eyes darted back to the easel. He chewed the inside of his cheek as he studied it. "They've been to my bach?"

"Sue, your wife, gave us permission," Constable Chadwick said.

Stead jerked slightly. Alexa thought mentioning the wife was a mistake.

"I found that greenstone fair and square."

"Tell us about it," the constable said.

He didn't look at her. "No one owns the rivers. The bloody *hori* taking what isn't theirs. Ngāi Tahu thieves."

Constable Chadwick stiffened. Alexa knew *hori* was a derogatory term for Māori.

The thwapping of a helicopter invaded the room. As Stead turned toward the door, Constable Chadwick rushed at the phone. Stead turned back and lunged at her. Alexa thrust herself between them. "Stead. The police are here."

He shoved her out of his way and grabbed Constable Chadwick's arm, jerking her off her feet. He dragged her to the pantry.

Alexa ran toward the door.

"Stop!" Stead yelled. His free hand whipped a knife out of the pouch. Constable Chadwick screamed and flailed.

A flash of red froze Alexa on the spot.

Stead heaved the thrashing constable into the pantry and locked the door. He pointed the knife at Alexa as he stepped closer, its stained tip hypnotic. "Let's go." He grabbed her by the wrist like Gina Granger had. She tried to speak, but her mouth went dry. She followed woodenly through the lobby, Chadwick's muffled screams tailing them. Alexa prayed Vince would be out front.

The porch was empty.

Where was everyone? Shouldn't Sergeant Kramer and Constable Bartlett come running at the sound of the helicopter? The deafening din drew her eyes upward. A yellow DOC copter hovered like a vulture above the lodge. Yellow.

Hazard. Obstacle. Dead end.

Damien Riggs was coming for Stead, and Alexa would make the perfect hostage. Or perfect ballast to jettison.

The helicopter lowered, disappearing behind the lodge. Alexa searched the sky. Where the hell was Bruce?

Stead jerked her down the porch stairs. She stumbled so she could grab the pruning shears from the bottom step. Stead's grasp tightened, but he didn't turn as he hurried to the helipad. She almost dropped the clippers as he yanked her around the side of the lodge and across the downdraft-flattened grass toward the chopper. She worked to get a better hold of the clipper handles.

She fumbled for the release notch and felt the blades release. "We should wait for Sergeant Kramer," she yelled.

His vise grip tightened.

She dug her heels into the soft earth, her hair flying wildly around her face. "Think about your kids!"

He wrenched her toward the decapitating rotors.

With no aim, she stabbed the steel blades at his wrist and squeezed with every muscle in her hand, feeling the crunch of his bone. Stead dropped her arm, grunting. They froze, mesmerized by the crimson fountain spurting from his cuff. The downdraft from the rotors dispersed the blood into spray.

She'd sliced an artery. Probably the radial.

Alexa jumped back. Stead dropped the knife to hold his wrist and collapsed to his knees. The sound of the whirling blades changed frequency. Large hands squeezed her shoulders from behind. She tried to break free until she heard Sergeant Kramer's voice. "Easy, lass, easy." He pushed her aside and yelled at Stead to lie flat. Constable Bartlett stood like an oaf, staring from her to the chopper lifting off.

"Apply pressure," she screamed.

Chapter Forty-Six

Sergeant Kramer ordered Constable Bartlett to call Medi-flight. Alexa flung the clippers from her grip and sprinted across the grounds and into the lodge. Constable Chadwick's muffled screams were music to her ears; she was alive. Alexa flung the pantry door open. The constable's eyes were saucer-big as she stepped out, holding a bloodied cloth napkin. The sleeve of her uniform shirt was crimson. "Where's Willis?"

"Sergeant Kramer has him secured. Are you okay?"

Constable Chadwick pressed the napkin back to her bicep. "I'm fine. It's just a nick. Are *you* okay?"

Alexa explained what happened, her recount as devoid of emotion as Gina's had been as she described stalking Diana. She refused to break down.

Constable Chadwick looked at her in awe. "Garden clippers?"

Alexa clenched her fists. Stead could bleed to death in less than five minutes. Suddenly she heard rotor blades. Again. Was Riggs coming back? Fight or flight coursed through her veins as she dashed to the windows. An army-green copter skimmed the trees and disappeared. "It's Bruce," Alexa said.

Constable Chadwick joined her at the window. "Who?"

"DI Horne." The pilot had probably spotted the yellow copter and was in pursuit. How did a copter chase work? Her mind reeled James Bond aerial chases. They always ended in a fiery crash.

Constable Bartlett rushed in. "Where have you been?" he yelled at Constable Chadwick.

"Locked in a closet!"

"Do you have a tourniquet?"

Constable Chadwick grabbed her first aid kit. Alexa knew she should follow the constables outside, see if Stead Willis was alive, but her legs wouldn't obey. She made it to a chair and collapsed. She hefted her knees up and hugged them close, bowing her head, a ball of remorse. She could feel the clippers in her hand, feel the crunch of carpal bones. "Science, science," she rocked. "I believe in science, not violence." What if Stead died?

After a few minutes she dragged herself to Stead's backpack in the lounge. She started to open it, but then caught herself and retrieved a pair of gloves and brought the pack into the dining room. She searched through it looking for her camera and jammed her finger on something hard. She was lifting the second rock out when she heard Charlie's voice.

"A helicopter crashed!" Charlie was red-faced, out of breath, his voice jerky. "I heard trees smashing and then an explosion."

Alexa ran to the dining room window. Mount Elliot preened in sunshine. There was no sign of a downed helicopter.

Charlie doubled over, hands to knees. "I saw the flames, Lexi." Her legs wobbled. "Where?"

"On the other side of the river. I couldn't cross it. Call 911."

Bruce, she thought. "What color was the copter?"

"I never saw the copter. Just heard a crash and saw flames. Call the police."

"The cops are by the helipad." But they were working on another emergency. Alexa's mind spun like rotors.

Charlie stepped closer to her. "Why is your face bloody?"

She pawed at her cheeks, dashed to the satellite phone, and dialed 111, New Zealand's 911.

"Emergency Call Center," the operator said. "What's your name?"

"A helicopter crashed!" Was Bruce dead?

"Where are you?" the operator asked.

"Pompolona Lodge, Milford Track."

Charlie flung his backpack off. "By the river. Tell them by the river," he huffed.

"How long ago did the incident happen?"

Alexa covered the mouthpiece. "How long ago, Charlie?"

"Ten or fifteen minutes. I ran straight here."

Alexa told the operator, her voice trembling.

"Are you at the scene?"

"No. We're at the lodge." When she heard the sound of yet another helicopter, getting louder, she thrust the phone at Charlie and ran through the lobby and out to the porch, crashing into Vince.

"What's going on?" he asked.

"Where have you been?" she snapped and tore around the building. She halted when she saw the large army-green helicopter touching down.

Bruce was safe. She took in the scene. Stead Willis, flat on his back, was being attended to by Constable Chadwick, who was elevating his arm. Constable Bartlett was covering him with a space blanket. Sergeant Kramer ran to meet Bruce, who ducked under the rotors and met him halfway. Instead of running to him, Alexa stepped backward, into the shade of the lodge, caught her breath, and steadied her emotions. She watched Kramer gesture toward Stead and Bruce gesturing toward the air. The pilot and police officer climbed out of the copter with a stretcher. Alexa watched them load Stead and carry him to the open bay, Constable Chadwick hovering by his side. There was jostling as they got Stead, and then themselves, buckled in. Alexa prayed Stead was alive. Bruce and Constable Bartlett climbed in last. The copter lifted, leaving only Sergeant Kramer behind.

Her ears thrummed. She thought she could smell smoke.

Sergeant Kramer looked stooped; the day's events had weighed him down. She stepped toward him. "Is Willis alive?"

He removed his cap and wiped his forehead. "Constable Chadwick applied a tourniquet. The bleeding stopped but he's gone unconscious. He needs a transfusion fast."

Alexa's heart sank. "Charlie says a helicopter crashed."

"It was Riggs. DI Horne said it looks bad. They'll drop him and Bartlett at the crash scene. Or as close as they can get. DI said it was like a fireball, that Riggs didn't have a chance. The Civil Aviation Authority are on the way."

Alexa thought of Gina Granger slashing her wrists and wondered if Riggs had crashed on purpose. "How did it happen?"

"Flying too low. The DI said a landing skid clipped a tree and flipped the copter."

Alexa tried to wrap her head around another calamity.

"CAA investigators will determine the cause. DI Horne said they'd get a coroner from Queenstown. He thought you'd been through enough."

For that, Alexa was grateful.

They turned together and walked toward the nearly empty lodge.

ONE WEEK LATER

Chapter Forty-Seven

Charlie and Alexa blinked in bright sunshine as they left Ruakuri Glowworm Cave. Charlie was flying home tomorrow. Alexa had taken a final vacation day so she could show him the cave. He was more excited by the limestone formations than the galaxy of bioluminescent larvae hanging from the ceilings.

As they crossed the parking lot, Alexa thought about the glowworm cave postcard Gina Granger had dropped at the ranger station. Had she wished she could go there with her Jerry? Alexa vacillated between sympathy and revulsion when she thought of Postcard Woman.

She and Charlie had been evacuated to Queenstown the morning after the helicopter crash. They had gone bungee-jumping off the Kawarau Bridge. Alexa had figured it was no biggie. She had survived Gina Granger and Stead Willis. She could survive being attached to a rubber band and jumping off a bridge.

The memories made her stomach clench.

On the drive back to Auckland, she asked Charlie what it was like when he climbed Mackinnon Pass.

"There were lots of switchbacks."

She had seen them from the air.

"Two-thirds of the way up the clouds cleared, and all I could see was blue sky, tiny lakes, snow, and mountains. It was windy as hell. At the top there's a place where you can drop a pebble over the edge and it falls for twelve seconds."

Alexa held her breath for twelve seconds. Last night she'd been sure she heard rotors and had dashed to her apartment window to search the empty sky.

"When I was at the top I decided to make things work with Mel. To forgive."

He hushed while Alexa pressed the gas pedal of her Toyota Vitz and passed a truck.

"I've been thinking about that guy who cursed you," Charlie said.

Alexa remembered the Māori elder, and the bones that rerouted the highway project. "He didn't curse me. He said looking at the bones would release evil."

"He was right."

She was going to miss Charlie. He'd leave behind a tiny tear in her heart.

"I did some research while you were at work yesterday."

She had been busy tying up Black Diamond and Bone Track threads.

"The Māori believe a curse is lifted when justice has been achieved," Charlie said. "You found the bird guy, Karl, by the river and used his teeth to identify him. You found the men responsible for killing him. The curse lifted."

Dr. Ana Luckenbaugh had returned to the bones and uncovered a partial mandible, four teeth intact. The X-rays Alexa took of them matched Karl Atul's dental records. Dr. Luckenbaugh also discovered the tip of a knife blade embedded in a fragment of rib. It did not match the knife Stead Willis carried on the Milford Track.

"We don't know which man killed him," she said. "Willis says he never met Karl Atul and that he took my camera because Riggs said I had a picture of them lifting a rock from the river."

The memory card with all the evidence was found in Stead's backpack along with two small boulders of greenstone.

"People in his town are defending Willis, including his wife," Alexa said. "They say he's saved several lives in his search-and-rescue work and that he has as much right to the greenstone as Māori."

"He won't be as fit to rescue people with only one hand," Charlie said.

Alexa's throat dried. Stead Willis would most likely lose the use of his right hand. The nerve damage was severe. He had been charged with greenstone thievery and attempted kidnapping. Other charges were pending.

"Is anyone defending Damien Riggs?" Charlie asked.

A large boulder of bowenite was found in the copter with Riggs's body. According to a newspaper article, its value was twenty-four thousand dollars. The Te Anau Police and Bruce were continuing their investigation of black-market *pounamu*.

"No. I can't figure out what would cause one of them to stab a stranger to death."

"I can imagine," Charlie said quietly.

Alexa didn't think he was referring to Riggs or Willis.

"The *iwi* chairperson said there's going to be a secret ceremony to return the greenstone rock to the river."

"That would be cool to watch," Charlie said.

ONE MONTH LATER

Chapter Forty-Eight

The green envelope resting against her apartment door had been hand-delivered, but she didn't know by whom. She'd opened and read the invitation on the spot.

Join the celebration of life for
Karl Arthur 'Kahu' Atul
15 March, Hokitika Wildlife Rescue Center
5:00 PM

Scribbled in a shaky hand at the bottom was: I have something for you. Mrs. Ngaio Atul.

Under the sheet, Bruce nudged her foot with his, pressed his hairy calf against her smooth one. They were tangled together in a California king overlooking the Tasman Sea in Hokitika. Karl Atul's memorial service was in one hour.

"It's beautiful," Alexa said of the green-gray water through the glass sliders of their room.

"And deadly," Bruce said. He nudged the sheet down, exposing more of her breasts.

She laughed but pulled the sheet back up. They didn't have time for round three. "Why deadly?"

"Crossing the Hokitika bar where the river meets the sea is

treacherous. After the service—if it's still light—we'll walk to the shipwreck memorial."

Round one had been two hours ago after they checked in. She'd been shy and warned Bruce as he unbuttoned her blouse. "My back. It's ugly."

He looked at her oddly, his fingers gone still, his eyes reflecting the sea.

"It's burned. Scalded. I…"

He put his finger to her lips, and then she let him complete his task. With his shirt and her shirt pooled on the floor, he caressed her scars and pulled her close. It hadn't mattered at all.

The Wildlife Center was a place to rehabilitate and release—if possible—injured or abandoned birds. She and Bruce were greeted by a line of Karl's *whānau*, or family—a sister, two cousins, an uncle, three nieces—in the traditional Māori way of pressing nose to nose and forehead to forehead. The last and oldest person in the line introduced herself as Karl's mother.

"I'm Alexa Glock. Thank you for inviting me." She wanted to say more to this woman with sorrowful eyes but couldn't decide what.

Mrs. Atul said, "Breath of life. I've been waiting for you. Kahu's spirit is with us."

"Kahu? Was that Karl's nickname?" she was able to ask.

"*Ae.* It means hawk." Mrs. Atul was maybe eighty. She put something smooth and warm in Alexa's hand and closed Alexa's fingers over it. "Don't look until Kahu is with you."

Alexa balled her hand into a fist. She felt strange sensations. Goose bumps, a whistling as if something was flying past her ear, heat from her palm.

Mrs. Atul motioned for her and Bruce to follow, past a large aviary full of chattering birds to the front bench of a small outdoor amphitheater. "Please sit here." They waited silently, Bruce's thigh against hers. She looked at his profile, caught a glimpse of his own sorrow. She wondered if he was thinking about his divorce—a sort of death minus the casseroles and sympathy cards. She wondered how Charlie and Mel were doing.

About twenty people took seats behind them. Alexa remembered that Karl had been described as a loner, and it had been five years since he'd disappeared. A photograph of him, kind eyes and bushy beard, a large hawk on a perch beside him, stood on a table. Surrounding it was a shrine of tools, stones, a nest, carvings, and a flax basket. The family filed in last, gathering on either side of Alexa and Bruce.

A man in a black beanie, his arms a swirl of tattoos, walked in front of the shrine. "I'm Aden Tauwhare, a stone carver and cousin of Kahu's." He closed his eyes, bowed his head, and began speaking in Māori. A prayer, maybe. When he lifted his head, he spoke English. "Kahu spent his life here on the South Island, on Ngai Tahu soil, and *pounamu*—the spirit stone— spoke to him from his ancestors: father Jon, grandfather Aden, great grandfather Karl; and by Ranginui, the sky father; and Papatūānuku, our earth mother." He nodded at Mrs. Atul. "He was guided by his ancestors as he breathed life into stone." He switched to Māori and told a story that made people around them laugh.

One of Karl's other cousins stood, embraced Mrs. Atul, and began speaking. "We were able to purify Karl's spirit when this young woman found his resting spot by the river." He gestured to Alexa.

Surprised and uncomfortable, Alexa squeezed the object in her hand and felt Karl's encouragement. She opened her palm slowly, and studied the translucent olive-green *pounamu* spiral. A *koru*, an unfurling frond. New beginning, life, and hope.

"Karl's spirit couldn't leave his body," the cousin continued. "Evil needed sloughing. Peace needed restoration." He smiled and looked skyward. Dappled light filtered through the tree canopy, and birds sang with abandon. "*Te ao* Māori. We went back to Karl, by the river—our source of fish and eel and *pounamu*.

The ceremony of *tuku* was carried out to free his spirit from his bones."

Alexa gasped when another man joined him. His arm was covered by a thick leather glove. A large tawny hawk perched on it. The man smiled and began speaking. "Karl took care of birds like Ruby when they were hit by cars or caught in nets."

The bird's yellow eyes stared at Alexa. It lifted one talon, and then the other. *And a bird like Ruby took care of Karl,* Alexa realized, thinking of the hawk circling Karl's grave.

"Kahu, or hawks, are messengers from the gods in heaven, and now Karl is free to wing his way along his next spiritual path." The man raised his arm upward. "Soar beyond the clouds, beautiful bird."

The hawk spread its wings and lifted. Alexa heard the bird, *kee-o, kee-o,* and watched it fly away.

Don't miss a single adventure with Alexa Glock!
Read on for an excerpt from

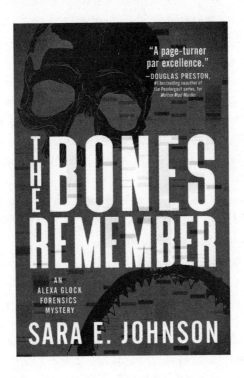

THE BONES
REMEMBER

"A page-turner
par excellence."
—DOUGLAS PRESTON,
#1 bestselling coauthor of
the Pendergast series, for
Molten Mud Murder

THE BONES
REMEMBER

AN
ALEXA GLOCK
FORENSICS
MYSTERY

SARA E. JOHNSON

Chapter One

Safe from the tempest, Alexa Glock dripped across the cement floor to the ticket counter. She scanned the price board: round trip Bluff to Stewart Island—$85.

"Stroppy, eh?" the agent said.

Alexa nodded, looking through the window at the pelting rain, slapping waves, and gusts that shook the building. The passenger ferry, tethered to the dock, challenged its restraints with each assault. It was dwarfed by a long, lean oil tanker one pier over. Alexa imagined the tanker breaking loose, crushing the ferry.

Mary, the one friend Alexa had made in her eight months in New Zealand, had called the whipping winds of Foveaux Strait *hau-mate*, Māori for "death wind."

Got that right.

"I need a one-way ticket." She hiked the crime kit strap securely up onto her shoulder and released the handle of her sodden suitcase, flexing her cramped fingers.

"Ferry is delayed." The agent, a wizened woman with sharp eyes, accepted Alexa's credit card. "No return, eh?"

The thought of no return induced a flicker of fear. "I don't know how long I'll be staying." She took the ticket and scanned the lounge. Her fellow passengers—locals, tourists, hikers—stared glumly out the window or at their phones. Alexa settled on a bench near a *Kiwi Experience* flyer. Stewart Island was a hot spot for the iconic birds. Another flyer advertised shark cage diving: "See Great Whites Up Close!"

Mary had planned to dive with sharks. "Come with me," she had cajoled. "*Mangōtaniwha.* The great white shark. Our guardian."

Alexa had laughed. "Yeah, right."

But now Mary was dead. She had died in a car wreck two months ago. Alexa mourned her new friend. And simmered with anger, too. Someone else leaving her.

A woman surrounded by a pile of shopping bags pushed herself up from the bench and came to where the flyers hung. She leaned in, frowning, and tore one down. "Rubbish," she said, crumpling it.

Kiwi Experience hung alone.

A tall man in gum boots and thick fisherman's sweater distracted Alexa. He shouted into his cell. "If they want it, they'll have to come get it." His halo of grizzled curls was a mini-storm, and he trailed the scent of salt and sea.

Struggling out of her raincoat, Alexa canvassed for coffee. No go. A caffeine desert. She had arrived late last night at the Vista Hotel and left it—and the breakfast buffet she had paid for—at dawn to catch the ferry. It had been a wild ride since yesterday when her boss at the Forensic Service Center in Auckland had popped into her cubicle. "Get packing. You've got your first away case. Stewart Island."

She had flipped a folder closed. "That's down south, right?" New Zealand was divided into two islands. Since moving here from North Carolina, she hadn't left the more populous North Island. Dan, her boss, explained that there was a third island. "Thirty kilometers off the tip of the South Island. Fly into Invercargill, bus to Bluff, ferry across Foveaux."

Dan Goddard, chief forensic examiner, had hired Alexa as a roving forensic two weeks ago. The six-month odontology fellowship that had lured her to Auckland was over, and she wasn't ready to leave the southern hemisphere. No one was waiting for her back home. She had completed a contract case in Rotorua—Detective Inspector Bruce Horne and his glacial eyes flashed in her mind—and then applied for a job at Forensic Service Center. Local police called FSC when they needed assistance, and she would travel to those places.

"What's the case?"

"Hikers discovered a decomposed body." Dan's eyes behind bookish glasses sparked with energy.

"Any idea who it is?"

"Ten months ago, Robert King, forty-four, from Christchurch, disappeared deer hunting. Never returned to the hut." Dan handed her a picture.

A fit-looking man held a dead deer by the antlers. His proud eyes stared directly at the camera. His hair—what little remained—formed a dark brown crown.

"That's King. The three blokes he was with looked for hours, then called it in. Massive searches, even recently with live tracking equipment. No sign. No body. Until now."

"Has the family been notified?"

"We need positive ID first. Get there ASAP. And…"

She waited, studying her boss, who wore red tennis shoes and untucked polos.

"…he has a bullet hole through the right zygomatic. The local ranger doesn't think it's self-inflicted."

Alexa fingered her cheekbone in the chilly waiting room. Out the window, the storm continued its vise grip on the harbor. Early December was the beginning of summer in the southern hemisphere, crazy as that was to an American, but the weather hadn't gotten the memo. She checked the time: almost nine. Sergeant Kipper Wallace of the Stewart Island Police Department was expecting her. First case of her new job, and she'd be late.

Dentals would be the quickest way to identify the remains. She remembered what Professor McBride at the dental school had said. "Forensic odontology has the potential to bring the forlorn to justice."

Robert King awaited justice.

She texted Sergeant Wallace, but the message bounced back undelivered.

Wind slammed the entrance door against the wall, making her drop the phone. A man and woman in matching high-vis rain gear, pulling suitcases, blew in as she retrieved it from under the bench. Damn. The screen had cracked. She wiped the phone on her jeans and watched the couple at the counter. The man asked if the ferry was delayed. Americans, Alexa could hear.

"For now. Not to worry."

"We have a meeting at noon," the woman said, shaking her hood off to reveal blond tresses.

"Aye," the ticket agent said. "Might be a tad late. Round trip?"

The couple pouted like preschoolers. Alexa watched with mild interest as they arranged themselves and their belongings on the remaining empty bench and then sat back to back, huffed and sighed, and pulled out their phones.

To pass time in a more constructive way than judging the Americans, Alexa considered the missing hunter. She retrieved his dental records from her suitcase and studied his X-rays. The top film, a periapical, showed upper teeth from crown to roots snaking below the gum line. A chill danced up Alexa's spine. If King had not shot himself, who was the root of such evil?

Chapter Two

Alexa stood for the entire hour's crossing, holding on to the interior rail of the ferry and staring at the heaving horizon while the captain calmly picked his way through swells, some exploding over the bow. Her queasiness was barely abated by the ginger tablets she'd bought from the ticket lady. She vowed to fly back, instead of taking the ferry, even if it meant chipping in some of her own money.

Now on terra firma, passengers dispersed like sea spray in the wind. Alexa, jerking her roller suitcase through puddles, caught up with the man in the fisherman's sweater. "Excuse me. Is there island Uber?"

"Uber?" His nickel-colored eyes focused on her wet Keds.

"Or Lyft?" A raindrop hit her squarely in the right eye, blurring the world. She shifted the crime kit more securely on her shoulder and rubbed her vision back to normal.

"There's the one taxi." He pointed up the road at vanishing taillights. "Best way to get around is to ten-toe it."

She needed to dump her stuff at the hotel and get to the police station, pronto. "How far to the Island Inn?" She had reserved a room ahead of time, conscious of her *per diem,* and wasn't expecting a Ritz-Carlton.

"Five-minute walk." He pointed a long finger to a building

perched above Halfmoon Bay. The rain distorted the inn into a cream-with-red-trim watercolor. "Heading that way. I'll drop you." Without waiting for an answer, the lean man strode toward a hulking black pickup truck in the parking lot.

What the hell.

Mr. Fisherman threw her suitcase in the bed of the truck, next to netting and rope.

The truck purred to life as Alexa arranged herself on the cold leather seat. She buckled up as the driver accelerated onto Elgin Terrace. Horsepower and rain drowned any chance of introductions. She glanced at the man's profile. Early forties, angular and weathered. In three minutes they arrived at the small two-storied inn.

"Thank you for the lift."

Mr. Fisherman nodded.

A group of people holding signs watched her from the patio area as she hauled her case out of the truck bed. It looked to be a mini-protest. Their screams of "Ban the cage, BAN THE CAGE" got louder as Alexa approached—as if she were going shark cage diving. Not. Happening. She squinted through the rain at the signs: *Paua Divers Aren't Bait,* CHILDREN SWIM HERE. Mr. Fisherman honked as Alexa scurried past and through the door.

An old-timey wooden reception counter stood at the far end of the lobby. The Americans from the ferry were already checking in. "I don't appreciate the greeting committee," the man said to the receptionist.

"Sorry about that," she replied, removing her glasses. "Caging is a bit of a stink on the island."

"The money we pay to dive with the sharks goes toward ocean conservation," the woman chimed in.

"Some of it," said the receptionist.

The high-vis couple snagged my taxi, Alexa concluded, unzipping her raincoat. Off to the right, a waiter carried a tray of fried fish and chips in the busy restaurant. Her stomach growled in protest. To the left an arrow pointed to Full Moon Lounge.

The Americans nodded at Alexa as they hurried off.

"*Kia ora.* I'm Constance Saddler, proprietor. Are you a shack diver too?"

"Shack diver?" It took her a second to decipher. "No. I'm not here to dive with sharks. I have a reservation. Alexa Glock." She fished her phone out to check messages. No bars. "Is there cell reception on the island?"

"Not to worry. On fine days." Constance looked a few years older than Alexa, early forties. Her blond hair, dark at the roots, needed a trim. "What brings you here?"

"Business. Can you give me directions to the police station?"

Constance's eyes widened. "It's number two View Street. A short hop." She took a map from a stack on the counter and circled a dot. "It's about the hunter, yeah?"

News had leaked. "I can't say."

"Right then." Constance checked the computer screen. "You've booked a studio. I'll take you there."

They exited out a side door, where a one-story wing had been added. "These are our private entrance suites." Constance unlocked Number Three with a key. "You have an en suite double, tellie, and wee kitchen." Constance cracked the window and approved when the curtain billowed. "Would you like standard or trim?"

Alexa was caught off guard again.

"Milk for your mini-fridge. Standard or trim?"

"Standard, thank you."

"I'll be back later with your milk." Constance paused. "It wasn't a local, you know."

Alexa watched through the window as Constance hurried away. She supposed on an island with fewer than four hundred residents that everyone would know everyone and there would be no secrets. She pulled hiking pants and socks from her suitcase and set her white Keds by the window—which she closed—to dry. She changed, combed her thick dark tangles into a ponytail, laced her boots, and grabbed a mini-package of biscuits next to the electric kettle. She would dine on her way.

The sea-green cottage at 2 View Street belonged in a children's picture book. Alexa checked the sign. Yep. *Police Station*. She climbed three steps to the front porch and turned toward the harbor. Through tapering rain, she could see the ferry leaving, causing her a flutter of panic. Stranded on a remote island. *And Then There Were None*, and all that. She swatted away such irrational thoughts of remote locales and killers among us and entered. Sergeant Kipper Wallace had expected her two hours ago. A uniformed woman in a cubicle turned. "Hello. How can I help?" Her name tag said Constable Elyse Kopae.

Alexa had learned Kiwis used the term "constable" instead of "officer." Same difference. "I'm looking for Sergeant Wallace."

"Are you from Auckland forensics?" The constable was young, maybe Māori, with dark, direct eyes. Her black hair was chin-length. She did not have a lip and chin tattoo like some Māori women. Neither had Mary.

"Yes."

"The senior is at the fire department. Waiting for the all-clear so he can take off."

"Senior" was another oddity. Instead of saying "sir" or "boss," police officers called their superiors Senior. Alexa couldn't bring herself to use it. "Take off?"

"To the location."

Constable Kopae pointed out the room's single window to another sea-green building. One side was an open garage housing an inflatable raft. Alexa's stomach flip-flopped.

She flew across the wet grass. A slightly overweight man opened the door before she knocked. "You made it. I'm Sergeant

Kipper Wallace." He was mid-forties and wore a bright orange jumpsuit with SAR on the breast pocket.

"Alexa Glock." She put the crime kit down and extended her hand.

"Glock, eh? Like the gun?" Mostly bald, the sergeant had patches of sandy fuzz above each ear.

"Glock, paper, scissors. That's me."

The sergeant's shake was firm. "Call me Wallace."

"Sorry I'm late. The ferry…"

"The entire island knows when the ferry is late. We've got to get going," Wallace interrupted. "The tide." He looked Alexa up and down. "You'll need a search-and-rescue suit like mine and overnight gear."

"Overnight?" She had become an echo.

"No roads where we are going. We'll fly, land on the beach, hike a couple kilometers to the body. Bush is dense. We'll bunk at the hunter's camp. My constable will rig you."

Back across the grass, Kopae pointed to an orange jumpsuit hanging from a hook in the unisex bathroom. "It will keep you visible. Don't need you getting shot."

"Who would shoot me?"

"There are hunters out there. You can use my rucksack. I keep it ready. Lost trampers, that kind of thing. It's got a torch, compass, water, tooth powder, towelettes, space blanket, and jumper."

"Thank you. I appreciate your help."

"Are you from the States?"

Alexa nodded and pulled the generous-sized suit over everything but her boots, which she slipped back on and laced, glad for thick, dry socks. "How many officers do you have on the island?"

"We're a two-person station, me and Sarge."

"Two people? How do you get time off?"

"It's all good," Constable Kopae said.

"Don't know what I'm getting into."

"It's rugged. Beast practice for you to have a tracker." She handed over an orange-and-black walkie-talkie.

Alexa was alarmed. "Beast practice?"

Constable Kopae frowned. "You know, using latest knowledge and technology. Don't you have beast practices in the States?"

Oh, Alexa thought. *The constable was saying* best. "Of course. We follow best practice procedures back home too."

"That's the SOS signal," the constable pointed. "And it's waterproof."

The burn scars crossing her back tightened as Alexa studied the tracking device.

ACKNOWLEDGMENTS

Many thanks to the following people who "hiked" *The Bone Track* with me.

Thank you to my agent, Natalie Lakosil of Bradford Literary Agency, who loves the Alexa Glock series and led me to the Poisoned Pen Press/Sourcebooks team. Thank you to my first editor, Barbara Peters, and to my new editor, Diane DiBiase. These women are astute guides and can see the forest when I am in the trees. Thanks also to assistant content editor Beth Deveny, who rocks at fact-checking and copyediting.

What would I do without my writing group? Thank you to our facilitator, Nancy Peacock, and my fellow writers, Lisa Bobst, Denise Cline, Linda Jassen, and Ann Parrent.

Researching forensics is fascinating. I owe a great debt to my forensic advisor, Dr. Heidi Eldridge, an expert in the field. Her guidance has been stellar, and she admits that she is "stupidly geeky" about features in her own fingerprints.

Thank you to track operations manager Shaun Liddy at Ultimate Hikes in New Zealand. He generously read the manuscript for accuracy. According to Shaun, the expression "she'll be right" sums up the Kiwi attitude to life: "The chances of something bad happening aren't that high. If something bad does happen, we can handle it. Kiwis don't sweat the little things and lead happier lives for it."

I acknowledge neuroscientist and author David Eagleman, who has written extensively about the brain and purports that we all die three deaths.

Triangles Sisters in Crime and the North Carolina Writers' Network have provided support and fellowship.

The poet Blanche Baughan declared the Milford Track to be "the finest walk in the world," and I agree. Some of the places in *The Bone Track* are real, and some are made up. Any mistakes are real and mine alone.

Thanks, always, to my husband, Forrest.

ABOUT THE AUTHOR

© Morgan Henderson Photography

Sara E. Johnson lives in Durham, North Carolina. She worked as a middle school reading specialist and local newspaper contributor before her husband lured her to New Zealand for a year. Her novels *Molten Mud Murder*, *The Bones Remember*, and *The Bone Track* were the result.